Faye

C000143715

By
Lilly Adam

ISBN: 9798613629459

Also written by Lilly Adam:

May of Ashley Green
Stella
Poppy Woods
The Whipple Girl
Rose
Whitechapel Lass
Daisy Grey
Beneath the Apple Blossom Tree

Dedicated to my wonderful readers; I hope you enjoy reading this book as much as I enjoyed writing it.

Who said that love was fire?
I know that love is ash.
It is the thing which remains
When the fire is spent,
The holy essence of experience.
By Patience Worth

CHAPTER ONE
November 1857

Some folk might have called it an ill omen, others a well-deserved punishment for her impetuous and foolish behaviour but on that moonless night, when neither man nor beast was brave enough to leave their shelter, Faye Butler made a desperate attempt to reach her grandmother's cottage, somewhere along the highway between London and Oxford. As the driving, icy rain pelted down upon her back, she winced from the stinging pains of labour. Her worn out serge dress clung to her body and her saturated woollen shawl was beyond serving any useful purpose. She screamed out into the hostile night sky as the next pain squeezed her tightly, forcing her to her knees on the muddy verge of the desolate road. Her pains were now coming fast and strong. She dug her fingers into the soggy mud, as the sudden urge to push her heavy load out into the dark and gloomy world overtook her entire being, confirming to her that it would be impossible to reach the safety of her grandmother's cottage in time for the confinement; she also knew that on such a treacherous night, nobody would venture from their homes, leaving her completely alone.

The loud crackling as a bolt of lightning pierced through the black night coincided with the first muffled cry from the tiny, slippery baby as she was born onto a sodden grassy bed, leaving her mother relieved from pain but shivering uncontrollably and desperate for help. The heavy rain was relentless. Faye ripped off her soiled petticoat to wrap the crying baby in, but there was no warmth to be found on such a bleak and angry night.

Daybreak arrived along with a weak sun and a flawless sapphire sky, wiping away the fury of the previous night. The only visible signs which remained were the copious puddles, dotted across the waterlogged thoroughfare, making a slow journey for the morning's travellers, of which there were very few at such an early hour. The two lifeless bodies, now covered with mud, were almost submerged into the bog-like verge. One of the first passersby who'd been vigilant enough to spot the discarded bonnet, as its damp brim fluttered like a trapped butterfly on top of the small mound of mud was Harry Fairbanks, who after losing a substantial sum of money at the gambling tables of London, was returning home to Oxford, where he was a prominent figure in society, a shrewd businessman and a property owner. He'd experienced far more rewarding gambling nights in his life, but tonight was one which had left his pockets empty of banknotes, replacing them with a thick bundle of I owe you notes. He would normally be snoring, in a state of satisfaction on his return from such an evening, but his mind was troubled and he knew it was time to stand back and take a look as to where his life was heading and to salvage what he could after such a foolhardy night.

As he stared hard at the site where Faye Butler and her newborn lay, a slight movement of the baby's scrawny arm seemed to wave to him. In an instant, Harry Fairbanks was pummeling the roof of the carriage with his fist and yelling for the coachman to bring the vehicle to a halt.

"*Stop man!*" he yelled, above the noise of the horses' hooves and the carriage wheels. "*Stop for God's sake!*" He'd already opened the carriage door and the sight of the rapidly passing ground caused him to feel dizzy, especially after having had no sleep since the previous night. "*Are you men both stone deaf?*" he screamed. "*Stop this carriage at once, d'you hear me?*"

The two London coachmen, who were in a hurry to take their passenger to his destination and return home, reluctantly pulled on the reins and commanded the horses to halt, presuming that their passenger merely wished to alight in order to relieve himself or to throw up, but sure of a decent tip from the wealthy Harry Fairbanks, they behaved as cordially as was possible on the chilly autumn morning.

"Is everything alright, Sir?"

"I'm sure I saw a young infant back down the

road...quite a few yards, I'd estimate, especially since you took so damn long in responding to my orders to bring these fine beasts to a standstill."

The coachmen glanced at each other and as if reading their thoughts, were all too aware of how tired and semi-drunk eyes had a habit of hallucinating.

"I'm sure it was just a fallen branch from last night's storm, Sir," assured the coachman, with his colleague nodding his head in agreement.

"What do you take me for, you imbeciles? I'm not a blithering idiot and if I say I saw a child on the verge you can rest assured that my eyes have not deceived me; now turn this vehicle around and drive on, this instant. It might also be advisable for you to remember who's paying you for your troubles too."

The very second that Harry Fairbanks' words had spilt from his mouth, he suddenly remembered that he'd left London without a single shilling in his pocket and now his plan of walking the last few yards to his house in Oxford, in order not to wake his wife, would have to be aborted.

As they neared the site where the discarded bonnet still remained flapping in the increasingly strong November wind, there was no mistaking the sound of a baby's distraught cries. All three men stood momentarily, aghast at the pitiful scene which filled their eyes. Harry acted quickly, pulling the half-submerged infant from out of her muddy resting place and spontaneously removing his jacket to wrap the scrawny baby in, before placing the bundle into the carriage.

"Right then, let's be on our way now!" commanded the coachman, impatiently. "There's no hope for the mother; she looks as though she left this world when her little bastard arrived."

Harry felt the blood in his veins heating up by the cold-hearted words which he was hearing.

"How dare you be so presumptuous, where is your heart man?"

The coachman wanted nothing more than to return home to the warmth of his bed, he'd had a long and arduous day and wasn't in the mood for any saintly actions from an Oxford toff.

His colleague, however, said very little and appeared quietly concerned by the devastating sight.

"Believe me, Sir, I'm not being presumptuous, but every picture tells a story and you wouldn't find a decent woman dropping her load at the side of the highway unless she was ashamed and fleeing in order to save her family from the shame. We've all seen this before...let's not allow our hearts to overrule our sense of propriety now."

"You Sir are a cold-hearted and inhumane bigot and I will make damned sure that your employer hears of your appalling behaviour.

You sicken me to the pit of my stomach and I have no wish to continue on my journey, with you at the helm."

The coachmen stared at each other in disbelief, as Harry quickly returned to the carriage and took hold of the baby again.

"But we're only five miles away from Oxford...we've gone out of our way and sacrificed sleep and a warm bed to bring you here," despaired the coachman, "you can't possibly expect us to simply return without payment!"

Not relishing in the prospect of a long walk carrying a screaming baby on such a cold morning where the bitter easterly wind seemed to reach the very marrow of his bones, Harry made a quick change of mind.

"Very well, we shall continue on our journey in five minutes, after I've done all I can for this poor unfortunate woman," instructed Harry, not taking his eyes off the sombre scene whilst speaking.

"What can *you* do? She's dead, for God's sake!" stated the coachman belligerently.

"We can at least leave her looking a little more dignified!"

"Doubt that she ever possessed such a quality when she was alive...if you ask me she doesn't deserve a second look."

"Well, I'm not asking you and I hasten to remind you that none of us knows anything about her nor of her fatal consequences. Now kindly give me one of your blankets."

"They're not ours to give, and if we return to the coach house minus a blanket, it will be us who ends up paying for it out of our wages and neither of us can afford that!"

"For God's sake man, where's your sense of humanity? Just give me your finest rug and I will see to it personally that you are reimbursed as soon as we arrive at my home."

The two men reluctantly strolled off towards the carriage to retrieve a blanket. Harry could vaguely hear them muttering to each other under their breath and was concerned that perhaps they might speed off without him. The final and depressing sight of this poor young woman seemed to rip Harry Fairbanks' heart in two...he hated to see a beautiful young woman wasted. He stared hard at her face; she looked peaceful even though her body was heavily bloodstained and her cheap clothes ripped and filthy. Harry laid the baby onto the grass bank as he carefully pulled her slight body out from the muddy bog, leaving it to rest on the roadside. He proceeded to pull her soiled skirt down to cover her modesty and placed her discarded damp bonnet onto her head of golden curls. A mud-covered reticule caught his eye, half-submerged into the ground and splashed with streaks of blood. He took out his pristine handkerchief and quickly wrapped it up before tucking it beneath his waistcoat. Whilst one of the coachmen sat holding the reins, waiting impatiently to embark on the final leg of the journey, his colleague returned to the morbid scene and handed a tartan blanket to Harry. "We're not taking a corpse in the carriage!" he stated sternly. "It's considered bad luck, you know?"

Harry could feel his fists clenching, how he would take great pleasure in throwing a hard punch into this insensitive, inhumane man, but knew that first, he needed to get the crying baby to safety. He stared at him in disgust, "One day, you might find yourself or a loved one in a similar tragic situation...It might be wise for you to reflect on that. We will stop at the undertaker's *en route* and with a small payment, I'm sure he will be more than delighted with the business," replied Harry, cynically.

The coachman smirked, turning his back on Harry to rejoin his colleague.

In all his thirty-five years, Harry had never before witnessed such a gloomy scene which had left an oppressive dark cloud overshadowing him. He held the tiny scrap of a child close to his body in a bid to generate some of his heat to her and as the journey continued, Harry found himself transfixed on the infant's tiny face which was only half visible where his jacket was wrapped around her body in multiple layers. He felt a pang of sorrow for the child who would never know or experience the true love of her mother, but he had come up with the perfect solution to her future and prayed that he might be able to convince his wife to take on the baby as their own. Even to himself, it sounded like an idea brought on by madness, but Harry had been deeply affected by the early morning's events and desperately wanted to infuse a little sunshine into its bleakness if it was at all possible. The more he thought about it the more it made complete sense. He and Delia had been married for six years and there had yet to be any sign of a family; Delia had not been the woman who he'd imagined he was marrying, which Harry blamed mostly on the fact that their marriage was proving fruitless. He couldn't remember the last time that he'd seen a genuine smile upon her face, she was turning into an iceberg and the time in which they spent in each other's company was diminishing with every passing year, which in itself was mostly his fault and the fact that he felt compelled to leave the dull atmosphere of his home to frequent the gaming tables.

Delia had become miserable and uninterested in every aspect of their lives and constantly nagged Harry about his gambling habits which she strongly frowned upon, consequently forcing him to lie about his activities but she was more observant than he gave her credit for and very little passed by her notice as she took to watching him like a hawk. Harry was a huge disappointment to her and when both her parents had passed away, her great aunt, who was reputed as a miserly type, hastily arranged the marriage between Delia and Harry Fairbanks, immediately after Delia's coming out ball. Not wanting to waste any more of her wealth supporting her, she had met Harry Fairbanks quite by chance at the roulette tables in London, where they had both endured a successful night and Delia's aunt saw a union between Harry Fairbanks and her charge as the ideal solution that would, at last, free her from her responsibilities which were biting into her finances.

At first, Delia welcomed the prospect of her own home and independence away from her aunt who she'd never been able to see eye to eye with. Harry Fairbanks seemed like the perfect match; at thirty-five, he was eight years older than Delia, which was considered an ideal age gap. A handsome and clever self-made businessman and one of Oxford's most eligible young gentlemen, Delia instantly agreed to become his wife, a rash decision which she soon regretted when it was too late. Soon after the initial honeymoon period, Delia came to realise that Harry's main love and passion was not for her, but instead for his uncontrollable gambling and games of chance, where so far, he had proved to be extremely fortunate by triumphing far more than losing. His pastime took him away from Oxford most evenings only to return in the small hours of the morning with a belly full of alcohol and wanting nothing more than to retire to his bed. Delia's life became lonely and boring and was made worse by her failure to become a mother. She yearned for a child and was convinced that it might change Harry's lifestyle should he become a father and encourage him to spend more time with her. When, seven months ago, the news of Queen Victoria's ninth child, Princess Beatrice filled the newspapers in April of 1857, Harry's insensitive remarks about Delia's failure to produce a child, broke her heart and caused an even wider rift in their relationship. Now, at the age of twenty-seven and with the passing away of her aunt two years previously, Delia felt as though her life had run headlong into a dark tunnel with not the slightest glimmer of light at the end of it. She felt trapped and totally betrayed by her husband and prayed that the future would soon change for the better.

CHAPTER TWO

Feeling a comforting sense of calm as Oxford's familiar lofty spires came into view, Harry prepared himself to leave the carriage and face what he knew would be a difficult confrontation with Delia. He hoped that she'd still be asleep; at least until he'd made himself look more presentable. He was in a dishevelled state and looked as though he'd spent the night taking a mud bath. As the coach approached Headington Hill's summit, Harry tried in vain to brush off some of the mud from his lower legs and once, gleaming boots but the sticky clay-like substance merely smudged in more to the fine cloth of his trousers. Harberton Mead house stood to the right of Headington Hill, surrounded by countryside; it was almost colonial in its design. A house of beauty with its pale green wooden cladding, symmetrical frontage and four pillars to the front porch it emitted an ambience of tranquillity. As the house came into view, the raised veranda which encompassed the entire house, immediately reminded Harry of cool drinks, long, balmy summer evenings and happier times when Delia wore her pretty gowns along with a smile and was most attentive towards him. They would talk until the dramatic sunset sky seemed to leak from the sinking sun like an artist's palette, before giving way to a starry scene of diamonds upon a black velvet cloak.

Being suddenly jolted out of his reverie as the coach came to rest along the worn track outside Harberton Mead, Harry was reminded that he needed to quickly find the necessary money to pay the coachmen or perhaps issue yet another *I owe you*, which he knew they'd not take kindly to and then there was the baby to consider; if she woke up before he'd had a chance to explain everything to Delia, his plans would be thwarted. Harry took out his pocket watch, it was already nine o'clock which meant that the maids, Maybell and Selma, would soon be arriving, but at least for the meantime, he only had Mrs White, the cook, to worry about. He wondered if this was how a soldier would feel before embarking onto the battlefield. Harry couldn't remember a time when he'd been so nervous about confronting his wife, but he'd never before had to explain a grubby, naked newborn to her and the more he thought about it the more the situation seemed to become unbelievable, even to himself; had he really returned home with a dead woman's baby? He questioned himself, had he completely taken leave of his senses?

"Wait there my good men, while I retrieve your well-deserved payment," Harry requested, as he alighted from the coach, temporarily leaving the baby on the seat.

Tired and eager to return to London, the coachmen's manners were quickly diminishing. They looked glum and sighed heavily, both hoping that their passenger wouldn't take too long and would present them with a large enough tip to make their sleepless and chaotic night seem worthwhile.

Harry intended to be as quick as possible. As soon as he stepped over the threshold his nostrils informed him that Mrs White was in the midst of preparing a fishy breakfast, he felt his stomach churning over and was immediately overcome with nausea. After quickly concealing the deceased woman's reticule beneath the drawers of his pedestal desk, he grabbed a wad of crisp white banknotes from the secret compartment, inside volume four of the leather-bound set of *successful business* books, then, hastily returned outside. Both the coachmen were satisfied with their payments and waited while Harry retrieved the, now crying, baby from the carriage.

"Good day to you, Sir," called out the driver in a loud voice, annoying Harry, who wished for silence until he'd had a chance to wash and change his filthy clothes. The sound of female voices in the distance made him turn his head and as he'd feared, the maids had just crossed over the style on the bottom field. He stood for a second to admire the herd of Longhorn cows as they grazed peacefully and then caught sight of

Mrs White who was leaning her head out of the front door, presumably looking to see if Maybell and Selma were on their way.

"I knew there'd be a clowder of cats arriving the minute they sniffed out the kippers!"

She stared curiously at Harry, her eyes not failing to notice the noisy bundle in his arms.

"Good morning, Mr Fairbanks, breakfast will be ready in fifteen minutes."

"Good morning, Mrs White...thank you."

The baby suddenly cried louder than she'd done since her rescue; he and Mrs White stared awkwardly at each other.

"So it wasn't cats that I heard then," she declared.

"No, er...it's a baby...I rescued her on my journey home."

The strangeness of Harry's words seemed to leave Ruth White speechless, which was quite uncharacteristic in itself, only adding to the bizarre morning's events. Maybell and Selma were now three-quarters of the way up the field and their sharp young eyes and ears had instantly alerted them to the fact that their employer was carrying a baby. They whispered between themselves, making scandalous assumptions as to how such a strange scene could have come about.

"Good morning Mr Fairbanks," they chirped in unison, trying to hide their churlish giggles.

Harry let out a peculiar grunt and hastened into the house as though there was nothing at all untoward about the morning's oddities.

Delia's voice could soon be heard as she moaned about the coldness of the house and the fact that nobody had yet lit any of the fires. Deciding to sit in the kitchen, with it being the only room where there was any warmth to be found, Delia immediately sensed that something was troubling Mrs White.

"Is everything alright, Mrs White?"

"That's not for me to say, Mrs Fairbanks," she replied sharply, shoving her clenched fists into the large lump of dough on the table and sending puffs of flour into the air.

"Oh dear, has Mr Fairbanks returned home? I *thought* I heard his voice. What's he done to upset you, Mrs White?"

"That's not for me to say, Mrs Fairbanks," she repeated once more, confirming to Delia that there definitely was something amiss and forcing her to leave the warmth of the kitchen.

"Maybell and Selma will soon have the fires blazing, Mrs Fairbanks," called out Mrs White, as if reading Delia's thoughts, "and I'll have a word with them...I can't see any reason why they shouldn't arrive here earlier in the mornings now that the weather is turning."

"Thank you, Mrs White."

As the unmistakable sound of a baby's wailing suddenly filled the house, Delia looked back to Mrs White in horror; she held her stare, not quite knowing what to say. In her mature years of fifty-two, it was a very rare occasion when Ruth White was lost for words and this was proving to be one of them.

"I pray that Mr Fairbanks hasn't brought about a scandal to Harberton Mead!" Delia overheard Mrs White uttering to Maybell and Selma after she'd left the kitchen and passed the maids on her way. Her heart dropped into her empty stomach as she made her way towards the source of the commotion.

Holding the baby, awkwardly, in his arms, Harry was pacing the study floor; barefoot in just his long-johns and shirt, with his muddy clothing and footwear discarded to the corner of the room. He immediately looked up, pleased to see his wife for once.

"Ahh, Delia, *my love*, thank God you're awake; I'm sure you'll be more successful at quieting this baby than I." His tone was that of desperation. Delia could hardly believe what she was witnessing and aghast by Harry's *matter of fact* sentiments to such an extraordinary situation.

"I hope to God you don't actually expect *me* to take care of one of your mistakes, Harry, because my duties as your wife certainly don't stretch that far!"

For the first time in what had been a long and distressing night, Harry found himself laughing at Delia's absurd assumption.

"It's no laughing matter *Harry*! Are you drunk as

usual?"

"Delia, if you would just administer some of your feminine and maternal touches to this screaming infant, I will explain everything; trust me, it is *not* what you think my darling."

Delia studied the scene before her eyes; curious to hear her husband's explanation, which she already knew would undoubtedly be a string of lies.

"You're filthy, Harry...did some angry husband push you into a ditch? You certainly deserve worse," she stated angrily. "I remember when you used to take such pride in your appearance."

"And I still do!" snapped Harry, impatiently. "Now are you *going* to help me, or should I take her to Mrs White in the kitchen?"

Delia eyed his unkempt appearance, a day's hair growth had given his face a sinister-looking shadow and his bloodshot eyes had sunk behind circles of darkness.

"I hope you're not warning me, Harry, because I refuse to be threatened by you and I hope you realise that it's an impossibility to keep a screaming baby secret; the maids are already putting two and two together and coming up with their own theories, which, I hasten to add, doesn't give you much credit."

"If you'd just hear me out, Delia, you'll realise how innocent I am, my poppet."

"I don't believe a single word, Harry, but for the sake of peace and quiet, I'll gladly take the child to Mrs White; I'm sure she has more knowledge of babies than you and I."

She marched briskly towards Harry, snatching the baby from him,

"It's soaking wet!"

"It is a girl, by the way," muttered Harry.

Delia took the baby directly to her bedroom, remembering that she had some tiny garments and a stock of baby paraphernalia tucked away in her bottom drawer from the early months of her marriage when she had eagerly anticipated become a mother. The water in her washbowl was still tepid and as she gently wiped away as much of the mud as possible from the small, fragile body, it seemed to have a calming effect and for a few minutes, there was a welcoming peace and quiet.

As expected Maybell was soon knocking on the door,

"I've come to light the fire Mrs Fairbanks, may I come in?"

Delia suspected that Mrs White was curious to find out what was going on and had sent Maybell up, mainly for that reason.

"Ooh...a baby!" she declared, trying to sound surprised.

"Yes, Maybell, how very observant of you; please ask Mrs White to heat some milk for her, and if she knows how to construct some kind of emergency feeding bottle, that would be greatly appreciated, then perhaps we might regain some temporary peace."

Delia proceeded to put a napkin on the baby and dress her in a nightgown before swaddling her in a thick crocheted blanket. The baby's deep blue eyes stared up at Delia for the entire time and as Delia admired her soft skin and light downy hair, she also reminded herself not to form any attachment with the sweet newborn child.

Mrs White had heated some milk for her and sent Selma to the nearest apothecary in Oxford, to purchase a feeding bottle. Meanwhile, she insisted on dropping small amounts of the milk from a spoon into the baby's mouth, to ease her hunger pains. No questions were directly asked as to where the baby came from and as to who her parents were, but Mrs White was of the same suspicion as Delia that Mr Fairbanks was the father and had been left to handle the terrible shame of the sordid affair.

Now in full fighting mood, having had time to go over the situation and possibilities in her mind, Delia returned to the study where Harry had attempted to smarten himself up by having a quick wipe down. He looked weary and bedraggled and searched Delia's face as she entered the room, trying to detect her mood.

"Thank you, my darling, I can't tell you how grateful I am to you and how relieved I am that the child has finally ceased her wailing; she must be in very capable hands."

"Please spare me your sweet tongue and don't patronise me, Harry, especially not when you've arrived home with your illegitimate child and looking as though you've had to fight your way out of a muddy ditch with her. I'm going to the drawing-room; both you and this room have a repelling odour about them."

"As you wish my dearest, but this entire house actually reeks of fish, how you can possibly smell anything else seems quite surprising!" exclaimed Harry, crossly.

"I've asked Mrs White to have some coffee sent to the drawing-room, my appetite has completely diminished."

"*Good God Delia*, I swear to you that I'm completely innocent in all of this. I rescued a newborn child who was half-submerged in a muddy bog, alongside her dead mother on the roadside a few miles from Oxford, anyone else would applaud and sing my praises, but *you*, my very own wife, can only see fit to make ridiculous speculations and judge and condemn me!" Harry's raised voice echoed through the house which was music to Mrs White's ears as she and the maids worked in silence with the door ajar, hoping to listen in on the anticipated argument.

Harry followed Delia into the drawing-room, where the tray had already been left on the coffee table. She sat on a rigid straight backed chair rather than sink into the sumptuous damask couch, wanting to keep a formal atmosphere until she was convinced by Harry's absurd explanation. Harry poured the coffee and retold everything which had happened over the last twenty-four hours, leaving out the fact that he'd lost a colossal amount of money and would have to spend the day playing with the figures and working out how to salvage enough funds to pay off the pile of I owe you notes which he'd accumulated throughout his long and unfortunate evening.

He suddenly remembered the woman's reticule and prayed that it might contain anything that would convince Delia he was telling her the truth. He leapt out of his seat, startling Delia, "I've just remembered, I retrieved the poor woman's reticule, it's in a bit of a soiled state, but you never know, it might shine some light on to who she was *and* if there are any relatives who would be able to offer a home to her daughter." For the first time since arriving home, a tiny glimmer of hope lifted Harry Fairbanks' spirits.

CHAPTER THREE

With the purchase of a feeding bottle, the baby had fed contentedly and was now fast asleep in the warm kitchen in a makeshift crib which Selma had made from the wicker laundry basket. They were still curious to know more about the baby, but Mrs White had issued strict instructions that until otherwise permitted, they were not to breath a word of what had gone on at Harberton Mead to their families or friends on their return home at the end of the day, an order which both Maybell and Selma knew they'd not be able to keep to themselves and could already picture the excited look of intrigue on their ma's face when they teased her with their scandalous secret from Harberton Mead.

Harry placed the damp reticule down onto the coffee table, it had dried off considerably and shards of dried mud fell easily from it. Delia eyed the brown, floral embroidered silk bag, as Harry fumbled around trying to untangle the soiled drawstring. He poured its contents out freely hoping that Delia would view this as a sign that he had nothing to hide. A shilling piece rolled across the table, dropping onto the floor. A small pile of papers and letters scattered the table, emitting an earthy damp odour. There was also a wedding band and a small amount of money, no more than four shillings in total.

Harry began to carefully open up each paper.
"I wonder why she wasn't wearing this?" mused
Harry as he put the wedding band to one side.
Delia remained silent, her thoughts now telling
her that perhaps on this occasion Harry was
telling the truth.

There was an employer's reference, written on
official headed paper bearing the name of
Belmont Hall in Faversham, Northamptonshire
and detailing the good character of a Miss Faye
Butler who had it seemed worked as a parlour
maid. Harry muttered a few of the sentences as
he quickly read the letter. Inside another
envelope was a strange assortment of lace and
bits of coloured ribbon along with cuttings of
printed love poems and poignant and romantic
sentiments of love and endearment, all written
in the same neat handwriting with minuscule
illustrations of hearts, lovebirds and flowers.

"Was she wearing a wedding ring, Harry?"
quizzed Delia, who was still pondering over the
gold band on the table.

Harry's brow was deeply creased as he picked
up the reference again.

"This is dated almost seven months ago...now
that *does* make more sense...but why wasn't she
wearing the ring?"

"So you *did* check her finger then?"

"*No, no* I didn't, Delia. The poor girl was lying
dead in a ditch on the highway with her
screaming child half-buried in the mud. Do you

honestly think that checking her fingers for rings was my priority? There's only one thing that I can tell you about Faye Butler, which is that she had fair curly hair; not unlike your own hair, as it happens."

Delia picked up the silver coffee pot and poured out two cups, her stomach was rumbling and she could feel a headache coming on. In the distance, she could hear the sound of the baby crying again and was suddenly overcome with sadness for the poor woman who must have endured a terrible and frightening birth and felt so alone.

"I think her daughter has that same fair hair too," uttered Delia, sadly.

Both Harry and Delia drank their coffee in silence before continuing to go through the rest of the letters. Harry was finding it increasingly impossible to suppress his yawns; his body ached but his mind was overloaded with worries; he knew that even if his head was to rest upon a pillow, sleep would evade him.

"So where is the poor woman now? Please don't tell me that you just left her on the roadside, Harry."

"Of course not; well initially, I had little choice. The coachmen were adamant that a corpse in their carriage would bring them a life of bad luck."

"Gosh, how terribly mean and heartless!" interrupted Delia in shock.

"My thoughts exactly, it took all of my persuasive powers to convince them to part with one of their threadbare rugs to cover the woman with, which, I had to pay for on arriving home."
"Why when you arrived home, Harry?" Delia snapped, "Oh, no, don't trouble yourself to answer that ridiculous question...you obviously gambled away every penny, last night!"
"I must admit, it wasn't one of my more memorable nights at the card table, but let's not worry about that now, my darling; we have far bigger problems at this minute." Harry instantly visualised the pile of I owe you notes which were now in his secret book compartment, reminding him that he'd have a long task ahead of him and had no idea as to how he would manage to settle his huge debts. Delia stared crossly into the corner of the room, her mouth pouting as she pondered as to why she'd been in such a hurry to marry Harry Fairbanks before she'd had long enough to be familiar with his real character.
"Anyway," continued Harry, disturbing Delia's thoughts, "as I was explaining to you; I insisted that the coachmen stop by at the local undertaker's parlour which was inundated with corpses ...I said that I'd fund the cost of the funeral, but was informed by the undertaker that he'd have to retain her body in the morgue until the police had been informed and made the necessary investigations."

The sound of the wailing baby grew louder, bringing Mrs White knocking urgently on the door. She appeared in a flustered state, her face bright pink and her mob cap hanging off the side of her head. The screaming baby was almost as red-faced as her and clearly in a state of distress, "I'm sorry, Mr and Mrs Fairbanks, but me and the girls haven't been able to console this baby since she woke and we've got a dozen and one jobs to attend to and at this rate there won't be a tidy, clean room, or even a sniff of luncheon, not to mention dinner. I don't know what's wrong with her, and none of us has much experience with babies...she just won't stop this terrible screaming!"

Delia immediately got up and relieved the distraught cook, taking the baby from her, "Thank you Mrs White, you've done a remarkable job with her, let me see if I can find a way to calm the poor little creature."

Mrs White's tensed shoulders relaxed as she was unburdened from the small noisy bundle. She pulled out the baby bottle from her apron pocket and pushed it into the crook of Delia's arm, "Maybe you can get her to drink some more milk, Mrs Fairbanks; she just refuses when I try."

Delia paced the drawing-room floor rocking the baby in her arms but it wasn't until she rested the baby over her shoulder that the crying eventually ceased and the baby released her wind leaving a small deposit of regurgitated milk on Delia's expensive silk dressing gown. Paying no attention to his wife, Harry was deeply engrossed in another of the letters.

"This letter has been written by a relatively local woman, who signs it Granny *'Butler'*...her address is Dove Cottage in Wheatley village. Do you think that was where she was heading to?"

"Well read it out...what does she say?" encouraged Delia, as she gently rocked the baby to and fro in her arms.

With his face screwed up and looking distorted Harry tried in vain to make sense of the letter, "It's severely faded and parts of it have been completely eaten away," he moaned. "She must have had this letter for some time...I can just manage to read the year on the date which is the year 1855. It really doesn't help that her handwriting is almost illegible, she presumably suffers from the shakes or wrote the letter in freezing temperatures, or perhaps even after a couple of sweet sherries!"

"*Oh Harry*, for heaven's sake; pass me the letter! Here, you take the baby!"

Harry froze, "Oh, God, *no*...You keep hold of her, you're much better at it than me; I'll hold the letter up for you to see."

In the flash of a second, Delia hastily dropped the baby into Harry's arms and snatched out the letter from his hold,

"*Stop being a coward, Harry!* You're the one who brought this baby into our home and our lives...

you were probably the first person to hold her, so don't start with your feeble excuses now!" Harry smiled sheepishly at Delia, a pang of sorrow suddenly struck him as he couldn't help thinking how natural she looked with a baby in her arms; she'd make a wonderful mother if only they were to be blessed with a child, he mused.

"Yes, I suppose I was...Do you think she'll subconsciously remember me forever?"

"I doubt that very much...what a ridiculous notion, Harry."

Delia carefully studied the delicate letter and discovered it to be a message of sad news, informing Faye that her grandfather had passed away. The grandmother insisted that Faye was not to take time away from her new position at the '*big house'* but to visit as soon as she was permitted a holiday.

"There's no mention of any other family members," announced Delia after she'd dictated what she could read of the letter.

"Oh dear, what a shame...this poor little creature is going to endure a tough life," muttered Harry as he stared hard at the tiny life in his arms.

It was a few hours later when Harry, who was methodically working his way through the account books, noticed the local constabulary's carriage heading towards the house. He quickly shoved his workings out, which presented a bleak outlook, back into the drawer and made his way to inform Delia, who was still patiently tending to the baby in the drawing-room. Pausing in the hallway, Harry wasn't at all impressed with his reflection in the looking glass. He presented an extremely rough image; he'd still not had time to shave, his tired eyes had sunk into his head and his hair hung greasily and reeked of stale cigar smoke. Delia was elegantly positioned on the peacock blue couch looking as beautiful as always and making Harry feel totally ashamed of his villainous appearance.

"Brace yourself, my darling, we're about to receive a visit from the local constabulary," announced Harry, on entering the room.

"We have nothing to worry about; you acted in a very noble way and probably saved this baby's life. That is of course if everything you told me is true to your word."

Harry gritted his teeth in anger, annoyed that Delia still had her doubts,

"What do I have to do to make you believe in me, Delia? I swear to God every word which passed my lips is a word of truth!"

Delia diverted her eyes, knowing that she was behaving a little cruelly to Harry, and also now quite sure that he was telling her the truth.

"Do you think that they'll take the baby with them?" she enquired, casually.

"I don't know, maybe. Do *you* want to keep her?"

"What are you saying, Harry...what do you mean? She's a human being, not a stray dog. It wouldn't be as easy as that and besides, why would we want the responsibility of somebody else's child. I want my own baby, Harry...can't you understand that?"

There was no time to continue the conversation as the rapping on the door was quickly followed by Selma announcing the arrival of the two constables, adding to the gossip that she would be able to delight her ma's ears with over supper that night.

The pair of constables wearing their blue swallow-tailed jackets towered above Harry and Delia even though they'd removed their tall stovepipe hats. They stood seriously faced in preparation to address the grave incident. Introduced as constables Morris and Webster, they had obviously worked together for years and began their investigations in perfect synchronization. Even the sleeping baby seemed to sense their presence and her gentle whimpering soon forced the questions to a halt while Delia rang for one of the maids to take the baby into another part of the house and try to console her.

Harry was reprimanded for not leaving the only evidence, being the deceased woman's reticule, at the scene of the crime, to which both Harry and Delia implored that there was no evidence of any crime; only that of an unfortunate woman who'd died in childbirth and that if he'd have left it behind it might have been lost, stolen or damaged even further from another possible downpour. Slightly red-cheeked, Morris and Webster said no more on the matter and proceeded to sift through the contents of the reticule.

"Can I offer you some refreshments Constables?" asked Harry.

They declined the offer saying as how they were far too busy to drink with the present fatality to deal with plus a robbery which had taken place during the night in a city alehouse. Half an hour had passed before Morris and Webster concluded that they'd continue to go through Faye Butler's meagre personal belongings down at the station and as they collected everything together and put it into a large brown envelope, Webster reminded his colleague that they would have to take the baby with them. Delia felt a sudden icy chill sweep through her and as Harry rang for one of the maids to return the baby to the drawing-room Delia was anxious to know where they would be taking the helpless newborn baby to.

"Don't fret, Mrs Fairbanks," expressed constable Morris, "I can see that you've taken good care of her and I dare say she'll be treated well in Bicester workhouse which is most likely where our Sergeant will instruct us to deliver her to."

"What about the baby's father...that poor woman's husband, he's more than likely waiting in their home for her to return!" cried Delia.

"Worried out of his wits; the poor man!"
The constables exchanged a glance, struggling to conceal their self-righteous grins,
"With all due respect, Mrs Fairbanks," he continued, "I doubt very much that there *is* a husband, let alone anything which remotely resembles a home...no, sadly, we've come upon this sorry scene all too often, it can be a cruel and wicked world out there, Mrs Fairbanks."
Still not satisfied, Delia continued to plead with Constable Morris, "What about the baby's grandmother? We've read the letter, you know, she lives in Dove Cottage just a few miles away!"
Both Constables Morris and Webster looked downcast as simultaneously they slowly shook their heads,
"Unfortunately, Constable Webster and myself were called out to '*old widow Butler's*' cottage about a week ago...I'm surprised you hadn't read about it...made the front page in the *Oxford Chronicle* you know. Some foreigner had turned up on the poor old woman's cottage and brutally struck the unfortunate soul. Old Mrs Butler was found stone-cold dead with the look of fear on her face as though she'd seen the devil himself. I'll never forget that day...not for the rest of my days and I hope I never live to see such a ..."
Constable Morris suddenly stopped in mid-sentence, noticing how Mrs Fairbanks appeared quite pale-faced all of a sudden,
"Oh, I do apologise, Mrs Fairbanks, I didn't

mean to be so descriptive...are you feeling ill?"
Harry hurried to his wife's side, just as Maybell
and Selma quietly knocked on the half-opened
door, bringing the baby with them.

"Please don't make a fuss, Harry, I'm perfectly
well. I've merely been sat too close to the fire; it's
become quite stuffy and overcrowded in here."

"Well I never," declared Constable Webster as he
glared at Maybell and Selma. "Now, tell me if
I'm mistaken, but are you two sisters and does
your ma work in the tobacconists and
confectioners at the end of Henley Road?"

Maybell and Selma nodded, coyly, as they
quickly glanced at Mrs Fairbanks, hoping that
they weren't in any kind of trouble.

"Well, I never...you young lasses are the image of
your ma!"

"Well done, Constable Webster, it's clear to me
now why you are employed in Her Majesty's
constabulary!" chuckled Constable Morris.

The sombre atmosphere in the drawing-room
was momentarily lightened but Delia could feel
her heart painfully contracting as she viewed
Maybell place the baby into Constable Webster's
arms. Delia quickly looked to Harry, his tired
face looked even more strained and Delia knew
that he was as despondent as her to watch as the
baby was being taken away to the workhouse in
Bicester.

"Wait!" called out Delia as the constables had
already left the drawing-room and were being

shown out by the maids, who were engrossed in a conversation about the delicious assortment of confectionary sold in the shop where their mother was employed.

"Allow *us* to look after the baby...just until you've had a chance to discover if she *does* have a living relative or a concerned father, even." Constable Webster viewed Mrs Fairbanks' suggestion as a narrow escape from having to handle a squealing newborn baby in the confines of the police carriage all the way from Oxford to Bicester and looked at Constable Morris with an expression which he hoped his colleague of many years would understand. Harry, meanwhile, was relieved to hear his wife's words of compassion and immediately voiced his thoughts,

"What a splendid and most sensible idea; the child will be perfectly safe and well cared for and it will save you an unnecessary journey to Bicester. What do you say, Constable?"

"Well, Mr and Mrs Fairbanks, it's not *normal* procedure and I'm not sure if our Sergeant will be in agreement; but you are a reputable gentleman around these parts, Mr Fairbanks and personally, I think it's a jolly good idea," expressed Constable Morris. "Very well, hand the baby back Webster and let's be on our way. You'll be hearing from us in due course, Mr Fairbanks."

CHAPTER FOUR

A long and tiresome week had passed, leaving Delia feeling weary from her disturbed nights and busy days. Baby 'Faye' as Delia had temporarily named the child was thankfully thriving and had already filled out a little into her wrinkly skin. Delia clandestinely delighted in her new and demanding role as a foster mother but kept her feelings close to her chest along with a stern face whenever Harry was anywhere near her. She continuously admonished herself against becoming emotionally attached to baby Faye, but could already feel the ties of love as they entwined around her heart like a clinging, climbing rose knowing that the day would arrive when her heart was painfully pricked by its sharp thorns. Harry, meanwhile had spent the week engulfed in his own self made traumas and for the time being had pushed the incident of Faye Butler and her baby to the back of his mind, considering it a Godsend that Delia was so engrossed in caring for the baby that she had little spare time on her hands to meddle in their appalling financial affairs.

There was no possible way in which Harry could repay his escalating debts which, with the extortionate, accumulating interest being charged, were set to double in two days time. During his sleepless nights, he had devised a desperate plan which would, with a huge helping of luck at the card and roulette tables of Brooks's Gentleman's club, hopefully, see him break even.

It had been an emotional day when Harry had shaken the hand of the property agent, sealing the deal on the sale of a business close to his heart. The modest but booming boatyard which was situated along the bank's of the river Thames by Iffley Loch had been responsible for the building of hundreds of punts over the years and had been purchased by Harry's late father just a few years before he'd passed away; leaving the world to re-join Harry's long-departed mother. Sensing how desperate Harry Fairbanks was for a quick sale, the property agent purchased the boatyard himself, knowing that he would make a handsome profit when he came to sell it on in the following year, during the summer months. Harry was not in a position to dispute about the rock bottom price and like the cunning property agent, knew that it was the worst possible time of the year to sell such a business. Having already gambled away any trinkets and jewellery of any substantial value which had also belonged to his late parents, Harry hoped to persuade Delia to loan him her pieces of gold jewellery which he'd gifted to her on various occasions over the years. Once he'd pawned them and put the money to good use, he would hopefully be in a position to reclaim them. Perhaps he'd not trouble her at the moment, he mused, since she was busy taking care of baby Faye; he would simply borrow them for the evening and hope she'd not notice. Presuming that the upstairs of Harberton Mead had already been swept and polished that morning, as Harry was carefully filling his inside coat pockets with the contents from his wife's jewellery box, the sudden arrival of Selma with a pile of fresh linen over her arm startled Harry, turning his pale and tired-looking face a bright shade of scarlet. Realising how suspicious he must have appeared, he froze on the spot as he silently prayed for a believable excuse to enter his head. For a brief time, both he and Selma were embarrassingly lost for words.

"Is it normal to be changing the bed linen so late in the afternoon, Selma?"

With her eyes still focussed on Mrs Fairbanks' open jewellery box, she watched as Harry casually closed its lid and placed the last item with the rest, into the pocket of his cashmere overcoat. There was a prolonged pause before she replied,

"Mrs Fairbanks was busy with the baby this morning...she said it would be alright for me to do my work now; but if you'd like me to go and come back when you've finished...when you've finished your work, that is, Mr Fairbanks."

Harry wished that it had been Maybell on bed linen duties; in his opinion even though Selma was the younger of the sisters, she was by far the sharper witted of the two and possessed a more inquisitive mind than that of her older sibling. The fact that she'd just witnessed him helping himself to Delia's treasure would more than likely trouble the girl's thoughts until she'd confessed to what she'd seen.

"It's a surprise for Mrs Fairbanks, Selma...I'm having some precious gemstones added to a couple of the plain pieces when I go to London later...so, *please*, not a word to Mrs Fairbanks...I'd hate the surprise to be ruined."

"Very well, Mr Fairbanks, you can trust me, I wouldn't dare to ruin your surprise."

Harry hurried from the bedroom and downstairs to his study where he stuffed the thick wad of banknotes from the boatyard sale, down the inside of his boot; it would be ironic if the one time when his carriage to London was held up by highway robbers, was the day when his pockets were filled with his entire funds. Carefully wrapping up Delia's jewellery in a handkerchief, he stuffed the package down the leg of his other boot and put some loose change into his pocket and a few banknotes into his wallet. The sound of baby Faye's crying echoed throughout the house and the mouthwatering aroma of Mrs White's delicious baking gave Harry no encouragement to leave the house on such a chilly and depressingly dull afternoon to embark on what would be a challenging and life-changing night at the gaming tables.

He found Delia sat deep in thought as she stared out of the drawing-room window, entranced by the fluttering autumn leaves as the strong gusts whipped them across the lawn, leaving them captive beneath the shrubbery. Harry coughed lightly to gain her attention,

"*Goodness*, Harry, you've been in and out of the house like a Jack in the box today! What's going on?" she stressed, belligerently.

Harry spoke timidly, "I've business in London this evening, my love. I doubt I'll return until the morning or later, perhaps, so don't wait up for me, my darling."

Delia eyed Harry from top to toe; he was well-groomed and dressed in his finest attire.

"You look positively, dashing, Harry. Who will be the fortunate *trollop* on your arm tonight, I wonder? Does this urgent night out have anything to do with the baby?"

Harry did love his wife but found her constant suspicious mind quite overbearing. In their early days of marriage, he'd relished in the way that his wife became jealous by a mere smile or polite and social conversation between him and another female. Delia presumed that every woman he was acquainted with was a former lover and insisted in grilling him about every single one, even the wives of his business associates. Harry felt that no other woman in the entire world could adore him as his wife did, but as the years progressed Delia's obsessive jealousy became like a third and intrusive person in their marriage and the novelty soon wore away only to leave a trail of bitter arguments and a relationship which seemed void of all trust.

"*Delia*, I have *extremely* important business to settle and I'll be perfectly honest with you, my love..."

Delia suddenly burst into a theatrical laugh, cutting Harry off in mid-sentence.

"*Honest? Honest, did you say?* That will be the day, *Harry Fairbanks!* That will be a day worth celebrating in style when you are honest with me. Where are you *really* going Harry? *Now* try to be honest!"

Harry swallowed hard, his mind ticking over like clockwork as he tried to decide if he should be totally honest on this occasion; preparing Delia for the worst possible scenario might just prove easier on him in the long run. He furtively glanced at the grandfather clock and realised there was little time to spare if he wanted to board the stagecoach to London. Delia would most likely become more enquiring than a high court judge and all of his plans would be ruined.

"I'm leaving now, to London, my dear and as I've already stated, it's strictly business. I assure you there will be no pleasure whatsoever in my evening on this occasion."

Delia pouted her cherry red lips as she rapidly blinked away her tear-filled eyes whilst she stared at Harry,

"Why weren't you honest with me all those years ago, Harry? Why couldn't you admit to me that you were a compulsive gambler? You tricked me into marriage and now it looks as though you're going to drag me down the road of destitution with you."

"Might I remind you, Delia, that you married me 'for richer, for poorer' and if you think that you were tricked into marriage, well, my sweet wife, let me remind you that your late aunt led me to believe that I was marrying an heiress. If you ask me, her death was perfectly timed...otherwise, you might be visiting her in debtor's prison!"

"Oh stop being so mean, Harry!" yelled Delia as she grabbed the closest item to hand and flung the onyx ashtray through the air towards Harry. "Yes, Harry, I did marry you for richer and for poorer, but not for self-inflicted poverty...and kindly do not speak ill of the deceased, especially when it's my dear late aunt."

Calmly picking up the ashtray from off the floor, annoying Delia even more with his coolness, Harry knew that if he hoped for any success that night, he'd have to make an immediate exit.

"We'll discuss this issue on my return, my love, now, I really ought to leave."

Without giving Delia the chance to respond,

Harry marched out of the drawing-room, placed his top hat onto his head of slickly oiled hair and spurred on by his anger, strode briskly towards the highway. He couldn't understand why Delia held her late aunt in such high esteem; she'd been ready to palm Delia off to practically any man who looked as though he had a healthy bank balance and had shown little concern for Delia's future happiness. It was fortunate for Delia, considered Harry, that he had been a decent, respectable and relatively well off husband.

Delia wiped away her tears, she felt miserable and unloved. Her life was empty and she had nobody apart from an untrustworthy husband who she was sure, no longer loved her and did very little to show that she was special to him anymore. Delia had had such high hopes when she'd become Harry's wife six years ago; she'd loved him, or at least she thought she had; he was handsome, kind and thoughtful and had been extremely attentive towards her during the early months, often surprising her with gifts and arranging surprise trips to the theatre. They had been inseparable during the beginning and both anticipated to see the fruits of their long nights of passion materialize. Delia had presumed that her happy married life would remain constant but having so desperately yearned for a child, every wedding anniversary which passed, became a cruel reminder that she was barren and that their marriage had not been blessed with children. Harry began to spend more time in London and over the years, Delia began to notice the disappearance of various items of any worth around the home, but with her not favouring Harry's departed mother's taste she was pleased to be able to replace the objects with ornaments of her own choice.

The nearing cries of baby Faye soon brought Delia out of her reverie, as Selma crept gingerly into the drawing-room.
"Good afternoon, Mrs Fairbanks."
Delia held out her arms, eager to hold and comfort the distraught baby,
"I'm sure her voice has become louder in the short time that she's been with us!" declared Delia as she watched Selma struggling with the wriggling baby.
"Mrs White said that Faye prefers to be nursed by you, Mrs Fairbanks...she just keeps crying whenever we try to rock her to sleep."
"*Really*, is that so?" Delia was more inclined to think that Mrs White and the maids simply lacked the patience to rock Faye to sleep. They knew that Delia would not allow the baby to cry continuously. Not sure if it was pure coincidence, or if there was some truth in Mrs White's theory, baby Faye immediately fell silent the minute that Delia cradled her.
"You see, Mrs Fairbanks, *it's true*, baby Faye

really does love you!"

Left alone with the baby in her arms, Faye's round, clear eyes fixed firmly on Delia's and for the very first time, Delia experienced a warmth which spread through her entire body; she felt the sudden urge to kiss the baby and knew, from that instant, that the ties of love had become firmly knotted, never to be broken.

CHAPTER FIVE

It was with great relief that Harry alighted from
the overcrowded and stuffy carriage. It had been
one of the longest journeys between Oxford and
London which he could remember embarking
on. The passengers, most of who were clad in
damp clothes after the previous heavy storm,
packed together uncomfortably beside each
other. The small inner space seemed to be
lacking in any fresh air and the overpowering
stench of body odour lingered in Harry's
nostrils, long after the stagecoach had
disappeared into London's bustling horizon and
the irritating sound of the young lad's whining
voice still echoed inside his thumping head.
Sometimes, thought Harry, it was indeed a
blessing that Delia had not presented him with a
string of rowdy children; there was much to be
admired about a life of peace and quiet.
His first port of call was to a reputable
pawnbroker in East London, not one of Harry's
favoured parts of the Capital, especially when
there was such a large amount of cash hidden on
his body. Notorious for its callous villains and
hardened gangs, the East End was rife in
poverty and in every street Harry was
confronted by the gaunt street urchins whose
starving, deep-set eyes were able to beg for food
and money without any words even passing

their sore and cracked lips. After pawning Delia's jewellery, Harry became paranoid that he was now being pursued and with every few steps, he looked back over his shoulder, convinced that the perpetrator was leaping into a dark alleyway or shop doorway on his every turn. He hailed a hansom cab the minute that he reached the main thoroughfare and as it neared St. James, Harry felt safe enough to discretely transfer the wad of banknotes from out of his boot and into his wallet. The familiar sight of the yellow Portland stone of Brooks's Gentleman's club was a welcoming sight, it was nearing eight o'clock and as the weather had progressively worsened since his departure from Oxford and the strengthening wind was causing the orange flames of the street lanterns to flicker and spit, he quickly stepped over the threshold into the warmth and luxury of Brooks's. With enough time to socialise a little before the more serious business in the gaming room commenced, Harry ran his tongue across his lips in anticipation of a warming whiskey to smooth his dry throat.

The thick layers of hazy blue smoke were sent into disarray as he strolled casually through the sumptuous lounge area upon the deep pile of the decorative red Persian carpet; all the while he was surreptitiously noting who was present from the corner of his eye. He chose to sit on a worn and well broken in, tan buckskin armchair, close to the stone fireplace, where a roaring fire crackled loudly as it sent huge leaping flames up into the chimney breast. Little time had elapsed before a smartly attired waiter arrived holding a silver tray. The orange flames reflected in the crystal glasses, changing the colour of the liquid which they carried. A group of men, who had gathered on the opposite side of the room, appeared to be consoling a middle-aged and overly distressed man who they surrounded. Harry could vaguely hear their sentiments of commiserations and assumed that the gentleman was probably in a similar situation as himself and had gambled away his entire wealth; he silently prayed that he wouldn't be in a similar state later on that evening. The double oak doors leading into the gaming room were soon swung open and not wanting to appear too eager to commence gambling, the men casually strolled towards the room, concealing their true feelings of excitement as any gentleman of integrity would.

With Selma and Maybell having left Harberton Mead to return to their family home for the night and the gentle sound of Mrs White's snoring emanating from her room, Delia decided to extinguish the lanterns and have an early night. Faye, who continued to sleep in the well-padded washing basket, which was now perched on the top of Delia's dressing table, was at last sound asleep. Delia paused by her side to admire the perfectly clear complexion of Faye's beautiful little face; her soft cheeks were slightly pink, matching her tiny love heart lips and a tiny lock of golden hair poked out from her woollen bonnet and rested upon her brow. Delia hadn't realised how exhausting taking care of a newborn baby would be, she'd always imagined them to sleep most of the time and only cry when in need of a feed. She had now learned that this was not the case; whenever any of the women in their circle of acquaintances had given birth, they only complained of the horrendous pains of childbirth and left *'nanny'* to deal with most other aspects of caring for their newborns.

After having lost more games of whist than he'd won, Harry moved into the adjacent room where the pace was considerably faster and money changed hands at the speed of the throw of two dice. The high barreled ceiling of the *'Hazard'* room as it was more commonly known seemed to trap the excited hollers of the rowdy gamblers, sending them continuously echoing and bouncing around the room. Men had been known to lose everything they possessed within an hour of indulging in the quick and addictive game and Harry was no exception; after winning the first few games, he became overconfident and flighty. Thinking that his winning streak would continue, Harry's stakes increased and his predictions of the winning numbers rolled, began to fail. With the steady consumption of whiskey throughout the night, it wasn't long before Harry became blasé and reckless which led to calamitous consequences.

Delia had been woken up in the small hours of the morning by baby Faye's whimpering; it was no surprise to see that there was still no sign of Harry and as she sat shivering in the cold kitchen, whilst waiting for the milk to warm, a disturbing image of Harry parading the night clubs of London with another woman, filled her with anger and jealousy and as much as she adored the baby he'd rescued, there remained a niggling thought that somehow Harry knew more about Faye's mother than he'd let on and now he was out living the high life in the West End, leaving her with all the responsibility of her husband's folly while he undoubtedly shared the joke about his accomplishments with a common woman of the night. Burning tears rolled down her face, she could feel her heart being ripped in half. She loved baby Faye and the reality that she'd soon be taken away from her was akin to her entire world coming to an end. She no longer wished to endure the sort of lifestyle that she and Harry had lived before the arrival of Faye; she wanted more and she wanted to continue mothering Faye; it was the only aspect of her life which filled her with a sense of importance and gave her life purpose.

"Well, I never" exclaimed Mrs White, all of a sudden..."I was in the middle of a terrible dream; the poor little child was crying so desperately and there was nothing I could do to comfort her, I couldn't even stretch out my hand to touch the poor little scrap and then I awoke to the sound of little Faye!"

Ruth White stood barefoot on the cold flagstone floor, wrapped in a thick dressing robe and squinting, in a bid to see clearly without her spectacles.

"I'm so sorry Mrs White," expressed Delia who'd been so indulged in her thoughts that she'd forgotten what had brought her to the cold kitchen in the middle of the night and by some miracle had managed to block out the sound of Faye's ruckus.

Suddenly rushing towards the stove, Mrs White rescued the boiling milk just in time before it spilt over the top of the saucepan.

"Oh, what's wrong with me? I can't even warm some milk for that poor baby who's screaming with hunger pains. Is it any wonder why God didn't bless me with my own baby?"

Mrs White had known Delia long enough to sense that the crack in her voice was not solely due to her being overtired, but that she was deeply unhappy; she sympathised with her, knowing exactly where Mr Fairbanks was at such a late hour and what he was up to; she frowned, thinking how he should be with his wife, supporting her, after she'd been so generous in accepting the responsibility of the child, *his* child she didn't doubt; there was very little that went on under Harberton Mead's roof which slipped unnoticed by Mrs White.

She also knew how he had taken his wife's jewellery with him and had falsely praised Mr Fairbanks when Selma had explained the *'secret surprise'* to her over afternoon tea.

"You go upstairs and fetch the little cherub; I expect a cuddle will suffice until the milk has cooled; I'll just go and find my spectacles and put the water on to boil...I think we could both do with a nice cup of tea and perhaps a slice or two of toasted bread with lashings of butter!" Mrs White was an angel herself thought Delia, she was blessed with the gift of making every miserable situation seem bearable and Delia loved her for it.

Delia wasn't the only one feeling melancholy during the lonely hours of the night; Harry had left the gaming rooms and was slumped onto a leather chesterfield couch, in a dishevelled state, but despite the copious amounts of whiskey he'd poured down his throat, the terrible reality of his financial situation induced a sobering effect upon him. The club was now quiet with most of the clientele having returned to their homes. A few of the whist tables were, however, still occupied by desperate gamblers, hoping to reclaim a fraction of their losses before facing the wrath of their wives. Harry had lost everything and had not even managed to clear a single one of his I owe you notes; it was, without doubt, one of his most tragic nights; he was a ruined man. He was suddenly distracted by the sound of quiet sobbing coming from the far, dark corner of the room; the armchair had its back facing Harry, so it was impossible to see who occupied it. Harry hoped that he wasn't acquainted with him; in his opinion, there was nothing more pathetic than a crying man, it showed a trait of feebleness and complete lack of backbone. As the hands of the huge ornate wall clock moved slowly around its dial, curiosity and the need for a little peace forced Harry to leave the comfortable couch and make his way towards the desperate-sounding man. A few half-empty tumblers of whiskey were scattered on side tables and in the deep window ledges; Harry poured a few of the dregs together and presented a full glass as an offering.

Clearly embarrassed, the man, who did prove to be unknown to Harry, immediately pulled out a neatly folded handkerchief and pretended to mop his sweating brow, surreptitiously dabbing his tear-soaked face at the same time.

"*My dear fellow*, I was of the impression that I was alone, I must apologise for my discourteousness."

Harry handed him the cloudy looking drink but had already realised that this extremely well-bred gentleman was not intoxicated, as he'd expected; he recognised him as the man he'd noticed earlier that evening when he'd first arrived at Brooks's.

"That's jolly decent of you old chap, but I'm not in the mood for celebrating."

"Did the luck of the gaming room not shine on you either, Sir?" enquired Harry, sympathetically.

"I didn't participate at the whist tables tonight, old chap, the truth is, that I find myself in tragic circumstances and simply can't bear to go home; I cannot tolerate hearing the sorrowful cries of my darling Marjorie; she is a woman in the deepest state of mourning and I am but a mere coward."

Shocked by the stranger's declaration, Harry was tongue-tied and beginning to wish that he'd left this man to himself.

"Shall I see if I can bribe a waiter to bring us a pot of coffee and perhaps a plate of whatever is left to eat in the kitchen?"

"God Bless you my good fellow, you have come to my mercy when those whom I considered loyal to me have chosen to desert me during my bleakest hour...Lyle Dagworth, and it is indeed a great pleasure to meet you...Mr?"

Harry's tiredness had slowed his reactions and for a few awkward seconds he could only stare down at the extended hand before grabbing hold of it,

"Harry Fairbanks, excuse my slowness, it has been an extremely long and drawn out night."

"Now, my good fellow, did my ears deceive me, or did I hear you mention a pot of coffee?"

Harry suddenly remembered his embarrassing financial situation and the grim fact that his wallet and pockets were completely empty.

"I do beg your pardon, Mr Dagworth, but in my haste to comfort you, it completely slipped my mind that this night has left me penniless and ashamed of myself to boot."

Lyle took out his wallet; it was swollen with banknotes, causing Harry's eyes to widen.

"Here you are Harry, go and see what you can tempt the waiters to rustle up with this," he pushed the crisp, white five-pound banknote into Harry's hand, "and my friends call me *L.D*, by the way, and tonight you have proved to be the only person worthy of my friendship; you're a decent chap Harry Fairbanks, *a decent chap*."

Harry left in search of a waiter, he felt suddenly refreshed and optimistic; was it pure fate which had guided him to enquire after the distraught man, he pondered; he certainly appeared to be a gentleman of wealth and status.

CHAPTER SIX

Curious to know Mr Lyle Dagworth's reasons for being in such a state of distress, for the time being, Harry put his own troubles to one side. It had been an easy task to persuade a weary waiter to make a pot of hot coffee and a plate of sandwiches, especially when the generous payment was waved before his eyes, he had also included stoking up the dying fire into the deal. Harry shivered as he returned to where Mr Dagworth was still sat in the same armchair, it was approaching dawn; Harry was tired, hungry and chilled to his bones but having already sensed that his new acquaintance was probably going to keep him occupied until he'd finished pouring out his troubles, Harry mentally prepared himself to be an earnest listener.

"I've managed to persuade someone to stoke up the fire, Mr Dagworth; may I suggest that we locate to the couch nearer the fireplace?"

"I must insist upon you calling me L.D, my good fellow, remember my words; from this night forth, I consider you to be a sincere friend."

"Very well, L.D, the waiter will be along just as soon as he's prepared our modest feast."

"I find myself with little appetite Harry, it's my darling Marjorie, you see, she has lost the will to live and cries day and night, begging to be united with our sweet angel in heaven. She has seen our little Phyllis, in her dreams; she is waiting at the gates of Heaven for her beloved mother and poor old Marjorie wants nothing more than to be with her; I no longer mean anything to her; she can't bear any more children, or so old Doctor Winston informs us and he's usually quite accurate in his prognosis; so you see, Harry my dear fellow, I'm surplus to requirement, an old *has been*. Even my wealth is of no consequence to her anymore."

Harry rubbed his aching head; his new acquaintance had given him an awful lot to think about and as much as he felt sorry for Lyle Dagworth he already regretted befriending him, especially when he had a mountain of his own troubles to contend with. He did appear to be like a man with the entire world on his shoulders though, causing Harry to feel, for the first time since he'd left Oxford, that *his* troubles *could* be overcome, even if it involved a few months, or even years, of hardship.

"Come along L.D," insisted Harry for the second time, "We will be more comfortable seated by the fire and I do believe that the waiter is heading towards us with a tray of refreshments!" Lyle followed like a wounded dog being led to safety by his master and slouched onto the couch while Harry relieved the waiter of the heavy silver tray and proceeded to pour out two cups of the steaming black coffee, it's tantalizing odour already awakening Harry's senses and filling his head with a plan which could prove beneficial to both him and his new acquaintance. "Here you are, L.D." Harry passed him the white, gold-rimmed cup and saucer. He took it eagerly and immediately began to sip the hot liquid but refused the offer of the sandwiches. Harry began munching his way through the silver platter of neatly cut, triangles, suddenly realising how hungry he was. The coffee and food had a sobering effect and whilst Lyle consumed his third coffee, Harry's thoughts were in turmoil as he tried to decide what the most convincing story would be, to tell Lyle, or if he should simply try to keep things less complicated and tell him the truth. He wondered how wealthy Mr Lyle Dagworth actually was, knowing that some of the members of Brooks's Gentleman's club had conned their way into gaining membership and were little more than undercover crooks out to swindle their way through life.

"Forgive me if I'm speaking out of turn, but shouldn't you insist on being at your wife's side during such mournful times?" asked Harry in a sympathetic tone.

"My dear good fellow, our sweet angel passed away some seven months since and we are no longer in mourning, although my wife fails to differ and has lost all sense of propriety along with her faith, I dare say. I fear that *I* myself will very shortly be in mourning for her if she continues to distress herself in such a punishing manner...her heart cannot possibly stand the strain from her constant grief, and neither can I."

Harry swallowed the last sandwich and poured some more coffee for them both. He wondered if *he* had aged overnight as the mysterious Mr Dagworth had. He was a scrawny man, quite tall with a protruding stomach, which he'd been unable to hold in as the hours ticked by and had now released the buttons to his tight-fitting waistcoat, allowing his belly to hang distastefully over the waist of his trousers. His face was camouflaged by an excessively overgrown mutton chop beard which had obviously been blackened and his brow was deeply furrowed, causing the top half of his head to appear years older than the bottom half. Harry deduced that he must be in his fifties, at least.

"Your wife has obviously felt the loss of your daughter far worse than many women would have...perhaps the opportunity to have another child might be the cure...how old was the child when she passed away?"

"She was just a mere and innocent, little baby, just five days old and already the light of my wife's eye."

"Oh dear, what a tragedy for you both!"

Lyle stared across the room in a trance, he looked tired and although Harry felt sorry for him, he remained dubious as to whether he should trust this stranger.

All of a sudden, Lyle turned to face Harry; his face appeared tense and angry, turning a hue of bright red.

"I do recall that I've already told you how another child is totally out of the question for my darling Marjorie...I fear, you are not paying attention to me, Mr Fairbanks and if that is the case, you might as well leave me to my misery this instant!" he declared in a booming voice.

Completely thrown by Lyle's fickle behaviour, Harry became slightly nervous in his company, "Forgive me, Mr Dagworth, but *I do indeed* remember everything which you told me in confidence, it is *you*, Sir who has jumped to the wrong conclusion, from my suggestion. Mr Dagworth, you find me in a similar state of emotional torture as yourself, you see, I am also in mourning; I am in mourning for my wife, who passed away, in childbirth, just a week ago!"

Lyle's bottom jaw dropped, he could only gawk in shock at his new acquaintance.

"You *do not* in the least resemble a man who has, so recently, suffered such a bereavement...why in God's name are you even *here*, gambling?"

"Because, a few weeks before my wife's confinement, she confessed to me that her unborn child had nothing whatsoever to do with me and that she intended to leave me, just as soon as she'd recuperated from the birth. She has been a slave to temptation and indulged in a sordid affair with a man who, it would now appear, has left the country, wishing to have nothing to do with his child and leaving in his tracks a trail of scandal and misery."

"So where is the child now? Is it a girl or a boy?" exclaimed Lyle, jumping up from his previous slouching position and now appearing wide awake after hearing Harry's revelation.

"She is at my home in the care of a nanny until I have decided what would be best for the reputation of my good family name, but I will not have any ties with the child; she is a damaging reminder of my late wife's infidelity and a burden that I wish not to be saddled with for the rest of my days."

Lyle's deeply furrowed brow became screwed up into a tight knot in the centre of his forehead; he was clearly thinking the very same thoughts as Harry.

"Marjorie would be restored to her old self if she was just given the chance to be a mother...*I'm certain of it.*"

"The question is, Mr Dagworth, how much are you prepared to pay for your wife's sanity?"

For a few, slow passing minutes, Lyle and Harry sat staring hard at each other, like a pair of wild animals about to embark on a territorial battle.

Then, Lyle burst into a bout of loud and almost hysterical laughter, his tears streaming uncontrollably down his face.

"My dear good fellow, you are a man similar to

myself. I *applaud* you Harry Fairbanks and I have a feeling that tonight will be a night to change both of our circumstances to the better. Name your price Mr Fairbanks, but know that I must insist on seeing the infant before a single guinea leaves my hand and if the transaction goes ahead, there will be no revoking our agreement; is that clear, Mr Fairbanks?"

Noticing the arrival of two middle-aged women who were busy polishing the numerous tabletops, Harry decided that perhaps it was time to leave the club.

"It appears that morning has arrived on us all too soon," he announced, just as the clock struck the hour of nine o'clock.

"Then we will continue our conversation in the comfort of my home, it is just a stone's throw away in Grosvenor Square."

From the moment when Harry heard Lyle mention that he resided at Grosvenor Square, he knew that he was a man of considerable wealth and was filled with a reassuring sense that for the first time in weeks he was backing a winner. The four-storey house was the second in the row to the left as they walked into the secluded square of fine-looking properties which enveloped an ornate well cared for garden in its centre. Lyle's ageing butler was in the lobby as they stepped over the threshold; a look of concern clearly visible on his serious face as he clandestinely inspected his master's unfamiliar guest. Following a night of stressful gaming and having had no sleep, Harry felt embarrassed by his scruffy appearance as he stood inside the grand home of Lyle Dagworth.

"Ahh, Johnson my good man, this is my *dear* friend, Mr Fairbanks, who will be staying with us for a while."

Harry was not expecting Lyle's generous hospitality, he merely wished to seal a deal and settle everything as quick as possible, including handing over the baby, but in fear that Lyle might have a change of heart if he refused his invite, Harry thought it in his best interests to comply and smiled cordially to his host,

"That's most generous of you L.D," expressed Harry, purposely addressing him in such a way in an attempt to convince Johnson that he was indeed a *'dear friend'* as Lyle had claimed.

"Not at all, Harry, after all, we are about to embark on a deal which will result in a lifelong bond. Now, Johnson, kindly show Mr Fairbanks to one of the guest rooms, I'm sure he'd like to freshen up before we proceed with any more business; find him some suitable clothes and anything else needed for his duration too."

"Yes, of course, Sir, I'll get on to it immediately."

"Shall we say coffee in my study in half an hour, my good fellow?"

"Er, yes, L.D, that sounds perfect," muttered Harry, already feeling a little out of his depth in the grand surroundings of Lyle's stately looking residence.

"Johnson, where's Mrs Dagworth?"

Johnson's face was void of any expression and his monotone speech was already annoying Harry; reminding him of why he'd never desired to employ a butler at Harberton Mead.

"I believe she's still in her room, Mr Dagworth, Lily has just taken up her breakfast tray, Sir."

"Thank you, Johnson, that will be all, please don't leave Mr Fairbanks, waiting any longer."

"Very good, Sir."

Eager to seal a deal and return to Oxford as quickly as possible, half an hour later, after a hasty wash and shave, Harry completely ignored the finely tailored suit which Johnson had hung up for him and left the luxurious room he'd been allocated, to go in search of Lyle. It wasn't difficult to find the study, Harry followed the pungent aroma of freshly brewed coffee and soon found Lyle hovering around in the doorway, waiting for his arrival and looking extremely dapper in his smart change of attire. Lyle viewed Harry with unease etched upon his face,

"I distinctly instructed Johnson to provide you with a change of clothing, my dear fellow...were they not to your liking?"

"On the contrary, the suit was perfect in every way, but I'm rather afraid that I will have to decline your generous hospitality; I have urgent business to attend to at home."

Lyle looked downhearted, "And where exactly *is* home, my dear fellow?"

The moment Harry blurted out that he resided in Oxford he knew it was a huge mistake; he should have given a false town or city; he inwardly cursed himself, crossly. He wanted to keep Lyle Dagworth at arm's length, especially after the deal had been secured.

"*Oxford indeed*, such a magnificent City, a beautiful part of our country, you are most fortunate, Harry."

"Unfortunately, Lyle, due to the scandalous circumstances which now surround my good family name, I will be forced to relocate just as soon as we have concluded our venture," declared Harry, in a solemn voice.

"My dear fellow, how crass of me to be such a blundering fool; your disastrous plight completely slipped my mind. Now, I beg of you, come and make yourself comfortable in my study, the draughty hallway is hardly the place to be indulging in such private matters."

Lyle Dagworth's private study was exactly as Harry had expected; a sumptuous room with luxuriously padded seating, oak-panelled walls and a well-stocked leather-bound library to one side of the room. Harry felt the rush of saliva fill his mouth as the aroma of coffee wafted through the room. They sat opposite each other in winged velvet armchairs, facing the bottle green, tiled fireplace, where the gentle sizzle of burning wood along with the radiating heat had a soothing effect on Harry; the lack of sleep had finally caught up with him as he struggled to keep his eyes open and restrain his yawns. Lyle was all too aware of Harry's condition and with a little persuasion, he convinced him that to return to Oxford that day would be pure recklessness,

"My dear good man, you must spend the remainder of the day relaxing and catching up on your sleep and tonight you will join Marjorie and myself for dinner. I would have had time by then to explain about the child to her, although, I must implore that no mention of the transaction of money must be mentioned; that will be for our knowledge only. Marjorie would detest the prospect of '*buying*' a child. Now, we will resume our business discussion tomorrow morning, when we are refreshed and up to the task. By the way, Harry, old chap, you're not hiding anything from me, I trust?"

"What on earth would I be hiding from you, Lyle? What sort of insulting insinuation is this?" questioned Harry, irately.

"Well, you know how these sinful escapades can materialize," uttered Lyle, timidly.

Harry gulped down his coffee in two mouthfuls, becoming increasingly vexed by Lyle's dictating behaviour.

"No, Lyle, I'm afraid I don't; what exactly do you mean, please *enlighten* me!"

"My dear good fellow, I mean no disrespect," expressed Lyle, sensing how he'd upset Harry. "I merely want confirmation that there are no defects or disabilities to the infant. I'm sure you can understand my concern!"

Harry found his thoughts wandering back to the night which now seemed like an age ago, the image of Faye Butler on the muddy roadside filled him with misery and made him question whether or not what he was about to embark on was the right course of action to take. He justified his actions by telling himself that if he'd not saved the baby, she would have undoubtedly lost her life; he knew that Delia still believed him to be the baby's father, so consequently she wouldn't object to him saving the child from a treacherous life in the Bicester workhouse, which is where she'd most likely end up after the police had finished their enquiries and returned to claim the child. Under the Dagworth's care, the infant would benefit from a privileged upbringing and if her mother's voice could be heard from beyond the grave, Harry was quite sure that she would be in favour of the life which Lyle and his wife would provide for her. The tidy sum of money would solve all of his problems and enable him to turn over a new leaf and concentrate on becoming a devoted husband to Delia, hopefully gaining her love and respect once more.

"I can assure you implicitly that there is nothing

whatsoever abnormal with the infant; trust me, Lyle; I am no liar," declared Harry in a raised and angry voice.

"Calm yourself, my good fellow, I mean you no disrespect, but when money is involved, one can never be too careful. I suggest that we both retire for some well-deserved rest. If there is anything whatsoever you require do not hesitate to ring for it. We will resume our business after dinner and when we both feel a little more relaxed." Harry was glad for some time alone and within a few minutes after lying down on the thick feather mattress, he was snoring blissfully.

CHAPTER SEVEN

Hall, Spencer and Lock were a notorious debt collecting company based in Whitechapel's Cable Street. It was predominantly Ed Hall, who ran the underhanded company in London's East End, with the help of a small band of ruthless, hardened criminals, many of whom had spent a spell in Newgate prison and now seemed to relish in seeing their fellow man suffer the same humiliating consequence as they had. Spencer and Lock were nonexistent, merely names added by Ed to make the company sound professional and hopefully attract extra business. Barely visible, the entrance to the tiny first-floor office was an unsightly battered-looking door with its once black paint now peeling and faded to a dull streaky grey. The concealed entrance was in between a secret opium den and 'Limehouse lodgings', a seedy lodging house which by night became a brothel. Cable Street was infamous for its houses of disrepute and wild alehouses, attracting some of the most devious villains and scoundrels of the East End to its vicinity.

Ed had overslept; the dark, cold mornings combined with his dawn hangover, were making it difficult for him to drag himself from out of the rat-infested hovel which he refused to call home, insisting that by the time he'd reached forty he'd be wealthy enough to change his lifestyle, and buy a cottage on the south coast. A dream which none of his associates believed would ever materialize; anyone who knew Ed Hall also knew that he was an Eastender to his very core and wouldn't last more than a few days away from its rough and violent streets. After splashing a handful of icy water over his face and fleshy bald head, Ed took out a freshly starched collar to attach to the off white shirt which had not left his body for eight days, a splash of strong bergamot and sandalwood cologne to his pungent underarms and a quick splash to his coarse dark bearded face made him feel ready for another day's work. His beady, bloodshot eyes suddenly caught sight of the leftover, previous night's whiskey in a tumbler next to his bed; he quickly picked it up and gulped down every last drop.

Ed Hall exited from the front door to Limestone lodgings, took four steps and turned his key in the door of the office of Hall, Spencer and Lock. Picking up a couple of letters as he stepped over the threshold, he climbed the creaky staircase and flung himself down onto the ripped leather upholstered chair behind his unorganized desk. The air inside the dingy cramped office was stale and dusty and with the occasional blast of soot falling from the chimney breast, which hadn't been swept in months, a sticky film of sooty residue covered every surface of the damp and excruciatingly cold room. There were three, shabby looking, desks in the office, each one within a few inches of each other; Ed's was the largest of the three, the other two were allocated to whoever turned up to work and needed the use of one, which was quite seldom since most of the men who Ed employed were illiterate. It was Rob Lopez who was the first to show up, which was pleasing to Ed as he'd just opened an intriguing letter from a well to do West End solicitor wishing to employ their assistance. It was the usual scenario, of someone gambling away more money than he owned and then proceeding to gamble on borrowed funds or possibly nonexistent funds. This case was different though due to the fact that the perpetrator resided in Oxfordshire. Ed hated to conduct any work that wasn't in London; it was outside of his comfort zone. His fearful reputation didn't stretch further than the north side of the Thames and it was a rare occurrence to receive work so far away too. He remembered Rob telling him that he'd been to visit a relative in that part of the country very recently. He couldn't remember much, though, due to the fact that he was in the foulest of tempers when Rob had turned up late for work and allowed the slimy villain, who they were in pursuit of, to give him the slip. Rob had changed since that day and Ed could sense that something disastrous must have taken place which seemed to have stripped him of his usual cheery character.

"Morning Gov,"

"Ahh, Rob, lad, don't bovver ter take off yer togs, I got a big job for yer an' it sounds just up yer street in Oxf'rd."

Rob felt his heart plummet,

"I ain't going nowhere near that place fer as long as I live, Mister Hall...sorry, but yer gonna 'ave ter get one ov the other lads ter do that job."

Ed couldn't believe his ears and glared angrily at the handsome, olive-skinned man who stood calmly in front of him.

"Yer might be able ter wrap all them pretty petticoats 'round yer finger, but that doesn't wash wiv me, Lopez. I pay yer wages an' if I decide ter send yer ter the Highlands ov bleeding Scotland, then that's where you'd be heading. But lucky fer you, it's just down the road, so if yer knows what's good for yer, you'll quit fussing an' be on yer way."

"Yer don't understand, gov, I can't go ter Oxf'rd...anywhere else, but not Oxf'rd," expressed Rob, with his spread out hands now resting on Ed's desk, as he spoke down to him, showing no respect.

Ed leapt out of his chair in an angry rage, standing up to face the insolent puppy who dared to disobey him. He stared hard into Rob's almost black eyes with a strong urge to pound his fist into his rigid jaw and knock it out of its perfectly formed shape, but in his head, he slowly counted to ten, whist his eyes continued to bore into Rob's.

"So tell me, lad, why can't yer do this job? Weren't you in Oxf'rd a few days ago? Didn't yer tell me that yer got family living there?"

"Well that's it yer see, Gov, me relative 'as since passed on an' it would be too painful fer me ter return there, so soon, like."

"Yer never mentioned anything 'bout it? 'Ow come?" probed Ed, suspiciously.

"Yer know 'ow it is, Mr Hall, some ov us like ter keep our sorrows locked away in our hearts, not shout about it, in the 'ope ov getting false sympathy. My entire world 'as fallen through since me recent journey, Gov."

"Are all Spaniards like you, Mr Lopez?" enquired Ed, unsympathetically.

"I wouldn't know, Gov, cos I don't know any other Spanish folk."

"What about that recently deceased relative then?"

"Well, that's a long story, Gov, but she wasn't a blood relative."

Rob could feel the sweat trickling down his back; his mouth was dry and his palms sticky and uncomfortable. He didn't like being put on the spot by his boss and had hoped to completely eradicate that disastrous day in Oxford from his memory, never imagining that he'd soon be requested to embark on a somewhat forced journey there. Still suffering from shock and a broken heart, if he hadn't have spent all of his savings recently, Rob would never have shown up to work, but in order to prevent Ed Hall from asking any more awkward questions, he knew that if he wanted to keep his job, he'd have to oblige.

"Can I see the letter, Gov?"

Ed released a shallow sigh and handed him the solicitor's letter, glad that Rob had at last seen sense.

"Just copy down the cove's address, this is a prize letter ter keep in the record book an' I don't wanna lose it; it ain't very often that Hall, Spencer and Lock are approached by such a topnotch solicitor from up West."

In a primitive fashion, Rob slowly began to copy down the Oxford address, his lettering was large and messy, with each word drowned in ink.

"For the love ov God!" yelled Ed, frustrated from watching, "didn't they bloody well teach you yer letters in that orphanage?"

"They did fer a while, but then the teacher decided that it would be wasted on the likes of me, an' sent me ter pick oakum instead. The teacher said that folk wiv my colouring would never need ter read anyway."

"Then yer teacher was a bloody wooden top. Come on; let's go down ter the chop'ouse before we start a day's work, it's bleeding freezing in this office, I can barely write meself, me 'ands are that bloody numb."

As they marched towards the chophouse at the far end of Cable Street, Ed suddenly arrived at the decision to accompany Rob on the journey; there wasn't much else going on and he knew that by midday someone was bound to drag him to the alehouse, an invitation, which he always found impossible to refuse. He already had a thumping head and a day away from the stench of the Thames which wafted up from the pool of the river with the slightest of breezes would make a welcome change. He also wanted to see for himself how the pretentious folk of Oxford really lived and if there was any truth in its highly regarded reputation.

The Cable Street chop house reeked pungently of coffee, eggs and fish, all merged together to create a stuffy obnoxious odour, but still not failing to deter its customers. Dark patches of grease were clearly visible through the sawdust-covered floor which felt sticky underfoot as the young waiter directed Ed and Rob to the smallest table with its two high back chairs at either side. Ed caught sight of a discarded bloater's head on the adjacent table, which immediately swayed him to order one of the tasty fish.

"Right, lad, fill yer belly, cos nowhere in the entire world will yer find victuals as tasty as in the East End, an' we're off ter Oxf'rd."

"Yer, coming wiv me Gov?" said Rob, excitedly, managing to conceal his sorrow.

"I figured that this might be a two-man job, now let's eat and go an' hire us a wagon."

"Ain't we going by railway, Mister Hall?"

"Don't be a bloody daft bugger; what if we 'ave ter take some ov this Fairbanks' furniture ter the auction 'ouse? we gonna balance it on the top ov our heads?"

"Oh yeah, Gov, I wasn't thinking," muttered Rob, his roving eyes now focusing on two young women who'd sat down at a nearby table.

"One day, Rob Lopez, yer gonna find that you've bitten off more than yer can chew. I was exactly the same in me youth; I know yer might find it difficult ter believe, when yer looks at me now, but once upon a time, I too cut a dashing figure of a man and had a fearful appetite fer every petticoat who caught me eye. It's a mug's game, Lopez, take me advice; all I ended up with was a broken heart an' not a woman in the district who trusted me; that's why I'm going on forty and without a wife, ter warm me bed and cook fer me. There ain't nuffing wrong in settling down an' living a life of marital bliss, young Rob. Think on that bit ov valuable advice else you'll end up like me, an' the rest ov those wasted old thugs who I employ."

Rob listened intently to Ed's words, wishing that he'd confided in him fully about the ordeal which he'd recently endured. His one and only true love had left his life forever; he knew that nobody would ever replace his beautiful golden-haired Faye; she was a unique girl with no faults; she was an angel, his angel and they had planned their future together, which was now nothing but a dream. Rob felt a painful lump constricting his throat and could only sit in silence until he'd persuaded his thoughts to divert.

Stiff from the biting cold winds and from sitting on the wagon for so long, it was four and a half hours later when Ed and Rob had reached the outskirts of Oxford. Rob cautiously eyed the wooden signpost pointing to Wheatley village and was immediately reminded of that awful day, when his plan had gone disastrously wrong.

CHAPTER EIGHT

The thin and gangly woman sat at one end of
the elongated mahogany table; swathed in
numerous layers of black silk, her cheeks hollow
and her eyes red-raw from their never-ending
flow of salty tears, Marjorie Dagworth looked
more like a woman in her seventies and had
managed to create an atmosphere of grief and
depression within the dining room. Not
accustomed to such dismal introductions, Harry
seemed to lose all of his social skills from the
moment he was shown into the room by the
frosty faced Johnson. Quickly releasing
Marjorie's hand, the instant he saw Harry, Lyle
smiled broadly, insisting that Harry sat opposite
him and on the other side of his *'beautiful wife.'*
Harry could see very little beauty in the austere
woman at the end of the table, who sniffed
continuously and dabbed her sore, red nose with
a limp handkerchief. After a hasty introduction,
Lyle insisted that they should commence dinner
without delay; Harry, who had only eaten a few
dainty sandwiches in the last day was now
starving and couldn't wait to devour the
succulent slices of pink beef that were in front of
him. He noticed how Marjorie took only one
roast potato and a carrot and like a sickly child,
she merely cut up the food into minuscule pieces
and proceeded to move them around her plate

as though she were playing some kind of strange game.

"Mr Fairbanks knows of a newborn baby girl, my dearest love, the poor creature is an orphan and when I heard of his heartrending news, I implored that he should meet you, my dear, just to witness the terrible torture which you endure daily, since our precious, little Phyllis was taken to heaven. The sudden clatter as Marjorie dropped her cutlery and let out a disturbing holler, turned Lyle's cheeks a shade of burgundy,

"My sweet, delicate baby was taken from me, Mr Fairbanks, snatched away before I had the chance to give her all of my love, leaving me with a broken heart, which I fear will never mend."

"I was so awfully sorry to hear of your sad loss, Mrs Dagworth, there can be nothing more crippling to the heart than to lose one's very own child."

Marjorie sobbed loudly, while Lyle, who had left his chair, had his arms wrapped around the pitiful woman, as he rocked her back and forth. Harry had never before witnessed such a scene and the sorrow which seemed to emanate throughout the entire dining room had a profound effect on his appetite, bringing dinner to an unpleasant and abrupt end.

"My darling girl!" exclaimed Lyle, "did you not take heed of my words? I suggested to my good

friend, Harry, that you would make the perfect
mother for this poor unfortunate infant; we
could adopt the creature into our home and into
our hearts...I believe this to be a miracle my dear,
delivered to us from the Almighty to ease your
suffering. God has seen how you mourn for our
dear departed angel and has chosen to replace
her. What do you say, my darling girl?"
Lifting her head, Marjorie gazed up to her
husband, her sad cornflower blue, eyes stared
into his face, searching and for the first time, her
lips curled at each end to such a minute degree
that the tiny smile upon her face was scarcely
visible. She reached out, clutching Lyle's wrist
with both hands,
"This isn't another one of your mean tricks is it
Lyle, because if it is, I swear that this time I
promise you that I *will* carry out my threat and
join my darling Phyllis in the next life! Tell me
you're not lying, Lyle...*give me your word.*"
"Calm yourself my love, calm yourself, what will
our guest think of us? Why; he might even
change his mind seeing you in such an
emotional state."
Harry felt the time was ripe for him to intervene
and put Marjorie Dagworth's troubled mind to
rest,
"Dear, Mrs Dagworth, I can see that you have
suffered immensely but I can emphatically
assure you that as we sit around your delightful
dining table, back in Oxford there is a perfect

baby just longing to be in the arms of an adoring mother like yourself and in the bosom of your secure, loving family."

Lyle was delighted by Harry's intervention and clandestinely gave a slight nod of approval, especially seeing how Marjorie's demeanour had immediately changed; she sat upright, quickly wiping away her tears and sliding off the black, lace head square to reveal a mop of unruly auburn hair, lacking in any style. The minimal change had already made Marjorie look years younger and Harry deduced that before Marjorie's bereavement, she must have been a fine looking woman and was quite a few years younger than her husband."

"*Do* tell me about the little darling, Mr Fairbanks...how old is she and how did she come into your care?" enquired Marjorie, excitedly.

Harry sensed that Lyle already had his own version of the story that he wished his wife to hear and at the risk of losing the deal, he insisted that Lyle narrated his own account to Marjorie.

"My dear fellow, I know how painful it is for you to tell your heartbreaking story, please accept our apologies for appearing so insensitive; we are simply excited by the prospect of a baby in our home, once again."

The room was silent as Lyle began his fictional tale.

"You see, Marjorie, old girl, this child is, in fact, a descendant of a brave officer and gentleman of the Oxfordshire Light Regiment. Now, Marjorie, do you recall me reading the newspapers to you; about the terrible Indian mutiny?"

"Oh Lyle, you know how I detest all things political...that's man's business, you should know me better by now, my darling."

Harry couldn't quite believe what he was hearing; even Delia had read the newspapers and shown concern about the atrocities occurring in India. He suddenly felt a great urgency to be with her, she was worth ten of this pretentious woman. He would make Delia's life transform to the better once he'd sorted out the business, he would take her on a surprise trip to Paris and allow her to purchase a dozen high-quality Parisian gowns and anything else which took her fancy.

Lyle continued, "This extremely brave officer was brutally killed in battle and when his poor unfortunate wife lost her life during childbirth, on the voyage back to our English soil, the child was immediately handed over to her Godparents who were, as you have probably deduced, my darling, Mr Dagworth and his wife. But with the tragic passing away of my dear friend's wife, he finds himself unable to raise this helpless orphan child, who has no other living family, so you see, old girl, it makes absolute sense for all concerned that we should raise her as our very own child."

"Is this *really* true, Mr Fairbanks? Has fate really

worked in my favour for a change?"

Harry's low opinion of Mr Lyle's wife was ever-increasing; she was proving to be a selfish and tactless female and if the yarn which Lyle was spinning her had any truth in it, he would have been on his way home by now, without waiting around to finalise a deal. But, fortunately, Dagworth's words were as false and pathetic as he was, mused Harry, and the sooner he was on his way home the better.

Marjorie had already rung for Johnson to retrieve one of Lyle's priceless bottles of champagne from the wine cellar, wishing to celebrate the turn of events in her true selfish style.

"Unfortunately, Mrs Dagworth, it *is* true and sadly, I have lost three very dear people in my life," announced Harry, feeling as fraudulent as Lyle, but not wishing to arouse any suspicions, although he was somewhat convinced that Marjorie's thick skin was oblivious to his supposedly tragic losses.

She smiled cordially at Harry, but already her thoughts were planning the refurbishment of the nursery and the list of items which would have to be purchased for the new arrival.

"My dear L.D, it is paramount that I return to Oxford on the early morning stagecoach; perhaps we could conclude the paperwork before retiring for the night?"

"Oh, yes, my dearest," interrupted Marjorie, as

she gulped down the champagne, already feeling its effects, "we mustn't keep Mr Harry any longer than is necessary, the sooner he toddles off to Oxford, the sooner he will be able to return with the child...or should we perhaps accompany you, Mr Harry and collect the sweet little creature ourselves...what do you think Lyle, my darling?" Marjorie finished her sentence with a loud hiccup, followed by a bout of giggles and a stern glance from Lyle.

"Come along my good fellow," insisted Lyle, "let us partake in a glass of port and a little serious business talk in my study."

The fire in Lyle's study had died down hours ago, leaving the room chilled and uninviting, but happy to have left the company of the obnoxious Marjorie Dagworth, Harry welcomed the fresh and sobering atmosphere of the cool room and knowing how Marjorie now had her heart set on adopting the baby, Harry had the upper hand when it came to sealing the deal, positive that Lyle would do almost anything to keep his wife content and put an end to her mourning.

Harry couldn't help notice the troubled look upon Lyle's face as he lifted the heavy, crystal decanter from its silver tray and poured out two glasses of the deep red port.

"I believe you have a *'trump card'* over me, my dear fellow, I trust you won't take advantage of the situation, after all, I think we are both doing each other a great favour here."

"That might be *your* opinion, *L.D*, but remember, *I'm* the one holding the baby, which I believe is the key to your happiness."

"Yes, yes, you're quite right, of course, Mr Fairbanks, now, take me out of my misery and state your price."

"A thousand guineas," announced Harry's firm and serious reply as the two men focussed on each other. Without batting an eyelid, Lyle immediately responded,

"Five hundred."

"*Six hundred*, not a guinea less and I want a hundred now to cover my expenses."

Lyle held out his hand to shake on the deal, "You drive a hard bargain, Mr Fairbanks, I hope I won't live to regret it in a few years time."

CHAPTER NINE

"Ahh, Gov, can't we leave the poor sod alone 'till the morning, it'll be dark before long an' I don't reckon there'll be any auction 'ouses open by the time we've finished loading the wagon, not ter mention dealing wiv the likes of that *Mr Fairbanks*. I reckon 'e sounds like the sort of cove ter come at us wiv a pistol or a bleedin' axe, so reckon it's best if we show up in broad daylight."
"Hold yer tongue, Rob, for God's sake, I can't even 'ear meself think, I swear yer like a nagging snot-nosed kid but there might just be a little bit of sense in yer ideas. I'm bloody well starving too an' I don't like the look ov that black cloud that's bin following us fer the last few miles."
"Yer see, Gov, reckons it's as wise ter listen to yer youngers as it is to yer elders!"
"An' reckon it ain't an 'anging offence ter give a young employee a slap 'round the head once in a while!"Joked Ed. "Anyway, ain't yer familiar wiv this neck ov the woods; where's a decent watering 'ole in this posh City then, Rob?"

Rob's cheery face immediately faded, as he remembered the beautiful woman who filled his dreams every night; the woman he'd set his heart on spending the rest of his life with. He was even prepared to take on her child as his own; she had been totally honest with him when it would have been quite easy for her to have kept silent and convinced him that it was his child growing in her belly. Folk considered him a flirt, a womanizer, but the truth of the matter was that he simply found it more pleasurable and easier to chat with women than the heavy-handed, crude speaking men who resided in the East End. He meant no harm and couldn't help his roving eye. Rob appreciated beauty when it fell before his eyes. Faye Butler had been in a distraught and desperate state when, on that spring day of 1857, quite by accident, Rob had collided with her on the corner of Angel Alley and Whitechapel Road; she was lost and had recently left her employment as a parlour maid in Northamptonshire, fleeing to London where nobody knew her and where she could hide from her shame. Raised by her grandparents who lived in Wheatley, a small village on the outskirts of Oxford, Rob instantly sensed her to be a young maid in distress when he first looked into her sad evergreen eyes; she looked weary and tearful and on viewing the brown carpet bag in her clutches, Rob knew that she was running away from something or someone. He had insisted on taking her to a nearby chophouse; she needed nourishment and Rob needed to find out more about this vulnerable young woman who he felt an instant magnetism towards.

May of 1857 was proving to be an extremely hot

month and folk were already predicting the arrival of a great heatwave in the coming summer months, which also meant an increase in diseases and consequently a high death toll. Rob couldn't help noticing how his new acquaintance was dressed in copious layers of clothing, topped by a thick winter coat. He could see the beads of sweat beneath the brim of her bonnet just waiting to spill over the fine lines of her brow and concluded that everything in the world which this young woman owned was either on her body or in her bag. Although reluctant to accept Rob's invitation, the cramping hunger pains which were causing her to feel quite faint, together with her parched mouth, persuaded her that the offer from the dark, handsome stranger would be harmless. After a somewhat coy introduction, Rob escorted Faye to one of his more favoured chop house, T.J. Melksham's situated just off the main road. After having eaten a huge portion of pie and mash an hour earlier, Rob forced himself to eat, solely for the sake of Faye, after which he vowed to abstain from food for the rest of the week. A little shy at first, Faye ate slowly and elegantly, savouring every mouthful of the sausages and mash which floated in a puddle of greasy gravy on her plate.

"So Faye, 'ow long 'as it bin since yer last ate?"

"Two days since I had a proper meal, but I've eaten a couple of apples and a chive of bread on my travels though."

"Where yer heading, if yer don't mind me asking?"

"Oxford," blurted out Faye, as she chewed on a mouthful of gristly sausage, "I've just left my job in service...it was at Belmont Hall in Faversham, that's in Northamptonshire, but I thought I'd come to London first before I go home. I'm going to have a baby you see..."

The shock of Faye's words and the calmness in which she spoke caused Rob to take a sudden intake of breath.

"What about the baby's father?" he gasped, surreptitiously glancing at Faye's hand in search of a wedding band.

"Oh, it's not like that, there was no love involved, quite the opposite, in fact, you see, the slimy creep of a footman managed to sneak up into the female quarters of the attic. He planned the whole sordid incident, just because I refused to walk out with him; he purposely staged an accident with a jug of custard, knowing that I'd have to go and change my mucky uniform. He had me cornered and there was nothing I could do about it, even if I'd have screamed my head off, nobody would have heard me at that time of day and as much as I kicked out and thumped the beast, I stood no chance against a brute like him. What's more, he had the blooming nerve to insist that I'd been leading him *and* all the other male staff on and that I was only getting what

I'd been asking for...*those were his exact words.*"
"What a *bastard*...sorry 'bout me foul tongue, but
that's bloody criminal, 'e needs locking up!"
"Can I have that sausage if you're not going to
eat it...seems a shame to go to waste?"
Amazed by Faye's flippant attitude, Rob gladly
pushed the sausage onto her plate, relieved that
he wouldn't have to consume the third one
himself.
"And were you?"
"What...leading him on...You must be joking; as
I said, he was a filthy, squirming pervert and I
was just having a bit of a laugh really, teasing
perhaps, but that's all."
"Does 'e know what 'e's done...I mean, that
you're now gonna 'ave 'is child?"
Faye looked aghast, taking a quick pause in her
meal, "*Of course not!* that would be like issuing
my own death sentence, he'd probably think he
had the right to march me down the
aisle...imagine that...makes me tremble just to
think of it."
"So what will yer tell yer parents then, when yer
get to Oxf'rd"
"Oh, I don't have any living parents, Rob, they
died of the fever when I was a baby. I was raised
by my grandparents, but it's only my
grandmother who's living now; I think she'll be
quite happy to have me and her great-grandchild
living with her...I expect she will enjoy the
company in her old age."

Faye appeared to have everything worked out and as she satisfied her hunger, her pretty face took on a new brightness and her eyes had soon lost their sorrowful look.

"Will you tell her the truth, Faye?"

Faye swallowed the last mouthful of her meal, washing it down with a beaker full of lemonade, "Thanks for the meal Rob, that was just what I needed...I hope I'll be able to return the favour one day; and no, I couldn't possibly tell Grandmother the truth, she'd say it were *all* my fault. She spent ten good years of her life warning me about being over-familiar with menfolk; In fact, they were the very last words which jumped out of her mouth when I left Wheatley, a few years ago. She always swore that it would get me into trouble one day and she was right, of course."

"Come, on, we best leave this place, I can see old Ma Melksham giving me the funny eye over there," stated Rob, "she 'as a sharp eye an' a tongue ter match, does that woman."

The unusually scorching sun, for the time of year, had already caused a putrid odour to waft into the air from the Thames, prompting Faye to cover her airways with the palm of her hand as the unbearable stink turned her full stomach. Whitechapel Road, as usual, was a hive of activity.

"Give me that bag, Faye an' take 'old ov me arm, so we don't get separated in the crowds."

"Where did all these people suddenly emerge from?" declared Faye in astonishment. "Don't think I've ever seen so many folk on one street at the same time, except on market day an' when the fair arrives."

"Ahh, every day's a market day in the East End."

"Where are you leading me to, anyway, Rob?"

"Back to me lodgings, if that's alright wiv you."

Faye froze in her footsteps, causing a couple of the women in the crowd behind them to trip up and inflict their angry feelings towards Faye, cursing her in a crude tongue which was the only language most of the ignorant and poverty-stricken folk knew.

"I'm not *that sort of girl*, Rob. I hope by telling you my plight that I haven't given you the wrong impression of me...because if that's what you're about, then I'd best be walking in the opposite direction to you."

"Don't be daft, Faye, I'm not that sort of man. I mean yer no harm, Faye; all I want is ter let yer put yer feet up an' take a nap. I've gotta go back ter work anyway."

Faye's cross expression immediately lightened; she was taking a liking to Rob and already felt that he was a man who she could trust.

Although Faye hadn't asked, Rob decided to enlighten her a little on his lodgings, in a bid to ease any worries she might be feeling especially as he considered the evil way in which she was snared by the bastard footman.

"You'll be safe, don't worry yer pretty little head none, I live in a house full ov women, yer know!"
"What!" cried Faye, "how does that come about?"
"Well I tell a lie, there does 'appen ter be one male, but 'e's only four years old!"
Faye felt an unexpected sinking feeling, it was as though the one and only star in the sky had suddenly faded.
"Oh I couldn't possibly impose on you and your family, Rob, but thank you for everything; it's been a real treat to find a genuinely caring man in this cold world for a change."
"Hey, steady on gal, I ain't got no family, them's me neighbours I'm talking 'bout, yer see, I 'ave a room above old Granny Isabel's haberdashery shop in Wentworth Street, well it's more like a large cupboard really, but it's me 'ome. Granny Isabel 'as 'er room, an' the other one is filled wiv Mrs Watkins and 'er brood ov seven noisy kids, 'er 'usband's away at sea an' only gets back once in a blue moon."
Faye felt the spring in her feet return. "Won't old Granny Isabel mind you bringing a female to your room, though?"
"Nah, in 'er eyes, I can't do nothing wrong...she's a wise old owl, who recognizes a trustworthy gent," teased Rob.
True to Rob's words, Granny Isabel *did* welcome Faye into her tiny but compact shop as though she'd known her for years. She was a nimble woman with a head of gunmetal hair, which was

styled into a tidy bun at the back of her head. Her washed-out eyes, although buried deep beneath her over-grown eyebrows, remained sharp as she peered out through her brass rimmed pincer spectacles.

"Any acquaintance of my dear Roberto's is welcome over me threshold an' under me roof," her crackling voice announced.

Hearing the chimes of Granny Isabel's clock striking the hour of three, Rob was all too aware of how he'd taken a much-extended luncheon and remembered that Mr Hall was waiting for his return to go out on a job.

"Sorry, Faye, but I gotta get back ter work...follow me! "

A wooden chair and a narrow wrought iron bed were the only items of furniture in the cramped room; overcome with weariness, Faye was eager to rest and quite glad that Rob had to return to work, giving her the opportunity to feel more refreshed when he returned. Rob said a hurried goodbye, assuring her that he'd return with food and drink by the early evening, before quickly racing back to Cable Street.

Even the din from the neighbouring children and the screaming baby, couldn't keep Faye awake as she laid upon Rob's palliasse. As she glanced around at his clothes, hanging from randomly placed nails, it took little time before she drifted off into a deep sleep.

CHAPTER TEN

Woken a couple of hours later by the stampede of children clambering up and down the wooden staircase; Faye gingerly left Rob's room in search of the lavatory. Two young girls were sat barefoot on the bottom stair, whispering to each other and giggling as they turned to gawp at Faye as she made her way down the stairs.
"Didn't your mother tell you that it's rude to stare?"
The girls giggled some more, muttering under their breath to each other.
"Would you be kind enough and show me where the lav is, girls?"
"She means the privy, Lucy," mumbled the older girl who, Faye deduced, couldn't be more than seven.
"Come on lady, we'll show yer. Come on Lucy you're coming too!"
Faye followed the two young girls down a narrow hallway, passing by the kitchen at the rear of the house, where Granny Isabel was lifting a heavy black kettle onto the stove.
"Can I help you with that?" Faye called out.
The old lady turned around, smiling, which Faye took as an invitation to enter the kitchen and relieve the frail woman's thin arms of her heavy load.
"Did yer 'ave a good kip, me darlin'?"
Faye had already taken a liking to Granny Isabel

when Rob had introduced them earlier, but now she was convinced that it wasn't just a false display of kindness for Rob's benefit.

"Yes, thank you... Mrs..."

"Yer must call me as all folk call me 'round 'ere, *Granny Isabel.* I know yer ain't from the East End, but as long as yer under my roof, as far as I'm concerned, yer one of our own kind and will be treated accordingly."

Granny Isabel peered over the rim of her pincers, looking down at Lucy and her sister, *"What you two nosey gals gawking at...where's yer manners! Left 'em upstairs I reckon."*

"Oh, they were just showing me to the lavatory," Faye quickly declared, not wanting to get the girls into trouble with the old woman.

Granny Isabel took a jar of toffees from off the kitchen shelf and offered them, along with a huge smile to the sisters,

"Ta Granny Isabel!" they exclaimed in unison, their faces radiant.

"Now, Lizzie an' Lucy Watkins, show this young lady where the privy is while I make us both a nice cuppa rosy lee."

By the time Rob returned from work that evening, Granny Isabel had thoroughly entertained Faye; showing her almost every single item which was on sale in her shop. Each cabinet, drawer and shelf were filled with ribbons, threads, buttons and yarns in every shade; pins and needles, shears and scissors and bolts of every type of fabric and yard upon yard of delicate lace. Everything a seamstress would ever need; it was like a treasure store of delights and in between showing her each drawer, there would be a customer stepping over the threshold. Granny Isabel proudly boasted how she'd purchased many a crate of supplies from the sailors who, in days gone by, used to lodge with her. She declared to Faye, with an exaggerated wink of her eye, that most of these crates were one's which had mysteriously gone missing from the docks. She told how she had paid a mere pittance for each crate and was still raking in the fortunes that they were selling for. Granny Isabel also offered Faye a job, helping out behind the counter. Feeling confused by the offer, if it hadn't been for her desires to become more acquainted with Rob, she would have immediately declined the offer and stuck to her original plan of making tracks to Oxfordshire but Rob intrigued her and although not wanting to openly admit it to herself, she knew that in the very short time in which she'd been in his company, she was already falling in love with him. She knew nothing about him, and could almost hear her grandmother's words of warning ringing in her ears; she also realised that being *'with child'* from another man didn't put her in a position to presume that it would be at all possible to have a proper long term relationship with Rob.

"Roberto Lopez!" greeted Granny Isabel in her best Spanish accent. "Come an' join yer young lady an' me fer a cuppa before yer goes up."

Rob smiled coyly at Faye, feeling slightly awkward for the first time in the company of a young woman, who looked even more beautiful now, since she'd rested, changed her clothes and removed the concealing bonnet, allowing her attractive head of corn coloured hair to tumble in gentle waves around her shoulders.

"I'll just go out back an' wash the day's grime away, Granny Isabel, it's a right sweltering day an' I wouldn't like ter offend you two lovely lasses."

"Well, that's a young lad aspiring ter impress, if ever I've seen one," stated Granny Isabel, grinning.

Rob quickly rinsed his head under the pump in the back yard and raced up the stairs to change his sweaty shirt. He had spent the afternoon annoying Ed Hall by his lack of attention and interest in work. Rob's mind had been in a quandary as he focused on one subject only and that was how he was going to persuade Faye to postpone her journey to Oxfordshire. Just the thought of having to say 'goodbye' to her cast a dark and gloomy shadow over him.

Following a fish supper, eaten in Granny Isabel's kitchen, it took little persuading before Faye agreed to stay on in Wentworth Street for a while, but she insisted on being totally honest with Granny Isabel, telling her the truth about her condition; she didn't fancy having to spend the coming months being unable to draw breath whilst being suffocated in a tight corset in order to conceal the swelling of her belly. Granny Isabel, although a little surprised, wasn't shocked and merely declared how she was too long in the tooth to be alarmed anymore and after using a few choice words directed at the loathsome footman and most men, in general, she continued the evening as though nothing untoward had passed her ears. Rob insisted that Faye should take his room and with a light-hearted warning from Granny Isabel, that he was not to get under her feet, she agreed to allow Rob to sleep on a palliasse in the corner of the kitchen. Faye gratefully accepted Granny Isabel's offer to help out in her haberdashery shop, deciding that it might be better for her to wait until after her baby was born before she showed up on her grandmother's doorstep, fantasizing that if her dream should come true, she might even turn up with Rob as her husband, saving her grandmother from ever discovering her shame.

As the stifling spring came to an end the predictions of a scorching summer became reality and London seemed to cook beneath the baking sun and the stagnant stretches of the Thames created a vile stench. There were times when Faye wished she was living back with her grandmother, where the summer air would be fragrant with the ripening barley; the fields would resemble a golden lake, the hedgerows would buzz from the sound of wildlife and the balmy summer evenings would be lit by a radiant moon amidst the glitter of an ocean of stars. The village folk of Wheatley would while away their time relishing in the season, where the warm evenings became social gatherings. There was many a time when Faye regretted ever leaving Oxfordshire and her grandparent's home; she had been impetuous in her haste to work in service and to widen the horizons of her sheltered village upbringing.

The summer of 1857 would always remain a summer which, for many reasons, Roberto Lopez would never forget. His ever-growing love for Faye grew in strength and Rob knew he couldn't bear the prospect of a future life without her. Faye, in return, also harboured the same powerful feelings but still feared that because of the baby she was carrying, there would be no hope for a future with Rob. It was one afternoon in early autumn when Rob found enough courage to propose to Faye; she was ecstatic. The surprise and sheer joy of his words caused her sea-green eyes to brim over with tears of happiness and relief. Her heart felt as though it was about to explode inside her chest at the prospect of becoming Rob's wife and embarking on a secure and blissful future with him at her side. Rob had never mentioned his new romance to Ed Hall; preferring to keep his work and social life separate was one reason, but the fact that Faye was carrying another man's child was the main reason. From the moment that Faye accepted his proposal, Rob was adamant that, when the time was right, they should announce to the world that the baby was his. They decided to marry after the birth, but sensing Faye's embarrassment, when they were out together when cruel folk searched her hand, Rob insisted she wore the gold wedding ring, which he'd devotedly spent most of his savings on. Knowing how much Faye missed her grandmother and village life, Rob was prepared to give it his best shot and live the *'country life'* after they'd married, but lacking any farming experience, he had no idea how he'd earn a living. Aiming to put an end to his worries, Faye had assured him that he could journey into Oxford daily, where there was bound to be some kind of work he could do. The plan was to leave the East End as soon as Faye had recovered from her confinement and after they'd had a quiet and relatively secret wedding. Faye would tell a white lie, making out that she'd written to her grandmother, explaining that she was getting married but her husband was unable to leave his employment in Northamptonshire for the foreseeable future. That would be the gist of her story, though her grandmother would never receive such a letter which would have been conveniently lost in transit, never to arrive at Dove Cottage.

As the time became nearer to Faye's confinement, Rob found himself worrying relentlessly about the huge responsibility of supporting a wife and child in a new and strange place, where he'd never set foot in before. During a conversation in a local alehouse one evening, a young Italian delivery man was telling his account of how he'd been ambushed when his work had taken him out of London and into the countryside. He claimed that folk outside of London were not accustomed to those whose skin was a darker shade and in their ignorance, the village folk had chased him out as though he were a leper. Rob was shocked and left questioning if it *was* a wise move to depart from London and if anyone would even give the likes of him the opportunity to earn a wage. His nagging thoughts remained with him constantly, day and night, until he decided that the only way to put his mind at rest was to make a secret journey to Wheatley village and Oxford. He had to find out for himself if he was about to make the right decision, to leave the only life and home he'd ever known.

The beginning of November arrived in typical East End style, bringing with it a chilling dampness and a continuous dense fog, which lifted only slightly by mid-afternoon.

Now looking as though her belly could swell no further, Faye's confinement was imminent, prompting Rob to embark on his intended trip. Reassuring Faye of how much he loved and cherished her, he lingered, not really wanting to leave, as he kissed her full red lips goodbye. He'd been forced to tell her a white lie; the very first he'd ever told her as they had always been totally honest with each other about everything. He declared that a man he'd met in a West End alehouse had informed him of a job in an Oxford printers' and that he'd advised Rob to go as soon as possible if he wanted any chance of securing the position. The look of excitement upon Faye's beautiful face sent a surge of guilt through his heart.

The rain pelted down violently as Rob rode out of London upon the hired chestnut stallion; he harboured a superstitious feeling that the East End was issuing a stark warning for him not to leave.

CHAPTER ELEVEN

It had taken Rob less than an hour after arriving in Oxford to sadly realise, that it was not a city where he would easily fit in and where he'd be made to feel welcome. Already feeling homesick, which wasn't made any easier by the fact that he was chilled to the bone, soaked through and in need of a bed for the night, with nothing but expensive and grand looking hotels within the city, Rob made his way back out of Oxford. Quite by accident, he stumbled upon an inn which was somewhere in between the City and the village of Wheatley. His money was quickly decreasing and with everything in the area being twice the price as it was in the East End; by the time he'd paid for his bed and a stable for the horse he was left with a meagre few pennies in his pocket. Hoping to find the City more appealing in the light of day, the following morning Rob returned into Oxford and took a stroll around the impressive looking University City, admiring the notorious buildings and finding the hideous gargoyles amusing, but still feeling like a fish out of water. Not used to riding frequently, his body ached from being in the saddle and he was already dreading the journey home. But the thought of being united with Faye very shortly inspired him to force the stallion into a speedy gallop; he could barely remember what his life had been like before Faye, she had truly taken over his heart and enhanced his life.

The dangerous power of curiosity dragged Rob off the main homeward-bound thoroughfare like a magnet. The battered wooden signpost, which was barely legible seemed to leap out at him; Wheatley village was three miles away and there was nothing he could do to stop himself, already picturing Faye's astonished expression when he told her how he'd met her grandmother and visited the village where she'd spent her childhood.

Dove Cottage was easy to locate, nestled in between two identical cottages, and mirroring the three cottages on the opposite side of the narrow dirt track, Rob immediately understood why Faye's face lit up every time she spoke of her village. It was serene in its simplicity, a place of calmness completely cut off from the entire rest of the world, and untroubled. Rob proceeded past the row of tiny dwellings, searching hard into the tiny windows of Dove cottage, hoping for a glimpse of Grandmother Butler, but all was quiet in the sleepy village. The narrow track opened out as Rob continued through the village, he passed a small chapel and a few more cottages and then an area of a thick copse, on either side of him, before the land altered into farmland. He counted four farmhouses within his sight, all with smoke puffing out of their chimneys, suddenly reminding him of how chilly it was. He pulled up his jacket collar, which made little difference with all his clothes still damp from the soaking he'd received the previous night. In the distance, Rob caught sight of a few inhabitants, probably farmers out feeding their beasts and most likely too busy to be bothered with an East End lad who hadn't a clue about country life. Steering his horse back around, he retraced his tracks and by a small miracle, watched as the front door to Dove Cottage slowly opened and a frail old woman emerged, carrying a willow flower trug; she proceeded to hobble down the garden path, completely oblivious to Rob's presence as she took hold of a pair of scissors and began cutting away the last remaining summer blooms.

"Excuse me!" yelled Rob excitedly, as he awkwardly dismounted the horse, catching his foot in the stirrup and nearly making a complete fool of himself. The old woman dropped her scissors as she stood rigid, seeming unable to move or breath. Rob suddenly remembered that he'd not removed his cap and quickly yanked it off, wanting to make a lasting first impression on Faye's grandmother, that he was a man of good breeding and manners.

"What do you want with me!" she screamed out, hysterically, the look of fear, clear upon her wrinkled face.

In his haste to reach Mrs Butler and ease her

obvious anxiety, Rob had vaulted over the low
garden gate without stopping to unlatch it.
"Stay away from me you filthy heathen," she
blurted out, her voice now crackling.
Rob felt his heart sink; it *was* true what the
Italian had told him. But he was still sure that
Grandma Butler would soon change her
uneducated opinion of him when she knew of
his relationship with her granddaughter. Rob
was so focussed on the old woman that he'd
failed to notice how the inhabitants of the
surrounding cottages had all emerged from their
homes and were now forming an audience.
"I'm a very dear an' close friend ov yer
granddaughter, Mrs Butler!" Rob continued,
trying to choose his words carefully so as not to
cause any more stress to the old woman.
"Oh, dear God! What have you done with my
Faye, *you savage*...is that why I've not heard a
single line from her all these months?"
"I ain't done nuffing Mrs...I wouldn't dream ov
'arming 'er," Rob pleaded.
"Don't worry, Mrs Butler, I've got my shotgun
ready if he so much as lays a finger on you!"
shouted out a neighbour, his declaration cheered
on by a gathering of men and women.
"Why isn't she at Belmont Hall, then? Tell me
that...they returned my correspondence and
nobody up there knows where she is...What
have you done with her?"
In a bid to comfort the distraught old woman,

Rob reached out his hand to her. Mrs Butler
flinched and collapsed onto the flower border,
her face quickly turning the exact shade as the
white chrysanthemums in her basket. Her eyes
were open wide, staring up at the gloomy sky
but seeing nothing and Rob instinctively knew
that she was dead.

"He's only gone and murdered our Mrs Butler!"

"Did *you* see that? he struck her!"

"He needs stringing up...*bloody foreigner!*"

"Quickly young Ted, go and fetch the
constable...take my cart, hurry now!"

"Let's put a rope around the scoundrel!"

The voices and chants of the lynch mob infused
sheer terror into Rob; he knew he wouldn't stand
a chance with these folk, they were out for his
blood, convincing Rob that they felt no guilt in
their false accusations. There was only one
option and that was to make a quick escape and
pray that he'd not be caught. Quickly glancing
back to where he'd alighted from the horse, his
fear was confirmed...one of the neighbours had a
tight hold on the reins, leaving Rob with only
one option which was to run as speedily as his
rigid legs would move. With clenched fists, he
swung a mighty right clout, bringing the burly
farmer, who stood in front of him to his knees, a
speedy sideways kick took the second man by
complete surprise, as he stood in shock watching
his neighbour topple over. One more right hook
sent the third man flying backwards, falling with

a loud thud to the ground, the blood already flowing from his nostrils. Grateful for his tough upbringing on the streets of London's East End, Rob sensed that his fearless approach and spontaneous actions had shocked the docile country folk of Wheatley village. As he hurdled over the picket fence, fleeing in the direction of the thicket which he'd spotted a little earlier, he ran with a speed, which even shocked himself, without looking back until he reached the seclusion of the woods, where he flopped to the ground, amongst the copious fungi and damp bed of musty smelling leaves. With the knowledge that the entire population of Wheatley village was pointing their fingers at him as the murderer of Faye's grandmother, Rob realised that there was no hope in him trying to prove his innocence; he was already a condemned man and worst of all, he now had to return to London and break the dreadful news to Faye. Why had he ever embarked on such a foolhardy journey, he asked himself furiously; he had ruined everything.

With a week passing and there still being no sign of Rob anywhere in London, Faye was becoming increasingly anxious and both she and Granny Isabel were fearing the worst, especially knowing that his line of work could have easily placed him in danger; nobody favoured a debt collector knocking on their door threatening them with a prison sentence. The ever increasing twinges across her belly were a constant reminder to Faye that her confinement was nearing and as sweet as old Granny Isabel was, without Rob by her side, Faye still felt like a stranger in the East End and yearned for her home and the love and support of her real Grandmother. Promising that she'd return one day if only to collect her bag of belongings which she was unable to carry, Faye left Wentworth Street on a bright but chilly November morning, leaving Granny Isabel with her grandmother's address and with the promise that she'd send Rob to join her just as soon as he arrived home, or on a more dismal note that she'd write to inform her, should she hear any news at all of why he'd not returned. Granny Isabel had tried everything in her power to try and persuade Faye not to leave in her condition, but Faye's stubbornness, as always, won the battle of words.

It had been a strange but beautiful six months, and as Faye passed by Angel Alley on her way to the main London to Oxford Road, she felt quite nostalgic as her thoughts drifted back to the day when she'd first met her forever love. She prayed he was safe as she wiped away a trickling tear from her cheek and pulled her shawl tightly around her shoulders as the raw wind sent a shiver through her body.
The overloaded stagecoach soon arrived and

Faye just managed to squeeze in between the sour-faced passengers, who eyed her in disgrace, all being of the same opinion that a woman in her condition should be at home and not travelling the highways of the country. Faye was also aware how everyone in the carriage was furtively glancing at her bare hand and jumping to the conclusion that she was a fallen woman. She felt like announcing the fact that her wedding band no longer fitted her swollen finger, but with second thoughts decided that these shallow folk were not worthy of an explanation, even though their assumptions of her were essentially true. An hour into the journey, the carriage came to an unexpected and sudden halt in the middle of nowhere; one of its wooden wheels had endured a deep split after crashing into a bolder on the track and was proving too dangerous to continue. After being informed by the coach drivers that there was a coaching inn just five miles further along the route the passengers were forced to endure the biting northerly winds as they alighted the vehicle and proceeded by foot. There would not be another stagecoach for at least three hours, and it would undoubtedly be full up, they had warned their angry passengers. After a long and lonely walk to reach the coaching inn, the heavy pulling of Faye's swollen belly was having an exhausting effect and the sharp contractions together with the dull ache in her back were a sure sign that her baby was eager to make an appearance into the world. The disappointing news that the carriage wouldn't be roadworthy until the following morning, prompted Faye in her decision to walk the rest of the journey, with the hope that she might be able to cadge a lift along the route. According to the innkeeper, Oxford was ten miles away which meant it was only about four miles to her village.

Within a short period, the bright sky quickly clouded over bringing heavy, dark and ominous clouds filling every blue space above. The strengthening bitter cold winds with their threat of an imminent downpour were unable to spur Faye on any faster; she shivered as the pains of her labour had brought her to a snail's pace, forcing her to stop every few minutes. Nightfall arrived along with continuous torrential rain and with the moon shrouded by charcoal clouds, Faye continued blindly, slipping and sliding on the muddy roadside. The drivers of the few carriages which passed her by failed to notice her or hear her desperate cries for help and before long, Faye submitted to the terrifying fact that there was no way in which she could prevent her baby from being born. Sliding down a shallow, muddy embankment, her body was overtaken by the powerful urge to push out her load.

"Reckon I'd 'ave 'ad more company if I'd brought a corpse along wiv me," remarked Ed, annoyingly, "Fer God's sake Rob, what's on yer mind?" he demanded, "You've bin as quite as a bleedin' church mouse fer the last 'alf hour!"

"Sorry Gov," exclaimed Rob, being jolted out of his reverie, "I was just trying ter remember where there's a decent place ter stay fer the night," he lied.

"Don't worry 'bout *decent*, lad...me mouth's as dry as a sheet ov sandpaper an' me empty guts are protesting! All I want, is a full belly an' a place ter put me head fer the night...now can yer help *Roberto* or not?"

No sooner had Ed's words left his mouth than both men spotted a welcoming looking inn on the corner of a nearby junction,

"The White 'Orse," read Rob out loud, pleased that it was quite a few miles away from Wheatley village.

"That will do, let's just 'ope they 'ave a couple ov beds fer the night an' I 'ope by the time morning arrives, that yer might 'ave a bit of a smile on that miserable face ov yours too!"

CHAPTER TWELVE

"Look Maybell, I do believe baby Faye is smiling at me!"

Maybell obediently turned her head as she drew back the curtains in Delia's bedroom; she found it hard to comprehend how her mistress could be so excited by the gummy smile of a baby, especially one which wasn't her own and whose father, according to Mrs White's speculation, was that of her philandering husband.

"Ahh, God bless her, Mrs Fairbanks, she's a right pretty gal and she certainly adores you," Maybell said what she knew would be pleasing to Mrs Fairbanks' ears; it was common knowledge between cook and her younger sister that Delia Fairbanks was besotted with the infant.

Turning her attention back to the world outside as she tied back the curtains, the sight and sound of a huge wagon approaching Harberton Mead made her deaf to Delia's continued *baby* chatter. The wagon was definitely heading towards the house and Maybell could see no sign of Mr Fairbanks anywhere onboard.

"Mrs Fairbanks!" she exclaimed, anxiously. "We have visitors!"

"It's most probably some poor devil who Mr Fairbanks has begged a lift from when most of the country's population was sleeping," uttered Delia casually, refusing to divert her eyes off the baby for one second.

Maybell hurriedly wiped away the condensation from the window with the corner of her apron; the wagon had drawn closer giving Maybell a clear view of the two men and proving to her that Mr Fairbanks was not among them.

"No, Mrs Fairbanks, there are only two strangers that I can see and my eyes don't usually lie to me. What could they want, Mrs Fairbanks?" cried Maybell, now in a state of alarm.

"I know every single face around Oxford, Mrs Fairbanks and I ain't ever set my eyes on two such terrifying men as those outside the house!" Placing the baby onto the bed, Delia let out an exaggerated sigh as she made her way to the window.

"Honestly, Maybell, you need to stop this silliness, nobody knows *everybody* in a city like Oxford, they're probably just lost tradesmen, it won't be the first time that such folk have branched off the main road in our direction." Delia's comments were spoken only in a bid to calm the anxious maid, who was clearly becoming panic-stricken by the strangers. Delia gazed down at the colossal wagon, which stood stationary; its rough-looking occupants were sat in conversation.

"I don't suppose Mr Fairbanks is anywhere to be found, is he?" enquired Delia, hoping that he may have sneaked in during the night and slept in another room. Maybell shook her head slowly,

"No, Mrs Fairbanks, he's not at home!"

"Right, Maybell, you're to go and ask Mrs White to find out what they want, while I quickly get dressed, but don't let them pass over the threshold, at least not until I join you downstairs, is that clear?"

Maybell wrung her hands, nervously behind her back.

"Don't worry about a thing, Maybell; I assure you no harm will come to you! Now run along."

"Yer sure this is the right 'ouse Mr Hall, it looks right fancy ter belong her some cove who ain't paid 'is debts...not our usual type of punter!"

Ed Hall looked at his prize letter from the West End solicitor, which somehow made him feel quite superior and proud, infusing him with a feeling of power; he'd gone up a peg or two and if he handled this job well, it could be the beginning to a whole new type of business.

"Yes, Roberto, this is it, now get yer lazy backside off of that seat, an' let's get going, we're already a day be'ind schedule, which ain't gonna bode well wiv them West End toffs. Wiv a bit of luck, the likes of Mr 'Arry Fairbanks will part wiv 'is possessions peacefully, wiv out too much ado. Now, come on then, let's go an' see what awaits us on the other side ov them fancy, lace curtains, young Rob; the sooner we gather enough funds tergether the sooner we can get back 'ome...That cove in the White 'Orse told me

that there's an auction down in Oxford terday."
Ruth White wiped her hands on her floral apron
and quickly checked that her curly hair was
presentable, at fifty-two, she already had a good
handful of grey hair framing her chubby face,
which she referred to as her *shades of grace*. She
had left Selma kneading the dough, but Maybell
who was hopping nervously from one foot to
another, followed closely behind with a rolling
pin concealed in the deep pocket of her skirt,
and although she'd assured Mrs White that she'd
be ready to protect her should the need arise,
Mrs White doubted that the jittery girl would
even manage to pull the weapon out of her
pocket, let alone strike anyone with it. But she
meant well, and that in itself was a comfort to
Mrs White.

Ed bashed the door noisily with his fist,
completely ignoring the polished brass door
knocker, believing that it was beneficial to put
fear into the debtor before he'd even had a
chance to open the door. Mrs White pursed her
lips, as she hastened angrily towards the noise,
complaining under her breath about the bad
manners that some people had been born with.
"Yes, can I help you...is there some kind of
emergency, or are you both blind to the presence
of a door knocker?"

Trembling in Mrs White's shadow, Maybell
couldn't believe cook's show of bravado as she
addressed the two heavily built towering rogues

in such a bad-tempered way.

"We wanna see the head of the house, not the bloody maid!" stated Rob, rudely, as he was suddenly reminded of the country folk who'd given him so much trouble in Wheatley.

"Alright, Rob, let *me* deal with this, I'm sure this fine woman will be most obliging," expressed Ed, as he offered his widest smile to Mrs White.

"For *your* information, the *head* of the house is not at home, and I'm the cook, *not the maid!*"

"Who is it, Mrs White?" called out Delia, as she hurried down the stairs, concerned by the coarse sounding voices.

"Well, Mrs Fairbanks, I can tell you, it's *no* gentlemen caller, *that's for sure!*"

Delia quickly took over from her cook, immediately disliking the look of Ed Hall and his young assistant, although she found the younger man a lot easier on the eye than his boss.

"Yes? Can I help you two gentlemen...have you taken a wrong turning? Are you lost?"

Ed liked the look of the fine figure of a woman; she had class and spoke softly, unlike the type of women he was used to back in London.

"If this is Harberton Mead, an' the home ov a Mr Fairbanks, then we most certainly 'avent taken a wrong turning...Mrs Fairbanks. I'm not one to presume, but reckon me ears heard yer maid address yer as Mrs Fairbanks. Would Mr Fairbanks be yer 'usband then?"

"Not that it's any of your business, but yes, Mr Fairbanks *is* my husband," affirmed Delia, crossly.

"Mr *'Arry* Fairbanks?" emphasised Ed.

Delia nodded, glad that she could still feel the presence of Mrs White and Maybell standing close behind her.

"Well, Mrs Fairbanks, I won't beat about the bush, 'cos I reckon yer looks like a decent sort. I 'ave an order from the London courts ter collect the outstanding debt of three 'undred an' eighty-five guineas or effects ter that value."

Delia swallowed hard; she could already feel her blood heating up and was livid that Harry had put her in such an awkward and embarrassing situation, not to mention the colossal dept he'd managed to accumulate. Where on earth was he, she mused angrily and how was she going to deal with these unscrupulous debt collectors. That was just typical of Harry not to be anywhere in sight when he was needed.

"How do I know that you're genuine, you don't strike me as reputable gentlemen, at all…"

"They look like a couple of common thieves to me, Mrs Fairbanks!" interrupted Mrs White, pushing her way back into the door frame next to Delia.

Ed pulled out the letter from his pocket, waving it triumphantly in front of Delia's face.

"I'm right sorry that yer 'usband's not at 'ome, we'll try an' make this as painless as possible, ma'am," stated Ed sympathetically, genuinely feeling for the poor woman.

"I don't suppose yer 'appen ter 'ave any cash, Mrs Fairbanks? "

"None that will make the slightest difference to my husband's huge debt, but I suppose I could let you have my jewellery, that's worth a substantial amount. It's mostly gold."

On Hearing Delia's words, Maybell was overcome with nausea as she remembered her sister telling her, only yesterday, of how she'd startled Mr Fairbanks as he was pocketing all of his wife's jewellery like a sly fox. Neither of them had believed the feeble excuse he'd told Selma, and their ma, who received daily reports from her girls, had come to the conclusion that what with the baby and now the lack of money, her daughter's might soon have to start looking for employment elsewhere. Both Selma and Maybell had decided to cross that bridge when they came to it, feeling quite sad at such a prospect.

"You'd better come in I suppose," invited Delia, reluctantly. Mrs White's sharp eyes studied the state of their boots, insisting they removed their mud-covered footwear.

Delia rushed up the stairs, eager to resolve the problem quickly and see the back of the two strangers. It took barely five seconds after discovering her empty jewellery box, for Delia to deduce that it had been Harry who'd robbed her of every piece of jewellery, and why not she mused angrily, after all, *he* had bought them for her in the first place, so, as with everything else in her life, nothing was rightfully hers; she owned nothing and was totally subservient to a hopeless gambler. She paused to gently stroke baby Faye's soft cheek; the innocent baby had a calming effect, easing Delia's anger a little before she marched downstairs ready to teach her useless and unreliable husband a lesson.

CHAPTER THIRTEEN

Delia stood motionless in the window recess, watching as nearly every item of furniture was loaded and secured with heavy rope onto the wagon, along with the household silver, save for the candelabras and candlestick holders, which Delia had requested to be left for safety's sake. The entire downstairs was soon emptied, the entire contents of Harry's treasured antique, *William and Mary* desk was dumped into the corner of the study and his thick Persian rug rolled up and added to the haul. The pile of I owe you notes had not gone unnoticed, but by now it was of no surprise to Delia, leaving her feeling as though she was drowning in darkness by the shattering events of late. Only a few choice items from upstairs were added, a *Queen Anne* dresser, with a matching tallboy. As heartbreaking as the scene was, Delia was completely shocked by the lack of empathy she felt towards her husband; she felt a strange and wicked sense of satisfaction and hoped that Harry would be guilt-ridden and wounded by the consequences of his folly; every family heirloom which he'd ever inherited was about to be sold off. By midday, the household was in an emotional state after the morning's events. The bailiffs had left to the auction; Mrs White had broken down into a snivelling wreck with May-

-bell trying to console her, while Selma was quietly protesting in the background, that she couldn't see how it would be possible for the Fairbanks' to afford to pay their wages after what had occurred. Baby Faye continued to sleep soundly through the entire hullabaloo while Delia paced from window to window in search of Harry, eager to give him a piece of her mind.

"Now I'm never going to be able to afford that beautiful tea set for my bottom drawer!" cried Selma, crossly.

"Be quiet, Selma, there are far more important things in life than your stupid bottom drawer, besides you don't even have a beau! And you're younger than me! I'm the one, if any, who should be assembling a bottom drawer!"

Mrs White suddenly let out a loud whimpering sigh.

"There's nothing wrong with being prepared, Maybell. I don't want to start my married life being short of anything...Ma thinks I'm wise too."

"Huh, you won't be short of anything except for a groom!"

"Wait 'till I tell Ma, you stupid...."

"*For the love of God*, girls, will you both stop your bickering," ordered Mrs White. "Just look at us all sat selfishly hiding in the kitchen when God alone only knows what poor Mrs Fairbanks is going through. A good, decent woman like her doesn't deserve to have endured what's happened today. *Maybell!* put the water on to boil, and Selma see if there's any of yesterday's bread left...with all the drama going on, the poor mistress hasn't even eaten breakfast yet, she'll be swooning like a broody hen soon! Selma put some eggs to boil too while you're about it. I'll go and see how that poor young woman is fairing."

With there still being no sign of Harry, Delia was now beginning to think that his financial collapse had caused him to gain one too many enemies who might have taken it upon themselves to teach him a lesson; not everyone would be prepared to accept an *I owe you* so politely, she mused. Her fears were suddenly increased as she stared in trepidation at the approaching police wagon. Her sharp intake of breath prompted, Mrs White to hurry to her side as Delia flopped backwards onto the wooden floor, forgetting that the armchair was no longer there.

"*Oh, my dear, Mrs Fairbanks,*" she exclaimed. "Did you take a funny turn...I wouldn't be surprised, what with the awful morning we've had and with you still not having put a crumb of food or a hot drink passed your lips! Don't you fret now, the girls are preparing an early luncheon as we speak, and that little baby, well, she's been as good as gold all morning...what a *little angel.*"

"Mrs White, I fear that our terrible morning is

about to become even worse!"

With a quick glance out of the window, Mrs White's hand shot up to cover her gaping mouth. "*Oh, Lord have mercy!*" she cried out.

"Do you think something has happened to Harry?"

"No, no, Mrs Fairbanks, don't you fret none, it's more likely to do with that business with baby Faye's mother," consoled Mrs White, praying that she was right. "Should I show them in, Mrs Fairbanks?"

Delia looked around at the sparse room, where only a few worthless ornaments, half a dozen newspapers and a battered writing bureau remained.

"Yes, Mrs White, I suppose we'll have to let them over the threshold."

Constables Morris and Webster were both unable to conceal their look of horror as they entered the bare drawing room and greeted Delia, their eyes surveying the room in disbelief.

"I thought I recognised that couch on the wagon we just passed by!" stated Constable Morris, his booming voice echoing.

"I trust that we haven't just passed by a couple of common thieves, Mrs Fairbanks?" added Constable Webster, noticing how flushed she appeared. He'd already, however, suspected the work of the bailiffs; thieves were never that organised and rarely showed up in daylight hours.

"Well you might as well know the truth, Constable, after all, I wouldn't dream of fibbing to a police officer. It was, as you have probably deduced, the bailiffs..."

Constable Webster drummed his fingers nervously on his helmet which he held, close to his chest; he felt genuinely sorry for Delia.

"I don't suppose you're here with news of my husband, are you? Only he left for London two days since and still hasn't returned home."

The constables eyed each other, thinking along the same lines that if Mr Fairbanks' finances were in such a sorry state of affairs to warrant the bailiffs already being summoned, he was probably laying low somewhere.

"I'm sorry, Mrs Fairbanks, we are here regarding the infant who was left in your care. Unfortunately, due to the absence of any living relatives, the law states that we have to take her into care. We can't thank you enough for putting yourself to such an inconvenience and taking the baby under your caring wing since her birth."

The empty room suddenly began to spin and Delia's ears were filled with the muffled sound of voices as her legs turned to jelly, bringing her crashing to the floor. Quickly intervening, Mrs White pushed the constables out of her way and joined Delia's side, lifting up her head as she took the tiny bottle of smelling salts from her apron pocket and waved the bottle under Delia's nose, quickly bringing her around.

"Constable, please could you hurry to the kitchen and tells those maids to bring the meal in as quickly as they can!"

"Of course," said Constable Webster, obediently making his way out of the room.

"It's a shame that women can't work in the constabulary, Mrs White, you'd make a fine Sergeant!" joked constable Morris, trying to lighten the mood.

Mrs White was not amused and looked daggers at him.

"Where do you intend to take her, Constable Morris?" said Delia, in a small voice.

"It will be Bicester workhouse, Mrs Fairbanks, it's one of the more favourable establishments in Oxfordshire, I'm sure she'll be well looked after there."

"She's an adorable little creature and I've grown so very fond of, Constable; it pains me to think of her being abandoned in such a daunting place," exclaimed Delia, tearfully.

Constable Webster popped his head around the corner of the door,

"Er, Mrs Fairbanks, your maids suggested that perhaps you'd prefer to eat in the kitchen, where there are a table and chairs."

Delia ignored the Constable she was far too concerned about the fate of baby Faye.

"Constable Morris, would you be kind enough to wait for the return of Mr Fairbanks before you take the baby away to the workhouse, only there *is* a possibility that we might wish to adopt her."

"Are you quite sure, Mrs Fairbanks? After all, we don't know a thing about the baby's father...it would be a cruel state of affairs if he should show up one day."

From his patronising tone, Delia sensed that the constable considered her to be an over-sentimental female, who was thinking with her heart, not her head. She glared coldly at him, all the time fearing that he had the authority to take baby Faye away from her. She loved that tiny, helpless baby as though she were her own flesh and blood and would surely lose her wits if she was parted from her, not to mention knowing that she was to live a dismal existence in such a treacherous place, as the workhouse.

"Why don't we all go to the kitchen for some refreshments before poor Mrs Fairbanks keels over again?" interrupted Mrs White.

"I'm afraid that Constable Webster and I have a busy afternoon ahead of us and must make haste, but I promise to *sweet* talk the sergeant and persuade him to allow you to keep the infant in your care for a couple more days, by which time Mr Fairbanks would have hopefully returned. Come along Constable Webster, I think Mrs Fairbanks has had one too many shocks for today; we'll take our leave of her now."

"Thank you, Constable Morris, you've been most understanding. By the way, has the baby's poor mother been laid to rest yet?"

"I wouldn't know, Mrs Fairbanks," he affirmed, as both constables simultaneously replaced their lofty helmets back onto their heads, "what with the increase of fatalities, due to the recent scarlet fever outbreak, the Oxford undertaker where she was initially taken didn't have adequate space. ...I think she was taken to Chipping Norton...or was it Woodstock?" he mused, rubbing his forehead as though it might improve his memory. "No, sorry, Mrs Fairbanks, it's completely escaped my memory, but I can certainly find out for you."
"Thank you, Constable."

CHAPTER FOURTEEN

No matter how tightly Delia tried to squeeze her eyes shut, sleep failed to overtake her body. Her mind was wide awake and filled with thoughts and worries. The main question which troubled her most was, did she really and truly love Harry and wish to remain by his side for the rest of her days? She had taken her vows to be his wife, no matter what misfortune and ill health fell upon them, but surely it was a violation of those sacred vows when he, in fact, had willingly sabotaged their marriage. Her life was in ruins, she didn't want to wait, like the dutiful wife, and listen to Harry's feeble excuses of how he'd lost everything he owned, she didn't want to struggle for however long it would take, knowing that as soon as Harry's head was above water again he wouldn't be able to resist the gaming rooms of the West End gentleman's club and the downhill spiral would begin all over again. It had dawned on Delia that throughout her six years of marriage, the tiny spark of love which might once have existed between her and Harry had not been given the loving fuel to ignite their relationship and instead the flames had self-extinguished, leaving in its place, a cold emptiness.

The gentle patter of rain upon the bedroom window distracted Delia's thoughts for a while;

the usual sense of cosy warmth was missing, she felt trapped and Harberton Mead no longer felt like her home or a place of security. She threw back the blankets and lit her bedside candle, a chill swept through her body as her bare feet touched the icy cold, floorboards. Baby Faye was moving slightly in the wicker laundry basket, her eyes remained half-closed but Delia knew it would only be a matter of minutes before her cries of hunger broke the silent night. After wrapping her thick bed jacket around her shoulders Delia pushed her icy feet into her slippers and crept downstairs to the kitchen in order to prepare some warm milk for her and the baby. She wondered how much money the bailiffs had managed to obtain from the auction as she glanced around the empty rooms; Harberton Mead was a mere shell and no longer resembled home to Delia. Just like her marriage it was empty and devoured of all love and attention.

Gazing down lovingly at Faye, as she contentedly suckled her milk, Delia came to her final decision which had been the source of her disturbance all night. She would not be parted from Faye and would do everything in her power to make certain of it. She would also leave her husband to fester in his own problems and never return to him. Today would mark the beginning of her new life, hopefully, a far happier one, where love would be no stranger.

By the time the first murky light of another damp day had arrived, Delia was already dressed and had filled a small leather case with her belongings. Although her jewellery box was now only good for firewood, the one consolation she had, was that she was still in possession of the gold chain around her neck, and a couple of gold rings plus her wedding band which adorned her fingers; she had also found three brooches of some value which she'd carelessly left pinned onto her hanging dresses. After going through the pockets of every one of Harry's expensive suits, Delia's futile search ended with less than ten silver shillings and a couple of silver sixpences. Most of the money would have to be divided between Maybell and Selma; they had been good housemaids and didn't deserve to be out of work and out of pocket, she would also sit and write two distinguishing character references, to ensure they'd have no trouble in finding employment elsewhere. As for Mrs White, she'd lived at Harberton Mead for more than ten years, leaving Delia unsure of how to deal with her circumstances, but she'd willingly allow her to stay on at the house and wait for Harry's return, after all, Harry had little experience of looking after himself. In her annoyance at how the Fairbanks' family were held in such high esteem amongst the people of Oxford, and yet here she was, scraping around for a mere pittance, Delia decided to pack every one of Harry's suits into a chest and take them with her; no matter how difficult a task, they would fetch a good price at the pawnbroker's and it would allow Harry to experience how it felt to have his personal belongings taken from him. It was a start, and would hopefully keep her afloat until she'd had time to organise her new life.

Ruth White woke early, disturbed by the noisy clatter as Delia dragged her luggage down the stairs. Surprised to see the suitcases and wooden chest by the front door and Delia fully dressed and in her finest bonnet and mantle; it didn't take long to work out what was going on.

"Good morning Mrs White, I'm so sorry if my noise disturbed your sleep. How are you?"

"You're surely not leaving are you!" she blurted out, completely ignoring Delia's polite greeting.

"Oh Mrs White, *dear Mrs White,* I assure you, I didn't intend to leave without saying my farewells to you *and* if you'd be so kind, as to share breakfast with me, I would be truly honoured, heavens knows when I'll have my next decent meal."

By the unhappy look on Mrs White's face, Delia could sense how perplexed she was.

"I'll put the water on to boil and scramble some eggs," she muttered under her breath as she quickly turned around and returned to the kitchen, leaving Delia feeling a though she'd committed a shameful crime. She followed her in the hope of easing Mrs White's obvious concerns.

"Those young girls will be devastated you know?" she sniffed. "They love being in your employ they're so fond of you and are so happy here."

"But, Mrs White, I'm quite sure they won't be happy to work for nothing; *you* witnessed what happened yesterday. Mr Fairbanks is penniless and up to his eyes in debt...he may even be forced to sell Harberton Mead, there is no future here, and I am leaving him."

"But he's your husband!" declared the extremely shocked looking cook. "It's against the law; you belong to him...you took your wedding vows, *remember?"*

"And what he has done is also against the law; he stole my jewellery, Mrs White and has left me destitute. Sometime today, baby Faye will be taken from me and thrown into the workhouse, to suffer a life of poverty, misery and loneliness, just like all the other poor orphans and in our present financial circumstances, there is no law in the land that will allow me to keep her. I love her, Mrs White and can't bear that thought, so I will take her with me and start a new life, a life devoted to her."

"Where will you go?"

"I'm sorry, Mrs White, for your own good, I have to keep that a secret," insisted Delia, even though she hadn't a clue herself, as to which direction

138

she would head to.

Mrs White pursed her lips as she poured the boiling water into the brown earthenware teapot. The smell of her creamy scrambled eggs opened Delia's appetite, she'd barely eaten during the previous day and was now famished.

"Let me come with you then; it's *too* much for you to handle, being alone with a young baby; the world is a wicked place you know and you've led a very sheltered life with your eyes being spared the ugly side of it. I could be a great help to you and besides, I don't fancy being left in this empty shell of a house to face Mr Fairbanks when he returns and as you just stated, he'll probably have to sell everything and may even be sent to the debtors' prison to boot."

Mrs White's unexpected request came as a huge shock, leaving Delia lost for words as she pondered over her suggestion, which did, after all, make a lot of sense.

"You mark my words, Mrs Fairbanks, there's safety in numbers *and* in having a mature woman at your side."

"But I wouldn't be able to pay you, Mrs White."

"I'm not after being paid, I want a new life too and a new adventure, just like you, and besides, it's been more than six months since Mr Fairbanks gave me any payment, but don't worry, I'm a woman of very modest means and have some savings tucked away for a rainy day."

"Why didn't you inform me, Mrs White, *that's terrible!…*"

"Oh, I didn't like to trouble you Mrs Fairbanks...I've got eyes and ears and I'm not unaware of what Mr Fairbanks gets up to when he's away from the home; it wasn't such a shock to me to see the bailiffs at the front door."

"I expect you know more than I do then, Mrs White. You are a saviour, *do you know that*, and I would be delighted to have your company, but I must warn you, that life will be a lot different from your days here at Harberton Mead."

Mrs White chuckled, the strain on her face disappeared and she had a sparkle in her eyes again, "Oh, Mrs Fairbanks, I haven't always been the cook in this house you know...I lived a full life and my eyes have witnessed far more than you could ever imagine. We'll make a jolly good team and that sweet little angel will be well taken care of and given all the loving which she deserves!"

Delia was intrigued, she'd never really envisaged Mrs White as anything other than cook at Harberton Mead house; she was like a part of the furniture but now Delia couldn't wait to learn more about this wholesome woman.

Mrs White proceeded to dish out the scrambled eggs and as they enjoyed their last meal under Harberton Mead's roof, they were both feeling a sense of optimistic excitement at what the future would hold for them.

Maybell and Selma arrived at their normal time and although shocked and saddened by the news, they were delighted that their final pay was unexpectedly healthy and that Mrs Fairbanks had taken the trouble, with all that had gone on in her life, to compose two outstanding references for them. Knowing what a gossip their mother was, Delia lied and told them that she was off to spend some time with an old friend on the coast, not saying which coast though and that Mrs White was also moving to pastures new. The maids were quickly hurried off the premises after saying their farewells, to allow Delia and Mrs White to make an early departure before the return of either Constables Webster and Morris or Harry Fairbanks.

"What on earth have you got in this blooming wooden chest, Mrs Fairbanks? Because I don't reckon we'll get very far lugging this heavyweight around!"

"It's full of Harry's suits; I thought I'd pawn them...sort of teach him a lesson...he *did* steel my only items of any value, after all!"

Mrs White's scornful looks caused Delia to feel like a spiteful and mean woman; she shook her head in disapproval but then totally surprised Delia by her suggestion,

"Why don't we treat Mr Fairbanks to coming home to a lovely warm home and put all of those fancy clothes in the stove, I doubt we'll get much from that old miser in town, and it will only delay our departure."

Delia laughed out loud, "Mrs White, you *do* surprise me!"

"I'm sorry to say it, but Mr Fairbanks doesn't appreciate what a fine life he's been blessed with and he certainly deserves all that's coming to him. Now, Mrs Fairbanks, where is your planned destination?"

"I thought London; it's where people go when they want to hide and make their fortune, isn't it?"

"Well, I suppose there might be some truth in that, but London's not paved with gold as many folk seem to think and it's a City rampant with crime, poverty and disease. But, on the other hand, there could be opportunities for us to earn a living in such a bustling place."

"*Earn a living?*" repeated Delia, naively, "that sounds quite daunting."

"Let's start with London, then, if it's not to our liking...well, there's nothing to stop us moving on, maybe into the countryside, or up north where there's plenty of mills and factories and plenty of money to be made."

After taking great pleasure in filling the burning stove with Harry's fine attire, Delia Fairbanks held baby Faye close to her chest and together the threesome left Harberton Mead house for the very last time.

CHAPTER FIFTEEN

Delia Fairbanks had always led a sheltered life, never having to fend for herself, which was a fact that Ruth White was well aware of. She'd lived for a while in London and knew that unless they found employment in a decent area of the City, it would prove a real eye-opener for Delia and one which she'd find impossible to cope with. As luck would have it, the stagecoach pulled in at the coach house in Dorking and wasn't due to continue to London for another hour. Delia immediately became annoyed by the inconvenience prompting Mrs White to suggest that they should stretch their legs and take a stroll around the market town.

"How jolly untimely," stressed Delia, crossly, "I simply want us to arrive in London in good time to be settled for the night and begin our new life in the morning!"

"With all due respect, Mrs Fairbanks, it's not going to be a piece of cake when we *do* eventually arrive in London. I'm not really sure that you fully understand what you're heading for."

"Oh, I see, are you suggesting that we return to Oxford, Mrs White, to that shell of a home and to my unreliable gambling husband!" Delia's tears ran freely down her cheeks, dripping on to baby Faye who was cradled in her arms, fast asleep and unaware of anything.

"Of course not, Mrs Fairbanks, I merely want you to be prepared for the worst, that's all."

"Well if you must know, I'm not prepared for anything, Mrs White!"

They continued walking in silence along Dorking's main thoroughfare until they spotted a small crowd outside the town hall. There were people of all ages and families too, most of them carrying luggage in scruffy-looking carpet bags and small bundles wrapped up in soiled rags. They appeared deprived and desperate; crying, barefoot children with barley a warm item of clothing on their scrawny bodies to keep out the bitterly cold November wind; men and women looking older than their age, their faces drawn and weary. Delia looked in horror, finding it impossible not to stare at such a pitiful and heartbreaking sight.

"What's going on, Mrs White? Do you have any idea?"

"It must be hiring day," she said in a small voice. "All these poor folk are homeless and if they don't manage to be hired by local farmers today, then they will likely all end up in the workhouse."

"*Goodness,* that's terrible!"

"It certainly is, Mrs Fairbanks and worth bearing in mind that we might find ourselves in the same situation very soon if we fail to find our fortune in London."

No sooner had Mrs White finished her sentence when they were suddenly alerted by the sound of approaching hooves and the voice of a man close behind them. He appeared to be addressing them and Both Delia and Ruth turned to face him, having to stretch their necks to view the middle-aged man, who sat high in the saddle upon his huge steed.

"I'm looking for a cook and a housekeeper, five shillings a week with bed and board included; you'll find me an easy man to work for and very accommodating when it comes to the young one in your arms. If you don't mind me saying so, you two ladies appear to be the healthiest and prettiest looking folk down here today. What do you think...Oh, and in case I didn't mention it, I run a farm, four miles west of here." The farmer spoke confidently as though he meant business, as he towered above them.

Just as Delia was about to open her mouth to protest, Mrs White quickly intervened,

"Thank you kindly, Sir for your most generous offer; could you just give us a few minutes to decide?"

"I'll give you more than that; meet me back here in an hour while I wash away the roadway's dust in the *Bull's Head*, but you'd be missing a great deal, should you decide to turn down my offer, which I'm sure you won't! My name's Jasper Heath, by the way." He smiled, cordially, doffed his cap and rode off.

"*Oh my Lord*, Mrs White, what are you thinking!"
exclaimed Delia, flabbergasted.

"I'm thinking that maybe you'd better start
getting used to calling me *Ma* if you really
want us to make any kind of success and not end
up in a filthy rat-infested hovel in the East End
of London, come nightfall; even then we'd be
considered lucky…I suppose there *are* always
the brothels if we get really desperate, but I
doubt I will attract any customers, so it will be
completely up to you, my dear."

Delia was convinced that Mrs White was
fibbing, sensing that she wasn't keen to travel to
London. Still with a look of utter shock upon her
face, Delia replied, "Do you seriously think that I
could be a housekeeper, Mrs White? Has it *really*
come to this?"

"You heard him Mrs Fairbanks; he runs a farm,
not a grand country estate, we'll be able to
muddle along nicely *and* have a warm place to
sleep at night. It will be far better for little Faye
too, just remember the copious outbreaks of
cholera, typhoid and scarlet fever there are in
London, especially in the sort of place where
we're likely to end up in; as hard as it may seem,
you've got to face the facts, Mrs Fairbanks; we
are homeless and have very little money. Can we
really afford to pass up such a generous offer
from that Mr…? Oh dear, I can't for the life of me
remember his name…don't know what's
happening to my memory these days!"

"Jasper Heath, that's what his name is. Please tell me your plan then, Mrs White. I'm going to put my trust in you, simply because you are older and know more of the ways of the world than I do."

"I'm sure this is the right move, Mrs Fairbanks; I can feel it in my bones. Now first things first, we must return to the coach house and collect our worldly belongings; we can discuss our story on the way ."

After a refreshing pot of tea in a Dorking tea room, they left to meet Jasper Heath as *'mother'*, *'widowed daughter'* and *'granddaughter'*. Delia's story was that she'd lost her husband to the fever when she was in the early months of pregnancy, and the supposedly Mr White and Delia's father, who happened to be a lot older than his wife, had passed away ten years ago.

Even after an hour of Ruth White's persistent persuading, Delia was still feeling reluctant and anxious about lying and pretending to be a widow *and* Mrs White's daughter.

"I'm really not sure it will work, Mrs White; first of all, I will *never* remember to call you *Ma*; you and I look nothing like mother and daughter and secondly, what happens when Mr Jasper Heath starts asking questions about our background, we're almost certain to slip up...we will end up looking like a couple of liars, not to be trusted and will undoubtedly be thrown off the farm!"

Ruth White knew that convincing Delia to go along with this scheme was essential in keeping them both safe and with a roof over their heads. Winter was just around the corner and they had a new baby to think of; Ruth already knew how Delia loved the little orphan child as though she was her very own baby.

"Don't worry so, my dear, we can discuss our story later tonight and make certain that it's flawless. I'm sure it won't be difficult, we can simply tell the truth about where we've been living and claim that we have now fallen on such hard times that we are unable to pay the rent and feed ourselves. It won't be too far away from the truth, anyway. We don't want to find ourselves homeless with winter on the way...we've got this little angel to take care of too."

Mrs White stroked baby Faye's soft cheek, she had woken up and would soon be hollering for a feed. "What a little darling she is!" she praised, lovingly. "Now remember, make sure you call me ma," she hurriedly whispered in Delia's ear, catching sight of Jasper Heath as he headed towards them on foot.

"I hope this means that you've decided to accept my offer," he asked, his heavily whiskered face looking delighted.

"We have, Mr Heath," replied Mrs White, taking charge, "so long as my daughter, granddaughter and myself can all share the same sleeping quarters."

Now, out of the saddle, Jasper Heath appeared shorter in stature and just half a head taller than Delia; he possessed a kind looking face and warm, milky brown eyes. Mrs White estimated him to be no older than fifty; he had a lean but strong-looking body and was obviously used to hard work she deduced, pleasingly; if there was one type of man which she couldn't abide, it was a lazy one.

"You'll find Mickleham Farm quite spacious, I believe, unless you've been used to living in a palace, that is," he joked. "There's a room suitable for at least four adults which I'll gladly let you have."

"Thank you Mr Heath, that's most considerate of you," replied Ruth.

"Good, now that's settled, two of my sons should be arriving any minute with the wagon, so you'll be able to ride back with them; we'll discuss other matters over a pot of tea back at the farm and in front of a blazing fire; it's a right cold day today; I reckon heavy snow will soon be heading down from the North." Jasper rubbed his hands together, as he stretched his neck, in search of his sons.

"Ah, Praise The Good Lord, here they come. That's good; at least we'll arrive home before nightfall."

Delia and Ruth watched as the wagon drew closer to them; the two lads were barely men, both as handsome as their father, they appeared bashful when introduced, their clean faces instantly turning a bright shade of red.

"Lads; these two fine women and their baby, will be joining us; take them home quickly to the warmth of our humble home and out of this icy wind."

There were courteous smiles upon everyone's faces; the two lads doffed their caps as they jumped down to load up the back of the wagon with Delia and Mrs White's luggage, together with the supplies which Jasper had purchased in town. Delia and Ruth were then assisted into the back and the tail end of the wagon was secured. In all of her life, Delia had never travelled in such an undignified manner, but trying not to let her disappointment show in front of Mrs White, she sensed that she was probably in store for far worse as a farmer's housekeeper.

The wagon squeezed through the narrow track, which was edged with tall, overgrown hawthorn hedges and blackberry bushes, now stripped of their fruit and looking desolate as the chilled wind ruffled their tiny leaves. The women huddled closely together in a bid to keep warm as they shivered. "That farmer seemed in an awful hurry to employ us, don't you think, Mrs White?" Delia whispered in her ear.

"Well, just take a look at how fine and healthy we looked, my dear, compared to all of those pitiful creatures who were desperately waiting to be hired; Jasper Heath knew he was on to a good thing and worried sick that some other farmer would make us a better offer. Mark my words, he wouldn't have offered any of those paupers five shillings a week! *And* for goodness sake!" implored Ruth White, becoming quite flustered, "you *must* start calling me *Ma*, and as impertinent as it might appear, from now on, I will call you Delia, and please don't forget that the child's name is Faye *Fairbanks*!"

"I feel as though I've been purchased from a cattle market," uttered Delia, sadly.

"Well, I suppose in a way we have *both* been purchased, but try and look on the bright side; at least we will be sleeping in a bed with a roof over our heads tonight and out of this unbearable coldness."

"Well, I hope so unless Mr Jasper Heath decides to put his newly acquired cattle out in the barn!"

"*Nearly there!*" called out one of the lads, "just around the corner and Mickleham Farm will be in sight!"

"*Oh Ma*, did you hear that, we're nearly there...how exciting!" declared Delia, sarcastically.

Mickleham Farm appeared attractive and boasted a larger than average sized farmhouse. It was situated on the edge of the roadway with its farming land stretching out behind it and to one side. The half-brick, half-stone building which over the decades had had extra rooms added to its rear, including a huge and modern kitchen with a working tap and huge, modern cooking range, was a welcoming sight for Mrs White; her aching joints now longing to feel some warmth on them, again.

As they all gathered in the spacious kitchen which was thankfully well heated, Ruth White deduced that this was a family who had lost its mother and since there had been no mention or signs of any daughters, the male-dominated family appeared to be crying out for some female intervention.

Jasper Heath couldn't believe his good fortune as he ushered Delia and Mrs White to make themselves at home around the table; these were fine well-bred women and not the type normally found outside the town hall seeking positions. He introduced his three sons; aged sixteen, nineteen and twenty. Noah, William and Adam were all handsome and polite young men and both Delia and Ruth, took an instant liking to them. It transpired that their mother had become ill two winters ago with bronchitis and had lost her long battle during the following spring. It was only now that Jasper had given in to his stubbornness and finally admitted that they were in need of extra help and a woman's touch around the farmhouse. He had also felt unable to allow another female to pass over the threshold and rule the kitchen so soon after the passing away of his beloved wife.

The three young men were besotted by baby Faye and she was passed from one to another; they all seemed to have a way with her and managed to keep her contented for a while, even though her feed time was overdue. Delia and Ruth introduced themselves according to Ruth's instructions which caused Delia to feel like a complete fraud when Jasper Heath, kindly and so sympathetically commiserated her on the loss of her husband. He suggested that Delia should take herself and the baby to the front parlour where she could have some privacy to feed the hungry baby and was quite shocked to hear that Delia was nourishing her young infant on cow's milk.

"Do you mind if I heat up some milk for the baby?" Mrs White intervened; worried that Delia might say something to expose their lies. "You see, Mr Heath, my poor daughter was left so distraught after giving birth, when the reality that she was without a husband finally sunk in, that her milk just disappeared. Apparently, it's quite common in such traumatic cases, so the doctor informed me." Noah, William and Adam had already gone red in the face, while Jasper, now slightly embarrassed was quick to retrieve a jug of milk from the pantry.

"Please Mrs White, there is no need to ask, this is as much you and your family's home now and you must treat it accordingly. I have a strong feeling that we are all going to get along just fine and your granddaughter *already* has three admirers, I'd say!"

It only took a week for the shyness to vanish at Mickleham Farm. Jasper Heath and his sons were soon eagerly waiting for the arrival of every mealtime, thrilled to be served delicious and varied dinners for a change; they had lived on fried eggs and bread and cheese for far too long, with the occasional boiled chicken and potatoes. The farmhouse was once again filled with the daily aroma of freshly baked bread and more often than not, there was always a pot of hot tea and a well-stocked pantry with delicious cakes and fruit buns. While Ruth was in her element cooking in the huge kitchen and counting her blessings every day that they'd not continued the journey to London, Delia still felt out of place and knew that she wasn't contributing her fair share of work, even though she tried to assist Mrs White and make herself useful as often as she could. She often slipped up and forgot to call Mrs White 'Ma' but thankfully, when this *had* happened in front of one of the Heath family Ruth had managed to make the excuse that she and her daughter used to play a childhood game where she would address her as such and now, because of her recent trauma, she sometimes unknowingly reverted back to her childhood days. Mrs White felt it inappropriate to allow Delia to involve herself in the running of the Heath household and encouraged her just to devote her time and attention to baby Faye. The three of them shared a large room on the ground floor, next to the kitchen, which proved extremely convenient, giving them quick and easy access to the kitchen without disturbing the Heath family who all slept upstairs. It also meant that baby Faye's increasingly louder cries went unheard by them. Their new life seemed very strange but Mrs White constantly assured Delia that as soon as they became familiar to their new surroundings and newly formed relationships, everything would turn out just fine.

CHAPTER SIXTEEN
April 1858

Mavis Glover prided herself on being the most devoted wife that any man of the cloth could be blessed with and on that memorable night in November, although it had pained her to sacrifice the warmth of her bed and brave the elements, when the young bedraggled messenger boy, who couldn't have been more than nine years of age, was hammering on the front door of the vicarage she insisted on standing by her husband's side and accompanying him to the local Woodstock undertaker's parlour. On that treacherous night, when the dark skies had been slashed open, giving way to the season's worst storm and the icy wind chilled the bones of any poor soul who was unfortunate to be out in such weather, the Reverend Barnaby Glover, together with the local doctor were beside themselves that such a dreadful mistake could have been made. The quiet whimpering from the supposedly deceased young woman, who'd been picked up by an undertaker on the Oxford highway and later transported to Woodstock, had initially caused the undertaker to think that on such a hostile night, a stray cat had taken refuge in the morgue; he'd searched every dark corner before his attention shifted to the recently delivered corpse which he'd decided to attend to in the morning; he hadn't even bothered to remove the thick blanket concealing the body and which was, most likely, a huge contributor to her survival. A young fair-haired woman whose face was as white as the winter moon and lips so pale that they were almost invisible had clearly not been separated from her soul and had the face of an angel concluded the undertaker after he'd gingerly peeled back a tiny portion of the blanket, before sending his messenger boy out into the wild night for help.

This poor young girl, who had miraculously survived and been blessed with another chance of life was taken into Mavis Glover's charitable care. She became the topic of conversation amongst her husband's devoted flock at every following chapel service, with Mavis, as always receiving nothing but praise and admiration for her kindness. After a few days spent in Woodstock's cottage hospital, Faye Butler was then transferred to the Radcliffe Infirmary in Oxford where after a few weeks of uncertainty, she began to shows signs of improvement. Once a week Mavis Glover travelled the twelve miles to visit Faye until she'd made an almost full physical recovery and was fit enough to return to the vicarage and reside with Mavis and The Reverend Barnaby Glover, in order to recuperate. Being left in a somewhat mentally disturbed and physically weak state,

Faye's fragile body had sided so close to death and lost so much blood that it had left her severely traumatized. Only time would tell if she'd ever recover fully, the hospital doctors had stated. It was clearly evident to the medics that the main cause of Faye becoming so close to death was the fact that she'd recently given birth. The details surrounding how and who had discovered her and how she'd been passed around Oxford like a mislaid parcel were still quite sketchy but with no sign of any baby and since nobody knew how long she'd laid on the roadside before being discovered, the devastating truth, concluded the doctors, was that the stench of blood had been detected by starving wild animals who'd tracked and snatched the baby; they were, however, convinced that the infant would most likely have been stillborn. Faye's distressing cries for her lost baby could be heard every day in the vicarage and even though Mavis did all that was in her power to comfort Faye, she sensed that this fallen girl was unmarried, believing it to be a mercy that her child had not survived, no matter how much it broke Faye's heart. Hearts could be mended, considered Mavis Glover, but the terrible sin of an illegitimate child might take Faye the rest of her life to wipe clean and she had decided to help her in every possible way, beginning with the daily prayers which Mavis insisted upon.

Faye had not only had to contend with her poor health and the loss of her baby but one day in April of 1858 she'd come across an article in an old newspaper, which related to the peaceful village of Wheatley being thrown into disarray by the appalling murder of an elderly resident who'd lived at Dove Cottage for most of her life. There was no mention of any names but Faye suddenly remembered her grandparents and her happy childhood days at Dove Cottage. It had also jogged her memory as to why and where she'd been heading on that wintery night when her body had been ravaged by the pains of childbirth.

"Mrs Glover," she suddenly cried out, with the newspaper crumpled up on her lap. "This article, in here… it's my grandmother's house, Dove Cottage; it's where I grew up before I went to work in Northamptonshire and before that damned weasel of a footman forced himself upon me."

Mavis looked up from her piece of needlework, "We'll have *no* swearing in the vicarage," scowled Mavis, shocked by the amount of intriguing information in Faye's brief sentence. "Let me see that newspaper," she ordered.

Faye sat watching as the expression on Mavis's face changed.

"This was printed back in November; it must have been just after you had your unfortunate accident!" Mavis Glover had always insisted that

Faye must have been run off the thoroughfare by some careless driver. As the muddled images in Faye's mind began to paint a clear picture, she felt as though her heart had leapt up into her throat as she remembered her darling love, Roberto Lopez; she could almost smell the scent of his skin and picture his dark smouldering eyes gazing at her. It had taken five months, but by simply reading those few memorable words in the newspaper, it was as though the flood gates had been pulled open and Faye's head was awash with her past life. Finally, she knew who she was and where she'd come from. The names of those people who'd been part of her life had at last returned.

"Oh my dear child, you've had an alarming shock, I can see it in your face...I will tell Reverend Glover to call Doctor Atkins at once!" Since the day when Faye had been discharged from the Radcliffe Infirmary in Oxford, Mavis had made it her priority to mollycoddle Faye, and although she meant well, at times Faye found it almost suffocating and as a glimpse of her past life reminded her of how free and independent she'd been; she had the strongest urge to escape the strict, conservative regime of the pokey vicarage.

"Mrs Glover, I'm fine… really…and I'm even confident that at last I am fully recovered from my ordeal, but this news is awful…I need to find out if my grandmother is alive, and whether this rotten newspaper is true to its words. I've also remembered that I have a beau, and we were supposed to be married by now," explained Faye, seriously.

"*Stuff and nonsense!*" cried out Mavis, her long skinny neck seeming to stretch out of her austere white collared, black dress. "Whoever you think your beau might be, Faye, I can assure you that he is *no* gentleman to allow such a tragedy to take place without even bothering to look for you! And why didn't he make an honest woman of you earlier for goodness sake? Sounds like a common blackguard to me, and you're better off without him in my opinion!"

"But how do we know that he *didn't* look for me?" Faye protested, "He is a decent man too, Mrs Glover…he wasn't the father of my baby, but loved me enough to stand by my side and support me. You don't know the first thing about him, so please don't jump to such false and unfair presumptions!"

"*Roberto Lopez*, did you call him? That's no English name is it, and this newspaper report states that there were witnesses who claimed that the perpetrator was a foreigner."

"Rob is no foreigner, Mrs Glover, he was raised in an East End orphanage, his parents just happen to have been of Spanish origin! Anyway, now that I'm feeling so much better, I simply *must* take a trip to Dove Cottage!"

"All in good time, Faye, and if the Good Lord

sees it fit for you to return to your past life, which, I hasten to add was a life not fit for any respectable young woman who expects to fulfil a decent future. You were saved, young Faye and delivered to the vicarage for a purpose and the sooner you realise and appreciate that fact, the happier you will be."

Faye felt as though she were talking to a brick wall. Overcome with fatigue all of a sudden and in need of a rest, she sensed that Mrs Glover had no intention of opening any doors which might allow her to return to the life she once had and to her grandmother if, by chance, there was the slightest possibility that she might still be living. "There must be a way in which we can find out about my grandmother," insisted Faye, "do you think the local constabulary might know anything...her name is Mrs Butler." Faye suddenly realised that she had no idea as to her grandmother's first name, for as long as she could remember, she'd always been referred to as *grandma* or *Mrs Butler*; even in the presence of her late grandfather, who also addressed her as 'grandmother'. "She lives at Dove Cottage in Wheatley village, a few miles outside of Oxford." Mavis had her annoyed face on; she shoved her delicate piece of needlework into the sewing box, next to her chair and stretched out her long legs, rotating her ankles in a clockwise direction, before rising from her seat and gliding like a graceful swan out of the tiny parlour, not daring to look back. Faye re-read the newspaper article, breaking down into tears as the thought of never being able to see her grandmother again weighed heavy on her heart. What had happened to Rob, and where had he gone to on that November day when they'd been so happy waiting for the arrival of her baby and for the day when they would marry and become a proper family. Faye could feel the return of one of her thumping headaches, the tragic news which had shaken her memory had suddenly taken its toll on her, still fragile, body. She knew how fortunate she was to be alive, even the doctors had not expected her to live after losing so much blood and being exposed to the elements and the cold slab of the morgue for hours, she'd also suffered from a high fever for three weeks, brought on by an infection, apparently not uncommon after childbirth, especially one which had taken place in such filthy surroundings.

Mavis returned to the parlour, along with her fake smile; she came bearing tea and sponge cake and words of false sympathy. Faye was adamant that she'd continue with her insistence in finding out the truth about her grandmother and nothing that her temporary guardians could do or say would deter her, she owed that much to her dear grandmother, she mused.

The following day was marred by heavy and endless April showers which filled the vicarage parlour with a gloomy darkness. Barnaby Glover had been forced to oblige his wife's night long nagging and had agreed that he'd endeavour to find out about Faye's grandmother. He felt he owed it to Mavis; in their eighteen years of marriage, she had always supported him through thick and thin, never refusing any of his requests. It would be an inconvenience and he wasn't prepared to waste his time travelling the twenty or so miles to Wheatley, to have confirmed what the newspaper had already stated but he left the vicarage, assuring both Faye and his wife that he'd return with the truth surrounding the events which had taken place all those months ago. After all, he reflected, as much as his wife didn't want to see Faye leave the vicarage, he was dreading such a day even more. Lately, he'd been deeply troubled by his feelings towards young Faye, but at the same time, equally excited by the overpowering thrill which he'd not experienced since being a schoolboy. Those everlasting, carefree days of summer, when he'd accompanied the rest of the young and inquisitive boys in his school year as they crawled through the tall bracken and stealthily concealed themselves amongst the thick, grass tufts to spy in awe as the women folk stripped off their outer garments and stockings, before bathing in the River Glyme. He was now a respectable man of the cloth in his mid-forties and as much as he knew his thoughts were surely immoral, he couldn't help himself from dreaming of Faye. It had crept up on him slowly; when he'd first set eyes on her he was shocked at how pitifully thin and pale she was and saw little more than a young, vulnerable and sick woman who had almost certainly been taken advantage of, but over the months Faye's presence seemed to fill the vicarage with a glowing light of excitement, she was young and spontaneous and giggled at the silliest of things which Mavis would merely frown at. She would even compliment him after he'd read an interesting sermon and her beauty was soon evident as her health returned and her thin and undernourished body filled out to reveal a shapely young woman, with a head of rich, golden curls which shone so attractively when the light caught them. Faye Butler thrilled him, and Barnaby Glover wasn't yet ready to resume his normal mundane life and would, therefore, encourage Mavis to use all her influence in trying to keep her living at the vicarage for as long as possible.

To keep Mavis Glover happy, Faye hid behind the heavy leather-bound Bible, turning a page every now and again; it was the perfect solution where she could allow her thoughts to recapture the past without listening to the constant unnecessary chatter of Mrs Glover. Everything was now coming back to her and she knew that her days of poor health were behind her. She remembered Granny Isabel and her haberdashery shop in Wentworth Street where she'd fallen hopelessly in love with Rob. He *did* love her, that, she was sure of and she hoped that the only reason why he'd not come in search of her was that; like the rest of the folk in Oxford he'd been informed that she was dead.

"I think we might make a missionaries wife out of you, Faye!" announced Mrs Glover, excitedly. "There are plenty of young and handsome clergymen who are desperate to take a good, God-fearing and devout wife to the darkest parts of Africa, where there is still, so much work to be done; you were born to undertake such a role, Faye...why do you think that the Almighty chose to bring you back from the brink of death, even though you had committed an unforgivable sin. He delivered you to this tiny country vicarage for that reason."

"As soon as I am fully recovered, Mrs Glover and find out the truth about my dear grandmother, I must return to my beau in London...he obviously believes that I'm dead...suppose he *did* go in search of me, only to be told by the Oxford peelers that I'd died on that awful night?"

" *Stuff and nonsense*, my dear. As difficult as it might be, you *must* forget about this *Roberto Lopez* and count your blessings," instructed Mavis. "*Oh look*, the sun has at last decided to put in an appearance, why don't you go and cut a bunch of daffodils from the garden; Reverend Glover *does so adore* the reminders of springtime upon the dinner table and then, perhaps, you could help me prepare the meal for when he returns from his arduous travels."

Glad to get away from the prim and self-righteousness of Mrs Glover's nature, Faye was beginning to feel trapped in her surroundings. Even though she was grateful for the way in which the reverend and his wife had so kindly taken her into their home and nursed her back to health, it was now becoming clear that they had already mapped out her future and it was a future which didn't appeal to Faye.

CHAPTER SEVENTEEN

Barnaby Glover hadn't needed to travel as far as
Oxford to discover the truth about Faye's
grandmother; by chance, he'd bumped into
Constable Grant during his daily beat around
the narrow lanes of Woodstock. Always ready to
take a break in the hope of divulging some
interesting gossip from the Reverend Glover,
Constable Grant was eager to be of help and it
gave him an air of importance as he filled him in
on the crime which had allegedly taken place in
Wheatley village five months previously. Even
though there was not a soul in sight, Constable
Grant spoke in a whisper, as the pair leaned up
against a drystone wall beneath the wide
umbrella of a mature oak tree, pausing
occasionally to glance furtively up and down the
lane. Barnaby Glover strained his ears, not
wanting to miss a single word.
"That's extremely charitable of you and your
good wife to shelter the poor fallen women
under your care, Reverend; I hope she fully
appreciates the kindness you've shown her. And
you say she believes it was *her* grandmother who
resided at Dove Cottage? Well, every police
station in the county received a full report about
the murder; we were all instructed to be on our
guard, just in case the perpetrator should
suddenly appear on our doorsteps, so to speak.

But then a couple of weeks following the incident, we received an update, informing us that after having undergone a medical examination by the doctor and after interviewing the entire village, who'd by all accounts all been watching when the confrontation took place, the new evidence was that the poor old woman's heart had simply given up. They reckoned that the young man who'd initially been labelled as a murderer must have been that scared, especially since he'd done nothing at all wrong, that he just scarpered. Some of the witnesses claimed that he appeared to know Mrs Butler, that he'd even called her by her name. There *was* the issue of his origin too...we've had, Italian, Spanish and even Indian mentioned, but I doubt we'll ever know now, and I wouldn't have thought that he'll ever show his face in Oxfordshire again."

"Thank you Constable Grant, your exceptionally well-informed report has saved me the untimely journey into Oxford. I do believe that our young, Miss Faye Butler is sadly correct about her grandmother. That poor young creature seems to have had nothing but misfortune during her life. I will have to break the sad news to her, but I'm sure the fact that her grandmother died of natural causes will prove to be of some consolation, at least." Barnaby spoke sadly, in front of the constable, hiding his relief that this news would hopefully keep Faye at the vicarage a little longer.

"She seems to have come on in leaps and bounds since she discovered that old newspaper in the vicarage," he declared. "I pray that the Merciful Lord will now guide her to a more rewarding life."

"Perhaps she is now well enough to visit her late grandmother's graveside," suggested Constable Grant.

"Yes, perhaps. Thank you kindly, for your help; now I won't hold you up a moment longer and by the look of those gathering black clouds, another shower looks imminent."

The constable chuckled, "I don't, for the life of me, know why they call them April showers, more like April downpours, I'd say!"

With smiles on their faces, the two men parted, heading off in opposite directions.

Immediately sensing the strained atmosphere on his arrival back at the vicarage, Barnaby's first instincts were to check on Faye. Mavis, who was obviously in one of her moods, was busy in the kitchen making sure that every pot, plate and utensil landed with a clatter. Faye was curled up at the end of the sofa, her pretty head resting in the palm of her hand. Her slight body took up little space and she reminded Barnaby of a vulnerable injured bird; he wished he could just scoop her up into his arms and hold her close to him. She looked up, aware of his presence.

Barnaby knew she'd been crying and it broke his heart.

"Good afternoon, Faye."

"Good afternoon, Reverend," she replied in a soft voice.

"Is everything alright? Only you seem to be missing your charming smile?"

His warm expression and benign words induced a faint smile upon Faye's face.

"I'm feeling a little down in the dumps today, that's all."

"Anything I can do to help?"

"Oh Reverend, you've done more than enough for me already...*and* not forgetting Mrs Glover, of course," she added out of politeness. Barnaby sensed that his wife *had* done or said something to upset Faye, but he decided to take advantage of her absence in the parlour. He perched down on the edge of the couch, already feeling his heart, pulsating strongly behind his rib cage. He looked into Faye's pretty soft olive green eyes and felt a sudden abnormal shyness; he hoped it wasn't transparent as he admonished himself to take control of his frozen tongue and break the silence.

"I have news of your grandmother, Faye," he blurted out, clumsily. A glimmer of hope shone through her eyes and Barnaby knew that what he was about to disclose would shatter her expectations. "I'm so sorry, I should have phrased that more appropriately; what I meant was that I have some news regarding your late grandmother."

Faye lowered her gaze, allowing Barnaby to continue, "I know there is *never* any good news from the death of a close loved one, but in your grandmother's case, I feel that the fact that she left this world due to natural causes will be a great comfort to you. There was, as reported, a gentleman of foreign appearance at the scene, but it was later discovered that your grandmother's heart gave up; he was no murderer and evidently appeared to know your grandmother; the poor man was unfairly misjudged, which must have caused him to flee from the scene. I'm sorry that I'm unable to bring you any joyful news, Faye."

"It's not your fault, Reverend, and after reading that newspaper article, deep down in my heart, I knew that there couldn't have been a mistake and that my grandmother *had* gone to join dear Grandfather in a much better place. I'm just so brokenhearted that I never managed to visit her since I left Wheatley to take up my position in service. After all that they did for me, I let them down at the end of their lives...I should have been at their sides, not miles away in Northampton and London," sobbed Faye. Overcome by the impulse to comfort her in a close embrace, Barnaby enveloped his arms around her, wishing in his heart that he was not shackled to Mavis and the Parish.

"You must continue to be strong, my sweet darling," he whispered in her ear, "I'm here for you now, and will protect you from all harm, please remember that, Faye." Barnaby couldn't resist the temptation to brush a light kiss upon Faye's soft skin; it felt like silk in comparison to Mavis's tough weather-worn cheeks and he knew that he'd live his life in pure misery if Faye was not part of it.

"I hope you've had the opportunity to admire the beautiful daffodils!" Mavis suddenly appeared from nowhere; her voice and presence instantly bringing Barnaby back to reality with a sour feeling. He wondered if she'd been watching him or if she sensed anything untoward. He turned obediently to glance at the vase of yellow and orange daffodils in the deep window recess. "I have indeed; they are delightful and fill the room with the essence of spring."

"Faye picked them! Didn't you, Faye?" announced Mavis, icily.

"Yes, I did, Mrs Glover."

"I was only saying to Faye, earlier, that she'd make the perfect wife for a young and ambitious missionary. What do you say, Reverend?"

"I hardly think that picking a bunch of daffodils qualifies poor Miss Butler to be married off and shipped off to some dark and foreboding part of the world to live in misery and poverty, not to mention the likelihood of contracting some

awful incurable disease. I think she's endured
enough hardships of late and deserves a more
genteel lifestyle, so I don't want to hear another
word said on such matters."

Mavis felt humiliated, how dare he speak to her
in such a way and in front of that little
guttersnipe, she thought, angrily. She wasn't
blind and could see that the return of Faye's
health was also bringing with it a beautiful and
flirtatious young woman and a somewhat flighty
one who, due to her past record, might seem like
an easy and available catch to many a man,
including her husband who it would appear,
had been bewitched by her devious ways. She'd
be keeping a close eye on him, that was certain,
and the sooner she found a husband for Faye
Butler, the better.

A tense atmosphere surrounded the dinner table
that evening; Barnaby felt reluctant to speak to
Mavis or even look at her and Mavis chose to
ignore Faye, almost as though she wasn't seated
at the table. Faye, however, was feeling relieved
that Reverend Glover had spoken against his
wife's foolish idea's and was now convinced that
the foreign-looking man who had appeared to
know her grandmother, was her darling, Rob.
As soon as she could lay her hands on enough
money to reach London, and felt strong enough
to embark on such a journey she would be on
her way, she surreptitiously decided.

That evening, Faye made her excuses that she

was feeling too weary to socialise and retired early to her tiny room in the eaves of the vicarage, but weary was the exact opposite of how she was really feeling. The sheer thrill of just knowing that she and Rob might soon begin their life together filled her with an impatient yearning just to flee from the vicarage at first light. Realistically, though, Faye knew how foolish it would be to risk a long journey when she still suffered from bouts of lethargy and the mere thought of walking along the highway engrossed her with panic and flashbacks of that harrowing night when she'd felt the life drain from her body. She decided that a meticulous plan would be the best way forward; she needed money and she also needed to smarten herself up a little; the few clothes which she was permitted to wear came from the trunk of donations meant for the so-called heathens who lived in tribes across the seas and who lived in ways which Faye found hard to believe when Reverend Glover had spoken of them; she couldn't envisage how anybody would have the nerve to go about their daily lives in a state of half nakedness. The dark green day dress which Mavis had given her was void of any shape and had a permanent odour of mildew and fish about it; she'd also given her a dark brown, woollen skirt which was at least three sizes too big and its coarse material caused her skin to itch profusely. The accompanying lace-trimmed blouse, although quite pretty, was old and threadbare and no longer its original colour of ivory, but a murky and most unattractive grey. Faye was quite convinced that Mrs Glover had picked out the worst of the donations, but already had a plan to sweet talk the prudish reverend's wife into allowing her to rummage around the trunk for herself. Faye had noticed how attentive the reverend had seemed towards her of late, and in such drastic situations, it would appear that a little flirting might be her one and only key to freedom. She'd have to be careful of Mrs Glover, though, she warned herself, it wouldn't do to rile her; first thing in the morning she'd bake a batch of scones and try to hold her tongue every time she disagreed with her. Gazing up at the rafters as she prepared to sleep, Faye placed the flat of her hand onto her belly, remembering the moment of relief when her daughter had left her body, she could still picture her sweet face even in the darkness, it was clearly visible and an image which would remain with her forever. She must have lost conscious shortly after she'd swaddled the baby in her petticoat and couldn't remember anything else. Her emotions were completely muddled when she reminisced on her loss, she *had* been heartbroken, but now she viewed it as a blessing...what if she had grown up to bear a resemblance to her father, that ugly scoundrel of a footman; what a terrible punishment that would be, but now she was free to start afresh and prayed that when she did find Rob, everything would be the same between them again and they would share a beautiful future life together. As her heavy eyelids could stay open no longer, Faye's last thoughts were that the following day, she'd write to Granny Isabel in Wentworth Street, in the hope that she'd be able to reply with some good news about Rob.

CHAPTER EIGHTEEN

Barnaby Glover walked into the kitchen beaming all over his face; the sweet aroma of freshly baked scones had filled the entire vicarage and opened his appetite for breakfast. Mavis soon followed, with an air of pride about her as she inspected the state of the kitchen before breaking a scone into two and examining its insides.

"Is this down to *your* teaching my dearest?"

"It is indeed and I must admit that these look like a jolly good batch of scones, but of course the proof will be in the eating!"

Unable to resist, Barnaby bit into a scone without even bothering to butter it. He chewed with satisfaction,

"Well my dear, I have to admit, that you are an *excellent* teacher!"

He smiled at Faye, before taking his next bite, "Well done Miss Butler!"

Annoyed that she'd received no credit and that Mavis had lied about her so-called *baking lessons*, which were nonexistent, Faye pursed her lips in order to prevent what was in her mind from flying out of her mouth. She reminded herself of her plan and thought only of Rob, which induced an immediate calmness about her.

"I was wondering if I might be allowed to exchange my clothes with a more summery dress, Mrs Glover; the weather has turned warmer now and I'm finding this thick material quite uncomfortable, plus it's far too big for me." Faye demonstrated by pulling out the extra hand span of material at her waistline.

As Mavis glared crossly, Barnaby appeared far more sympathetic,

"She could accompany me to the chapel after breakfast since I have some paperwork to attend to and then, perhaps, choose her own gown. What do you think Mavis?"

"In my opinion, it's rather premature; we're only in April and it hasn't been unheard of for it to snow during this month."

Faye could sense that Mrs Glover clearly didn't want her to have a change of clothing and was simply making feeble excuses; she couldn't understand why though.

"In that case, how about we see if there are two suitable gowns!" beamed Reverend Glover, ignoring his wife's scowl. "One suitable for spring and one for summer, wouldn't that make more sense?"

"Have you put the water on to boil and prepared the teacups for breakfast Faye?" Mavis's tone was cold and bossy.

"I'll do it right away, Mrs Glover." While Mrs Glover and the Reverend disappeared into the parlour Faye quickly went about preparing the tea, glad to be spared from looking at Mrs Glover's unpleasant face for a few minutes but determined to keep her composure.

"Steady on now Mavis!" she overheard the Reverend, "the poor girl's only recently recovered and you *must* remember, that she's not our paid parlour maid, you know...remember your charitable duty my dear."

The breakfast was eaten in a subdued atmosphere, but Faye was happy with the Reverend's suggestion that they should walk across the small garden which separated the vicarage from the chapel, just as soon as they'd eaten, to delve into the trunk of donations.

Feeling far more relaxed in the company of The Reverend Glover, Faye walked by his side, enjoying the warm early morning sunshine upon her back. The overly long hem of her skirt had already become heavily soaked by the dew which didn't go unnoticed by Barnaby as he couldn't help himself from clandestinely eyeing Faye from head to toe as they indulged in conversation about the beauty of spring flowers. "Spring flowers are rather like the first course of a meal," Reverend Glover explained," they are an appetizer for the huge anticipated summer feast and a sign from The Almighty that after their winter demise, there is rebirth and new life." Impressed by his theory, Faye admired his easy and relaxed character. Within a couple of minutes they arrived at the neighbouring chapel, Barnaby led her down the aisle to the rear of the musty smelling building, Faye noticed a couple of puddles.

"It looks as though there might be some holes in the roof, Reverend Glover!"

"Yes, that's quite true; it's a job which must be attended to this summer. Now, Faye the trunkload of donations along with an assortment of other relics is kept in the crypt. I hope that doesn't discourage you, but rest assured, that as far as I know, nobody is actually buried there...it's a somewhat tiny space."

Behind the battered-looking arched, oak door, Faye had to duck her head in order to gingerly follow behind Reverend Glover with his burning lantern, down the worn, stone steps which reached deep beneath the chapel. The temperature immediately dropped, leaving Faye's skin covered with goosebumps. The tiny space was the living quarters for numerous clusters of spiders; dusty cobwebs dangled from the low ceiling and adhered to the obscure interior stonework together with strange but beautifully formed mushrooms, which sprouted out of every crevice, their overpowering aroma dominating the already musty air. The absence of clean air in the underground pit had already sent Faye's heart racing.

"Why do you keep the donation trunk down here, Reverend? It's such a gloomy place."

Reverend Glover laughed, "Mrs Glover is of the opinion that nobody would attempt to venture down here so it, therefore, makes for a secure storage space."

"But the horrid stench becomes infused in the clothes and ruins them...this dress still smells and I've washed it at least half a dozen times."

"Ah, but you must remember, dear Faye that these supplies are destined for the hot climate of Africa and beyond...A few hours beneath their scorching sun will soon rid them of their stuffy aroma."

Faye thought it odd that he'd called her by her first name, he appeared at ease when not in the presence of Mrs Glover and his smile became almost permanent. She studied his face as he struggled with the lid of the rotting trunk, his green eyes bulged, causing them to appear almost amphibian-like, but they had a hidden sparkle about them, which she'd only noticed when Mrs Glover was absent. Faye wondered if The Reverend Glover and his wife had ever shared a passionate relationship, she couldn't imagine so and presumed that their marriage had been arranged and one of mutual convenience. With the lid of the trunk suddenly flying open, throwing Barnaby off balance as his boot caught in his long jacket, he only just managed to take a grip of the trunk to prevent himself from landing unceremoniously on his backside. His cheeks took on a bright scarlet hue and Faye couldn't suppress her giggles.

"I'm so glad you find me so entertaining, Faye!"

he joked.

He'd called her Faye again. "I'm sorry Reverend, but you did look so funny!"

He stood up straight, his dark attire was covered with dust and fragments of old webs but he made no attempt to brush his clothes, instead he focussed wholly on Faye. He took her hand in his,

"Do you realise, Faye; that is the first time I've ever heard you laugh. You *too* are blossoming just like one of our garden's flowers. I think perhaps, that you are, at last, over the worst of your ordeal."

His expression was serious; his eyes penetrating and the way in which his large hand was completely engulfing hers caused Faye to become wary of the situation.

"Yes, you're right, I believe it *is* the first time that I've laughed," agreed Faye, her voice quivering. With reluctance, Barnaby released her hand.

"Take a look through the trunk, Faye. I hope we don't just possess all the plump ladies' cast-offs," he joked.

It was impossible to reach the bottom of the huge trunk without risking toppling in head first, the huge assortment of dresses, nightgowns and various accessories, all reeking of mildew would take a while to sort through and not wanting to remain in the eerie environment of the crypt for any longer than necessary, Faye prayed that she'd soon come across something suitable. Barnaby stood to one side holding up the lantern as he watched her every move. His red hot desire to take Faye in his arms, teased him as he repeatedly warned himself to remember his position in society; Faye has no interest in you, he told himself, she is young and in love with another. Do you really want to jeopardize your entire life's work for a moment of passion? Do you want to commit such a wicked and sinful act? His mind was in turmoil. "Perfect!" declared Faye, bringing Barnaby out of his reverie. "Can we go now; I really don't like it down here."

"Of course we can. I think a cup of tea is needed to rinse away all the dust we've been subjected to," suggested Reverend Glover.

Relieved to be back out into the sunny spring morning, Faye couldn't wait to wash her new summer dress and bonnet and the new undergarments which she'd also discovered in the trunk. After which she intended to sit out in the garden and write a letter to Granny Isabel. Back in the vicarage, The Reverend reverted to addressing her as Miss Butler again and Mrs Glover inspected Faye's choice of attire, with the conclusion that the cream and deep lavender, floral dress might be rather too colourful for the conservative confines of the vicarage, but for the time being, she decided to keep her opinion to herself.

CHAPTER NINETEEN

It was a Sunday afternoon and with the prolonged showers and overcast skies, nobody was inclined to hang around the chapel for long at the end of The Reverend Glover's sermon. Mavis was also eager to hurry back to the vicarage in order to baste the capon which she'd left roasting and prepare the vegetables; she grabbed Faye's arm telling her to stick close by her side beneath the shelter of her broken umbrella; once again feeling quite righteous as she made yet another comment on Faye's flimsy and unsuitable summer dress. Barnaby was left behind to put away the hymn books, tidy up and lock away the money on the collection tray. His cubby hole of an office which was adjacent to the crypt entrance was where he usually secured anything of value. Although he'd only just delivered his sermon about the falling standards of morality in the modern-day, he found it impossible to prevent his overactive mind from daydreaming of Faye; she had appeared even more attractive today, dressed in the pretty dress which she'd chosen; its colour reflected in her bright eyes, causing them to darken slightly, becoming even more alluring and the perfect fit of the gown emphasised her well-proportioned figure. How he'd love to buy a small gift for her, he thought, as the temptation to take a few shillings from off the silver collection tray became too much of a temptation for him to resist. It wasn't entirely his fault, he argued with his conscience, if Mavis hadn't always insisted on taking full control of every penny he'd ever earned since they'd been married, he wouldn't now find himself under her scrupulous eye where the household finances were concerned. He hesitated slightly before grabbing a handful of coins and quickly dropping them into his pocket. The sin had been committed; he'd stolen the charity money, donated by his flock beneath the roof of God's house; what could be worse, he thought, feeling suddenly nauseous. His flock had been most generous today, his sermon must have squeezed out the guilt in them; no man was free from sin and the cause was one of three, he concluded; money, power or women. He wondered if folk believed he was beyond such temptation because he wore a collar and stood preaching at the pulpit every Sunday, they'd be nothing but fools if that was the case, he was still a man beneath his pious cover and until recently *had* managed to remain strong-willed and able to close his eyes to temptation. But it was different now, Mavis had insisted on bringing Faye to the vicarage to recuperate, so once again, she was to blame. How could she have been so thoughtless as to put a pretty, young and flirtatious woman under his nose, morning, noon and night and not expect her presence to have the slightest effect on him? It had become like torture in the last few weeks when Faye's health and spirit had begun to improve; he had found it impossible to curb his active mind of sinful thoughts and now, it was completely intoxicated with only one thought, and that was to lay with this woman before he lost his wits forever.

He had already seen the tortoiseshell vanity set in the shop window; he would purchase it tomorrow and watch Faye's pretty face light up when he presented it to her.

After the Sunday roast was eaten, Mavis went out into the garden to tackle some of the weeds before the next shower, and while the soil was soaked and manageable; Faye announced that she was going to write a letter to Granny Isabel in London and politely asked Mavis if she could have the penny for the postage stamp. Mavis didn't respond to her request, she could only envisage Faye's return to London with her downfall and after all the work and effort she'd put in, just knowing that Faye was eager to hurry back to the seedy streets of the East End and into the arms of that no good Spaniard, angered her. Barnaby also had his reservations about Faye's yearning to reconnect with her past life and had already aimed to make it as difficult as he could, not daring to think of a day in his life when Faye wouldn't be part of it. He dozed off in the armchair, whilst frantically trying to think of ways in which he could prevent her from returning to London.

Roberto Lopez was a man who was an expert at concealing his emotions and Ed Hall was completely oblivious to his young assistant's plight, but as long as his men showed up to work every day, he tended to stay out of his employees private lives, especially Rob's; he was young, handsome and in Ed's opinion, more than capable of looking out for himself and gaining the affections of any available East End lass who might take his fancy. He had however noticed a certain quietness about him in the past few months, and a loss of interest and usual banter with the young women folk. It had worsened since their journey to Oxford and Ed began to wonder about Rob's connection with the deceased relation who he'd spoken of. Was it his sweetheart perhaps? He would endeavour to find out exactly what had caused Rob to lose his spark. It was Sunday, always a long and boring day and made worse by the continuous April showers. Having filled his belly in his favourite chophouse Ed decided to take a stroll along to Rob's lodgings in Wentworth Street.
Met by Granny Isabel who was sat on a chair outside the shop, enjoying the intermittent sunshine upon her wrinkled face as she watched the young children playing out on the street, Ed was surprised to discover that Rob lived above a

haberdashery shop.

"Can I 'elp you young man?"

It had been a good few years since anyone had called him a young man.

"Good afternoon, misses..."

"You ain't a peeler are you?"

"I'm Ed Hall."

"Cos if you are, yer be wasting yer time."

Ed could only presume that the old woman was hard of hearing.

"I'm Ed Hall!" he repeated in a louder voice.

Granny Isabel stared hard at him,

"That name don't ring no bells ter me, an' there ain't no need ter shout! What d'yer want wiv me, anyway?"

"I mean yer no disrespect grandma, but it's yer lodger Rob who I've come ter see."

"You *are* a bleedin' peeler ain't yer!" Granny Isabel yelled, causing a nearby group of children to halt their games and stand to gawk at Ed.

"Quick, let's leg it...'e's a Peeler!" they all bellowed in unison, before tearing off to play in the next street.

"Now look what you've gone an' done...ruined me fun fer the day that's fer sure!"

Beginning to wish that he'd not bothered to seek Rob out, Ed was losing his patience,

"I'm not a bloody peeler, fer heaven's sake; I'm Roberto Lopez's boss....'e works fer me down in Cable Street!"

Granny Isabel fixed her stern gaze on him, but in

the bright sunshine it was impossible to see his face clearly; she squinted but could only make out Ed's silhouette.

"Come 'n' stand over this side ov me fer a minute," she ordered.

Ed obliged.

"Yer can tell a lot about a man by 'is face," she announced as she stood up to inspect Ed.

"Hmmm..." was the only sound she made after staring hard, causing Ed to feel quite uncomfortable. "Wait 'ere an' don't yer dare run off!"

Ed sighed, "I'm no street urchin, misses an' not in the 'abit ov running off like one!"

Granny Isabel ignored his protests and hurried inside the door. Ed caught the sound of the bolts being slammed tight, he laughed to himself; she was a funny old bird he mused.

Five minutes passed before Ed heard the door being unbolted and welcomed the sight of Rob, returning with his landlady.

"Gov!" he declared, clearly embarrassed by his landlady's actions.

"Can we talk Rob?"

"Take 'im inter me parlour, Rob; don't reckon the pair ov you'd fit inter your room," suggested Granny Isabel.

"Is she yer landlady or yer jailor, lad?" joked Ed when they were out of her earshot.

Still a bit shaken by the fact that Ed had turned up on his doorstep; Rob laughed it off casually.

"She's a good woman is Granny Isabel."
"She certainly looks out fer you, I noticed...anyone could easily be mistaken in thinking that yer might be a wanted man...are yer?"
Rob paused for a while, wondering if now was the time to disclose what had taken place in Wheatley village all those months ago. Ed decided to change the subject but sensed that there *was* something which Rob was keeping to himself.
"This is a right quiet place ter live, lad…got yerself a little piece of heaven 'ere, I'd say."
He followed Rob into Granny Isabel's compact parlour where every shelf and cupboard top was crammed full of knick-knacks.
"Yer chose the right day ter come; it's usually like a bloomin' zoo 'round 'ere but Mr Watkins is 'ome from sea fer the weekend an' 'e's taken his misses an' their brood ov kids out fer a treat," Rob briefly explained. "Granny Isabel only 'as tea, can I get yer a cup, Mr Hall?"
"Ed, please, we ain't at work now lad and no ta but I brought a little something ter wet me lips wiv." Ed pulled out a dented, silver hip flask from his inside pocket. "Bring yerself a cup an' join me lad. Tell me what's eating yer, Rob...I know there's been something on her mind lately."
"Alright then, Ed, but this is strictly between you an' me...only me landlady knows what

'appened on that day."

"I guess that explains the grilling she gave me when I turned up!"

"Yeah, *she* knows I ain't no murderer."

"*Murderer!* Bleedin' 'ell Rob, you've gotta bigger problem than I ever expected!" Ed immediately took a huge swig from his flask and wiped his lips with the back of his hand.

"I never even laid a single finger on the old woman...*I swear*, Gov, she just collapsed in front of me. It was the band ov neighbours who gathered like a vicious lynch mob, out ter get me and accused me of killing 'er. I just ran from the place like a bloody terrified rabbit. It was on the outskirts of Oxf'rd; a village called Wheatley."

"Ahh, so that was why yer was so set against the job we were assigned ter last year. But surely if yer didn't touch the old woman, it would 'ave bin discovered...yer can't murder someone by just looking at 'em, after all...there wouldn't 'ave bin a mark on 'er body."

"Well, them crazed village folk were ready ter string me up then an' there."

"Then *they* were the ones in the wrong, an' besides, I never spotted a single '*wanted fer murder poster*' when we were in Oxf'rd...did you?"

"I guess, but I might as well be swinging at the end ov a rope, cos that old woman was the grandmother ov the only woman who fills me dreams at night an' who owns me broken heart."

Rob swallowed hard, feeling his tears welling up; he turned his back on Ed, not wanting to let Ed Hall witness his weak side. Granny Isabel's timing was impeccable,

"I just this minute wetted the tea leaves if you boys would like a cuppa Rosie Lee," she announced, poking her head around the half-opened door.

"Boys!" laughed Ed, "I've taken a right shine ter your landlady; she's made me feel young again.

"You two *are* both young...just wait 'till yer reach my ripe old age...an' don't yer even dare ter ask, cos I ain't got the foggiest anymore," she called out from the kitchen.

After Rob had explained his story to Ed over tea, with Granny Isabel joining them, adding the bits which Rob had omitted and also describing to Ed what a lovely young woman, Faye Butler was and how she had transformed Rob into a contented young man, Ed left Wentworth Street with a lot to think about. He'd taken a strong liking to Granny Isabel and had made a solemn promise to her that he'd do everything in his power to discover whether or not Rob really was a wanted man, though he already strongly believed that he was innocent. He could sense how much Rob had loved Faye Butler and wished that Rob had introduced him to her. She was definitely the cause of Rob's missing spark, and by the sound of it, they had shared an unbreakable bond of love with each other. Rob was now suffering from a broken heart and felt that his life would never again see a day of joy; Ed knew that young damaged hearts could be repaired, it just took time but for someone as sensitive as Roberto Lopez it might take longer than many.

By the time Ed had reached Cable Street, he'd already decided that another journey to Oxford might at least allow Rob to be able to walk like a free man again and not spend his days constantly looking over his shoulder; he hoped to be able to ease Rob's conscience, but mending his heart was out of his hands.

CHAPTER TWENTY

Work was slack in the office of Hall, Spencer and Lock and, thought Ed, there was nothing that Rob wasn't capable of handling on his own or with the help of 'Red' or Palmer if those lazy thugs ever decided to show their ugly mugs. Ed felt duty bound to find out more about the actual events which occurred during the previous year; Rob was a good and honest worker and he wanted to put his mind at rest, or if the news turned out to be as grim as Rob had told it, to help him get away and start a new life without the risk of one day being the next victim of the hangman's noose. Rob and Granny Isabel's words had troubled him all night and it had taken more than his usual half glass of whiskey to bring about any sleep.

 "I'm going to Oxf'rd, Rob...don't know when I'll be back but while I'm away, you're ter be captain ov the ship." Rob had barely put one foot over the threshold and Ed's plans took him by complete surprise.

"Is there another job in Oxf'rd then, Gov?" asked Rob, sheepishly.

"Don't be a bloody daft bugger, Rob, I'm going 'cos of what yer spouted ter me yesterday, or 'ave yer already forgotten!"

"Course I ain't, but yer don't 'ave ter put yerself out on my account, I don't reckon nobody will bovver ter look fer me 'ere in the East End."

"Well, I'm gonna find out the truth, Rob, so that yer can stop yer fretting an' start living again."

"I told yer yesterday, Gov, me life is already over now that I don't 'ave me darlin' Faye 'ere ter share it wiv." Rob hung his head, part of him wished he'd never told Ed about his troubles, he didn't wish to be reminded of Faye every day, not by Ed Hall, he'd never met her after all and probably imagined her to be just like any of the other flighty petticoats who he'd flirted with in the past. Faye was a rare and indescribable flower, one which only came along once in a lifetime.

"Cheer up, lad; just take care of things 'till I get back an' 'ope I return wiv some good news; yer can't spend the rest of yer life with such a burden resting upon yer. Take it from someone who's been in your boots before."

"What d'yer mean Gov?" Rob instantly enquired, his head lifting as his dark eyes searched Ed. Rubbing his palm over his fleshy bald head, Ed disclosed how he'd once been in a brawl with someone; the man's young son, of only ten years, had stepped in to assist his pa and been sent flying by Ed's punch. He'd lain as dead as a cold rock on the floor, blood trickling from his head. The crowds were shouting and yelling that Ed was a murderer and should be strung up immediately.

"They showed me no mercy, Rob when in fact it

was an accident. But, I *did* strike the boy, unlike you, who never even touched that old woman. I ran like a coward; I saw the anger in all ov their faces an' knew that if I stayed ter claim me innocence, they'd beat me to a pulp."

"Was 'e dead?" uttered Rob.

"Thank God, no, I saw 'im an' 'is pa down the market a few weeks later; as right as rain 'e was. So yer see, Rob, I only carried that worry fer a few weeks an' that were like a bleedin' lifetime, so God alone knows what yer going through."

Faye came down to breakfast the following morning filled with a great feeling of optimism; she had composed a letter to be proud of to dear Granny Isabel and had tucked it safely away in her dress pocket. Hopefully, it wouldn't prove too difficult to ask for a penny and to persuade Mrs Glover that she was fit enough to walk the short journey to the postal and telegrams office in Woodstock's High Street. The cloudless sky and bright sun made Faye feel happy to be alive and worked like a tonic on her weak health.

The Reverend Glover and his wife, who were seated at the table, didn't appear to be in such high spirits, they'd obviously argued or disagreed on something; with long faces reflecting their solemn mood. The plate of toast and pot of tea remained untouched.

"Good morning," said Faye, cheeringly, in a bid

to lift the heavy atmosphere.

Mrs Glover, whose miserable face reminded Faye of an old turnip, glanced up at the clock on the mantelpiece,

"We've been waiting five minutes for you to come down, young lady! You're not sick anymore and tardiness is no longer accepted under this roof! Do you understand, Miss Butler?"

"Sorry Mrs Glover, I don't have a timepiece; it was only the smell of toast which hastened me downstairs; I actually thought it was earlier. Isn't it a gorgeous day...there's not a rain cloud in sight."

Mrs Glover wasn't prepared to let the matter rest, "The Reverend Glover and I have been polite enough to wait for you and now the hot water and the toast are tepid. Good manners, are free you know, but perhaps *your* sort don't know any wiser. The East End of London has a lot to answer for."

"That's quite enough said on this matter; Miss Butler *has* apologised and it isn't really her fault now is it?" expressed Barnaby, sending Mrs Glover's angry expression to a higher level.

"Perhaps we could purchase a small clock or a watch for her," he suggested, "now, shall we say grace so that we can all eat this bountiful meal which the Good Lord has provided for us?"

Breakfast was consumed in an uncomfortable silence, with the usual plans for the day not mentioned. Faye cleared away the table, washed the dishes and prepared the vegetables hoping to put Mrs Glover into a more cordial mood, before daring to ask for a penny. Whilst scraping the carrots, Faye recalled her small embroidered reticule, she wondered what had become of it and its contents, she remembered having a few shillings in it, plus her personal letters and keepsakes and most importantly of all, it contained the wedding ring which Rob had bought for her. Had it been left on the roadside she wondered, had anyone found it? Sadly, she would probably never know.

Mrs Glover had shown little appreciation for the many chores which Faye had completed; she'd reluctantly left the vicarage mumbling about how it had been imposed upon her to visit a nearby farm where the farmer's wife had endured a difficult birth leaving her quite melancholy. Glad to see the back of her, Faye decided to approach The Reverend for a penny before he also left the vicarage. When he wasn't anywhere to be found, Faye presumed that he also had a busy morning scheduled. Satisfied that the vicarage was clean and tidy and would meet with Mrs Glover's approval when she returned, Faye decided to sit out in the garden and take advantage of the pleasant sunshine whilst waiting for the return of either Mrs Glover or The Reverend. The small hook on the back of the cupboard door had worked its way loose and as Faye attempted to hang up the feather duster it fell out completely, dropping to the floor and bouncing out of sight. There was a selection of jars at the bottom of the broom cupboard which contained a variety of nuts and bolts, nails, and screws; after moving them aside, to her relief, Faye also found one containing hooks. A black-painted jar caught her attention; unlike the other old jam jars, she couldn't see what it held but it felt far heavier than the rest of them and her curiosity forced her to unscrew the lid, bringing a smile and a sense of victory to Faye. Full to its brim with pennies, halfpennies and farthings, surely one penny wouldn't be missed, Faye thought and it would enable her to take a quick walk to the postal office and be home again before the others returned. For a split second, she was tempted to take far more than a meagre penny, there was surely enough to take her back to London and she'd reach Granny Isabel in Wentworth Street before the arrival of any letter. She froze, pondering on the prospect. It wouldn't be stealing, she considered, as she'd send the money back just as soon as she arrived and Rob would reimburse her, she was sure. But, Faye knew she was no longer the same overly confident girl that she'd been before her near-death experience, she had been weakened not just in body but in spirit and the thought of being alone for long, especially in the dark hours terrified her; she needed a guaranteed cushion of security, which for the time being, she found living at the vicarage. She couldn't be sure what or who would meet her in Wentworth Street, should she simply up and leave...it had been five months since she'd left and she feared that everything there might have changed. Maybe Rob had also moved on with his life and found somebody new to love. Faye suddenly felt her heart racing as though a herd of wild horses were galloping across her chest. Breathing became difficult, her head throbbed and her hands were shaking. Unable to screw the lid back on to the jar, the notion that she might soon be caught red-handed and labelled as an ungrateful little thief only increased her frantic state, as she wrestled with her body, pleading for calm to return.

It was The Reverend Glover who'd discovered Faye's body, out cold on the flagstone floor, surrounded by the assortment of jars and the feather duster. Barnaby threw down his parcel and hurried to her side, praying out loud as he tenderly lifted her head and shoulders to rest upon his lap. Her body felt as cold as ice, he quickly took off his jacket to cover her with. He anxiously felt her wrist and neck for a pulse; he couldn't find one and was now convinced that the life had left her; his spontaneous cries emitted from deep within his heart and filled every corner of the vicarage with grief. Holding her head tightly, he pledged his love to her as he kissed her face, his tears dripping uncontrollably, wetting Faye's face.

Barnaby had broken down into sobs and had no recollection of how long he'd been huddled in the same position, still holding Faye's head. He was unaware that she'd opened her eyes and had regained consciousness. She let out a loud cry, momentarily thinking that somebody was trying to squeeze the life out of her. Barnaby's sobs subsided, as he lifted his head in disbelief. Taken by shock as she witnessed the normally composed reverend in such a distraught state, Faye struggled to free herself of him, sensing that all was not as it should be. Her head ached and suddenly without warning, she emptied the contents of her stomach across the clean kitchen floor.

"I wasn't going to steal the money, *honestly*, Mr Glover...I just needed a penny...for my letter."

Barnaby had no idea what Faye was talking about and could only presume that she'd become delirious.

"My dear, *sweet* Faye, you've obviously had a rough morning; I don't know what happened to you, my darling, but I can't even begin to tell you how relieved and delighted I am to hear your voice again; for a terrible, terrible few moments, I feared that you had left this world," with his voice cracking and his eyes filling up, Faye was alarmed by The Reverend Glover's behaviour and his sentiments. What was going on, she mused, as she tried to pull her body up off the cold flagstones. She surreptitiously replaced the jars back into the broom cupboard, amazed to find that she still had a tight hold of the penny in the palm of her hand; Barnaby was trying to compose himself, drying his face and running his hand through his wild-looking hair.

"Come and sit down, Faye, allow me to mop the floor; you are clearly still in poor health," he insisted.

"*Goodness*, Reverend, I couldn't possibly let you clean up my mess, that's completely out of the question!"

While Faye struggled to return some order to the kitchen, wincing at every move from the sharp pains in her head and quickly tiring, Barnaby made a pot of tea.

"I hope this modest gift will help you to recover, Faye," uttered Barnaby, as they sat on the couch sipping tea. He placed the brown package onto her lap, nervously awaiting her reaction; he felt like a schoolboy and wanted nothing more than to witness a sincere smile upon Faye's beautiful face. He wasn't disappointed; Faye was immediately cheered by Barnaby's gift. Holding up the tortoiseshell mirror, she let out a quiet moan, unhappy with the pale and drawn face which stared back at her, she pulled the matching hairbrush through her fair hair, catching Barnaby watching in admiration.

"Do you like it?" he asked, eagerly.

As Faye looked into The Reverend Glover's face, she suddenly realised that she hadn't imagined hearing his affectionate words and his heartrending cries when she'd been in a semi-conscious state. She could feel her heart racing again; The Reverend had some kind of insane infatuated with her and she *had* to put an end to it. Images of the malicious footman at Belmont Hall suddenly flooded her vision, she couldn't take another man attacking her in such a way again and even if this was different in the way in which The Reverend Glover obviously had genuine feelings for her, Faye knew that nothing other than disaster could evolve from it. She would now *have* to make a hurried departure from the vicarage, but to where, she asked herself, knowing that should she show up in Wheatley, she wouldn't receive a warm welcome from any of the neighbours after not having returned when both her grandparents had passed away. They would not welcome her and probably even thought her to be dead too, so maybe it would be better to leave it that way. Faye was quickly bought out of her reverie as she felt the touch of The Reverend's fingertips stroking her cheek; she edged away from him, nervously.

"This is a lovely gift, Reverend Glover, but I couldn't possibly accept it...it's far too lavish for the likes of me and what would Mrs Glover say?

Maybe *she* is the one who you should be giving it to; she *is your wife,* after all."

Barnaby leapt up from the couch as though a bolt of lightning had struck him,

"*No, no* Faye, don't you understand? She may be my wife, but it is *you* who I love. You have filled my heart and I will love you until the night stars cease to shine, my darling." A solitary tear fell from Barnaby's face, splattering noisily onto teapot in the deathly silence. Faye had never in her five months at the vicarage ever wished for Mrs Glover's presence more than she did at this very awkward and emotional moment.

"Do you realise, Reverend that I am only nineteen years old; you are probably old enough to be my father...we would wish for completely different things in life and three people would end up unhappy and broken-hearted. Mrs Glover is a kind and generous woman whose love for you is stronger than iron."

Barnaby's expression was one of hurt; he looked down as he mulled over Faye's sharp words.

"No, Faye, you're mistaken, Mavis has never really loved me...she was nothing more than a left behind spinster of twenty-five with no suitors to speak of...I was *her* last opportunity and *she* was the wife I needed to enhance my work with the church. It was a marriage based on nothing but mutual convenience. There has and never will be anything other than a sense of duty between us. Surely you can see that, *can't you?* I'm forty-eight, Faye, but my heart and soul are young and you, my darling, have awoken them and given a whole new meaning to my life."

"But I *don't* love you!" protested Faye, feeling more and more trapped by every excuse and reason which The Reverend Glover continued to assert. She took the letter out from her pocket, holding it up in front of him, "My heart belongs to Roberto Lopez, and nobody will *ever* take his place...don't you understand? He is young and before my accident, we had planned to spend the rest of our lives together, to grow old and grey together…exactly how marriage is *meant* to be. Now, I'm going to walk down to the town and buy a stamp and hopefully, it will be the first step to reuniting me with my betrothed."

Barnaby stood silent and motionless as Faye quickly raced upstairs to fetch her boots and bonnet eager to leave the vicarage, even though she was feeling weak and ill. Perhaps a stroll in the sunshine would be the medicine she needed, she mused, but no matter how poorly she felt, she had to put some distance between herself and Barnaby Glover, until at least he'd gathered his composure once more. Hopefully, Mrs Glover would be home by the time she returned too.

CHAPTER TWENTY-ONE

Ed Hall decided to alight from the carriage before reaching Oxford City. He'd spent the journey mulling over in his head who to approach in order to make his enquiries without causing any suspicion and had arrived at the perfect solution; he would call at Harberton Mead house to enquire after The Fairbanks'; although having never met Mr Fairbanks, he could still remember how pretty and polite his wife had been. He'd simply explained how he was conducting some business in the area and had decided to enquire after them. It was a beautiful spring morning and Ed was surprisingly enjoying the country walk and being away from the filth and stench of the East End streets, at least he didn't stand a chance of having the contents of somebody's chamber pot tipped out onto his head here, he laughed to himself. He was feeling good about himself today, he'd worn his best suit for the occasion with a clean shirt and collar and since only four days had passed since he'd visited Whitechapel's communal baths, he smelt relatively fresh. On this day, Ed considered himself more akin to a noble detective; it was by far a more respected title than that of a debt collector and a title which he could easily become accustomed to.

Nestled in the midst of the countryside, the

distinctive, eye-catching Harberton Mead house suddenly came into sight, along with a huge *'for sale'* notice which towered like a beacon for everyone to view. An unusual twinge of guilt struck Ed; he'd never realised just how much debt Mr Fairbanks was in and it certainly appeared to be a lot more than the cost of the household items and furniture which he and Rob had taken to auction months ago. A lonely looking bedraggled man was sat out on the veranda staring out across the fields to where a herd of cattle were grazing contentedly. Ed hesitated for a while, pondering on whether or not he should continue with his plan, but before arriving at an answer it was too late and the man had stood up and was heading towards him with a welcoming smile upon his weary-looking face. He held out his hand to him and Ed immediately shook it.

"Harry Fairbanks," he announced confidently, "and I presume, you are Mr Gordon from the land agent's."

Ed ceased the handshaking. "Sorry to disappoint yer, Mr Fairbanks, but I'm Mr Hall and I'm nothing to do with the land agent." Ed was concentrating on talking more like an Oxfordian rather than an Eastender, he knew how difficult folk found the rough accent to comprehend but he detested speaking in such a rigid manner. Mr Fairbanks appeared puzzled.

"I must apologise if I appear somewhat remiss,

only I find myself under the impression that I should know you, Mr Hall."

"It's quite alright, Sir, I 'ad the great honour ov meeting yer delightful wife, last year."

"*My Wife!*" exclaimed Harry, "Are you quite sure it was my wife...Fairbanks is not such a rare name, you know."

Ed removed his bowler hat; he could feel the beads of sweat rolling down his back as he stood awkwardly with the warm sun beating upon him.

"Let me explain, Mr Fairbanks...I was hired to remove and auction yer house contents...back in November, it was..."

"*Yes, yes, yes,* I am well aware of the day when I was illegally robbed...and if you've come back for more, I'm sorry to disappoint, but there is nothing but my bed and a few worthless items remaining and as you have probably noticed, my home is now up for auction too."

"I'm sorry, Mr Fairbanks, but I am merely here to ask after you and your family's health. I was in the area, you see."

Harry Fairbanks flattened down his moustache; he looked bothered and appeared lost for words.

"Well, Mr Fairbanks, I can see it's not a good time for you, so I'll bid you a good day..."

"*No, please*, Mr Hall, what must you be thinking...I may have lost almost everything, but I still have my manners even if they appear to have momentarily vanished. Please Mr Hall, do

come in and refresh yourself, there are a few
questions I'd like to ask you too."

"Well, ta very much...er, I meant thank you, I'm
obliged. There are also a few questions which I'd
like to ask you too, Mr Fairbanks, that's if you
don't mind, of course."

"Hmm, I'm intrigued, Mr Hall and by the way,
I'm quite familiar with your colloquial accent, so
please don't struggle on my behalf! "

"Well, thank God fer that!" laughed Ed, as he
followed Harry into his bare home.

Little had changed inside Harberton Mead since
Ed had last set foot over the threshold; none of
the furniture had been replaced and a fine
coating of dirt and dust covered the wooden
floor. There didn't appear to be anyone else in
the house, Harry led Ed through to the back and
into the kitchen, where the kettle was already
throwing up a plume of hot steam into the air.
Ed was astonished as he watched Harry
Fairbanks, expertly make a pot of coffee and
neatly arrange the crockery onto the kitchen
table.

"We will take our coffee here, in the kitchen, Mr
Hall, because, as you are well aware, there is no
furniture in the house and this is the only table
and chairs remaining."

Ed wasn't sure if Mr Fairbanks sounded angry or
sarcastic, but he sat obediently at the table,
placing his bowler alongside him.

" 'Ave yer staff got the day off, then Mr

Fairbanks?"

"*Staff!* That's a joke if ever I've heard one...I'm a broken man Ed...You *did* say that was your name didn't you?"

"Yeah, that's right."

"Please Ed, you must call me Harry or, if you like, '*Arry*!"

They both laughed, breaking the strained ambience.

"Mrs White disappeared with my wife and our young charge shortly after your visit back in November and my two maids were apparently paid off and discharged. To be frank with you, Ed, I have not seen or heard from my wife since then, in fact, you were probably one of the last people to have seen her in Oxford. I arrived home from my business in London to find my house empty of everything and everybody."

"That's bleedin' terrible, 'Arry, I 'ope yer don't blame *me* fer what 'appened, 'cos I was only doing me job, yer know, an' as far as I recall, yer wife seemed as right as rain on that day."

"Of course I don't blame you my good fellow; it is me and only me who is to blame...I have been a fool, Ed, and now, when once I had everything, I find myself with nothing. I have no idea of my wife's whereabouts, but I'm certain that she's experiencing a far happier life and perhaps one day she might find it in her to forgive me and return. Now, Ed, how do you take your coffee...milk and sugar?"

Ed nodded, his thoughts mulling over the disappearance of Mrs Fairbanks and where she could have gone. Harry poured the coffee, apologising for being unable to offer his guest any food.

"Now Ed, enough of my troubles, what questions did you wish to ask me...I trust it has nothing to do with my diminished finances!"

"Oh, no, 'Arry, I'm wearing me detective's hat terday, an' me journey ter Oxf'rd 'as nothing ter do wiv me role as a debt collector but I'm in search of some vital information about an incident which took place just before I came 'ere, back in November...Did yer ever 'ear 'bout an old woman who lived at Dove Cottage in Wheatley village, by any chance, 'Arry?"

Harry stared at Ed, as the events of the stormy night in November claimed his thoughts.

"I did, as a matter of fact. What do you wish to know and why, if you don't mind me asking."

Ed had spent the entire journey going over in his mind how he could ask such questions without mentioning Rob in the conversation. He had been hoping that it would be Mrs Fairbanks who'd help him with his enquiries."

"I'm interested ter find out how she met wiv 'er death; was she on 'er own or were there any suspicions surrounding it?"

Harry was intrigued; what relationship with *Grandmother Butler* could this man possibly have? Did he know about the baby perhaps and then, the sudden, disturbing thought that this rough Eastender could, in fact, be baby Faye's father sickened him. The thought of that sweet looking, petite young girl, being subjected to the likes of this rogue turned his stomach; maybe it was *him* who she was fleeing from on that unforgettable night when she so tragically lost her life.

"D'yer mind if I pour another coffee, 'Arry?"

"Er, no, no, not at all, be my guest Ed."

"Yer feeling alright, 'Arry?" asked Ed, noticing Harry's sudden change of mood. "Can I pour you another?"

"Oh yes, please do, Ed."

"Do you happen to know her name, Ed?"

Ed paused for a while as he lifted the coffee pot, wondering why Harry Fairbanks had asked this question.

"I read somewhere that she was a Mrs Butler…I also read that she could 'ave bin murdered.
A client ov mine knew 'er granddaughter yer see…she 'ad a little un on the way yer see an' he'd like ter know exactly what went on in November; I'm afraid that's all 'e was willing ter tell me."

Harry suddenly had another train of thought hurtling through his mind; he remained focussed on Ed, wanting to catch his reaction when he asked his next question,

"Tell me honestly, Ed, do you know a certain, *Mr Lyle Dagworth*?"

There was nothing but an expression of confusion upon Ed's face as his forehead tensed into furrows. A sense of relief washed over Harry, as he realised that this man was not working for the unforgettable *L.D* to whom he still owed a hundred pounds *and* a baby. He was quite sure that the continuously weeping Marjorie Dagworth was a force to drive any sane man over the edge and do anything for peace. One day he would return the hundred pounds deposit which Lyle had paid him, along with some kind of explanation as to what had happened to the baby, but for the time being and until he had sold Harberton Mead and sorted his life out again, he was giving London a very wide birth.

Ed scratched his bald head, "Never even 'eard of the cove, 'Arry...why....should I know 'im...does 'e 'ave anything ter do wiv Grandma Butler?"

"Forget I ever mentioned his name Ed."

Ed gulped down the last dregs of his coffee, the dainty bone china cup looking awkward in his cumbersome hands.

"If I tell you everything I know about the old woman who lived in Dove cottage, Ed, do you promise to tell me the whole truth and the real reason why you've travelled this distance for the information?" Harry's look was stern and foreboding; it usually took a lot to shake Ed Hall, he'd confronted ruthless thugs built like battleships in the past, but here in his new and

unfamiliar surroundings, alone with Harry
Fairbanks he felt on edge, as he stroked his
beard in a self-comforting way.

"Blimey 'Arry, yer don't appen ter be a beak do
yer, 'cos yer don't 'alf sound like one!"

Harry was amused by Ed's comical assumption,
"Look about you Ed, do you really take me for a
'beak', I'm nothing but a fallen businessman and
an unsuccessful gambler, but I was raised as a
gentleman and am a man of the world, with a
wealth of knowledge tucked away inside of my
head and as hypocritical as I'm about to sound, I
detest liars and have no time whatsoever for
them."

"So is yer confessing ter me that you're a liar
'Arry?"

"It's one of the main reasons why I find myself in
such a sorry state of affairs and why my dearest
Delia chose to run away as she did. If only I was
given one more chance to put things right, Ed; if
only one could turn back the clock. "

"I doubt yer the first person ter say that, 'Arry,
an' 'appen yer won't be the last. But maybe we
could 'elp each other. I may not 'ave yer posh
ways, but in me own right, I too am a man ov
the world, an' can move in circles where you'd
stick out like a sore thumb."

For the first time in a long while, Harry
Fairbanks felt a flicker of hope about his future;
he considered the mere fact that such a man like
Ed Hall had turned up on his doorstep was not

to be ignored. Maybe *he* could help to track down Delia. Maybe they could help each other. Harry leant across the old, battered kitchen table with his hand outstretched. The two men shook hands once more. "Let's start again *Ed Hall*, I trust that *is* your real name?" said Harry, cordially.

"Of course it is, 'Arry; I ain't no liar yer know, just a man who treads carefully where the need arises!"

"Spoken like a real gentleman, if you don't mind me saying so!" Harry joked, "I have the feeling that we are going to make a good team!"

CHAPTER TWENTY-TWO

Mavis Glover had returned to the vicarage in one of her moods, a day wasted, she considered, and failed to understand how any woman could behave in such a downcast manner after being blessed with the gift of a beautiful new baby. Some women just didn't realise how fortunate they were and took their fertility for granted, she scolded. Her head was splitting after sitting in a stuffy, hot room with the fire blazing all day long, listening to the afflicted woman's constant outbreaks. Mavis felt as though she'd used up her entire year's sympathy in one day. She detected a rancid smell about the vicarage, as she marched through the parlour into the dining room and then to the kitchen. Everything looked in order, but a lingering sickly smell told her that something had happened in her absence. Noticing that the broom cupboard had been left ajar, she hurried to check on her savings, breathing a sigh of relief after finding it intact and just how she'd left it; she did, however, discover the source of the stink and immediately discarded the mop to the outside, closing the door quickly as though the mop was capable of finding its own way back in. Thinking that Faye had taken to her bed, she reluctantly climbed up to the small attic room to check on her. The room was empty and Mavis couldn't think where she'd gone; it wasn't like Faye to go out, but perhaps she'd been taken so poorly that she'd gone in search of Barnaby; she would be fine, Mavis consoled herself, Faye was probably feeling a lot healthier than she was, she thought as she curled up on the couch praying that her dreadful headache would soon subside. Placing her hand down the back of the couch to investigate the sharp object which had dug into her, body, Mavis pulled out the tortoiseshell hairbrush; she studied it curiously, suddenly realising that it was the one she'd admired every time she'd passed by a certain shop window in town.

She dozed off to sleep in the midst of wondering where Faye had found the money to pay for such an extravagant and unnecessary item, for she was positive that it *was* Faye who'd bought the brush; Barnaby wouldn't dare to cross the threshold of such a shop and his weekly allowance wouldn't cover its expensive cost.

It was a relief to be out of the vicarage and away from The Reverend Glover; Faye's troubled thoughts were firmly focussed on how she was going to handle the delicate situation when she returned. Regretting not having taken more than the one penny, she knew that it would be foolhardy to risk making her way back to London so unprepared, she hadn't even brought her shawl with her and even though the days felt summery, the April night's could still deliver a covering of frost. She rested for a while on a large sawn-off log, not used to walking so far, her legs were aching and she felt weakened by the morning's ordeal. What should she do, she mused; should she go straight to Mrs Glover, perhaps? Would she believe her or would she be dim-witted enough and presume that it was the other way around and that she was the one obsessed with her husband? He could and probably would deny everything and who would believe a young woman in her circumstances and with a history such as hers? Faye was quickly brought out of her reverie as she heard the Reverend calling out to her; he was running towards her, his face flushed with a trail of sweat trickling down it.

"Faye, I suddenly realised that you have no money for a stamp!"

Faye couldn't reply without admitting to stealing from the hands which fed and cared for her.

"I know; I was simply taking a stroll to clear my head a little."

The Reverend Glover stared into Faye's weary face, "Oh, dear, what have I done? You look quite unwell, Miss Butler and I find myself guilty of being the main cause for your relapse. Can you ever find it in your kind nature to forgive a foolish old man? I really don't know what came over me back at the vicarage, but my behaviour was atrocious and I feel *so* ashamed of myself. Can we pretend that this morning's silly episode never took place and never mention it to a living soul? I think I may have had a dose of spring fever, Miss Butler! "

It was music to Faye's ears, to hear him addressing her formally again but she wasn't sure if he was being honest, or simply wanted to prevent her from destroying his reputation, along with his marriage, however much he claimed it to be of no importance. But with little choice in the matter, she reluctantly accepted his apology and prayed that he'd now realise that she wasn't in the least interested in him and that this would mean an end to his pestering her.

"Very well then, Reverend, we shall start the day again."

The Reverend's tensed shoulders immediately relaxed as he smiled jubilantly. Faye, however, still felt inwardly annoyed; he was a ridiculous man, she concluded and he and Mavis Glover deserved each other. It was in that instant that Faye made her decision that she'd take the jar of small change from the broom cupboard; it was worth becoming a thief in order to break free of these eccentric people, as soon as possible.

After going through all of his pockets, the Reverend made the declaration that he didn't have a single penny on him and suggested they returned to the vicarage. He promised Faye that it was the least he could do, as a way of an apology, to personally post her letter later on that day. Feeling too tired to object to his suggestion she reluctantly agreed and accompanied him back to the vicarage. Overcome with fatigue, Faye left the letter to Granny Isabel with The Reverend and retired to her room where she soon fell asleep only to be woken by the sound of loud and angry voices which filled the normally peaceful vicarage. Praying that the argument had nothing to do with her and that The Reverend hadn't confessed anything foolish to his wife, Faye left her bed and opened the bedroom door. It didn't take long before she understood that the argument was about the tortoiseshell vanity set which Mavis Glover had discovered. She sounded more vexed and concerned about where The Reverend had got the money from for such an expensive gift; he had claimed it was a present for her for being such a wonderful wife, but Mavis Glover obviously knew her husband better than he gave her credit for and didn't believe him.

"You've *always* been foolish where money is concerned, Barnaby. You *know* your weaknesses, and you have me to thank for keeping you out of trouble for all these years. Honestly, you're worse than a silly little boy, *Barnaby!*"

"It's *not* right, Mavis, it's embarrassing. I'm a man of standing in this neighbourhood and I shouldn't be walking around without a penny in my pocket; you treat me like a child when I'm a grown man!"

"Oh, *stuff and nonsense*, you only have to inform me what you need money for, and as you well know, Barnaby, if it's for a worthwhile cause, then you'll find me most generous."

Faye could barely take in what she was hearing, and no matter how badly The Reverend had behaved, she felt sorry for him. Beneath her facade of the perfect dutiful Reverend's wife, who was the soul of the community, Mavis Glover was an overpowering, tyrant of a woman.

"Well, my dearest, I hope it won't keep you awake at night to know that I was *forced* to steal the generous donations of my devoted flock. I have sinned Mavis and *you* are to blame!"

"*Stuff and nonsense*, you ridiculously feeble-minded man, *you* and *only you* are accountable for your actions and I suggest that you return your pointless gift back to the shop and make penance. I didn't ask for a fancy vanity set, my late mother's one, God rest her soul, is perfectly adequate."

The vicarage became silent, followed by the slamming of the front door. Faye watched from her window as a clearly demoralized man, his head and shoulders hanging in shame, walked out of sight towards the direction of town. She decided to venture downstairs and wondered if The Reverend had taken her letter with him to post.

Mavis Glover appeared her normal self; she offered a hint of a smile and then concerned herself as to whether Faye had read the Bible and said her prayers. Faye lied, knowing that Mavis was probably not in the best of moods even though she wasn't letting on that she'd endured a terrible day.

"Would you like me to prepare the vegetables, Mrs Glover?"

"Not if you're feeling unwell, Faye," she replied, in a soft voice. "Only I had to throw the mop outside earlier."

"I'm sorry; I will clean it properly tomorrow."

"No, Miss Butler, you will go and attend to it this instant and *I* will peel the potatoes."

Faye was still in the garden when The Reverend returned home; he came in the back way, pausing to enquire why Faye was outside when the sun was setting and a cool air had descended. She was more concerned to find out if The Reverend had posted her letter,

"What are you doing out here, Miss Butler? You'll catch a chill. Is this Mrs Glover's doing?" His speech was stiff and formal.

"It's fine, honestly, Reverend, I'm nearly finished anyway and I'm not cold. Did you post my letter?"

"I did, Miss Butler...Now do hurry back inside." Alone once again, Faye was left feeling wary of the Reverend's fickle behaviour; she wasn't relishing the thought of sitting down at the table to eat supper with him and Mrs Glover. Whilst cleaning the threadbare mop, her mind had been plagued by what she'd heard earlier and it had given her an idea; she too would steal the collection money on Sunday, it would be easy, she simply had to remain behind after the service to put the hymn books away and then quietly slip away whilst The Reverend was chatting to his flock and Mrs Glover was gloating over the ladies' Sunday compliments about her artistic flower arrangements in the chapel. It might not even be construed as stealing, she told herself; she was a kind of charity case, after all.

Supper was consumed quietly with only Mavis attempting to make small talk. Claiming she was still not feeling herself, Faye expressed how she was in need of an early night. It was only Thursday and as she lay in her bed, excited by the thought that very soon she might find herself wrapped in Rob's embrace and back on the familiar streets of the East End again, Faye knew that she'd have to act normally during the next few days which was going to be extremely difficult where The Reverend was concerned. She really couldn't comprehend how that strange man's mind worked and wasn't convinced that after pledging his love to her and announcing that he was willing to sacrifice everything to be with her, that he could simply brush all of his feelings aside and carry on as though nothing had ever happened and no words had ever been spoken. He was an odd one, that was for sure and she needed to tread very carefully and avoid being alone with him, she concluded.

After their earlier argument, Mavis and Barnaby had nothing to say to each other and as the evening slowly drew to an end and they sat in the parlour, Barnaby kept his head in a book and Mavis busied herself with a pile of stockings which needed darning.

"I've endured an absolutely beastly day, Barnaby," she announced, leaving her seat to make the bedtime cocoa, "and farmer Lowe's, ailing wife wasn't completely to blame for it." She issued one of her hostile glares towards Barnaby, who refused to lift his head.

"As much as I hate to bring up the subject again, Barnaby; I trust you've returned that extravagant item back to the shop, and returned the money to its rightful place."

She marched to the kitchen, her lips pursed, leaving Barnaby once again feeling like a naughty schoolboy. He took out Faye's letter from his pocket and threw it into the dancing flames in the fireplace, unable to bear the thought of not seeing Faye every day and as deceitful as it seemed, he couldn't help himself.

The clement spring weather made for a Sunday service which packed every single pew in the chapel with happy folk, grateful that, at last, the winter was behind them and there would be many more delightful days to look forward to before its return. Faye had already heard The Reverend's sermon; he had asked her to accompany him to the chapel on the previous day to listen while he practised, telling her how he wanted to be sure his voice was projecting to the far back of the chapel and for her valued opinion on its content, which ironically was about loyalty and the miracle of how God had placed love for one another in the hearts of mankind. Feeling wary at the prospect of being alone with The Reverend again, Faye warned herself that if her plan was to be a success she had to act completely normal and besides, Mrs Glover was just a stone's throw away in the vicarage where all the windows and doors were open. After listening to the sermon and complimenting The Reverend, he explained excitedly how he had a surprise for her. Immediately feeling every fibre of her body in a state of alarm, she didn't welcome any surprises from Barnaby Glover, especially after the last one, but it seemed that she was pleasantly mistaken and The Reverend proved that he *had* accepted the fact that Faye's heart belonged elsewhere.

"I received a box of wedding gowns...They once belonged to The Sisters of Mercy in Oxford and I thought you could have first choice, for when you and your beau get married. I've had a quick look at them; I'm no expert of course, but they look quite presentable and I'm sure at least one of them will fit you."

"That's very kind and considerate of you Reverend, thank you," exclaimed Faye, the mere thought of her and Rob marrying producing a radiant smile upon her face and a warm inner feeling.

"Can I take a look at them now?"

"Tomorrow, after the service...they're down in the crypt and Mrs Glover has the key on her at the moment, plus she is preparing afternoon tea; and I daren't upset her again."

"Quite right too," agreed Faye, hoping that this wouldn't make it too difficult for her to keep to her plan of stealing the collection money.

The following day, while Faye was left alone in the chapel as The Reverend and Mrs Glover were busy saying their goodbyes to the Sunday flock, she hastily collected the hymn books and replaced them into the book cupboard. Her eyes were constantly drawn to the silver plate of coins, she wondered if The Reverend had made a mental note of roughly how much was there, she felt nervous; her palms were sweaty and her legs had suddenly turned to jelly; she peered towards the entrance; it was impossible to see anyone, but she could still hear the gentle murmur of conversing voices in the distance.

Without any more to do, Faye emptied half of the money into one of Mrs Glover's serviettes. She lifted up her dress, quickly shoving the package into her stocking top and flinched at the sight of The Reverend, as she suddenly caught sight of him stood in the doorway. Faye feared that he might have witnessed what she'd done. He walked towards her, slowly but with a smiling face which immediately put Faye's mind at ease. He took out a key from the pocket of his long Sunday cassock.

"I'm afraid you'll have to make another journey down into the crypt again, Miss Butler. I hope you don't mind?"

Faye did mind and wished that he'd forgotten about the dress which she didn't even want and was merely co-operating to keep everything looking normal. She hated that stinking, spine-chilling place and had no wish to venture down there again. Barnaby could read her mind;

"Oh dear, I can see you're reluctant...very well, Miss Butler, I will retrieve the dresses and you can try them on in my office. How does that suit you?"

Faye breathed a sigh of relief. "Thank you, but I won't need to try them on...I can tell by looking which one will fit me."

The Reverend gave no response; he fumbled nervously as he tried to fit the oversized key into the door. Faye noticed his hands shaking. The key fell out of his grasp, onto the stone floor, he hurriedly picked it up again, and Faye distinctly heard him cussing under his breath.

"Are you feeling unwell, Reverend?"

"Just a tad dizzy, that's all, Miss Butler." He sounded edgy, thought Faye.

"Why don't we leave the dresses until later...there's no hurry, Reverend."

Taking no notice of Faye's suggestion he successfully pulled open the tiny, squeaky door, picked up the lantern and made his way down into the abyss, leaving Faye alone in the chapel.

After a long and boring wait, there was still no re-appearance of The Reverend. Faye stood at the top of the winding, stone steps and called out to him; he failed to answer. There was a dull glow from the lantern which, assumed Faye, meant that he'd reached the crypt. Maybe he just couldn't hear her; she called out again, louder and once again there was nothing but silence. Had he been suddenly taken ill, she thought; he *was* shaking quite a lot earlier...perhaps he'd collapsed, had a heart attack...he could even be dead; she panicked, not sure of whether she should run for Mrs Glover or go down into the crypt and see for herself what had become of him. She quickly ran into the office and picked up the jug of water, hoping that it just might be what The Reverend needed, it was a very warm day, after all, and he'd been on his feet all morning delivering his sermon. Treading carefully down the precarious steps, she continued to call out to The Reverend and then, as she reached the last few steps, she caught sight of his feet, sticking out from behind a wooden crate. Still unable to see his face, it was obvious that he'd collapsed; there was neither any sound nor movement from him as Faye hastened towards him, spilling the water on her way.

All at once, Faye released a piercing scream as The Reverend bolted upright and grabbed her arm, pulling Faye down on top of him; she immediately knew what was in store for her, it was the nightmare episode with the footman all over again. She kicked out in every direction, and screamed as loud as she could, but knew that in the depth of the crypt, her voice was inaudible.

"Get your mucky hands off me!" she demanded, but Barnaby Glover's hold became stronger and painful. At last, he spoke,

"I didn't intend it to happen like this, my sweet flower, but you left me with no choice, did you?" He had manoeuvred her body and pinned her down on to the uneven floor as he straddled over her, his amphibious eyes presenting a wicked and hungry glare. Unable to move her limbs, Faye spat at him; he laughed deliriously, "Quite the feral cat, aren't you, my little kitten! "

"You disgust me, *Barnaby Glover*...you are *no* man of the cloth...you're a fraud and a hypocrite and don't deserve the respect you're given and *if* you dare to have your wicked way with me, I will make sure that you are ruined for life.

"Faye, my darling, you are so naive...do you think I'm *that* foolish to allow you the opportunity to slander my good name? After all, since I fell in love with you, I have sinned more than during my entire lifetime. I have nothing to lose, I'm already doomed to be thrown into the eternal pit of Hell; I might as well make it worth my while."

"You are sick *Barnaby Glover* and you won't get away with it you know, someone will come in search of me, eventually!"

"*Who, exactly?* All of your friends and family are either dead or presume that *you* are dead!"

The sudden realisation that this malicious man hadn't posted her letter to Granny Isabel caused Faye to shudder; he was right, who *would* bother about her?"

She jerked her body violently only to feel the crippling squeeze of Barnaby's strong grip. She felt like a defenceless dear, caught in the claws of a ferocious lion. Barnaby was a well-built man and Faye knew that if she had any hope of surviving, she'd have to make use of her wits because her strength in comparison to Barnaby's was nonexistent.

"What if we come to some kind of deal and I give you my word that I will leave here and never return?"

"That's better; I knew you'd be sensible about this, my darling." Barnaby stood up slowly, still keeping his large hand pressing down on Faye's ankles.

"I must be sure that you won't attempt to run away...do I have your word, or am I going to have to bind your slender ankles together?"

"I won't attempt to run away, provided I have your word that you'll let me go and not kill me!"

"*Kill* is a *very* strong word, my sweetheart...how could I possibly kill the only flower in the world who I love...you must make sure that you don't do or say anything which might cause me to forget that I left you down here in the crypt, where you could so tragically waste away."

Faye now knew, for certain, that she was in the grips of a mad man; one who made no sense and was probably having some kind of mental breakdown. She remembered her grandmother's warnings to her and wondered if she'd inadvertently given off the wrong signals to him. She watched as Barnaby dragged out a box and opened it, all the while he kept his eyes firmly on her and looked ready to pounce if she dared to try and escape. He pulled out a white, lacey wedding gown and passed it to her.

"Put this on, I'm going to make an honest woman of you. You *will* be my wife."

Unable to comprehend Barnaby's logic, Faye decided to obey him rather than protest and contradict him.

"I'll be back just as soon as my mother is asleep, then we will become husband and wife, my beloved."

Faye inwardly cringed as he kissed her lips before disappearing up the stairs. Thankfully he'd left the lantern behind and as she quickly followed him, her prayers that he'd not locked the door behind him were in vain.

CHAPTER TWENTY-THREE

There had been little sleep at Harberton Mead as Ed Hall and Harry Fairbanks spent the entire night in deep conversation. They both kept to their agreement of being completely honest with each other and as the sun eventually rose above the rolling fields of Oxfordshire they had arrived at some very intriguing revelations and it dawned on them that they had more in common than they could have imagined. Ed was completely taken by shock, he'd presumed that the baby in Delia Fairbanks' arms was her own and that Harry was the father; he would never, in a month of Sundays believe it to be the child of Roberto Lopez's sweetheart. For Ed, though, the best news of all was that there was no ongoing murder enquiry surrounding the death of old, Mrs Butler and it had been evident that she'd died of natural causes.

Harry was warming to Ed Hall and decided to make him an offer just as soon as he'd walked down to the grocery and purchased some essentials on which to feed his guest.

Ed Hall now wished that he'd brought Rob along with him; he was going to set about finding Faye Butler's burial place, so at least Rob could say his final goodbye and hopefully proceed with his life.

Harry had made a pot of extra strong coffee and

haphazardly sliced up a loaf and fried half a dozen eggs. The smell triggered Ed to leave Harry's bed where Harry had insisted he tried to get at least a couple of hours sleep, but sleep was the last thing on his overloaded mind. He felt such a desperate need to confide in Rob.

"Good morning my dear fellow. Did you manage to get some sleep?" Harry was in a jubilant mood, despite his rough appearance due to the lack of sleep.

"Mornin' 'Arry, I won't tell a lie; I didn't manage a single wink!"

"I presume that our all-night discussion was to blame?"

"That, and the sweet smell of fried eggs" joked Ed.

"Then you must come and join me. I have also come up with a proposition which might prove pleasing to your ears, my good fellow."

Harry sensed Ed's eyes on him as he painstakingly tried to clean away the coffee which had dropped onto the lapel of his jacket.

"Did I forget to mention, last night, that my dear, sweet wife felt the need to fill the burning stove with *every one* of my suits before she abandoned me?"

There was nothing Ed could do to prevent himself from exploding into a fit of laughter...it was infectious and the two grown men laughed until tears filled their eyes.

"I suppose I deserved it!" spluttered Harry.

"Ah, 'Arry, my friend, there ain't nothing more lethal than an angry woman!"

"That brings me to the little matter which I'd like to discuss with you, Ed," said Harry, in a more serious tone.

"I *am* guilty of mistreating my wife, and sadly it's taken such a tragedy for me to realise how much I love her and how meaningless my life would be if I fail to find her and bring her home."

Ed's brow furrowed.

"I know what you're thinking, Ed, that very soon, I will no longer have a home to bring her to, but you see, Ed, when I sell this place, I *will* be able to pay off all of my debts, buy a more modest dwelling *and* pay you for the work which you are going to do in locating her and discovering where that poor young woman, Faye Butler is buried. I will help you as much as I can; you can live here and I will of course purchase a new bed for you..."

"Sorry ter interrupt, 'Arry, but make it two mattresses instead and let me send word an' get Rob ter join us...we need someone young an' on the ball like 'im. Reckon he'd make a good detective."

Harry's face lit up, "So you *will* accept my offer...that's music to my ears, my dear fellow. *Yes*, you must send for Roberto, immediately. I can see that we're going to make a brilliant trio and everything will turn out just fine."

"Hmm, would be a whole lot finer if we could

bring back the dead, 'Arry."

"Poor Mr Lopez, he must be a broken man from the loss of his sweetheart. It cuts into my heart like a sharpened blade whenever I remember that beautiful, young woman's body, covered with mud and blood on that bleak November night."

"It might be better if yer don't mention all that, when 'e gets 'ere, 'Arry."

"*My dear man*, I wouldn't dream of it, what do you take me for? My own heart pines for my darling Delia, and God willing, she is alive, well and safe somewhere. I would *never* be so reckless in my account of Faye Butler...but he *will* have to know that it was I who discovered her."

"Of course, 'e 'as ter know the truth, an' anyway, as I told yer last night, Faye's baby 'ad nothing ter do wiv Rob...I'm sure that dear, little baby is in the best place wiv yer good wife."

"Her heart melted for that baby as though it were her very own, Ed, she loves little Faye and I know that wherever she is, that baby will be adored and well cared for by my dear wife"

"It's a right sad affair all 'round, 'Arry; let's just pray that it ends cheerfully an' we can track down Mrs Fairbanks. I'll write ter Rob, tell 'im ter get 'imself ter Oxf'rd in an 'urry, like. Yer got any paper, 'Arry?"

"You must arrange for a telegram to be wired to him, my dear fellow, the sooner he arrives, the better. Please, allow me to pay for it," insisted

Harry, digging deep into his trouser pocket. "Yer right 'Arry we *do* need ter get 'im 'ere fast like but I will pay fer the wire, thanks all the same."

"Rob, Rob my boy, wake up, this 'ere telegram as just come for yer...It could be a bit ov good news, Rob!" Granny Isabel's boney knuckles had turned scarlet from rapping so hard on Rob's door, her inquisitive nature itching to find out who'd sent it and what was written inside. Promptly opening the door, Rob stood baring his tanned and well-toned torso causing Granny Isabel to blush as she quickly diverted her eyes. "Sorry, I forgot me shirt, Granny!" Rob laughed, taking the telegram from her outstretched hand, hoping that it would be written using the few words which he'd mastered over the years. He closed the door, leaving Granny Isabel on the other side,
"I could 'elp yer read it Rob," her small voice called out. Rob put on his shirt and opened the door again.
"Come in Granny Isabel," he invited, smiling at his favourite old lady.
"Ain't enough space in there ter swing a cat, lad, how 'bout I go an' put the kettle on ter boil an' yer join me fer breakfast?"
Knowing he'd get no rest from Granny Isabel's nagging until she'd satisfied herself with the contents of his telegram, Rob struggled to keep a

straight face as he accepted her offer.

"Don't ferget ter bring that wire down wiv yer, now," she reminded him.

Rob tore the envelope open and stared at the neatly printed words. It was from Ed, he noted, feeling relieved. He concentrated on the line of print, reading it aloud like a child;

Rob, you must come to Oxford today. Harberton Mead House. Ed Hall.

He read it three times before being assured that he wasn't making any reading errors.

An hour later, Rob was sat upon the wooden slatted seats in a third-class compartment, leaving his beloved East End behind him. He adored the colossal steam engines, everything from their billowing clouds of steam to their rhythmic sound as they hurtled along the track like a herd of out of control stallions. He had questioned over and over again why Ed wanted him in Oxford so urgently. The compartment was packed full with an assortment of folk; a couple of hungry babies screamed above the sound of the locomotive and a jovial woman handed out rough-looking fruitcakes from her basket as she proceeded to inform everyone of how she'd not seen her dear sister in Oxford for over twelve years. An old wizened man was snoring in the corner, while the young lad squashed alongside him, studied him closely before feeling the sting from his ma's slap as she

scolded him for being rude. A plump, brown
hen bobbed her head up and down from inside
the secure wicker cage; her owner, an elderly
woman held on to it tightly, every now and
again whispering words of comfort to the
nervous chicken. Suddenly, the deafening
screeching as the engine pulled on her breaks
brought an instant silence in the compartment as
it grounded to a halt at Oxford Railway station.
Rob soon found himself in the heart of the city
and according to the railway porter, *'a good few
miles'* from Harberton Mead house. Feeling
hungry he made his way towards Cornmarket
where the porter had also recommended an
inexpensive restaurant. Impressed by the clean
and tidy streets of Oxford and its well-dressed
inhabitants, Rob's mood was disturbed by his
memory of Grandmother Butler and the sudden
realisation that he *could* be a wanted man in this
part of the country and until he met up with Ed,
he decided it would be best not to hang around
and to make his way immediately to Harberton
Mead house.

A dark and gloomy sky had replaced the earlier
brightness and Rob arrived at Harberton Mead
house along with a heavy downpour. Hearing
the approaching horse and trap, Ed was taken by
surprise to see Rob as he glanced through the
window; he'd not expected him until the
following day; but, at least, it meant that he'd be
able to talk in private and tell him the good news

that he was a free man, while Harry Fairbanks was taking a nap

Greeting Rob, warmly, Ed implored him to keep his voice low so as not to wake Harry. The heavy burden which had cast a constant black cloud over Rob during the past five months was instantly lifted when Ed broke the good news to him, bringing a genuine smile from his heart once again. He couldn't thank Ed enough for discovering the truth and also viewed the news that they were to work as detectives and endeavour to find Delia Fairbanks, with great enthusiasm.

"We'll also look inter where that sweetheart of yours is buried, Rob. I doubt she 'as anyone tending to 'er grave, so 'appen that could be a job fer you, lad."

"I reckon I would be comforted ter visit 'er resting place, Gov. I could put a bunch of flowers on it and maybe come ter Oxf'rd every year ter pay me respects."

"Great idea lad; let's pray that our work don't prove too difficult, eh an' that it won't take a lifetime ter track down the elusive Mrs Delia Fairbanks!"

"So was she kidnapped then, Gov?"

Ed laughed out loud, "*Yer daft bugger*, reckon yer bin listening ter too many ov Granny Isabel's wild tales! Course she wasn't kidnapped this is 1858, Yer fool, she ran off wiv the cook an' wiv yer sweetheart's baby!"

Rob's jaw dropped and for a few seconds, he couldn't be sure that he'd heard Ed correctly. "Come on through ter the kitchen, lad, yer look as though yer could do wiv some victuals!" insisted Ed. "Fairbanks is taking forty winks upstairs, it will give me time ter fill yer in on what's bin going on in the tranquil countryside ov Oxf'rd!"

While Ed did most of the talking, Rob satisfied his hunger with the remainder of the loaf and eggs which Harry had bought earlier that day. He cast his mind back to the day when he and Ed had first visited Harberton Mead house to clear it of its furniture; he remembered seeing Mrs Fairbanks with the tiny newborn in her arms, never in million years would he have believed her to be the baby which he'd witnessed growing as Faye's belly had become more and more swollen during their time together. In a bizarre way, he'd grown to cherish that unborn baby too; it was part of Faye and he'd adored her with every fibre of his being; the fact that she had no attachment to its father somehow made it easy for his heart to accept the idea of becoming the baby's stepfather when it was born. He felt jealous; jealous that after the intimate and loving times he'd spent with his darling Faye, it had not been him who'd held her baby in his arms, but instead, Harry Fairbanks, the gambler, whose reputation in the West End gentlemen's clubs had become the subject of scandal and ridicule and was spreading like wildfire, especially with the help of one Lionel Dagworth, who by all accounts was out for Fairbanks' blood.

"I don't understand, Gov," stressed Rob, as he champed on the chewy crust. "Why *does* Fairbanks want 'is wife back? She clearly doesn't love 'im or wanna be wiv 'im, or she'd be at 'is side. If we do find 'er, what makes Fairbanks think that she's gonna drop 'er new life an' return?"

"*That's a very good question,* my dear fellow!" The sudden appearance of Harry in the doorway and not knowing for how long he'd been listening in on their conversation, caused Rob and Ed to turn red-faced.

"*Arry!* I thought yer was napping. Yer must 'ave smelt the coffee!"

"Or perhaps my ears were burning, Mr Hall? I presume that this young fellow is *Roberto Lopez?*"

"*Rob!*" exclaimed Ed, nervously, "I'd like yer ter meet our new employer Mr 'Arry Fairbanks."

"Employer *and* friend I hope, Mr Lopez," expressed Harry as he shook Rob's hand.

"Now, please allow me to elaborate on my dear wife's situation." Harry poured himself a coffee before continuing, his face and tone remaining serious. "My dear wife left my home with the cook and with a young baby. I *know* that she was penniless and I doubt very much that Ruth White had more than a couple of shillings to rub together, so to speak, so I'm sure that wherever my wife has ended up, she is desperately unhappy and longing for me to rescue her...and I know what you are both thinking...why doesn't she simply return of her own accord? And this is why; because her departure was the only way in which she could protest about my despicable gambling and the fact that I've inadvertently ruined her life. But believe me, *my dear chaps*, wherever she is, she waits eagerly for me, and is no doubt, counting the days until we are once again united! *Now*, do you both understand?"

Both Ed and Rob were dumbstruck; Harry Fairbanks made no sense to them but without saying a word, they both presumed that the rich probably had a different way of handling their relationships. "Right, well that's sorted then," said Rob, breaking the uncomfortable silence. "The sooner we start, Gov, the better, I'd say, sounds ter me like yer wife needs rescuing quickly, before she pines away."

Ed glared crossly at Rob, wishing he'd keep his mouth shut and let him do the talking.

"So, 'Arry, d'yer 'ave any ideas as ter where she could 'ave gone...what about old ma cook, she got any relations? Does yer wife 'ave friends or family where she might be staying?"

Harry continued to drink his coffee, his thoughts seeming far away,

"I think it's a firm *no* to all of those questions, my dear fellow."

"Hmm, 'ow 'bout places she's spoken ov where she might like ter visit one day?" continued Ed, feeling more like Sherlock Holmes and proudly admiring his own clever-sounding questions.

"Well, there's, Paris and Venice of course," uttered Harry. "But as I've already told you, her purpose was *not* to put a huge distance between us, but merely to prove a point."

"Nah, she'd never 'ave gone abroad, not wiv cook *an'* a baby," agreed Ed. "She didn't 'appen ter 'ave a secret admirer, did she 'Arry, if yer get me drift?"

Harry slammed his cup down, splashing the coffee dregs across the table,

"Don't you dare to insult my wife ever again, do you understand? Men like you are two a penny, you know and my wife only has, or ever will have eyes for me. I suggest you never mention such an absurd idea again if you know what's good for you."

As true as Ed knew that men like him and Rob *were* two a penny, he also knew that it had slipped Harry Fairbanks' mind, that he was broke.

As good as his word, Harry left the house to purchase two mattresses. It was decided that Ed and Rob's search would begin in earnest the following morning, but whilst Harry was out, they discussed between themselves the great difficulty that they would endure in tracking down Mrs Fairbanks; she could be anywhere in the entire country and Ed knew that Harry's funds to pay their wages were reliant on the sale of Harberton Mead.

"Tell yer what we'll do Rob, lad; we'll begin our search in Oxf'rdshire an' then we could try an' find out where Faye Butler is buried. If Mrs Fairbanks *is* just kicking up a bleedin' fuss 'bout 'er lot in life, an' she *is* expecting Fairbanks ter trace 'er an' bring 'er back 'ome, then I doubt she's travelled too far from this area."

" 'appen yer might be on ter something there, Gov. I 'ope it ain't gonna take too long 'cos I'm already missing Whitechapel an' I don't like leaving Granny Isabel fer long wiv no man under 'er roof, while Mr Watkins is back at sea again."

CHAPTER TWENTY-FOUR

Barnaby stood in the parlour doorway, staring at the small dining table which was positioned alongside the window and faced the vicarage garden. The delicious smell of the roast lamb and potatoes wafted through the air, filling every corner of the vicarage but it did nothing to tempt Barnaby's taste buds, his mind was too occupied by other thoughts. He felt his stomach rumbling but he didn't want to lose the sweet taste of Faye's lips which still lingered upon his. He knew he had to try and act normally, but his head was spinning and as he stared at the sour-faced woman who sat at the table, for a split second her name had slipped his mind. She looked up at him, curiously,

"Why haven't you taken off your cassock, you'll drop gravy down the front of it...you know how messy you are."

"Sorry *mother*, I forgot!"

"Don't be so ridiculous, Barnaby, your words could be construed as sinful *and* it's a Sunday, in case you'd forgotten already...honestly I'm convinced that there *is* such an illness as spring fever and that *you* have caught it. I don't know what's got into you lately. Where's Faye...don't tell me she's taken all this time to put a few hymn books away...I can see that's another job I'm going to have to do myself in future."

"Yes, it will be, because Faye Butler has *gone!*" declared Barnaby, boldly.

"*Stuff and nonsense*, she has nowhere *to* go and it's a Sunday.

"Yes, so you keep reminding me, dear," replied Barnaby wryly.

"She's most likely daydreaming somewhere and forgotten the time...She's *another one* with spring fever...I'm beginning to think that I'm the only one wearing a sensible head these days. Come and say grace, I'm starving and I can't wait a moment longer. Faye will just have to eat her dinner cold and serve her right, the ungrateful little minx."

"Don't you *dare* to use such harsh words on her...I will not hear of it...Faye...Miss Butler is a free-spirited young woman who doesn't set her life to a mundane routine." Mavis was, once again, shocked by Barnaby's odd behaviour, but being eager to consume the meal which she'd spent hours preparing, chose to ignore his foolishness, sensing he was in a cantankerous mood and looking for a quarrel.

The temperature down in the crypt was a good ten degrees below that above ground. Faye had hurled the wedding dress across the room in rage; she'd found a woollen skirt inside of the trunk and had draped it over her shoulders like a shawl. Reeking of old, mouldy mushrooms, the damp garment *did* make her feel a little warmer. The lantern flickered and Faye was all too aware that before long it would extinguish, leaving her in total darkness. A giant, hairy black spider suddenly sped across the stone floor and disappeared into one of the cracks. Faye immediately jumped up, convinced that these black, crawling creatures were on her clothing. She brushed herself down vigorously, simultaneously breaking down into tears. There was no way in the world that she was going to let that repugnant Barnaby Glover have his wicked way with her…She would put up the toughest of fights, even if it killed her. She knew he would return and when he did, she wanted to be ready for him, but her resources were limited. Telling herself repeatedly to keep calm and think of some kind of plan, she knew she'd have to act quickly before either Barnaby returned or the complete blackout arrived. Searching every dark corner of the crypt she put together a modest collection of items which might be of use. A collection of broken bricks and rubble were piled up in one corner and there was also an old metal casket and some heavy old and tarnished candle holders, unfortunately without a trace of a candle inside of them; there was also, the crate of mouldy garments.

Frantically pulling out every item from the crate, Faye lowered the lantern down inside and decided that she'd feel a lot safer and perhaps warmer, sitting inside of it, especially after the lantern had gone out. She went through the clothes, which she concluded, had all once belonged to plump women; probably wealthy ones too. She pulled on the five pairs of bloomers, one on top of another, securing them tightly with a sash from one of the gowns; if *The Reverend Glover* was eager to devour her body, then she would make it as difficult as possible for him. She pulled her legs through the long sleeves of another gown and secured the remainder of its material with another makeshift belt. It wasn't long before she appeared five times larger than her size, but at least she now felt warmer and her nostrils had become so accustomed to the stench of mould that it no longer bothered her or turned her stomach. Regretting not wearing the layers of clothes after the next part of her plan, Faye struggled up the winding steps. She had collected a handful of tiny stones and bits of old broken off cement and began filling up the keyhole with as many as she could force into the small hole. Then stuffing small scraps of material into the gaps, she was soon satisfied that by the time Barnaby had broken through the first line of defence, he'd be exhausted. Placing a brick or a piece of rubble on to each step, Faye concealed the obstacles by draping the leftover clothes on top of them. Satisfied that the stone stairway was now as dangerous as she could make it, especially to a nervous man who would, no doubt, be in a hurry and with only one thought on his mind, she climbed into the crate and sat in wait.

Barnaby ate slowly with no enthusiasm, while Mavis consumed an extra helping of dinner plus two extra slices of apple pie, complimenting her own cooking with nearly every mouthful.
"That silly girl's dinner is stone-cold now...I wonder *where* she could have gone."
"I already told you; she has left *for good*...She told me herself and I watched her head off towards the main road to Oxford."
Mavis studied Barnaby's face, there was something peculiar about him today, he'd been acting strangely for the past few days and she was convinced that he was telling lies.
"Don't be so ridiculous, Barnaby, she hasn't taken her shawl, she doesn't have any money and I'm sure she'd not leave without saying goodbye to me."
"I expect she thought you'd persuade her to stay," replied Barnaby, calmly.
Mavis hurried from her chair to the broom cupboard, her lips pursed as she expected to find her jar of pennies gone, but was instantly comforted as they appeared exactly as she'd last seen them. She returned to the parlour; Barnaby was sat staring into space.
"Tell me *exactly* what she said to you, Barnaby...don't you care about what happens to her, after all that she's been through and after

all our hard work and care to bring her back to health again?"

"Of course I care about her...more than you know, but she has chosen to fledge our little nest and you must remember, Mavis, she isn't our kin and is as free as a bird! If you *must* know, I gave her some of the money from the Sunday collection tray, so you can stop worrying about her welfare...at least she won't have to sell her body in order to survive!"

"Don't be so crude Barnaby, it doesn't become you!"

The tense atmosphere in the vicarage was too much for Mavis to bear; it was a glorious spring day and she felt the need to take a walk in the peaceful countryside and be apart from Barnaby for a while. She donned her slightly tatty straw bonnet and left quietly, while Barnaby pretended to doze off in the armchair. Outside, the sunshine immediately lifted her spirits and she decided to put all her worries behind her and enjoy the afternoon. A walk through the nearby woods would be like a breath of fresh air and prepare her for the well overdue heart to heart which she intended to have with Barnaby on her return.

As much as Barnaby was tempted to return to the crypt, he knew that he'd have to bide his time patiently and wait for nightfall when Mavis would be snoring and dead to the world. He continued napping in the armchair, reminding himself that he needed to look his best and reserve his energy for when he walked down the aisle in the midnight hour with his beautiful young wife to be. The very thought of Faye's flawless body in his arms made it difficult for sleep to overcome him.

There was not one room in the Dagworth's residence in London's Grosvenor Square, where Marjorie Dagworth's weeping could not be heard. There was nothing that anyone could do or say to console her and ever since the promise of Harry Fairbanks' baby had not been fulfilled she considered it to be yet another bereavement in her life and deserving of even more mourning and wailing. Her thin and undernourished body was barely visible as she lay upon her huge feather mattress surrounded by dainty, damp handkerchiefs. Lyle had had more than enough and couldn't even bear to look at his eccentric wife, let alone listen to her constant snivelling. She had become a complete and utter embarrassment, he concluded, angrily. *"For God's sake*, Marjorie, can't you shut up...I can't hear myself think anymore. You are sending me into a state of insanity and driving the staff away too!" Lyle marched towards the bed; he grabbed Marjorie's puny shoulders and shook her body, *"Shut up woman*...stop this damned racket before I'm forced to leave you, Marjorie. Is that what you want, you *foolish* woman. I hope you realise that I've become the laughing stock about London...I'm the idiot who was taken in by that country bumpkin, *Harry Fairbanks* with his ridiculous lies and trickery and the word in Brooks' and White's gentlemen's clubs is that his wife, who he told me had died has up and vanished. I'll get that *worthless cad*, and when I do, he'll rue the day that he ever dared to utter a single word to me! To think that I even trusted him to sleep under our very roof!"

"Will you bring me the baby then?" pleaded Marjorie, pathetically.

*"You stupid, stupid woman...*There *is no* baby...*don't you understand*...Fairbanks simply invented his story in order to rob me! Why oh why do I even bother to waste my time and energy trying to explain anything to you, Marjorie?"

Lyle viewed his wife with sympathy; she was in the midst of some terrible mental breakdown and he feared that she might end up in the lunatic asylum bringing even more embarrassment upon him. She was a pitiful sight and that bloody leech Fairbanks had been a huge contributor in worsening her mental state. He would pay for it, Lyle decided angrily and he would send Marjorie away to the coast, for a peaceful and relaxing break, somewhere tranquil where she might make some kind of recovery. He took another look at her, she was wasting away; he'd felt only bones when grabbing her shoulders, there was but an ounce of flesh covering her skeletal body. Lyle felt guilty, he shouldn't have lost his temper with her, he mused, her mind and body were not that of the woman he'd married and it was his responsibility to care and nurture her back to health. He walked back towards the bed, picked up her thin hand and kissed the back of it.

"I'm going to help you my darling girl and I'm going to teach that blackguard Fairbanks that he can't mess with people's lives and get away with it. I'm going to send you to the coast, my little adorable kitten; a few weeks away from London and away from the memories, which haunt you, will do you the world of good and I'm going to pay Harry Fairbanks a visit too."

Marjorie's sunken eyes stared hard at Lyle as she considered his words,

"Will you bring the baby back from Mr Fairbanks'?"

Lyle sighed loudly, "I'm going to bring back my money, my dearest, not because I am in need of it, but as a matter of principle."

"But Harry Fairbanks seemed like such a *good* man, and he *did* promise us a baby, remember?"

"Here you are, dry your tears, and don't waste your thoughts on Harry Fairbanks, you're confused, my darling." Lyle handed her a large handkerchief from his pocket, there was no use at all in trying to explain to her, he concluded; it was as though her mind had ceased to understand any kind of logic and had become trapped in a sticky web, making him even more determined to seek out Fairbanks. Lyle knew that if he was stood before him now, he would take the greatest of pleasure in throwing his clenched fists at him.

Mavis admired the bunch of bluebells which she'd picked during her afternoon walk, they added a colourful touch of spring to the dreary parlour, she thought. Blowing out the last of the candles, she allowed the light of the full moon to guide her through the parlour and up the stairs to her bedroom, where Barnaby had already retired to, half an hour earlier, after declining his evening cocoa and complaining of feeling nauseous. Mavis was worried about Barnaby, he'd not been his usual self for a few weeks; his behaviour was odd and he came out with the most bizarre of sayings. She continued past the door to her bedroom, pausing briefly to listen for Barnaby's snoring; he was quiet. The next few stairs led up to the attic and to another issue which had played heavy on her mind all afternoon and evening. She looked in at Faye's room; the bed had been made, but her nightgown still hung over the back of the chair, and a bonnet, her shawl and a pair of stockings still hung from the hook on the door. It was quite obvious to Mavis that Faye's sudden departure had not been planned and she wondered if perhaps Barnaby knew more than he was letting on. She closed the door quietly, deciding to include a special pray for Faye's wellbeing with her bedtime supplications; she wasn't a bad girl, just a little flighty perhaps and she'd certainly paid a heavy price for her shortcomings.

Barnaby was as still as a corpse in the bed, he kept his eyes firmly closed and waited patiently for the sound that Mavis was fast asleep; she'd taken much longer to settle, he mused annoyingly. His thoughts went to Faye; he imagined her waiting excitedly for his return and eagerly anticipating the moment when she would become his wife; he had yet to decide where he would take her to live after their midnight ceremony, knowing that Mavis would be unhappy with his choice of bride. Mavis had become such a bane in his life recently, always disagreeing with him and accusing Faye of being no better than a harlot, but he knew otherwise and intended to protect her for the rest of his days.

The prolonged spell of lying completely motionless had caused Barnaby's leg to cramp; he couldn't remain still for a second longer and was forced to leap out of bed and hop around the bedroom as he rubbed the afflicted leg. At last on the verge of nodding off, Mavis bolted upright to observe, as he raced crazily around the room.

"What's wrong, Barnaby? Is there anything I can do to help you?" she expressed with concern.

The cramp had subsided and in a state of relief, Barnaby dropped down on to the floor.

"I'm just fine, *Mother*, don't worry about me, just go back to sleep."

Shocked, but a little unsure as to whether she'd heard correctly, Mavis declared, crossly,

"*I beg your pardon*, Barnaby, *who* did you just refer to me as?"

Barnaby ignored her question as he rubbed the back of his leg.

"Sorry to wake you, go back to sleep; it's late."

Mavis had had enough of Barnaby's ridiculous behaviour; Sundays always proved to be a very arduous day, but this one had been overbearing and all she yearned for now, was a good night's sleep and hopefully when Monday morning arrived it would also bring the return of Faye Butler and the return of her husband's wits.

CHAPTER TWENTY-FIVE

According to Harry Fairbanks, his supposedly devoted wife was hiding out somewhere quite nearby, so after gathering all the local information which might be of use and a map of the area, Ed Hall and Roberto Lopez left Harberton Mead at first light, leaving Harry at home to attend to his so-called '*business*'. Harry was completely disillusioned, concluded Ed and the devoted Delia probably had no intention or wishes of returning to him. However, it suited both Ed and Rob, for just the two of them to endeavour on the mission, where they would make locating Faye Butler's resting place a priority. Harry said his farewells to them with the promise of another feast of fried eggs on their return.

"What does 'e bloody well take us for?" complained Rob as they headed off towards the City of Oxford. "Does 'e reckon that we live like beggars on the street, back in the East End?"

"Yer 'ave ter remember Rob, lad, that 'Arry Fairbanks is a toff an' even though 'e's fallen on 'ard times, 'e still reckons that 'e's a cut above the rest ov the world. In all fairness, Rob, 'e ain't as bad an' not 'alf as pompous an' stuck up as some of the toffs that I've 'ad ter deal wiv in me life."

"Well, the sooner we get back 'ome the better in my opinion. I don't reckon I would ever 'ave been 'appy living 'ere in the countryside, not even wiv Faye. The East End will always be 'ome ter me."

They continued in silence for a while, Harry having the exact same feelings as Rob, but keeping them to himself. Before long, they arrived at the undertaker's parlour, its black-painted facade looking unwelcoming. There was no sign of anybody inside and the door was still bolted.

"I guess nobody in Oxf'rd snuffed it last night then," declared Rob. "Reckon these fancy folk are a lot healthier than us, don't you 'Arry."

"Nah; there's just less ov 'em an' they ain't all crammed inter every nook and cranny, like rats. We'll come back later. Now 'ow about we go an' do a bit ov what Fairbanks is gonna pay us for."

"I don't reckon we'll ever see a single shilling from that cove, Gov, 'e owes money ter 'alf the population ov London yer know."

"Ah, don't exaggerate, Rob, 'e's bound ter 'ave a small fortune once 'e's sold that bleeding great 'ouse ov 'is."

"What? Yer mean after 'e's bought 'imself a brand new place and some posh furniture ter fill it wiv fer that devoted wife ov 'is? I don't trust 'im, Gov, just like all them coves back in London who e's in debt to. If 'e does 'appen ter win back the heart of that poor Mrs Fairbanks, well 'e's gonna want ter spend a bit on 'er too; fancy petticoats like that one don't come cheap, Mr

Hall."

"I never knew yer were so knowledgeable 'bout the ways of the wealthy, Rob!" laughed Ed. "'Ow 'bout we go an' find somewhere ter get a bite or two whilst we wait fer the undertaker ter show up? Yer can fill me in a bit more wiv yer vast knowledge!"

It took Lyle Dagworth the entire morning to find the information which he needed to make his journey easier; Harry Fairbanks was indeed a shrewd sort and had been careful not to disclose his address to anybody, especially those whom he gambled alongside. But having more money than could reasonably be spent in a lifetime did have its advantages and even the wealthy manager of Brooks's gentlemen's club hadn't proved overly expensive for Lyle to bribe and secure that vital piece of information. In Lyle's experience, he was all too aware that no man was to be trusted where the exchange of money was involved. A quick visit to a nearby coach-house and he was soon sat upon the superior royal blue, velvet seats in the latest gleaming carriage, which was about to make its debut upon the thoroughfares of the West End. As the two black stallions gathered speed, galloping out of the City, Lyle relaxed a little and for the first time in a long while, felt a sense of freedom to be heading in the opposite direction of his troublesome wife. Away from the annoying and constant sound of her pathetic whimpering which had become wedged inside of his head, Lyle was, at last, able to think clearly.

Harry Fairbanks had come along with his false promises and made Marjorie a hundred times worse when she might possibly have recovered from mourning the loss of their child. Harry had lied, cheated and robbed him too and even though the hundred guineas, which he'd taken, was a mere drop in the ocean to Lyle, it was the principle and the irreparable damage that he'd caused which had provoked him to seek Harry Fairbanks out. Lyle had no idea what he was going to do when he finally met up with Fairbanks, his emotions had been erratic lately, his temper sometimes uncontrollable and that troubled him; it was completely out of his character to shake his wife violently, as he'd done, he'd been raised as a gentleman and taught never to raise a hand to the fairer sex. He felt his nerves were slowly fraying at the edges, and the urge to strike out had never been so strong in his life and the thought of removing Harry Fairbanks' sickly smile immediately caused his fists to clench tightly.

Rob and Ed drank their way slowly through a pot of coffee in the St Clements' coffee house. From where he was seated, Ed had a clear view of the front entrance of the undertaker's parlour and kept one eye sharply focussed for any signs that someone had arrived. The pretty waitress had informed them that he usually arrived at ten o'clock every morning, unless there was a rush on, so with only another twenty minutes to wait, they left the coffee house and took a stroll. The gathering clouds were a sure sign that the day was likely to see copious April showers, Ed had lost count on how many times he'd had a soaking since his departure from London, but at least his jacket now looked and smelt fresher. The middle-aged man emerging from one of the cottages and dressed from head to toe in black immediately attracted Rob and Ed's attention; he proceeded towards the undertaker's parlour, followed by Rob and Ed, who kept their distance.

"We'll give 'im a few minutes ter do whatever undertakers do when they arrive at the office," whispered Ed, as quietly as he could, which still managed to turn the undertaker's head.

"I ain't too keen on them sort of places, Gov..."

"Oh, an' I suppose I love a room filled wiv corpses do I? We're in this tergether, lad, so where I go, you do an' all."

Rob was quiet and praying that he wasn't about to come upon any ghoulish sights to haunt him. He'd often stumbled upon dead bodies in some of the rougher parts of Whitechapel and witnessed the sight and stench of bodies which had been dragged out of the muddy banks of the Thames. The harrowing scenes never failed to fill his dreams at night causing him to wake abruptly, terrified and in a cold sweat.

A strong odour of lavender filled the immaculate office of the undertaker's parlour. A shining wooden floor looked and smelt recently waxed; the undertaker sat behind a highly polished pedestal desk with a leather, veneer top in moss green. Rob counted five upholstered, high back chairs, all placed neatly around the sides of the office; there was also one in front of the desk, but to his astonishment, there was not a dead body to be seen.

The undertaker wore a sad and very serious expression as he stood up to greet them, his hand quickly outstretched in readiness to shake and commence business.

"May I offer my deepest condolences at such a sad time," he declared in his monotone speech.

Ed, smiled, "We ain't lost no-one, Sir...well, not recently that is, but we'd be most appreciative ov any assistance and information that you might be able to enlighten us wiv."

It always amused Rob when Ed tried to talk like the better folk, it just didn't sound natural somehow, but with the greatest of respect to the nature of the business which he was standing in and with his darling Faye at the forefront of his thoughts; Rob remained straight-faced and focussed on the matter in hand.

The undertaker's demeanour eased and he smiled, for the first time.

"If you gentlemen would care to take a seat, I'll do my best to help you, if of course, it's within my capability." He ushered them towards the chairs.

"Please, Sir, if you'd care to explain further." Ed swallowed hard, his mind working fast to arrive at the most accurate words.

"It's 'bout me lad, Rob...well, not 'im, but 'is betrothed. She tragically lost 'er life somewhere on the highway near Oxf'rd. We were told that she was brought 'ere, but then taken somewhere else. We're trying ter find out where she was eventually buried...yer see, Sir, young Rob wants ter pay his respects."

The undertaker looked confused; his brow furrowed deeply as he eyed Rob and Ed.

"When exactly did this fatality take place, because I don't recall having to send a body away from my parlour?"

"Ah, sorry, Sir, I should 'ave said. It was back in November...apparently during the night of one of the worst autumn storms."

"*Yes!*" he exclaimed, "I remember that night very well indeed, in fact, we named it notorious November and I do recall telling my apprentice to take two of the deceased to another undertaker. You see I only have room for six out the back, eight at a push, and that was the dreadful month when we had the frightful outbreak of scarlet fever. So many young lives were lost...such a tragedy!" He shook his head solemnly as he spoke. "My parlour was full to bursting on that stormy November night, I was at my wit's end, as were most of the local undertakers...If my memory serves me well, I *do* believe that my apprentice had to ride as far as Woodstock where the outbreak hadn't yet reached."

"*Woodstock!* Ain't there a palace down there?" enquired Ed, slipping up on his accent.

"That is true, Sir, *Blenheim Palace*, which is a *splendid* structure; constructed early last century and was a gift from Queen Anne to the 1st Duke of Marlborough…I believe he was called John Churchill…yes, that's right…*John Churchill*."

"So would me sweetheart be buried there, d'yer reckon?" Rob intervened.

"I would have imagined so...but why, if you don't mind me asking, have you not looked for your sweetheart's resting place before now! Did she not have any close family that you could have also asked?"

"The poor girl was an orphan," announced Ed, "she 'ad no family, apart from a grandmother who also lost 'er life 'round the same time. We all live in London yer see, an' we just presumed she'd come down 'ere ter visit 'er grandmother...it's a bit of a long an' confusing story."

"Yes, quite; I'm sorry I couldn't be more helpful."

"You've bin *most* 'elpful, now we just 'ave ter trace which undertaker she went to in

Woodstock, an' then, young Rob, can pay 'is long-awaited respects."

"Are you father and son, if you don't mind me asking?"

Both Ed and Rob were amused by the undertaker's question, knowing there was no resemblance between them...even their skin was a different shade.

"We're as good as father an' son, but we just work tergether."

Rob liked Ed's reply; he didn't know what it was like to have a father but thought that lately, Ed Hall had shown some true fatherly characteristics where he was concerned.

The undertaker nodded, his smile still set firm upon his kind face.

"By the way, there is only one undertaker in Woodstock, so your search will, hopefully, be straightforward. I wish you luck, gentlemen."

Ed and Rob stepped over the threshold and out into the fine drizzle, feeling victorious. It was only ten-thirty and they'd already accomplished a great deal.

CHAPTER TWENTY-SIX

The full moon's bright glow guided Barnaby along the short distance between the vicarage and the chapel, a journey which he was capable of treading blindfolded since he'd made it copious times. But he'd never in all his years made his way to the chapel with such unholy thoughts mulling through his head. The vicarage clock had just struck the hour of two, Mavis was, at last, in a deep sleep and Barnaby was jubilant that his plan was going just how he'd foreseen it. Feeling nothing of the night chill, Barnaby was sweating and his legs were shaking beneath him, causing him to trip up over his own feet. *'Calm yourself,'* he muttered crossly, under his breath, 'every groom feels excited about his wedding night.' He pictured Faye's body; her sensual curves, and young breasts, he knew her skin would feel like silk against his own and her hair as soft as down. He quickly wiped the dribble from his chin; his lips were anxious to devour every inch of her body; he hastened his steps and soon arrived through the arched doorway of the chapel. There was nothing but silence; an eerie silence which was suddenly broken by his own footsteps as he hurried up the aisle. He stopped at the altar to light a lantern, there would be no moonlight in the depth of the crypt and Barnaby was yearning to fill his eyes with his beautiful new wife; he hoped she was waiting as he'd instructed, dressed in the fine wedding gown. Fumbling in his pocket, his quivering hand pulled out the long key. Quickly patting down his wild hair and smoothing his overgrown whiskers, Barnaby admired his own masculinity, feeling strong and strangely youthful all of a sudden, as though he could take on the entire world. The key fell noisily on to the flagstones as it refused to enter the keyhole. Putting it down to nerves, Barnaby took a quick glance around, he could feel his heart racing; beads of sweat trickled down his face and he felt his undergarments adhering to his damp skin. He tried again, this time guiding the key in with two hands. There was something not right, holding the lantern close to the door, he squinted as he studied the key, thinking that perhaps he'd picked up the wrong one. Peering through the keyhole on bended knees, the darkness made it impossible to gain a good view.

"Damn it, bloody damn it!" he cried out.

"Don't you worry my sweet angel, we will soon be united, my darling love."

In a panic, he tried for the third time, thrusting the key into its hole with all the strength he could muster.

"Why the hell aren't you going in?" he yelled, tossing the key and sending it flying across the

chapel. Barnaby's erratic temper had caused a disaster. The key was now nowhere in sight and in the dim light emanating from the short wick of his lantern it was impossible to see clearly beneath the rows of dark wooden pews.

"My sweet dove, *please* forgive me...I'm doing all I can...please don't fret my love...have faith in your *dearest Barnaby*." Keeping up a continuous dialogue with Faye, as he crawled around on the dusty floor, feeling for the lost key, another half an hour passed before it was in his grasp, once more.

"*Oh my love!*" he cried out loudly, "our time is near...I *will* make this damned key work and you *will* be in my arms before long...Oh my Darling, sweet angel, can you ever forgive me for keeping you waiting like this? Do you *ache* for me as I do for you, my love?"

"***Who on earth are you talking to?***" Mavis was stood just inside of the chapel watching Barnaby as he quickly pulled himself up off the floor. In the darkness, only Mavis's face was illuminated by the flame of her candle. Barnaby stared at her; she looked old, her face drawn and her hair a state; tied in white rags and covered with a piece of netting. She looked more like his old deceased grandmother, he thought, as he grappled with his memory, trying to work out who this old woman was. She'd annoyed him, whoever she was; he couldn't recall inviting anyone to attend his wedding...It was to be a strictly private affair.

"I beg your pardon, madam. Do I know you? And do you have my permission to be here on my wedding day?"

"*Stuff and nonsense...**Barnaby Glover**...*have you been drinking? I'm extremely worried about your peculiar behaviour. You've lost your wits!"

As it suddenly came to light that it was Mavis standing in the chapel, Barnaby burst out into a fit of laughter.

"You ridiculous woman...you know for a fact that I never have and never will allow a drop of alcohol to pass my lips! What are you doing here anyway...go back to bed. Can't a man of the cloth have a conversation with his Maker without being interrupted by a sour-faced old hag?"

Mavis stood scowling, shocked by Barnaby's cruel and hurtful words.

"I left you snoring, *woman*...what in God's name are you doing following me anyway?"

"Well, Barnaby, since you're so concerned, I had to leave the bedroom and go to the outhouse, because *you* didn't put the chamber pot under the bed as I asked you to, yesterday. I was worried where you'd got to, in the middle of the night and quite honestly, Barnaby, I wish I'd never bothered."

Barnaby's bulging eyes bore into her, a look of disgust masking his face.

"Well, now that you've been assured as to my whereabouts, *Mother*, you can return to your *sweet* dreams."

Mavis flinched, there was unquestionably something not right with Barnaby; twice in the last twelve hours he had referred to her as *'mother'* and his odd behaviour, his rudeness and disrespect were completely out of character. "Goodnight Barnaby, don't stay out here too long, the nights can still get very cold you know."

"Yes, goodnight," replied Barnaby, abruptly, as he continued to stand motionless, waiting for Mavis to leave.

The second that she'd stepped back out into the crisp April night's air, Barnaby rushed to the crypt door. Mavis stepped back inside, crouching down as she quickly hid behind a pew. She lifted her head to gain sight of Barnaby and watched with intrigue as he began to kick and thrust his fists against the crypt door, hollering out like a wild beast. A sudden chill swept through Mavis, she'd never before felt afraid of Barnaby, but tonight he appeared like a man possessed and having more strength in him than she'd ever witnessed before; he was clearly conversing to an imaginary being or was it the devil who'd invaded his life, causing the string of outrageous and bizarre actions. In a state of trepidation, her spontaneous action was to run up behind Barnaby and bash him over his head with the heavy brass candle holder which she carried. Barnaby cried out as he swayed, unaware of what had hit him, before crashing to the ground. Mavis immediately pocketed the key, which had fallen from his grasp, before she surveyed the damage to Barnaby's head. He was out cold and Mavis didn't have the strength to drag his heavy body back to the vicarage.

"Oh, Barnaby...what have I done to you?" she muttered as she inspected his head. His flesh was still intact, but she could feel a large protruding lump where she'd struck him. Quickly fleeing back to the vicarage, she returned with a blanket and cushion. It was the dead of night and she didn't want to fetch the doctor just yet. But if forced to, she'd simply say the same to him as she would to Barnaby when he came around; that she'd found him out cold in the chapel. Before Mavis had the chance to make him comfortable, Barnaby was already struggling to lift his body, holding on to his head as his face winced from its painful throbbing.

"Thank God," said Mavis, in a small voice, relieved that she hadn't knocked the life out of her husband.

Disoriented and shivering, Barnaby allowed Mavis to help him make his way back to the vicarage. She lovingly wrapped the blanket around his shoulders and sat him on the couch while she kindled the fire and prepared some hot tea, laced with honey. He remained quiet and in a trance which Mavis considered normal since he'd been rendered unconscious for a time. Barnaby, however, was deep in thought, trying to piece together the events which instead of leading him to the arms of his beautiful sweet Faye, had brought him back to the vicarage, with Mavis nursing him. It suddenly dawned on him that Mavis *did* know of his plans and that she was capable of stretching to great lengths to sabotage them and ruin his happiness. She was an evil woman, he concluded and something had to be done to stop her.

As Mavis handed Barnaby a large beaker of tea, he remembered that tonight was his wedding night and that he shouldn't be here at all, but in the arms of his enchanting wife. He felt confused, not sure if he'd told Mavis about his wedding plans...and not sure if she'd agreed to them and given her blessing.

"What is it Barnaby, you appear so troubled, are you in pain my dear husband? Shall I go for the doctor? I wish you'd let me know what's been troubling you of late; you just haven't been yourself at all. Did Faye say something cruel to upset you before she left? Was that why she left so suddenly without even saying a proper goodbye? Please tell me Barnaby, I'm sure I could help, you know."

Barnaby hauled his body up from the couch; there was fire in his eyes as he towered above Mavis.

"*You stupid old hag!* What do you want from me? You are the heavyweight that hangs upon my wings; you are the poisonous viper who whispers in my ears and you are the shackles which make me no better off than a condemned man." The heavy strike from Barnaby's hand created a gust of wind as it came down upon Mavis's shocked face. She fell instantly, without as much as a cry. Barnaby stared down at his victim, he watched her shallow breathing and felt his heart plummet, knowing that she was still alive and would only continue to ruin his life. He had to think, he told himself, but the inside of his mind felt fuzzy...nothing was clear to him anymore; who was he? He questioned himself and why had he committed this wicked sin? In his fickle state of mind, his emotions became uncontrollable; laughing one minute, sobbing his heart out the next. He raced up the stairs, losing his balance a few times; his head remained dizzy. Viciously, he pulled out every drawer from the chest and ransacked the wardrobe; he knew that Mavis must have a stash of money hidden somewhere; his money, which he'd earned and which he intended to retrieve. With the entire contents of the wardrobe and drawers spewed across the floor, Barnaby had failed to locate a single penny. He yanked the mattress from off the bed and began to pull up the floorboards one by one, cussing loudly at the stubborn ones which refused to budge. Left in a state of exhausted, he'd found nothing and dashed from the bedroom to begin searching the kitchen. That was *her* domain, he mused and most likely to be where she'd keep anything of value hidden. He was suddenly struck by the falling mop as he opened the broom cupboard and in a rage hurled it across the kitchen. He came upon the jar of pennies, halfpennies and farthings and laughing crazily out loud, he chucked the jar at the wall, laughing even more as it shattered, freeing the small change.

"Where have you hidden the money you stupid bitch?" he yelled. "I *will* find it, I bloody well *will*, if it takes the rest of the night."

Cupboard after cupboard was emptied and Barnaby's rough and hurried handling of their contents left most of the treasured crockery, which Mavis had collected over the years, in a state of disrepair. Barnaby didn't care; his mind was set on one thing only, which was to find his money, it had even temporarily slipped his mind that Faye Butler was imprisoned in the depth of the crypt. A row of five, fancy, bone china teapots were displayed high on a shelf; teapots gifted to Mavis over the years in appreciation of the kindness and care she'd often given to many of the womenfolk in Barnaby's flock. He glanced up at them, wondering why he'd never seen any of them pouring out tea. Quickly scraping a chair across the flagstone floor, he climbed up and retrieved each teapot.

"You, sly thieving snake! What were you going to do with *my* money? You dare to leave me with a few shillings in my pocket year after year while

you have your own bank under my very nose. You thieving bitch, how dare you, bitch! Bitch! Bitch! I should have killed you!"
Barnaby counted nearly forty pounds, neatly rolled up and divided into each teapot. In his fury, he smashed every one of the expensive pots across the floor and dashed out of the vicarage, his pockets filled with the crisp white banknotes. He hurried back to the chapel, remembering that Faye was still waiting for him.

Now freezing cold, starving and thirsty, Faye was no longer able to feel her limbs. Squashed in the wooden crate, she felt weak and unable to move. Her mouth was dry and foul-tasting and with flashbacks of her trauma back in November ever-present in her mind, her heartbeat increased rapidly filling her ears like the thumping beat of a drum. Was this part of Barnaby's evil plan, she wondered; to leave her trapped in this abysmal place for so long, until every ounce of energy was drained from her, making it easy for him to claim her. Knowing that she was unable to put up any kind of fight Faye prayed that Barnaby would fall victim to the cluttered and dangerous stairway before he reached her.

As the rosy, dawn slowly surfaced, Mavis opened her eyes. Her swollen face throbbed painfully. She gently stroked it as her thoughts instantaneously went to Barnaby; she felt afraid of him for the first time in her life, fearing that he might be lurking around in the semi-darkness, waiting to kill her. Feeling as though she'd had her soul beaten out of her from Barnaby's crippling blow, Mavis was in a state of shock; nobody had ever lifted a hand in anger to her before. She tip-toed unsteadily to the kitchen, only to discover that the noises which she'd thought were merely part of her dreams, were, in fact, a reality; her eyes overflowed as she viewed the destruction. The high kitchen shelf was empty and Mavis knew that Barnaby had discovered her life time's savings and had probably fled with them. Although feeling a little safer, she couldn't relax until she'd checked the entire vicarage, just in case he was lying in wait with the intention of ending her life. After surveying the trail of mess and destruction which Barnaby had left behind him, Mavis stepped outside, she noticed that the door to the chapel was slightly ajar. Could Barnaby be inside, she wondered; should she try and help him, he was definitely showing all the signs of some kind of breakdown. As she neared the door, treading carefully and keeping a constant lookout in every direction, Mavis soon heard the sound of Barnaby's feral and crazy sounding voice; he *had* lost his mind, she feared and needed urgent help before he did any more damage. Rushing to the door, still holding her throbbing face, she let out a sigh of relief that Barnaby hadn't removed the key from the chapel door. She turned it, locking Barnaby in.

CHAPTER TWENTY-SEVEN

It was mid-afternoon when Lyle's impressive
hired coach pulled up outside of Harberton
Mead house. He climbed down from the
carriage, instructing the coachman to enjoy a
couple of hours at his leisure before returning.
Harry Fairbanks' country retreat was indeed an
impressive home, regarded Lyle as he stood for
a while enjoying the delightful chirping of the
provincial birds as they packed the air with their
splendid chorus; a sound he seldom heard in the
streets of London. Harry Fairbanks didn't
deserve this little spot of paradise, he mused.
There didn't appear to be anyone about the
place, not a single stable lad or a gardener. Lyle
prayed that he'd not had a wasted journey but
was quite content to relax in the pleasant sun
and enjoy the bird song if that were the case. His
footsteps invaded the tranquillity as he marched
up the wooden stairs, reaching the veranda.
Harry, who'd been doing little more than
walking aimlessly from room to room with his
troubled thoughts, suddenly stopped in his
tracks to peer out through the lace curtains. He
wasn't expecting anyone and it was certainly too
early for Ed and Rob to be returning.
"*Good God!*" he exclaimed, as he caught sight of
the unmistakable thin and lanky Lyle Dagworth.
Quickly retreating from the window, Harry

wondered what had brought Dagworth all this way. Surely a man with his wealth wasn't missing a hundred guineas, he pondered as he contemplated whether to open the door to him or sit quietly in the hope that he'd leave peacefully. He could hear his footsteps walking around the veranda; no doubt he was trying to pry in through the windows on his way. Thank God for Delia's insistence to dress the windows with the heaviest, pleated lace curtains, praised Harry. His attention was suddenly drawn to the sound of the back door being opened; Harry could have kicked himself for leaving it unlocked. What if Dagworth and the rest of his creditors had drawn lots on who should descend upon Harry? What if he was armed with a pistol, what if...?

"Mr Fairbanks!"

It was too late, Harry stood like a snared rabbit in his bleak and empty parlour. He suddenly felt very insignificant and vulnerable. Lyle studied the empty room, as he scratched at his bushy whiskers.

"I see now, why you've not shown your face in London for a while, Fairbanks. The *'For Sale'* notice didn't escape my notice either."

"Are you often in the habit of creeping in, uninvited, through the tradesmen's entrance, Mr Dagworth?"

"My *dear* fellow, you mysteriously disappeared from society, leaving many of your so-called acquaintances fuming and after your blood! I consider my gentle approach to be most generous, especially after our little agreement and the promise of the infant, which my poor dear wife is still hankering after...believe me, Fairbanks, there has been many a time when I have felt like strangling you with my own bare hands and if you resided in London, you would likely be in your grave and I with my neck in the hangman's noose!"

Harry viewed the strange-looking man; he didn't look capable of strangling an old hen; his belly had grown even larger since he'd last seen him which made his legs twig-like and seemingly struggling to support his body.

"Well, Dagworth, as you can see for yourself, I am in no position to return a fraction of what I owe you, not until I've sold my home at any rate. I am not even in the position to return your hospitality."

Lyle edged nearer towards Harry, "You lied to me Fairbanks, you made me look a fool in front of everyone; my wife has been left with her state of mind greatly impaired and you have the audacity to stand before me like some poor innocent, mistreated puppy. You deserve a bloody good thrashing, Fairbanks, you deserve to be expelled from society and if I'm not mistaken, it would take little effort to ensure you a spell in debtor's prison. You should indeed count your blessings that your debtors are not in a desperate need for their funds and they have the courtesy not to report you."

Harry could feel his fists clenching in anger as this pathetic man stood before him making threats and insults. He was quite convinced that one clout from his right hand would send him into oblivion but he would much prefer to settle this dispute peacefully and see Dagworth off his premises uninjured.

"How could you tell such a foul and wicked lie about your poor young wife too, Fairbanks...what possessed you, man? Is it any wonder that she has left you?"

"Just leave my wife out of it, Dagworth, you know *nothing*...why don't you return back to that fancy home of yours and worry about Mrs Dagworth; if I recall, *she* is the one in need of help."

"Is there no truth in the rumour that your wife has left you then, Fairbanks?"

"My wife has simply gone to stay with relatives."

"Is she aware, that you spread the word of how she'd lost her life giving birth to her lover's child?" questioned Lyle, cynically.

Harry took a long stride towards Lyle and grabbed hold of his silk cravat, pulling tightly as he glared up at his hideous face.

"Take your filthy hands off me you despicable runt before I'm forced to do something regrettable!"

Harry knew he was calling his bluff, Dagworth was a spineless sort, probably never thrown a punch in his entire life, he looked more the type to beat his wife; Harry knew his type well."
He let go of him with a hard shove which surprisingly didn't cause Lyle to move an inch; it was as though he had heavyweights in his boots. Maybe he'd underestimated this man's strength, thought Harry.
"I must admit, Fairbanks, I left London earlier with the sole intention of giving you a good beating; your pitiful living conditions and the state of your filthy attire do not infuse the slightest of sympathy towards you, in fact, I'm quite surprised that nobody else has beaten me to it. You are collecting many enemies, Fairbanks, and the sooner you sell this grand home and pay off your debts the better."
"Did I ask for your advice, Dagworth?" interrupted Harry, belligerently. "Don't you realise, that I'm in the process of doing just that?"
"Well, you might be furtively planning to disappear and restart your life somewhere new, where you believe you won't be traced...I'm telling you Fairbanks that won't be advisable. But I do have a proposition to make and I don't think you are in a position to ignore what I have in mind."
Lyle licked his dry lips, "Damn it, Fairbanks, aren't you even in possession of some coffee

beans...I'm parched you know and your little strangling escapade hasn't helped!"

"Come into the kitchen then, where I can keep an eye on you. *Of course, I have coffee.*"

Lyle laughed, mockingly, "Has it escaped your notice Fairbanks, that you have nothing left for me to steal even if it was my desire which I can assure you it isn't!"

Harry stared coldly at him, "You think you're so clever don't you Dagworth? I like to keep those whom I don't trust under my nose and you certainly fall into that category, dear fellow!"

The more of Harberton Mead which Lyle saw, the more persuaded he became that it would be the ideal country retreat for Marjorie, where she could recuperate. Not too far away from London too and surrounded in peaceful, scenic beauty. It was an ideal, tranquil place for someone in her fragile state of mind and when she'd made a full recovery, she could become acquainted with the ladies of Oxford's social circle...She would love it here away from the hustle and bustle of London. With a kind-hearted companion, a cook and a couple of their London maids, Marjorie would soon revert to her old self. He could travel to Oxford for the weekends too; yes, Lyle concluded it was a splendid idea and would solve many problems.

"I'd like to make you an offer on your fine house, Fairbanks. What do you say?"

Momentarily shocked by Lyle's announcement,

Harry mulled over his suggestion. He detested the thought of Lyle Dagworth and his pathetic wife living in his home; it was *his* home and even though it was on the market, he would be far happier if it was sold to a complete stranger. "If you *do* wish to make an offer on Harberton Mead, dear fellow, you'll have to proceed through the proper channels and take it up with the land and estate agent in St. Aldates. Don't presume that you're entitled to special treatment or a reduction, simply because I owe you a hundred guineas. Rest assured that you will get your money back, as will all the other vicious, barking dogs in London. Now if you don't mind, I have business to attend to, so I'd appreciate it if you would hurry up and drink your coffee and take your leave of me."

"I won't take up another minute of your precious time, Fairbanks and quite frankly your coffee is tasteless."

"Then it must mirror my taste in acquaintances then, Dagworth. Please make sure you close the door behind you!"

Feeling his blood heating up, Dagworth knew he'd not be satisfied until he'd wiped the egotistical smile from the face of Harry Fairbanks. Knowing that he was younger and stronger than him, Lyle didn't want to end up coming off worse, so he had no choice other than to strike when it was least expected.

Lyle stretched out his hand towards Harry,

"I expect we shall meet again when I have secured the purchase of your fine house, Fairbanks; no hard feelings I trust? "

Harry reluctantly accepted Lyle's handshake; he wanted nothing more than to see the back of him. What happened next took Harry by complete surprise, as the two men shook hands Lyle swung back his leg and thrust his booted foot into Harry's shin. Yelling out, from both pain and shock, Harry spontaneously released his hand only to feel the full force of Lyle's right hand as it pounded heavily into his face. Harry slumped to the floor, humiliated but too slow and maimed to retaliate.

"Now I can return to London a happy and satisfied man, Fairbanks...no hard feelings I hope!" Lyle Dagworth walked calmly out of Harberton Mead, leaving Harry fuming as he nursed his wounds.

The lavish carriage was already stood on the driveway waiting to take Lyle back to London.

"There's been a change of plan, my good man; we are to go to St Aldates...do you know of its location?"

"Yes Mr Dagworth, it's just a couple of miles from here, Sir."

"Excellent, excellent."

CHAPTER TWENTY-EIGHT

Faye sensed that either something had gone wrong with Barnaby's plan or that something had happened to prevent him from returning. Although it felt as though she'd been imprisoned in the crypt for days, Faye's logical train of thought told her that it merely seemed like ages. It was, however, an awfully long period to be without food, drink and clean air. Becoming weak and lethargic, her mind repeatedly presented a picture of the precious baby who, on the night of her birth had left an imprint of her pretty round face upon Faye's heart; that image would remain with her forever. She could see it clearly, tiny and vulnerable, a new life arriving into the world searching for her mother and it had been out of Faye's hands to do anything but wrap her in a cold and sodden rag. She hadn't even managed to suckle the poor baby. Faye didn't fear death, life these days was harsh and cruel and everyone she'd ever loved and held close to her heart had departed from the world, leaving her feeling lonely and neglected. Her mind drifted to Rob, had he abandoned her too, she pondered; it certainly felt that way. Did he ever truly love her in the same way as she loved him, or was he simply momentarily besotted with her and with the idea of becoming a family man; he was as an orphan, after all. Maybe he'd long forgotten her, erased her from his heart and mind even. He probably had a new life now, with a new girl, while she was left in this dire situation, terrified by the prospect of being assaulted by a crazed man and locked in some abysmal underground prison inside a stinking crate, awaiting her fate.

Faye's self-pity suddenly turned to anger, causing a huge surge of adrenaline to pump through her veins. There was a whole world outside of this chapel and beyond Woodstock, she told herself, she was young, relatively pretty and had her life to live and live it she would. She was not about to let some backward man of the cloth, and his weaknesses, ruin her life; she would fight him with her body and outwit him with her mind to eventually be free from him. Feeling better already, Faye climbed out from her confined prison, stretching her numb body. In the darkness of the crypt, it was even impossible to see her own hand as she held it in front of her face. She felt her way towards the stone steps treading extra carefully so as not to fall over her own traps. It felt good to be moving again and the feeling soon came back to her limbs. Clearing each step of its obstacles one by one, she put a couple of hand sized stones into her pockets in case she might need them as weapons to throw or knock out Barnaby with, should he be waiting to pounce upon her. She wondered if he'd already, unsuccessfully tried, to open the door and smiled; proud of her clever thinking to block up the keyhole. Overcome with exhaustion after clearing her way up to the top step, she sat for a while. The heavy door to the crypt was as thick as three doors put together, but as she rested her head against it she immediately knew that Barnaby was on the other side. His familiar voice was troubled, he was shouting too, although it sounded distant as though he was stood far from the door. As the noise and commotion increased, Faye sat puzzled, wondering what was going in the chapel. Barnaby was ranting and raging like a wild animal in captivity but Faye couldn't make out a single word which broke the silence. Comforted by the chunky door which separated them, she decided that for the time being, at least, she wouldn't attempt to dig out the debris which plugged the keyhole.

The destruction inside the vicarage, caused Mavis to break down into fits of raging sobs; Barnaby had ruined her well cared for and beautiful home and destroyed most of her treasured possessions. How was it even possible for a man such as Barnaby to change so drastically over a short period of time, especially when nothing traumatic or out of the blue had taken place, she wondered? The human mind

was very frail indeed. Having decided to leave
him alone for a good few hours to calm down,
Mavis now realised that he was no longer the
gentle and placid man she'd been accustomed to
all these years and was capable of inflicting
harm on her and in fact, probably on anyone
who stood in his way. She would bring both the
police and the doctor to the chapel in due course,
and perhaps a couple of strong young men to
restrain him, should the need arise, which she
was sure it would. She would also leave the
inside of the vicarage untouched as evidence for
all to view; she was all too familiar with menfolk
and how they joined forces together against the
fairer sex; she didn't want them labelling her as
an overreacting, neurotic woman, who had
merely had a minor disagreement with her
husband and blown it out of all proportion. She
doubted that anyone in Woodstock would
believe that the quiet, well mannered, Reverend
Glover was capable of such actions as he'd just
committed.

Having exhausted himself and in agony from his
wounded head and from punching and kicking
both the chapel and the crypt doors repeatedly,
Barnaby stretched out his body along one of the
narrow pews and quickly fell asleep. His
swollen knuckles were split open and dripped
blood upon the chapel floor. Aware of the
sudden silence, Faye placed her ear against the
door. She could hear nothing and presumed that

Barnaby had left the chapel. He had obviously given up in his attempts to fit the key into the blocked keyhole which brought about a sudden, cold fear that she might be forgotten and left to die in the crypt. She imagined someone stumbling upon her skeleton in years to come and in a state of sheer panic, attempted to painstakingly remove as much of the debris as she could, wishing that she was in possession of a hat pin as her small fingers became sore and bleeding.

In the hope that Harry might accompany them on their journey to Woodstock, Ed and Rob returned to Harberton Mead. The talk of Faye had put Rob into a downcast mood and nothing Ed could say made any difference. There was no sign of Harry, downstairs, so presuming he'd taken to his bedroom for an afternoon nap, Ed and Rob searched through the bare cupboards with the urgent need to satisfy their hunger. "Who'd ov thought that a fancy place like this wouldn't 'ave any victuals in the bleedin' kitchen! I swear the kitchen in Whitechapel work'ouse 'as more food than 'ere!" complained Rob. "Don't suppose yer know 'ow ter make bread do yer, Gov? 'Cos I've found a sack ov flour!"
Ed chuckled, "I ain't got a clue, lad!"
The sound of knocking and Harry's voice, coming from upstairs, abruptly ended their

search. Hurrying to his room they presumed he was either sick or drunk.

"Bloody 'ell, 'Arry, who did this to yer?" yelled Ed, shocked to see the Oxford toff looking more like one of 'is own sort after a street brawl, usually over something trivial. Harry's face was bloody and swollen; his moustache, thick with dried blood and his perfectly straight nose was disfigured; his bare shin was badly grazed and displaying a huge red lump.

"One of my many enemies, old chap and I pray to Almighty that he doesn't spread the word of my whereabouts and send an army of them to quell their anger at my physical expense. They are all after my blood Ed, every single one of them!"

"Reckon it's more like yer money they're after, 'Arry, or should I say *their* money. Rob! Go an' search the place fer some whiskey or something similar," he ordered, in his next breath.

"You won't find a single drop, dear fellow; don't waste your time on my account."

Ed pulled out his treasured silver hip flask from the inside of his jacket, "Probably a spoonful left in 'ere," he declared.

"Save it, my good man, your need might be more than mine one of these days."

"Ah, yer fergettin' 'Arry, unlike you, I knows 'ow ter look after meself, I was born an' bred in the back streets ov London's East End...they'd 'ave a right old laugh at you laid up like an old crone after one little beating!"

Harry was not amused and not at all used to physical violence, he felt proud that he was always able to resolve any disputes diplomatically or with the help of a meagre payout.

"Go an' make us some more coffee or tea, Rob, or whatever yer can find in this bleedin' stark palace!"

Suddenly reminded of Lyle Dagworth's insulting words about the coffee, Harry laughed out loud, now finding it quite amusing.

"The fellow who did this to me took a dislike to my coffee, would you believe?"

"Is that what you toffs fight over then?" joked Ed.

"Well, there was that, and also the fact that I promised his ridiculous wife a baby...at a price. I also still owe him one hundred guineas."

Rob left the room angrily, knowing that it was poor Faye's baby that he was selling, as though she was some kind of expensive trinket, not a tiny human being. It was tantamount to slavery, he reflected, crossly. He felt glad that Harry's wife had run off with the baby, it proved that she loved her and would take good care of her...Faye would be happy with that. He hoped that Harry would never be united with his wife again and that he and Ed failed in their quest to trace her.

"Right then, 'Arry let's get yer cleaned up an' walking on that leg, yer don't want it her go rotten now do yer? An' by the way, me an' the lad are bloody starvin' yer know. I don't think too highly ov yer working conditions, Fairbanks!"

"Forgive me old chap, I'm struggling in life without a cook and maids you know. Let Rob go down to the grocery shop in Headington and stock up the kitchen. You'll find some money in the study, there's a pile of books in the corner, look inside the one called *successful business*. By the way, my dear fellow, did I mention that the scoundrel who did this to me wants to buy Harberton Mead; also, don't judge me to be a feeble coward, that bastard took me by complete and utter surprise just as he was about to leave."

Ed stared, intrigued by Harry's bizarre way of life and unable to fathom how he'd allowed his finances to become into such a dire state.

With Harry out of action, and complaining nonstop about his wounded body and drowning in self-pity, Rob and Ed left for Woodstock without him, early the following morning, assuring Harry that from their business in Woodstock, they'd begin, in earnest, to search for Delia Fairbanks, even though they knew it would be like looking for a needle in a haystack, especially since both Delia and her cook seemed to keep themselves to themselves. There was simply nobody to ask without looking like complete fools. Ed had even suggested to Rob that they should just lay low for a couple of days and then admit to Fairbanks that they'd given up with the mission. They'd both had enough of the countryside and yearned to return to Cable Street and to the work with folk which they were more familiar with; they also hadn't had a decent meal since leaving London.

Lyle Dagworth had returned home, jubilant in the anticipation of telling Marjorie all about the delights of Harberton Mead and its beautiful surroundings. He was sure that she'd be as excited as he was when he declared his intentions to buy the property. Surprised by the sound of stranger's voices as he stepped over the threshold, he was greeted by a serious-faced maid in the vestibule. Wondering what had been going on in his absence, he enquired, rhetorically,
"Do we have guests, Lily?"
Lily glanced downwards, unable to make eye contact with her employer.
"In the drawing-room, Mr Dagworth; there are two detectives waiting to speak with you, Sir."
Lyle's immediate thoughts were that somehow, Harry Fairbanks had arranged to pay him back for the beating he'd so recently afflicted upon him by sending one of his cronies to rob him in his absence. Lyle immediately regretted not

inflicting more serious damage on him.

"Is Mrs Dagworth dealing with them?"

Lily faltered, "N…no Sir."

After disposing of his jacket and top hat, Lyle caught sight of his hand; he'd completely forgotten about his grazed and tender knuckles, from where he'd struck Fairbanks and quickly pushed his hand into his pocket.

"Why *are* there two detectives in the drawing-room, Lily? What's been going on in my absence? Has there been a robbery?"

Lily shuffled nervously from one foot to another, trying to find the appropriate words. The door suddenly opened, bringing Lyle's butler, Johnson, out into the vestibule, the signs of tension clearly showing on his face.

"Mr Dagworth! You're home!" he declared in a shaky voice.

"What in heaven's name is going on Johnson? I leave London for one day and return to absolute pandemonium! "

Lily scurried off back to the kitchen, leaving Johnson to deal with Lyle.

"I'm afraid there's been a dreadful accident, Sir, involving Mrs Dagworth."

"Oh Dear God! Where *is* the poor woman…has the doctor been to see her? And why the detectives…I'll murder that damned Fairbanks if he's behind my wife's injuries." Lyle was in a flustered state and obsessed with the idea that anything which had occurred in his absence must be down to Harry Fairbanks.

"I don't wish to sound impertinent, Mr Dagworth, but you should be careful what you say, Sir, what with the detectives so close by," advised Johnson, warily.

"Oh, I've had *quite* enough of this," expressed Lyle, sharply as he barged into the drawing-room to face the detectives.

The smartly attired detectives were sat close to each other deeply engrossed in a whispered conversation. As Lyle glanced towards them, he suddenly became aware that since he'd entered his home, there was one sound missing; the distant sound of Marjorie's constant wailing. The house was far too quiet and as the detectives broke the news of how his wife's broken body had been discovered in the garden, directly beneath her bedroom window, Lyle had already sensed that something fatal had happened to his, poor, heartbroken Marjorie. Strangely overwhelmed with a huge feeling of relief, for her sake, more than his, he knew she'd gone to a better place where she'd be united with their precious baby Phyllis and beyond the torturous prison which had claimed her mind for so long. He glanced at the daguerreotype upon the piano; Marjorie was in her youth and looking radiant in one of her many alluring ball gowns, it was an image that Lyle would treasure for the rest of his days, as he remembered all the good days that they'd shared together.

CHAPTER TWENTY-NINE

It had proved to be a huge blessing that Lyle
Dagworth had visited the Land and property
agents in Oxford; they would be able to bear
witness of his whereabouts at the time of his
wife's fatal accident. He was convinced that
Harry Fairbanks would take great pleasure in
disclosing how the raging Lyle Dagworth had
intruded, uninvited and given him a good
beating, making it sound even more convincing
that he'd been on some kind of aggressive
rampage. Lyle didn't mention that he'd been to
Harberton Mead, only that he'd passed by the
house and noticed it was for sale and thought it
would be an ideal home to aid Marjorie in her
state of depression. It took little time for the
detectives to interview Lyle's staff and the land
agent in Oxford before reaching their conclusion
that Marjorie Dagworth had taken her own life
and was in an impaired state of mind.

Ed and Rob arrived at Windthorpe's surprisingly
overcrowded Woodstock funeral parlour by
mid-morning, only to find an extremely
distraught woman who was seeking the
assistance of the local doctor, who these days
was a familiar face at the undertaker's
parlour. Since that unforgettable night back in
November when one of Windthorpe's corpses

had terrifyingly come alive, Mr Windthorpe refused to bury another body unless Doctor Atkins had confirmed for a second time that there was no sign of life left in the deceased. As Ed and Rob waited in the doorway, Mavis Glover implored that the doctor should accompany her to where she'd been forced, for her own safety, to lock her husband in the chapel.

"I find it quite impossible to believe that there is any truth in what you're saying, Mrs Glover," said Doctor Atkins, as he tried to calm Mavis, "Reverend Glover is by all accounts one of the most peaceful men I've ever had the pleasure of being acquainted with; what you have just described seems rather out of character for such a placid man of the cloth."

"Exactly, Doctor Atkins, hence my urgency to seek you out and beg of your help...*that crazed man in the chapel is not my husband*...just look at my face, Doctor, is it in his nature to strike me and cause such an injury as this?" Both Doctor Atkins and Mr Windthorpe studied Mavis's swollen, scarlet face.

"I must admit, that I'd never have thought it possible for our very own Revered Glover to behave in such an ungentlemanly manner. Something is amiss here...I did think that he appeared quite burdened during Sunday's sermon. There was a distinct strain in his voice." added Mr Windthorpe.

"Yes, exactly, I've noticed a gradual change in him for a few weeks, but now I fear that he has finally lost his mind," expressed Mavis.

"I thought he appeared quite normal...I can't see what all the fuss is about...probably just a simple misunderstanding," said Doctor Atkins, "but I should probably come and take a look at him and give you my professional diagnosis if you really insist, Mrs Glover.

Mavis pursed her lips, annoyed that these two men who'd she'd known for many years, didn't appear to be taking her seriously.

"Yes, Doctor Atkins, that would be wise and wiser still if you brought along a couple of strong men to restrain him, he's quite unhinged, you know."

"Come now, Mrs Glover, let's not blow this out of proportion."

"If you'd excuse me," interrupted Mr Windthorpe, as he glanced to the rear of the parlour, "I need to attend to these two gentlemen who have been waiting so patiently." Until Mr Windthorpe's declaration, Ed and Rob had gone unnoticed amid all the commotion but now, all eyes fell upon them; they were strangers to Woodstock and Mavis, Doctor Atkins and Mr Windthorpe were left feeling embarrassed that they'd conversed so openly in front of them.

"Good afternoon, gentlemen, can I be of service to you? I'm afraid you've arrived at a rather busy time."

"We won't take up much ov yer time, Sir; we just wanna bit ov information 'bout a young lass who was buried in these parts at the end ov last year."

A suspicious silence descended upon the small parlour as Ed and Rob's rough-looking appearance and Ed's even rougher accent was taken into account.

"You're not from Oxfordshire are you?" stated old Mr Windthorpe. "I recognize that accent though...*you're Londoners* if I'm not mistaken."

"That's correct Gov; you've 'it the nail right on the head, so ter speak; from the East End ter be precise."

Mr Windthorpe's face lit up, proud by his accurate deduction.

"Perfect timing, young men," declared Mavis. "You both look like strong and able men and could come along to the vicarage to assist Doctor Atkins with my poor dear husband who, as you've probably already overheard, has become somewhat deranged."

"Please Mrs Glover, I'm sure these gentlemen haven't travelled from London to hear of your troubles, perhaps you would be wiser to return to The Reverend Glover, he might well be feeling a lot better by now," instructed Mr Windthorpe.

"Nah, we don't mind do we, Rob? But if yer could just tell us where me lad's sweetheart is buried first, that would be right 'elpful, Gov."

"That's most kind of you, thank you," stressed Mavis. "Now please hurry up Mr Windthorpe, shall I help you go through last year's record books?"

"That won't be necessary Mrs Glover, I'm quite capable. Now, do you happen to know if it was November or December of perhaps October and can you inform me of the full name of the deceased too?"

Rob took a step forward and cleared his throat, "Miss Faye Butler," he announced in a clear but sombre tone.

Mavis took a sharp intake of breath as her hand shot up to cover her gaping mouth, while Mr Windthorpe turned a sickly, pale hue all of a sudden and had to be seated. Rob and Ed could only exchange furtive glances to one another.

"Is there anything wrong?" asked Ed, "She *was brought* ter this 'ere parlour wasn't she! That's what we was told in Oxf'rd."

Doctor Atkins broke the awkward atmosphere, "In which way did you say you were associated with Miss Butler? I'm sorry, but I wasn't paying any attention to your conversation until her name cropped up."

"She was me betrothed," said Rob in a shaky voice.

"Yeh, that's right, they was sweethearts," added Ed, puffing out his chest, "Is there a problem?"

"Then *you* must be *Roberto Lopez!*" announced Mavis, finding her voice once again.

"Allow *me* to explain," insisted Doctor Atkins, "I've been professionally trained for situations like this. Perhaps you have a drop of whiskey for these young men, Mr Windthorpe."

"I'm the one in need of whiskey," objected Mr Windthorpe. "I've had untold nightmares about that night in November, now it's all suddenly flooding back to me…it's a wonder my frail old heart hasn't stopped beating by now."

"Your heart is as strong as an ox, Windthorpe," acknowledged the Doctor.

"Can one of you just tell us what's going on an' what all the bleedin' fuss is about! 'ow is it that yer knows Rob's name an' all?" Ed butted in, becoming increasingly annoyed.

"Very well then, have it your way, but I'm warning you that you are in for a shock because although Faye Butler was brought to us to be buried here in Woodstock, she was not actually dead!"

"*Faye's alive?* Is that what yer saying?" cried out Rob in alarm.

"She was extremely poorly for a couple of months and left so terribly weak, as you can imagine; she'd suffered an awful lot, not just physically but mentally too. The loss of her baby sent her into a very murky place but with the kind and tender care of Mrs Glover, here," Doctor Atkins gestured to Mavis who was stood wondering where Faye had vanished to as she stealthily eyed the famous Roberto, who'd she'd heard so much about over the months.

"And of course, The Reverend; they took her in as though she was their very own flesh and blood and nurtured her back to health."

Rob was completely dumbstruck; he couldn't believe what he was hearing, thinking that perhaps he was in the midst of a dream.

"What 'appened to 'er baby then?" asked Ed.

"Well, there was no trace of the little tot, so it was presumed that some wild animal had got wind of the smell of blood and savaged the child...dreadful business, indeed." Doctor Atkins appeared heartbroken as he shook his head in dismay.

Ed's smiling face shocked everyone in the tiny parlour, he was euphoric, to come in search of Rob's poor sweetheart's burial place and to find that she was still alive and well, was a pure miracle, but the fact that Rob could now inform Faye that the baby she'd been mourning for all these months was also alive was the biggest blessing any mother could ever wish for and Ed was finding it difficult to contain his jubilant emotions.

"That's where yer all wrong, yer see; Faye's baby is alive, she was rescued from the place where 'er body was found an' she's being well-cared fer by a fine woman who believes 'er ter be an orphan."

Everyone was in such a stunned state in the poky parlour that the problem of The Reverend

Glover had been temporarily forgotten. Then Mavis announced the dismal news, "I'm sorry to have to tell you this Mr Lopez, but young Faye left the vicarage a couple of days ago and we have absolutely no idea as to where she's gone."

"But I saw her at church on Sunday!" declared Dr Atkins. "We even had a little chat...She looked healthier than I've ever seen her!"

"That's right, I noticed how pretty and summery she looked in her flowery gown, quite the young lady," added Mr Windthorpe.

Rob had become very quiet, his thoughts were spinning inside his head; he was shocked by the news but troubled by the fact that Faye had not written to him in all this time, to tell him what had happened and where she was living. Had she fallen out of love with him he questioned? Did she really ever love him as he'd adored her or was she merely taking advantage that he was willing to become the father of her child and provide for her? Now that she believed her baby to have died, why would she want to get in touch with him?

" *Rob, Rob*, stop bloody dreamin', we're going wiv the Doc an' Misses Glovva ter check out 'er old man! "

Rob didn't verbally respond, but followed the group like a sad, neglected dog, feeling as though he'd been winded, and knowing that Faye Butler would torment him for the rest of his life.

"What's up wiv yer?" scolded Ed as they headed towards the vicarage, "yer've got a face on yer like a mouldy turnip! *Yer just discovered that yer sweetheart is still alive!* Where's yer smile fer God's sake?"

"There ain't nothing wrong, Gov...I'm just shocked that's all!"

"Well, yer best 'urry up an' change that bloody sour look on yer face, 'appen yer might scare that sweet young lass inter the arms ov another."

"Didn't yer hear what was said?" snapped Rob. "She ain't 'ere no more, an' that old woman 'ain't got a clue where she went!"

"Ahh, come on Rob! We'll find 'er...maybe she's hiding from the crazy Reverend, sounds as though 'e's lost 'is bleedin' marbles!"

As Doctor Atkins, Rob and Ed waited by the chapel door for Mavis to bring forth the key, all three men glanced inquisitively at each other as their ears picked up on the quiet sobbing coming from inside.

"Wait!" instructed Doctor Atkins, sternly, "I have an idea. Please Mrs Glover, I mean no disrespect, but could you not utter a single word; I want him to think that I'm here alone."

Mavis obediently took a step away from the door, with her lips tightly pursed.

Doctor Atkins proceeded to knock on the door, his rapping becoming heavier in order to gain any response from inside.

"Reverend Glover, is that you in there? It's Doctor Atkins," he called out.

The sobbing abruptly ceased and within a few seconds, Barnaby had brought himself closer to the door.

"*Doctor!* Thank the Good Lord for sending you to my rescue...I'm locked in and my young bride..." There was a pause, as Barnaby appeared to have broken down into sobs again.

"Tell me what your problem is Reverend," encouraged the Doctor, calmly. "I will do my best to get you out and help you. Are you injured?"

"*It's my young bride, Doctor Atkins*...you see; my wicked mother stole my money and *forbade* me to marry her!"

The confused-looking doctor ushered Ed, Rob and Mavis away from the door.

"I think that your diagnosis might possibly be correct, Mrs Glover," he whispered. "Tell me; was *your* mother against your marriage to the Reverend?"

"Not in the least, Doctor; but Barnaby *does* keep referring to me as his mother, which I find very disturbing. Initially, I took it as a harmless joke, but of late, it has become quite out of hand. You must come and witness for yourself, Doctor Atkins, the terrible destruction which he inflicted on the vicarage before taking our life long savings; I've been saving up for years you know!"

Ed and Rob waited outside while the Doctor followed Mavis into the vicarage to view the damage.

Ed sighed heavily, "Don't reckon I'll ever wanna leave the East End, once we're 'ome again, Rob. There's something not right 'bout these country folk!"

"Yeah, too much bloody fresh air an' fresh victuals, if yer ask me. I miss 'ome, Gov. What am I gonna do?"

"*We're* gonna do the best we can, Rob, an' wiv a bit ov luck, everything will turn up trumps!"

Ed sensed the turmoil that his young assistant was going through, but with age came reasoning and he was convinced there was a good reason behind all what had happened.

As they sat upon the damp grass in between the chapel and the vicarage, in quiet contemplation, Ed came to thinking about the bizarre situation.

"Rob!" He blurted out, "If Faye was so well treated 'ere over the months, it don't seem right that she would just up an' go wiv out saying where she was heading. Something fishy 'as bin going on, I reckon, an' I reckon that so-called *'man of the cloth'* is behind Faye's disappearance. Reckon 'e might 'ave done something to 'er an' is making out that he's gone mad ter protect himself!"

The colour immediately drained from Rob's face, *"What are yer saying Gov?* That 'e's done away wiv 'er? Oh God. I should 'ave come in search ov

'er burial place sooner...I'm ter blame fer
everything...if it wasn't fer me, Faye would 'ave
gone ter live wiv 'er grandmother long before
she gave birth, an' none of this would 'ave
'appened."

"Don't blame yerself, Rob...Faye loved yer an'
yer never forced the lass ter stay in Whitechapel,
did yer?"

CHAPTER THIRTY

When Ed voiced his suspicions about The Reverend Glover, he could tell immediately that it had given Mavis good cause to ponder on his words. They were all still stood a few yards away from the chapel door whilst Doctor Atkins continued in his attempts to make some kind of headway through conversing with Barnaby. Convinced that the elderly Doctor Atkins was feeling a little scared of the apparently crazed and savage like man on the other side of the door, Ed valiantly offered to enter the chapel with Rob and restrain Barnaby, if needed.

"I ain't no doctor, but I reckon yer can get a better picture ov this man if yer speaks wiv 'im face ter face," advised Ed.

"I think the gentleman is quite correct, " agreed, Mavis, who'd had time to reflect on Ed's suggestion; it had dawned on her that Faye's disappearance had come around the same time as she'd found Barnaby using such foul language whilst trying to open the door to the crypt. He'd also referred to her as *'mother'* at the same time and acted extremely hostile towards her. Everything seemed to suddenly fit into place and make sense.

"I think I know where Faye is!" She suddenly exclaimed, in a raised voice, loud enough to make Doctor Atkins turn his head.

"Quickly, we mustn't waste a minute longer; I have a strong inclination that Faye's down in the crypt! "Her hand shot up to cover her mouth as she let out a piercing cry of distress.

"That *poor, poor* child, I think she's been there for two days! Nobody could survive such a plight...it's a ghastly place!"

"Don't yer think he'd 'ave let 'er out by now though?" stressed Rob, urgently.

"*I have the only key!*" cried Mavis, holding the old metal object up high for all to see.

All pandemonium broke out when the four of them stepped out of the bright sunny daylight and entered the dark chapel. Covered in dried blood, his eyes bulging from their sockets far more than usual, Barnaby's foul mouth suddenly dispersed a barrage of vile language and insults to every one of the group. It took every grain of energy and strength for Ed and Rob to hold him down while Doctor Atkins and Mavis struggled in vain to open the crypt door. Mavis quickly ran to Barnaby's small office where she remembered seeing an old discarded bell rope a few weeks ago. Lifting her head up high, she prayed that they were not too late.

Ed made sure to gag the Reverend with his grimy handkerchief, whether he was a man of the cloth or not, Ed considered his language and disturbance quite unsuitable beneath the roof of God's house. Rob also received a stern warning from Ed who had to remind him where he was, although he totally understood Rob's fury with the corrupt Reverend Glover and turned a blind eye when Rob's hand *'slipped'*, falling heavily into their prisoner's stomach.

"I'm sure this is the right key!" cried Mavis in distress. "It was definitely the one which Barnaby was using!"

"But did you ever see him open the door with it?" questioned the Doctor.

"Oh Heaven's above...we must be using the wrong key...where did Barnaby put the key? *Oh Good God*...he's obviously forgotten, otherwise, I'm sure he'd have opened it!" Mavis was becoming more distraught with every passing minute; her voice had increased an octave as she shook nervously.

"Let me 'ave a look at yer key." Ed had come upon many a key which refused to fit their keyholes whilst trying to gain access to debtors and he knew this old trick of jamming up the keyhole all too well.

"Reckon she's plugged up the key'ole, Mrs Gluvva...she's a clever lass an' a quick-thinking one too!"

Rob's knuckles turned white as he clenched his fists, wishing that he could lay into Barnaby and put the fear of God into him as he must have done to his darling Faye.

"She must 'ave been terrified ov that bleedin' so-called righteous man!" yelled out Rob, angrily.

"My dear young man, I was terrified of *that* man...*and I'm his wife!* And please curb your language; remember where you are!"

"*Rob!* stand 'ere by the door an' call out ter yer sweetheart, she might be reassured if she recognizes yer voice. I'm gonna search fer a tool ter dig out whatever she's blocked the key'ole wiv."

"Ooh, I have knitting needles *and* hat pins," declared Mavis. "Will they be of any use?"

"Yeah, they're just the ticket, Misses Gluvva!" replied Ed, gratefully.

It took barely two minutes before Mavis returned from the vicarage, puffing out of breath but with her sewing box, containing a dozen or so needles and long hat pins. Ed wasted no time and very quickly had managed to push enough of the debris through and out to the other side, allowing the key to finally turn in its lock. Now slumped on one of the pews with his head resting in his hands, Rob was convinced that this time, Faye really had left this world and he knew that he'd never forgive himself.

Mavis waited at the doorway with the glowing lantern, as she issued warnings to Ed and Doctor Atkins of the hazardous stairway. Immediately hit by the foul stench of the foreboding crypt, Ed led the way, holding the lantern up high.

"What a stench! It beats the Thames on a hot day does this!"

"I doubt that the devil himself would set foot

down here!" added the Doctor.

Nearly treading on what looked like a pile of rags at the foot of the stone stairway, it was the Doctor who caught a glimpse of Faye's distinct golden curls, barely visible amongst the copious folds of material.

"*Stop Ed*," he shouted, "I do believe the girl is beneath that heap of clothing, I can see her fair hair."

It was a shock to discover that Faye was actually wearing all of the clothes; it made it difficult to find her limbs. Doctor Atkins searched for any place on her body where he would be able to locate a pulse, as he warned Ed not to lift her body yet, just in case she'd tumbled down the stairs and had broken bones. Her face was now visible, and Ed studied her beauty as the Doctor felt her neck.

"*Faye, Faye, Faye Butler!*" Ed repeatedly called out and whilst Doctor Atkins mumbled under his breath that they were too late, Faye opened her eyes and stared hard at Ed.

"*Doctor!* She's awake, look! She's opened her eyes, look, look Doctor!"

It wasn't long before Doctor Atkins issued the all-clear that Ed could carry Faye out of the crypt; they were welcomed with loud cheers of delight from Mavis. Rob could only stare in disbelief. Faye's eyes had closed again; she was severely dehydrated and weak but knew in her heart that she'd been saved.

Back at the vicarage, Mavis set about removing the many layers of outer garments which Faye was wearing. Rob was reminded of the first time that he'd met her when again she'd been dressed in layers of her own clothes as she'd fled from the danger of the footman whose criminal actions had been the cause of so many consequences in Faye's life. Rob wished more than anything, that he could take Faye in his arms and pledge that he'd keep her safe and protected forever. He felt the strongest urge to express his undying love for her, but in the strange surroundings and with Mrs Glover fussing over her, protectively, Rob suspected that Faye hadn't even realised his presence. With Doctor Atkins satisfied that Faye was once again in the very capable care of Mrs Glover, who was no stranger to nursing sick folk back to health with her delicious broths and sweetmeats, he asked Ed and Rob to assist him with Barnaby Glover. It was the Doctor's opinion that he'd suffered a mental break down and not wanting him to be admitted to a lunatic asylum where he'd probably never see the light of another day and with the local cottage hospital being unsuitable, he had decided to find a room for him in Oxford's Radcliffe Infirmary. Ed and Rob agreed to escort Doctor Atkins and his patient to Oxford; they had to return to Harberton Mead anyway, but something told Ed that Rob might just decide to travel back to Woodstock with Doctor Atkins.

There hadn't been a lot to bring Harry Fairbanks any pleasure of late, but when Ed broke the miraculous news to him that the woman he'd pulled out of the muddy bank some six months ago was still alive and had probably been saved with the help of the warm blanket which he'd been so insistent upon, Harry was euphoric. "We must travel to Woodstock and pay her a call!" he declared. "This is incredible news, Ed and the most unexpected news that I ever could imagine hearing. Rob must be the happiest man on the planet! Where is he, by the way? At her side, I should hope!" Harry's tangled sentences tumbled excitedly out of his mouth; he had jumped up from the kitchen chair and was pacing up and down like a restless child. "This is cause for something a little stronger than coffee and that bloody cad, Dagworth, was quite correct in his analysis of these cheap coffee beans...they are unpalatable!" he complained. "Sorry 'Arry, but me flask is as dry as an old bone! "
"*Damn it!* It's a bloody nuisance being so poor. I'm not used to being so miserly Ed; I wish to buy Faye an expensive worthy gift."
"Steady on 'Arry, we don't want young Rob ter be jealous now, especially when she finds out that you were the knight in shining armour who

rescued 'er!"

"What a ridiculous notion, Ed, your train of thought is proof of why *you* live in the East End of London in lodgings, while I reside in comfort and luxury in Oxfordshire!"

"And you've just proved what a bleedin' stuck up toff you are!" retaliated Ed, belligerently. "But, Mr Fairbanks, at least I ain't in debt, without even a couch ter sit me arse on. Yer seem ter 'ave forgotten too, that it were me an' young Rob that were the bailiffs who 'ad ter watch that poor little wife ov yours suffer in silence when we loaded every scrap of furniture on ter our wagon."

Harry went quiet, there was nothing but the truth in Ed's words, he felt ashamed of himself; if only he could turn back time, he'd never put a foot over the threshold to any gaming room, he'd devote himself to Delia and life would have turned out so different and so sweet.

"Let's not fall out now, old chap, when we are in the midst of such good news. Help me search every nook and cranny of this place, Ed, there's bound to be something of worth which I can sell to tied me over until that pompous Dagworth puts in his offer, which I know for certain he will. That sly bastard can't wait to sit and gloat when he and his pathetic wife take over Harberton Mead!"

Their search ended as soon as Ed had discovered a box of old discarded silver cruet sets which had been dumped in the garden shed, tarnished and in need of a good polish, but never the less, worth a few pounds.

"Well done, Ed," expressed Harry, as he rummaged through the box, failing to remember ever having used any of the items before.

"I do believe that *you* are the best man to take these to the silversmiths, you probably know more about these type of dealings than I. They would no doubt short change me."

"An' they'd no doubt fetch the peelers, an' presume that I'm a common thief wiv this little lot in me possession!"

"Oh, very well then, I suppose it's no longer any secret that I'm financially ruined...I expect Maybell and Selma's mother has been sounding off all my private business like a foghorn and gaining a healthy turnover for her employer into the bargain. I can't see that I have anything to lose, and then we'll make tracks to Woodstock. I can't wait a moment longer, Ed. To think that I left her for dead on the roadside...I hope she will be able to find it in her heart to forgive me."

"Reckon she forgave you months ago, 'Arry, after all, you weren't the only person to presume she was dead an' in fact, it was you who made sure she was as warm as toast, an' not many folk would 'ave taken so much care with a corpse."

A look of panic suddenly spread across Harry Fairbanks; he flinched and grabbed hold to the door frame for support,

"How damned remiss of me!" he declared with a break in his voice. *"Faye's baby*; it had completely slipped my mind...Oh dear Lord, how will I break the news to her that I have no idea where my wife has taken her and if she is still with her? What if she chose to put the child into the workhouse...She was always suspicious that I was somehow personally involved with young Faye, she was even under the impression that I was the child's father. She could be anywhere by now...She could have travelled as far north as Scotland! "

"Calm yerself, 'Arry, first of all, Faye was told that 'er baby was dead months ago, so ter find out that she's alive will be pure music to 'er ears. But I thought yer told me an' Rob that yer wife was bound ter be close by...you've changed yer tune a bit ain't yer? *Scotland?*"

Harry flung himself into the seat of the hard wooden chair, covering his face in his palms, "Oh, my dear fellow, I'm nothing but an arrogant fool...I've lost everything; I've made a huge mess of my life and I deserve everything that befalls me. I had it all and was too blind to notice and too spoilt and stupid to appreciate what I had...now it's all gone, like water through my fingers and I am dried up and finished."

Ed felt awkward, he wasn't used to such dramatic displays of self-pity, most of the destitute folk who he had to deal with would vent their anger by using their fists on the next person they came upon and nine out of ten times, that person would be him, but he'd be on guard and ready to defend himself. He rested his hand on Harry's shoulder and gave him a couple of reassuring taps.

"Come on now Gov, this ain't the way forward now, is it? Who knows what's waiting 'round the corner, eh? Now 'ow 'bout we go an' flog this box ov fancy silver, yer might feel a bit better wiv a few crisp banknotes in yer pocket!"

"Hmm, if only, Ed; if only it were that simple," muttered Harry, under his breath.

CHAPTER THIRTY-ONE

Throughout the scorching summer of 1858, Ed Hall made several weekend journeys back and forth from London to Oxford. He had struck up an unusual kind of friendship with Harry Fairbanks, with Harry depending on him more these days, especially when it came to smoothing things over with Harry's many debtors. Ed's quick call at the grand residence of Lyle Dagworth uncovered the reason behind the Land and Estate agent's in Oxford not having heard any news about his impending offer on Harberton Mead. Harry, however, was not shocked by the news, Marjorie Dagworth had struck him as an extremely highly-strung woman who was losing her sanity. He did, surprisingly, feel a little sorry for Lyle, even though the faint signs of bruising were still visible upon his body from their last meeting. He knew how it felt to lose a dear wife and wondered how Lyle was coping, but at least he'd not lost his wealth too, considered Harry, as he wondered whether or not Lyle would still be chasing him for the hundred guineas which he owed.

The strong bond of love between Rob and Faye had only increased during their months of separation. As Rob's watery eyes struggled to hold back his tears, he explained everything that he'd endured since the day he'd left London to call on Faye's grandmother. Faye had always thought that Rob had presumed she was dead but was shocked to discover how he'd actually heard the news of her so-called death whilst being in Oxford. She spoke of the letter which she'd written, but it didn't take a lot of thought to realise that Barnaby Glover had purposely failed to post it. Faye had spent many hours in conversation with Harry, every time, pleading with him to describe every little characteristic and antic of her baby. As far as Harry was concerned, one baby was much the same as another in appearance, but he remembered Delia words when she'd told him that baby Faye must take after her mother and had fair hair. Faye wanted to know every detail surrounding the night of her daughter's birth and Harry retold the events to her almost every time they met. She was touched by the way that during such a bitterly cold night, Harry had sacrificed his jacket to wrap her baby in and cuddled her close to his body in the hope of keeping her warm and alive. She thanked him on countless times and would often kiss his cheek. He had not only saved her baby's life but his insistence to go out of his way and provide a warm blanket to cover her body was a lifesaver for her as well. Although Rob had not taken any notice of the baby cradled in Mrs Fairbanks' arms when he and Ed had removed the furniture from Harberton Mead, he claimed to Faye that it was impossible not to notice such a sweet and beautiful baby who he admitted had been the prettiest infant he'd ever set eyes upon. His words were pleasing to Faye, even though she was often frustrated and deeply depressed by how little time had elapsed since Mrs Fairbanks had left Oxford with her baby and she had been discovered in Woodstock by Rob and Ed. All those months of mourning for her baby, in which she'd tried hard to convince herself that it was for the best and how she'd not want to be reminded of the baby's father every time she looked at her were now instantly blown away. Faye yearned for her baby more than anything in the world and if it took the rest of her life and she had to travel the entire world, she felt she would never find true happiness until she was united with her firstborn. As disillusioned as Harry tended to be in his opinion that finding Delia would be a piece of cake, Rob and Ed had conversed with Faye in a more serious and frank way, explaining how difficult and lengthy it might prove to locate her. Speaking with Faye alone one day, Ed advised Faye that she should not let her missing child take over and ruin the rest of her life, telling her that she'd already suffered more than many at her age and how he felt sure that Delia Fairbanks adored the baby as though it were her own, otherwise she'd never have burdened herself whilst fleeing from her husband. Faye's tangled thoughts were slow to unravel, but when she put everything into a logical perspective, she knew that Mr Hall's advice was probably the right one to follow. She had an instinctive feeling that one day she would be united with her baby and it was comforting to hear how Delia Fairbanks had been so desperate for a child of her own. Faye was sure that her sweet baby was in caring and loving hands.

Rob had brought Faye back to Wentworth Street, where together he and Granny Isabel nursed her back to health. Physically it took only a brief period of time before she was strong again, but her traumatic experience in the hands of Barnaby Glover, a man she had put all her trust in, seemed to plague her night and day. She had become nervous of any man and her nights were often disturbed by vivid nightmares. Granny Isabel voiced her beliefs, that coming so close to death on two occasions would be enough to send most folk *over the edge*, as she phrased it; she admired Faye, with her determined spirit to conquer her fears and return to a normal way of life. Whilst Ed was leading a double life as a debt collector in London and so-called private investigator in Oxford, Rob was given more responsibilities and took over as acting manager at Hall, Spencer and Lock. Meanwhile, Faye assisted Granny Isabel behind her shop counter.

In the autumn, when Mr Watkins returned from sea the death of an uncle left him with a modest inheritance and the opportunity to take over the lease at his uncle's boatyard. It was the start of a new chapter in the life of Mrs Watkins and her large brood and with Granny Isabel, deciding that she'd had enough of the noise and mess that went hand in hand with renting out her two largest rooms to such heavily burdened families; she came up with a proposition for Rob and Faye.

Aware that it was approaching the month of November when Faye had lost her precious baby, Granny Isabel knew it would be tugging harshly at her heart; she detected such a sadness hidden in the depth of her beautiful sea-green eyes and knew that Faye would shed her tears in private, making out to her and Rob that she was coping with life. Granny Isabel, felt that it was up to her to do a bit of moving and shaking in the lives of these two young sweethearts, who seemed to be stuck in an emotional quandary. Even though Rob was certain that they still shared the same love for one another, he was of the impression that Faye was no longer in a hurry to marry him, now that she'd lost her child. Faye too had feelings of doubt and was convinced that in the past, Rob had simply been doing the decent act by offering to marry her so quickly. On the other hand, Granny Isabel had heard both sides of their worries and thoughts and knew that it was up to her to manoeuvre their relationship and get them back to how they'd been together a year ago.

Faye seldom attended church on a Sunday anymore, the trust she'd had in The Reverend Barnaby had left her with a fear of such men even though everyone had tried to persuade her that no human in the world, including the most religious of preachers, was immune to madness. Faye, however, refused to accept that Barnaby Glover had gone mad but was simply besotted by her and his lustful cravings had taken over his senses. He was an evil and wicked man, not a mad man; he'd known exactly what he was doing and she thanked God a thousand times a day that he'd not managed to fulfil his smutty desires. She now preferred to pray at home and thanks to Mavis Glover's influence, continued to read the Bible as often as she could. But on this particular Sunday, Granny Isabel had begged both Rob and Faye to accompany her to the church of St Mary Whitechapel before joining her for Sunday dinner. She had sold the butcher's wife six yards of fine Chantilly lace at a discount price for her daughter's forthcoming nuptials and had been rewarded with a prime cut of succulent beef.

The three of them returned home in a jubilant mood; the delicious aroma of the roasting meat and potatoes had overtaken the entire house on Wentworth Street, causing their mouths to water and their stomachs to rumble the second they entered. Faye laid the kitchen table and helped Granny Isabel with the vegetables and gravy. The meal tasted every bit as good as it had smelt and when their plates were empty, Granny Isabel grabbed Faye by her arm as she attempted to clear away the dishes.

"Let the dishes wait for a while me darlin', it's not often that all three of us sit down tergether an' 'ave a good old chin wag, now is it, an' besides, I don't want yer falling over that bloomin' palliasse which Rob still insists on sleeping on, even though I said 'e could move inter one ov the Watkins' old rooms."

Rob lifted his head, "It's not right that I should 'ave a huge room all her meself when you sleep in the back parlour an' Faye 'as me tiny old room. Yer could get a new lodger in an' make some money."

"*Or*, you and yer beautiful young sweetheart could be wed an' take the upstairs rooms, one as a parlour and one as a bedroom...there 's even a little cooking stove in one of them rooms, you'd be right comfy up there."

As Faye sat blushing and Rob fidgeted in his chair, annoyed as to why Granny Isabel had blurted out such an offer without first warning him, Granny Isabel merely rested her chin on her bony elbows and glanced from one to another.

Rob suddenly took Faye's hand in his, "We'd always intended ter wed, hadn't we...let's not let that bleedin' reverend put us off our life tergether. Yer know 'ow much I love yer Faye, an' I promise that if yer *do* still wanna be me wife, that I'll never stop searching fer little Faye, where ever she might be."

"Of course I still want to be your wife, Rob," replied Faye immediately."I thought it was you who'd had a change of heart! I'm nothing but bad luck, it seems to follow me like a begging dog...are you sure you want to spend your life with someone like that?"

Granny Isabel, chuckled, "Ah, you two love birds...just listen to yerselves...I'm gonna put the kettle on ter boil, we'll celebrate the good news with a cup of Rosy Lee."

"Marry me, Faye Butler, an' make me the happiest man in the world. I promise you'll never regret it." Rob had left his chair and in true tradition was on one knee at Faye's side. Her face blushed profusely as Granny Isabel stood watching from the other side of the kitchen, enjoying every second as her eyes became watery.

"I love you too, Roberto Lopez and I always have, since the moment we bumped into each other on the corner of Angel Street. I'd love to be your wife."

Granny Isabel's sudden loud holler infused laughter and merriment into the small abode on

Wentworth Street.

"Granny Isabel, yer always so quiet...is this a hidden side to yer that we ain't seen before?" joshed Rob.

"It's years since I've 'ad anything worth celebrating an' if me bones weren't so old and decrepit, I'd be dancing a jig across the room!"

If it was a quiet wedding which had been intended by Rob and Faye, between Ed Hall and Granny Isabel they saw to it that the word of this wintertime nuptial was spread throughout the East End. The story of Faye's miraculous return to life had already been one of Granny Isabel's talking points to every single customer who stepped over her threshold; it not only did well for business but made the somewhat aged and forgotten granny feel as though she was once again in the hub of the community. Ed had also found it difficult, when clients and associates had enquired after Rob, not to disclose the captivating story; he took great pleasure from the look of astonishment on folk's faces as his tale unravelled.

When news spread of their wedding and many churchgoers had heard the bands being read, nobody could resist being part of this uplifting story with its fairy tale end.

Despite the sub-zero temperatures of December, nothing deterred the crowds arriving with parcels of food and their blessings for the happy couple. One of the local alehouses had gifted two barrels of ale and Granny Isabel supplied endless pots of hot sweet tea all evening. Faye's English rose beauty was never more apparent, she resembled a 'snow princess' in her heavy white brocade dress which was topped by an ivory, fur-trimmed mantle; her golden curls were highlighted beneath the orange gas lights, as they fell softly around her heart-shaped face and the frosty air had given her fair cheeks a natural rouge. Rob's dark and striking looks were emphasised by his unusually dapper clothing, Ed had insisted on a new dark grey suit; found in one of the many Whitechapel pawn broker's shops and purchased at a friend's rate for the popular Ed Halls, who everyone in business felt inclined to stay on the right side of. It was the perfect fit.

Broad smiles were permanently fixed upon Rob and Faye's delighted faces and the terrible ordeals which Faye had experienced during the past twelve months had been swept to the back of her mind on this special day. She was now Rob's wife, and she had a job in Granny Isabel's haberdashery shop and decent lodgings too. Life, at last, was looking rosy and who knew what the future might hold for her, she mused as she admired her handsome husband interacting politely with their uninvited but most welcome guests. Harry Fairbanks had declined to attend, claiming how he'd be like a fish out of water at an East End wedding. He had however promised them a special wedding gift when his finances were sorted. Both Ed and Rob knew that little would change in Harry Fairbanks' life until he'd sold his home and found his wife. The freezing temperatures drew an early end to the rowdy wedding party just as the very first winter snowflakes descended like white butterflies tumbling from the night sky. Rob took Faye's hand in his, smiling as a flake landed upon her nose,

"Come along Mrs Lopez, let's sneak away quickly. I want me beautiful wife all to meself!"

CHAPTER THIRTY-TWO
October 1863

"I want me mamma; it ain't fair, Nanna, why can't I go upstairs? I won't get in Mrs Swift's way, I promise...cross me heart...please, Nanna!" Four-year-old Billy Lopez folded his arms crossly as his bottom lip quivered. Not only had he inherited his father's dark and handsome looks, but he had the same stubborn streak running through his veins. Granny Isabel couldn't find it in her to be cross with the adorable young lad who she looked upon like her very own grandson; in fact, she felt a twinge of sorrow for him knowing that very shortly he'd have to share his mother's love and devotion with his baby brother or sister. From the moment when Billy had arrived into the world, ten months after Rob and Faye had married, Faye seemed to be making up for everything which she'd been deprived of, after being separated from her firstborn. In five years, there had been no word of the elusive Mrs Fairbanks and the search for her, baby Faye and Ruth White had slowly wound down over the years with the only consolation being that Faye understood Delia Fairbanks to be a woman of good character and that she cherished her baby as though she were her own.

"Now, now, Billy, me little darlin' be a good boy

fer yer Nanna, an' I'll find me box of buttons, we can make a picture on the table wiv 'em."

Tears rolled down Billy's plump cheeks; it was dark outside, and he'd not seen his mamma since the night before; how would he go to his bed without her cuddle and bedtime story, his young mind worried. He quickly wiped away his tears with the sleeve of his jumper; his pa would be home soon and be sure to scold him for crying like a sissy. Granny Isabel pulled out her tin of buttons and placed them in front of Billy, she stroked down his soft curly hair and cupped his tearful face in her hands,

"I'm sure you'll get ter see yer mamma soon, me little treasure an' yer pops will be 'ome before yer know it...now, how 'bout I fry yer the last sausage...would that put a smile on yer 'andsome face?"

"It might," snivelled Billy."Why is Mrs Swift hurting Mamma? You said she was nice."

Granny Isabel had run out of answers. Since the arrival of Mrs Swift a few hours ago, when Faye's labour pains had reached the extreme and she was no longer able to keep quiet, Billy had not stopped with his continuous questions, some of which were completely impossible to answer, to a four-year-old.

Granny Isabel was suddenly aware that there was, at last, an end to Faye's distressing cries; she hurried to the foot of the stairs, cocking her ear until they were filled with that miraculous and heart-warming sound of a baby's first cry. She thanked the Lord for the infant's safe delivery and prayed that all was as it should be with Faye. Billy had left the kitchen and was shadowing his Nanna, with his small hand taking hold of hers,

"Can I 'ave me sausage now Nanna, I'm 'hungry."

A few seconds later, Mrs Swift was hanging her head over the banister, looking quite flushed, but smiling widely. Granny Isabel's heart lifted; she knew that mother and baby were both doing well.

"Could I trouble yer to some more boiled water, Granny, an' per'aps a cuppa fer the mother? It's another boy an' they're both doing splendidly!"

Granny Isabel cried out a whoop of delight," you've gotta little babby brother, Billy!" she declared joyfully.

"Can I go an' see?"

"After yer eats that sausage, lad, now let's go an' wet some tea leaves for yer mamma, I bet she's gasping fer a cuppa Rosy Lee."

As Granny Isabel poured the tea and wrapped the sausage in a thin slice of bread, Rob arrived home; his face was tense with all the signs of an anxious father to be etched upon it. As always, Billy ran to him and Rob hauled him up into his arms, kissing his face and hugging him.

"I gotta brover...Pappa!" he announced eagerly. "Can I go an' see 'im now...an' Mamma?"

Rob's eyes diverted to Granny Isabel, a spontaneous wide smile replacing his worried look.

"Already!" He sounded shocked; he remembered Billy's birth as though it was only a few weeks ago and that had taken nearly twenty-four worrying hours.

"Are yer sure?" he questioned foolishly, causing Granny Isabel to chuckle out loud.

"The new babby was crying Pappa," confirmed Billy.

"Sit down an' 'ave a cuppa Rosie Lee, Lad, the midwife's still up there any 'ow, an' yer don't wanna be getting in *her* way."

"Do yer want some ov me sausage Pappa?"

"Don't fret now Rob, Faye will be thrilled ter bits wiv another boy, an' it might be a girl next time!"

"Steady on Granny Isabel, I ain't even seen the new arrival yet!"

"Ahh that's life lad; I reckon you'll 'ave at least 'alf a dozen, mark me words; take advantage of what the Good Lord Blesses yer wiv, cos if I'd 'ave wed when I was a lass, I'd 'ave wanted as many little uns as would fill me 'ouse. They're the sweetness of life, without a doubt!"

Mrs Swift came bustling down the stairs, her arms full with a large tin load of soiled rags, to be put in the burner. Permission was given for Rob to take Faye a cup of tea.

"Now, I must get me skates on," she stated

urgently," Mrs Maple at number seven is getting ready ter shift 'er heavy load, but it's 'er first so 'appen I might be in fer a long night.
Congratulations Mr Lopez, yer got a fine strong lad, an' yer dear wife is a real star; now yer know where ter find me if yer got any problems."

With Mrs Swift leaving the house like a whirlwind, Granny Isabel, suggested for Rob to go up on his own, while she occupied young Billy for a little longer.

Poised elegantly in their bed, Faye looked tired but radiant as she held the swaddled, sleeping baby in her arms. Rob felt an uncomfortable lump in his throat; he felt euphoric as he viewed the beautiful scene before his eyes. His love for Faye caused his heart to swell; she was the perfect wife and mother and had now given him two adorable sons. He could just glimpse the head of dark hair peeking out from the white blanket, exactly the same as when Billy was born. How had he ever survived through those months of darkness when he'd believed that Faye was not alive? It was a memory which always filled him with despair.

"Another boy! Just like 'is big brover too! Are you alright me darlin', yer ain't too put out that it wasn't a lass this time?"

"Rob! Just take a good look at him, he's gorgeous and now I will have two strapping lads to protect me in this God-forsaken part of the country."

"One day, my sweet wife, we *will* find yer daughter an' we'll find that house in the country that yer pine for...I promise. I love yer Faye, more than you'll ever know."

"I love you too Mr Lopez."

"Let me introduce meself properly to me little lad," he whispered, as he took the small bundle into his arms, looking slightly awkward, but with eyes brimming with adoration. "'E's just perfect, the spitting image ov our darlin' Billy!"

A tiny polite knock on the door amused Faye and Rob, "At least he's given us *five* minutes to ourselves, Rob!" giggled Faye.

"Is that the coalman knocking so late at night, cos if it is, we don't want no coals, ta very much, come back termorrow!" teased Rob.

"I ain't the coalman!" stressed Billy seriously, not quite comprehending his father's joke. "It's me, *Billy Edward Lopez!*"

Rob and Faye's smiling eyes glanced lovingly at each other. "Open the door, Rob, stop teasing the poor lad, he's had a rough day too, being parted from his ma for so long."

Although not too impressed with his new brother who he'd imagined would arrive into the world ready to play games with him, Billy's permanent beaming smile for his mother as he snuggled up close to her was heartwarming. He timidly touched the tiny baby, as though needing to make sure he was real and was shocked by the loudness of his cries.

"What's 'e crying for Mamma?" he asked worriedly.

"'E's 'ungry, Billy," explained Rob.

Billy's eyes lit up, "I didn't eat all ov me sausage, 'e can eat that!"

"Come on Billy lad; let's give yer ma, some peace an' quiet, 'ow 'bout we go down the pie shop, I'm sure yer ma is starvin' too."

"Can we buy me brover some mash?"

Granny Isabel arrived just in time, with some more fresh tea and a healthy slice of cake,

"Did yer see that sweet babby, Billy?"

"Yeah, but he's 'ungry an' being a right sissy *and* 'e ain't got no teeth!"

Granny Isabel threw back her head in fits of laughter, "Well, there's a blessing in there somewhere young Billy, at least 'e won't be after yer dinner!"

Looking somewhat confused, Billy pulled on Rob's hand; he'd seen his ma and had had more than enough of all the fuss which surrounded the new baby and the journey to the pie and mash shop suddenly felt even more appealing. It dawned on Rob and Faye that they'd yet to name their new son and since Faye had spent her entire pregnancy convinced that she'd give birth to a girl, only had girl's names ready; they decided to put their heads together later that evening, on a full stomach.

The following day, Ed insisted on accompanying Rob home from work with a bouquet of expensive, hothouse blooms for Faye, and a bag of mixed sweets for Billy; not forgetting his favourite Granny, who he presented with a small bottle of Medicinal rum. He had also sent a telegram to Harry Fairbanks in Oxford, who had remained a good friend over the years. He was always intrigued by any news of Faye, feeling a strong bond towards the young woman who he'd dragged from the muddy bank all those years ago believing her to have lost her life. With there still being no word or sighting of Delia Fairbanks, Harry had at last accepted the cruel truth of the matter that she must have stopped loving him and would never return to Oxford. He presumed that she must have fled as far away as possible and had decided to devote her life to bringing up Faye Lopez's firstborn. As far as Ed and Rob were concerned though, their search for Delia Fairbanks would never end until, for the sake of Faye, they'd found her first child who would now be six years old. For obvious financial circumstances, it was impossible for Ed and Rob to concentrate exclusively on this search, but their eyes and ears were always peeled for any talk which might possibly draw them nearer to finding her. Shortly after Faye and Rob married, Harry took Harberton Mead off the market. Inspired by Ed's sharp thinking, after he'd fetched far more than expected from the sale of the box of battered and tarnished silver, he'd searched in places which he didn't know existed in the house and had discovered quite a haul of treasure hidden in the attic and various cubby holes in rooms which had seldom been used in the past few decades. It brought him nowhere near as wealthy as in days gone by, but it was a start; he was still in debt to many people but they were rich folk and he hoped that unless their rich worlds suddenly crumbled they wouldn't be in hurry to cash in on Harry's pitiful I owe you notes, which with a little luck, might have been lost or misplaced by now. By closing off most of Harberton Mead, Harry was able to buy a few pieces of essential furniture, second hand of course, but he was increasingly finding the world of buying and selling more interesting and was becoming quite a dab hand in the art of bartering, which he'd also learnt from Ed Hall.

A genuine surge of joy raced through Harry's body, putting a huge smile upon his face when he read Ed's telegram. Dear sweet Faye, she was like his own daughter; he felt there was a strong bond between them and was quite sure that Faye felt the same way too and looked upon him as a father figure. Deciding to take the next train into London, Harry was also elated at the prospect of spending some time with Ed and Rob. He'd buy chocolates for Faye and that sweet old Granny and a small toy for young

Billy, he decided excitedly as he took a quick check on his available cash.

Later that evening after the latest edition to the Lopez family had been shown off and admired and Billy had finally succumbed to tiredness after sitting with the men and feeling very grown-up, Granny Isabel had insisted that they all kept their voices down so as not to disturb the new mother as Harry Ed and Rob, chatted into the small hours. They came to the downhearted conclusion that in the last five years, apart from Rob's growing family, nothing had really changed in their lives. Ed's vision of receiving work from a wealthier clientele after he'd worked on the case involving Harry Fairbanks had not materialized. He and Rob were now the only two working at Hall, Spencer and Lock, and Harry couldn't understand why he'd not changed the name to include Rob's, especially since Spencer and Lock were nonexistent. That evening was the first time too that Harry openly admitted that there was no future for him and Delia and that it was now obvious that she no longer had any feelings for him. He still wanted the search for her to continue though, knowing how important it was to Faye to be united with her firstborn and he also wanted to settle legal matters with Delia and arrange for a divorce. Harry did, however, have an idea that he wanted to put to Ed and Rob, but after witnessing how at home they were, living in the East End, he already doubted that they'd jump at his proposition as he'd imagined. Not wanting to ruin what had been a pleasant and memorable evening, he decided to wait until morning and leave them with something to think about while he travelled back to Oxford.

Faye was sat nursing the baby when Rob eventually tiptoed into the bedroom. Somewhere in the distance they heard a clock strike the hour of three o'clock, it was icy cold and the bedroom fire had died out hours ago. Rob could see his own breath as he exhaled and declared that he was going to fetch some coals and light the fire.

"I'm fine, Rob," insisted Faye. "It's warm under the covers and you'll wake everybody up, going up and down the stairs now!"

"No, I won't, sweetheart, I'll be as quiet as a mouse, I promise." Rob gently stroked the baby's forehead, as he fed hungrily from his mother. "You two need ter keep warm, an' it feels more like the street in this room!"

There was no arguing with Rob, he was, as always, stubborn and so Faye voiced no further objection.

"I've thought of the perfect name for our little darlin'," announced Faye when Rob returned with the coal-scuttle. "Bobby!"

"Bobby!" repeated Rob. "Hmm, but some folks call me Bobby! Won't that be a bit odd?"

"But that isn't *your* name though is it and we

can't be put off by those stupid folk who don't know the difference between Roberto and Bobby!"

"'E does look like a 'Bobby', yeah, it's a good East End name, Faye, I love it. *Bobby Lopez*...falls easily off me tongue too."

CHAPTER THIRTY-THREE

Struggling to wake from her disturbing dream, Faye endeavoured to push off the blankets which were burning her body and making her feel so hot. She opened her eyes to find the room illuminated with ferocious flames, quickly making their destructive journey up the curtains. It had taken barely five minutes for the flames to take hold of the clothes which hung over the back of the chair; leaping high up the walls they rapidly spread across the bedroom, taking hold of everything in their path. Faye opened her eyes in horror; her cry was pitiful against the loud crackling of the fire.

"*Oh Dear God...Rob! Rob! Quickly*, wake up, the house in on fire!"

Rob bolted upright, suddenly feeling the intense heat burning his skin.

Quickly grabbing the baby from out of his crib, Faye yelled at Rob to rescue Billy from his corner of the room, which was divided by a curtain. The curtain was already alight as Rob urgently yanked it down from the ceiling.

"*Mamma, Mamma!*" Screamed Billy, as he was about to jump out of the narrow truckle bed and run towards Faye.

"*Stay there, Billy!*" Hollered Rob as he jumped about frantically, stamping on the blazing curtain, not feeling the searing flames melt the skin on his bare feet and legs and catch his nightgown alight. Billy opened his mouth and screamed continuously until being succumbed by the thick, choking smoke.

"Get out ov 'ere, Faye! I'll bring Billy! Just take the baby an' get out ov the 'ouse."

Harry, who was spending the night in Rob's old box room, had been mulling over how he was going to persuade Ed, Rob and Faye to consider his idea. The sound of the ruckus from the neighbouring bedroom immediately troubled him and as he leapt from his bed and opened the door, he was met by an extremely distraught Faye, dressed only in her nightgown, barefoot and in a state of sheer panic,

"Oh Harry, thank God you're still here...*Rob and Billy are in the bedroom...*" Faye didn't need to continue with her explanation, the billowing smoke and heat escaping from her and Rob's bedroom said it all and within seconds Harry had made a heroic dash through the blazing door frame, promptly returning with Billy in his arms.

"Quick as you can, Faye, evacuate the building and make damn sure you take Granny too!" Harry's sweating face was bright red from the intense heat and streaked with black smoke trails.

"*Rob! Where's Rob!*" cried Faye frantically, with tears streaming down her face.

"Don't worry! He'll be alright but I'll need to

carry him; *now hurry for God's sake!* "

The sound of both children crying so distressingly had already woken Granny Isabel and it didn't take more than a few seconds for her to realise what was going on. The elderly woman had the foresight to grab her life's savings; the blankets off her bed and her jar of biscuits keep to Billy quiet.

The small house took little time before it stood out like a beacon on a foggy night. The immediate neighbours had gathered in the street, some bringing feeble jugs of water with them, which made little difference and merely teased the lofty flames.

"Rob and Harry are still inside!" screamed Faye.

"Pappa!" sobbed Billy; pushing Granny Isabel's tin of biscuits away. *"I want Pappa!"*

One of the neighbours had hurried to the corner of the end house to fetch the escape ladder which was fixed to the wall; the fire wagon had also arrived with the group of firemen, who were all local costermongers and quickly set about using their metal hand pumps in a bid to dampen the flames and surrounding walls to prevent the fire from spreading.

"The staircase 'as been destroyed!" Faye heard one of the firemen yell out. She watched with her hand on her heart as a brave neighbour speedily scurried to the top of the ladder as it leant against the burning house. The window was already open, with Harry just visible through the

smoke; he had Rob slung over his shoulder. He quickly but carefully passed him out to the neighbour. Thankfully he was a tough and muscular dock worker, used to hauling far heavier weights than that of Rob's body. Harry followed behind down the ladder; he was a hero and had saved Rob's life.

Faye held on tight to Billy's hand to prevent him from closely witnessing his pa's terrible burns. Baby Bobby had cried himself back to sleep in Faye's arms and Granny Isabel, who had demanded a pat of butter from one of the neighbours, was rubbing it into Rob's badly burnt legs. Faye felt utterly helpless as she stood with a thick blanket draped around her shoulders. If only she'd stopped Rob from lighting the fire, was all that she could think of as she saw her sheltered world, once again, disappear before her eyes.

"Don't worry Faye," voiced the comforting words of Harry, "I'm sure Rob will be fine in a day or so. He's inhaled plenty of smoke and has burns to his legs, but I'm sure he'll heal in no time, he's young and strong. "

"You saved his life, Harry...we owe so much to you...thank you."

"I only did what any other man would have done, Faye. I'm no hero."

" Oh yes, you are... You have saved both our lives now and that certainly puts you in the highest ranks of a hero in my eyes, I have a good mind to write a letter to Queen Victoria, herself and recommend you for a medal, Mr Fairbanks." Harry had a twinkle in his eye; Faye's kind words had made him feel quite bashful.

"Let me hold on to the children for a while, Faye while you go and give your husband some encouragement."

"Thank you, Harry; I'll be quick, I'm sure Granny Isabel has more medical knowledge than me." Harry took the swaddled baby out of Faye's arms and held Billy's hand. He had become far too quiet and Harry's heart contracted as he viewed the pain in his eyes. The baby began to cry again, obviously sensing that he was no longer in the arms of his mother. It seemed that the only babies he'd ever held, were Faye's, thought Harry.

With the fire at last extinguished, leaving behind a black and smoking skeleton of a house after its ruthless destruction, the kind-hearted and generous neighbours were busy handing out cups of hot sweet tea and making arrangements to accommodate the now, homeless family for the rest of the night. Harry decided to walk to Limehouse and wake Ed up. He felt the urgent need to disclose his plan, even more now, after what had happened to his dear friends during this dismal night.

The night women of Cable Street hung around vacantly, offering their services to any man who happened to cross their path. The brothel near Ed's lodgings was a noisy riotous place; drunkards hollered obscenities at the top of their voices and men brawled unashamedly about trivial matters. It was the human race in its lowest form, thought Harry as he brushed aside a drunk and grotesque looking woman eager to be of service to him. He prayed that Ed was still awake as he rapped loudly upon his door. As luck would have it, Ed had yet to turn in for the night, the sight of Rob's beautiful young family had disturbed him; he realised that at the age of forty-five, he yearned for his own family, he was sick and tired of the loneliness of his bare and unkempt lodgings and wanted to return from work to a smiling wife and a brood of children. He'd had enough of being a bachelor and enough of the lonely life. He suddenly felt the most urgent need for a true and wholesome love, the need for a partner who he could share the rest of his life with and children who would look up to him and show him humility when he reached old age. The heavy knocking on the front door to his lodging house broke his daydreams, bringing him back to reality. It sounded urgent, he thought as he quickly poured the remaining drop of whiskey from his glass down his throat. Harry Fairbanks was the last person he expected to see on his doorstep; his dishevelled state and the strong odour of smoke immediately told Ed that a calamity had taken place.

"Bloody 'ell, 'Arry! What's 'appened?"

Harry stepped over the threshold and followed Ed into his room, where Ed spontaneously poured out two healthy glasses of whiskey. Harry rubbed his brow, his face looked ready to crumble and even though Ed had witnessed his friend in a few predicaments over the years, he'd never before seen such a disconcerting look of alarm in his eyes before this night.

"Sit down, 'Arry, an' get this down yer throat," ordered Ed as he quickly swiped the pile of newspapers and clothes from off the chair.

"Something terrible 'must ave 'appened," stated Ed.

Harry didn't beat about the bush and by the time he'd emptied his glass, he'd also disclosed the evening's events to Ed.

"Thank God that everyone managed ter get out alive. That family seems ter 'ave more than their share ov tragedies...I 'ope Rob ain't too badly burnt."

Harry looked around Ed's room, thinking how little he had for a man of his age.

"I'm sure he'll mend, Ed. But the family is homeless now and poor Granny Isabel's business and home have been reduced to a pile of smouldering ashes."

"How did Granny Isabel seem?" enquired Ed.

"Well, that's the strangest thing, she appeared to take it all in her stride; didn't say a word about losing everything, only jubilant that everyone got out alive and was busy rubbing butter into Rob's legs. Quite a remarkable woman indeed!"

"Ah, she's a true Eastender in every way, is old Granny Isabel. They don't make folk like her no more!"

"Ed, I wasn't going to bring this up until the morning, but in the light of everything that's happened, I feel that now is as good a time as any to make my suggestion to you and please hear me out before you interrupt."

Viewing Harry's serious expression, Ed sensed that what he was about to suggest wasn't a spur of the moment idea, but something which he'd thought about long and hard.

"I promise I won't interrupt 'Arry, but wouldn't yer like ter wash all that soot off yer face first...I feel as though I'm entertaining the coalman! And while yer do that, I'll go an' make us a brew."

Standing up to look into Ed's small shaving mirror, Harry was shocked by his grey streaked face.

"I'm quite surprised that I received a proposition from one of your neighbouring whores, looking like this!" he blurted out.

"Don't let it swell yer head 'Arry, most ov 'em ain't bothered 'bout a man's looks, an' she was most likely in a drunken stupor an' all! Now stop being so bleedin' vein, an' get cleaned up. There's a bowl ov clean water on the dresser!"

It was ten minutes later when Ed returned to the room, with two mugs of steaming hot tea. Harry was sprawled out on his bed, snoring loudly. Smiling to himself, Ed removed Harry's boots, covered him with a blanket, and made himself a makeshift bed on the floor already knowing that what little was left of the night was going to be long, cold and very noisy.

CHAPTER THIRTY-FOUR

"*My dear good friends!*" announced Harry
Fairbanks to the large party, as he sat in the
Whitechapel Road, chophouse at the head of the
conveniently assembled three tables, which had
been pushed together. "Firstly, I'd like to express
my heartfelt and sincere gratitude that you are
all feeling well enough, following last night's
catastrophe, to accept my invitation to this fine
hearty breakfast and I hope that what I am about
to propose, will delight you and be the
beginning of a new way of life for most of us."
Ed, Rob, Faye and even Granny Isabel were all
extremely curious to hear Harry's speech. Billy
sat on the high chair swinging his legs, as he
studied his surroundings trying to see what
others customers in the chophouse had on their
plates. Harry continued, focusing on Rob to
begin with, "My dear friend, Roberto, you are
without doubt, a brave and heroic man and
during any future conversations with young
Billy, when he is old enough to fully understand,
I will explain to him what a brave and selfless
act his father performed in order to save him
from the raging inferno. I pray that you are not
suffering too much pain this morning, my dear
fellow."

Still shaken from the previous night's events,
Rob felt quite the opposite of a hero; he knew
that if it wasn't for Harry's bravery and if he'd

not been staying with them, he and Billy would have perished in the fire, leaving Faye a widow with a young baby to bring up by herself.

"*You* are the real hero, Mr Fairbanks an' once again, I will be indebted to yer for the rest of me life, thank you, from the bottom of me heart!"

Harry smiled bashfully, "Let me continue, I know how hungry we all are, especially young Billy!... I'd like you *all* to move to Oxford and share my home, not just as a dwelling place but as a business too. I think that between Rob, Ed and I, we could create a lucrative business in the field of buying and selling, perhaps specializing in antiques and perhaps fine art."

Harry took a brief break, his throat was still hoarse and sore from the smoke damage and he needed to gulp down a glass of water before continuing, every word he spoke was painful but he was determined to enlighten everyone to his idea. He had managed to bring about complete silence around the table, all apart from Billy, who was becoming more impatient with every passing minute, wishing that the adults would put an end to their talking and allow him to fill his empty belly. Looking pale and tired, Faye held baby Billy in her arms as she mused over Harry's words. The thought of leaving the East End had never appealed to her more than today; she'd visited Harberton Mead and adored it and Oxfordshire was her home. She knew that if Rob was set against Harry's brilliant and generous idea, then she'd do all that was in her power to persuade him otherwise; they were now homeless, and Granny Isabel's place had been like a palace compared to what they might end up living in if they remained in London; she wanted more for her family than growing up in a rat-infested tenement building and watching Rob grow old prematurely as he worked every hour that God sent, in order to earn a mere pittance. The countryside would put colour on their cheeks and healthy flesh upon their bones. Away from poverty and disease, and living at Harberton Mead was far too good an opportunity to decline on account of being born and bred in the East End.

"Let me just explain a little more about my idea, and then we can eat, I promise!" Harry directed his speech towards Billy once again, admiring his exceptionally good behaviour; it would be a pleasure to watch him and his young brother grow up around Harberton Mead, he mused.

"We will divide the house up so that you all have your own living quarters and privacy but we will share the kitchen and one communal room; I was hoping that perhaps the women could take the cooking into their very capable hands. At this point though, I'm not sure how our dear Granny Isabel feels about leaving her lifelong home and friends."

Granny Isabel urgently waved her hand in the air, "Young man, believe me, I will be first in the queue ter leave the squalor an' disease of the East End be'ind me, an' all me friends are sitting right 'ere. Yer words are like the sweet strings of an 'arp upon me old ears!"

Faye was thrilled to hear, Granny Isabel's strong opinion; now they just had to get the menfolk to see sense.

"Well, Granny Isabel you are most welcome and I know that your willingness for change will be a great influence and a fine example for Ed and Roberto! Now, if you'll permit me to continue, I thought that initially we will use part of the stables as a workshop and storage area but I'm quite optimistic that it won't take long before we will be able to lease a more predominant showroom in the High street of Oxford. I know that both Ed and Rob are experts in the world of wheeling and dealing and are familiar with the ways of the auction houses and I have the business and economic expertise. We will all learn from our mistakes, and muddle along as best we can and with all of our joint efforts, I'm sure that we will prove successful."

Harry had given everyone a lot to think about and with Ed now being the only one left with a roof over his head, the decision to take Harry up on his offer seemed like a golden opportunity arriving at the perfect time.

The chophouse was filled with excited chatter and laughter as the new venture was discussed. There were still many unanswered questions but

Harry sensed that at the end of the day, his friends from the East End would be swayed to make the journey to Oxford. Billy was at last rewarded for his patience and given his favourite meal of a plate load of sausages.

"When are we leaving then? Cos I don't fancy another night kipping down on the floor of the Fletcher's draughty hovel, as much as I appreciate their kindness in our time of distress, me an' young Faye got less than 'alf an 'our's kip between us an' 'ave now got the stiff joints an' aching backs ter prove it." Granny Isabel was in fine fighting form, having already decided that like Faye, this was a marvellous opportunity and the answer to all their problems.

Ed and Rob, however, were more dubious about Harry's plans and felt they needed more time and a private meeting with him, away from the womenfolk. There were a dozen or more questions which were on both their minds and they weren't prepared to up and leave the East End on a mere whim. So it was decided, that for the time being, Ed would temporarily close Hall, Spencer and Lock and that between the modest office and his lodgings everyone would move in and make do until their final decision had been made. Harry was to spend the rest of the day, before returning to Oxford with Ed and Rob in their office, answering all of their questions and listening to their suggestions. There was also the question of what if Delia Fairbanks should decide to return home to her husband one day, but Harry assured them, that even if she did, she had no claim on Harry or his property since she had deserted him; Harry told of how he intended to appoint a lawyer to start the proceeds of a divorce as soon as his financial situation improved. Knowing how Faye and Granny Isabel were both eager to move to Harberton Mead, Harry was relieved that it was only Rob and Ed who had to be convinced; women could be very stubborn when they were dead set against something. Harry suggested that Ed should continue to pay the rent on his office and lodgings for another two months, by which time the new business would hopefully be showing signs of its success, and then Ed and Rob could make the ultimate decision of where they wanted to live and work. It was a good idea, thought Ed and gave them all a safety net, even though Rob and his family would be without a home should they decide to return, but that was a bridge they'd cross if the need arose. Rob and Ed were conservatively excited about the new venture and they did have a soft spot for Harry's beautiful home in Oxford and sometimes, they both concluded by the end of the meeting, a risk and a change in life were worth chancing.

By the end of the day, Harry had left London and Faye and Granny Isabel had turned Ed's lodgings into a comfortable place to sleep, considering it only proper that Rob and Ed should sleep in the office for the time being. Faye was exhausted; so much had taken place since she'd given birth and with all the stress, Granny Isabel warned Rob and Ed that the poor young woman needed bed rest for at least two days, with good food and nothing at all to worry her head about. Rob and Ed were in agreement and listened obediently to Granny Isabel's words of wisdom. They had a plan, and so after Rob had made sure that Faye had everything she needed, he left her sleeping soundly in Ed's bed, with Billy on the table next to her in one of Ed's empty drawers, they took Billy with them and travelled across the Thames and into West London, where, although there were fewer pawn shops which were far more expensive, there were fine and clean clothes to be found. Everything had been lost during the fire, but although the generous neighbours had donated a few necessary items, Granny Isabel insisted that they all purchased a few sets of finer clothes to wear when they turned up in Oxford.

"We don't want that posh lot down in Oxford thinking that they're too fancy fer the likes of us, now do we? an' we don't wanna start a flea outbreak in that nice Mr Fairbanks' 'ome by clothing ourselves out from them pawn shops 'round our neck ov the wood!" expressed Granny Isabel as she marched along the clean pavements of St James, clutching hold of Billy's hand.

"You're quite right, as always Granny Isabel, I reckon we all need ter learn 'ow ter speak proper too, if we're gonna be living in Oxford," suggested Rob.

"Well yer need ter take more notice ov Faye, then, cos she speaks right proper. At least I can put on a posh sounding voice if I need ter!" Ed stated, proudly.

Rob and Granny shared a sly smile; it never failed to amuse them when Ed spoke in his '*posh*' accent.

"Well 'appen we should pay more attention to you Ed Hall, wiv yer fancy ways," joshed Granny Isabel.

The sign displayed on the double-fronted window read, '*London's Finest second-hand clothing*', there were already a couple of customers inside of the well-stocked shop; Granny Isabel peered through the tiny square leaded windows, squinting her eyes.

"Reckon they might 'ave all we need in 'ere, lads!"

"Reckon this place is just full ov fancy petticoats an' the likes," said Rob, as he joined Granny Isabel, sticking his head close to a window.

"Why don't we 'ave a wander, while you go an' buy what yer need, Granny? Me an' Rob can meet yer 'ere later," Ed suggested as he took a handful of silver coins from his pocket.

"That's a grand idea, but yer can keep yer money

though, ta very much...I got me own, yer know," exclaimed Granny Isabel proudly.

"Yeah, Ed, Granny Isabel was quick thinking enough ter save 'er jar ov savings from the fire."

"Well even so, I'd like ter contribute," insisted Ed.

"Oh, go on then, if it makes yer happy!"

"Am I gonna get new clothes too?" Billy joined in, feeling as though he'd been forgotten.

"Ov course you are, me little darlin', yer ma won't recognise yer, you'll look so smart. Now you lads come back 'ere in an 'our, an' don't be late, cos I ain't so familiar wiv this part of London."

"You be a good lad fer yer Granny, now Billy, d'yer 'ear?" warned Rob.

"I will, Pappa, I promise."

As Ed and Rob strolled blindly, deep in conversation about their future in Oxford, they soon found themselves in Grosvenor Square. Due to the gloomy skies and threat of rain, the public garden in the centre of the square, was deserted. It was bleak at this time of year, but the wrought iron seats seemed to call out to Rob. "Let's go an' sit in there," he suggested. "Me feet are fair killing me an' I don't think I can walk another step without resting 'em fer a while."

"I should 'ave insisted that yer stayed at 'ome wiv Faye," said Ed, solemnly.

"What's going on over there? Ain't that where that bleedin' cove, *Dagworth* lives," exclaimed Rob, as he viewed a trail of men and women entering the house. Ed stretched his neck to see over the bushes, which surrounded the perimeter of the garden.

"Yeah, yer right there, Rob, that *is* the famous Lyle Dagworth's place, d'yer reckon yer can make it over there, or d'yer wanna wait 'ere, while I take a better look?"

"No, I'm coming wiv yer, this looks too good ter miss, reckon there's some kind ov sale goin' on inside."

Rob's presumption had proved correct and there was, in fact, a house contents sale taking place. They stepped over the threshold and mingled with the many dealers and inquisitive neighbours who filled every room. Lot numbers were attached to almost every removable item inside the house in preparation for the auction, which was to take place later, in the afternoon.

"Reckon 'e must have snuffed it then," whispered Rob.

"Yeah, that'll please our dear 'Arry, that's fer sure."

"D'yer reckon 'e wrote it down anywhere, that Harry Fairbanks owes 'im a hundred guineas?"

"Don't be a daft bugger, Rob, that bleedin' pompous ass was loaded; just get an eye full ov all these priceless treasures. And now he's under the ground, probably laying next ter that crazy

wife ov 'is, an' 'aving ter spend the rest ov
eternity listening to 'er crying."

"Ah, that's pretty sad, ain't it, Gov! That man 'ad
everything in 'is life except fer a child, an' ter
think that if 'Arry's wife 'adn't left 'im when she
did, all this would belong ter Faye's firstborn."

"Ain't yer forgetting, though; if Mrs Dagworth
was given the baby, she might not 'ave thrown
'erself out of the window as she did, all them
years ago," corrected Ed.

"No matter what though, it would 'ave all
belonged to 'er eventually."

"Makes yer think though, don't it, that as much
as we all spend our lives trying ter get rich,
money don't make yer happy...it's family, loved
ones an' dear friends, they're the real honey ov
life."

"Reckon being under this roof 'as done
something to yer brain, Gov; that don't sound
like the Ed Hall, I know, talking!"

"Let's get out ov 'ere Rob, this place is making
me feel right ill."

"We should take a little keepsake; a gift fer 'Arry,
what d'yer say?"

"*Bloody daft bugger*, I ain't coming back 'ere again
this afternoon, the sooner we get back 'ome the
better."

A monogrammed cigar cutter caught Rob's eye
as they made their way out of Lyle Dagworth's
study: it was calling out to him and although
he'd not stolen anything since he was a young

boy and only then as a necessity to survive, he stealthily swiped the cutter off the shelf and pocketed it.

Looking extremely delighted for someone who'd so recently lost her home and business, Granny Isabel was waiting with Billy outside of the shop when they returned. Stood next to them was a pile of neatly wrapped parcels. Billy was jubilant and dressed in a warm and extremely smart new jacket and munching on a piece of sweet candy.

"I reckon, that out ov all ov us, Granny Isabel is the most excited about our new life," whispered Ed as they neared the shop.

CHAPTER THIRTY-FIVE

It was a week later, during the first week of December that Rob and Faye, together with their two sons and Ed and Granny Isabel arrived at Oxford Railway station, all smartly turned out in their new second-hand attire to be greeted, enthusiastically, by an overly excited Harry Fairbanks. He had purchased an old horse which still had a couple of working years left in her and had, with his own hands and much to his own astonishment repaired and painted the rusty old horse cart which had been discarded in his disused stables for many years. The entire party was euphoric, eager to begin their new lives and all determined to do their best to make Harry's idea work. It was the first time that Granny Isabel had been to Harberton Mead and although Faye had described the outstanding house to her, Granny's imagination failed to conjure up such a picture; she had spent her entire life in the East End and although she spoke little of her early life, it was clear to everyone that she'd always considered herself to be most privileged to be living in her tiny dwelling in Wentworth Street.

"That's never one 'ouse, it can't be. It's bigger than the bloomin' Palace!" declared Granny Isabel as they turned off the main thoroughfare at the foot of Headington Hill, bringing the

impressive Harberton Mead house into sight.
"Oh, Granny!" laughed Faye, as she lovingly
linked arms with her, "I assure you it's nowhere
near as immense as the Queen's Palace."
"Well the sight of that grand building has
certainly filled me eyes and even made me
forget 'ow bloomin' nippy it is terday; reckon
there's frost in the air. I hope ter God that I won't
get lost in there!"
By the time the wagon came to a standstill at the
front of the house, Granny Isabel had everyone
laughing at her sudden, amusing outbursts; she
had become like a young child, as she viewed
her new surroundings. Her eyes had never seen
such a vast space and she'd never, in all her life,
lived anywhere where the houses weren't
packed tightly together and overcrowded. The
vastness of the surrounding fields and the sight
of the grazing Longhorn cows caused her jaw to
drop; for a brief moment she was speechless and
Faye detected tears in her aged eyes. Billy, who
had fallen asleep in his father's arms, awoke as
soon as the horse's gentle motion came to an
end, his excitement and the immediate barrage
of questions made up for Granny Isabel's silence.
"I do believe that the very old and the very
young have much in common!" whispered
Harry, jokingly, into Ed's ear.
"Yer quite right there, 'Arry, but they're also the
sweetest of folk!"
"That's indeed very true, my dear fellow; now

there is much to be done and I dare say you are all hungry and exhausted after your long journey, not to mention having had to endure sleeping in improvised beds since the night of the fire, so I suggest, that women and children head straight for the house, while we unload and unhitch the nag!"

Harry then suddenly jumped down from the horse-cart, holding up his hand in order to gain everyone's immediate attention,

"I would just like to say, welcome to your new home, where I hope you will all be very happy and where are futures will be filled with health, wealth and contentment!"

It was later during that evening when everyone had eaten and now knew which room or in the case of Rob and Faye, rooms, were theirs that Rob surprised Harry by giving him the cigar cutter. Harry turned the small silver gadget over in his hand, the engraved letters, *L.D.* immediately flooded his head with memories of the night when he'd first become acquainted with Lyle Dagworth. He felt a sickening feeling in his gut and a black and dismal cloud seemed to overshadow him, transporting him to the darkest of places.

"How did you come by this Roberto?" he questioned abruptly, bringing Ed and Faye out of their peaceful mood as they relaxed in the drawing-room.

"Well, there was an auction, at Dagworth's place,

reckon 'e must 'ave snuffed it; everything was being sold off. Don't think yer need ter worry 'bout that debt yer owes 'im anymore neither."

Harry looked troubled, "Thank you Rob, but I can't take this, in fact, everything about *that cad, Dagworth* sends an uncomfortable chill through my body; I wish to forget about him forever. It was, without a doubt, a wretched day when our paths had the misfortune of crossing. He was a conniving maggot of a man and not, as many considered him to be, a gentleman."

The atmosphere for the rest of the evening was strained; Rob felt as though he'd committed the most terrible crime and Ed, knowing that Rob had stolen the memento kept quiet but issued Rob with a look of warning, assuring him that he'd not heard the end of the matter. Shortly afterwards, Faye took herself off to bed, announcing that she could hear little Bobby whimpering upstairs. Rob quickly followed, leaving Ed to smooth out any bad feelings, which he'd caused.

"The lad meant no 'arm, 'Arry, 'e's young an' thought that 'e was doing a good thing, a bit like you folk when yer goes off hunting an' hang some poor stag's head on yer wall. It was bought for you as a kind ov trophy, that's all."

Harry stared into the distance, with the same vague expression upon his face.

"I realise that now, Ed, but there was nothing in my power to prevent my spontaneous reaction from causing me to behave as I did. It seemed to bring that ghastly period in my life rushing back like a flooded river. Memories of Dagworth and his snivelling, eccentric wife but worst of all, the reminder that I was actually prepared to sell them Faye's precious baby. How could I have been so cold and insensitive, what right did I presume I had to sell a helpless, innocent baby, Ed? Did I actually have a heart in those days?"

"Now yer being too 'ard on yerself, 'Arry and fergetting that six years ago, yer didn't even know Faye, in fact, like many folk, yer were convinced that she'd left this world; ov course you 'ad a heart. You 'ave *the best ov hearts*, 'Arry otherwise you wouldn't 'ave even bothered ter bring that little baby inter yer 'ome, an' yer certainly wouldn't be bringing us lot from the East End ter share yer 'ome an' life wiv yer!"

"You are a good fellow, Ed, and I'm a man who is still consumed with guilt!" cried Harry, his voice edgy.

"There yer go, that proves what I said is true; yer do 'ave a heart, cos if yer didn't, yer wouldn't feel the slightest twinge of guilt!"

"Maybe, maybe, but I know that until I have successfully united Faye with her daughter, I will live my life beneath the darkness of a shadow."

Ed poured out a glass of whiskey and gave him a reassuring tap on his shoulder, "Reckon we gotta think a bit more 'arder ov a way ter find

Mrs Fairbanks, then."

"Yes, my dear fellow, tonight I've realised that it is a problem which must be resolved before I can expect to endure any true happiness in my life again; guilt is a most disagreeable feeling, Ed."

"Well, at least you've got one less person ter worry 'bout, now."

"Have I?" quizzed Harry, looking confused.

"*Dagworth*, ov course; doubt anyone will bother ter take notice ov an I owe you, besides, who's ter say that yer ain't already settled it?"

"Ah yes, *Lyle Dagworth*, excuse my absent-mindedness, it has been a long but exciting day and high time I turned in for the night, but I'm looking forward to tomorrow and the first day of our new venture. By the way, Ed old fellow, what do you think about, '*Fairbanks, Hall and Lopez; dealers in furniture and fine art*'?"

Ed rubbed the back of his bald head, "It's a bit ov a mouthful, but at least everyone will be pleased, including me."

"Should we add *Butler* too?"

"*Stone the bleedin' crows, 'Arry!* I never thought the day would come when I'd be telling *you* not get be a *daft bugger!* Faye is a *Lopez* now, why not add Granny too, though I ain't got a clue as to what 'er full name is!"

Harry laughed, Ed had already succeeded in cheering him up, "Thanks, Ed, you are indeed an inspiration and have already managed to shift my depression. Perhaps Granny Isabel has forgotten her full name."

"Well that will be the first question for her ears in the morning, now turn that lantern out, we don't want any more fires; Good night, 'Arry."

"Good night, Ed, and God bless you, my dear fellow."

In the small hours of the icy cold morning, Faye was sat up in bed listening to the unfamiliar sounds of her strange new surroundings while little Bobby worked up a sweat as he suckled vigorously, satisfying his hunger; Faye couldn't take her eyes from him; he filled her with contentment and a special love; unique between mother and child, which knew no boundaries; she smiled as the tiny drops of sweat collected on his brow, he was going to be as greedy as his older brother thought Faye. The sudden realisation that her firstborn, her darling, daughter had spent her first few days under the very same roof infused Faye with an overpowering urgency to hold and kiss her. She had missed all of those special days of babyhood which were now gone forever. The very thought pained her and sent an urgent feeling of longing through her entire being. She wondered if she *was* still with Harry's estranged wife and if she still went by the name of Faye Butler; tears rolled down her cheeks, dripping on to Bobby's face, he carried on with his feed, dozing off intermittently, but not letting go of his mother's breast. She pictured an image of her daughter; she would be six years old now and Faye already knew that she had fair hair like her own, quite a contrast from her dark-haired sons. Faye hoped that she'd not taken after her loathsome father in any way, as she said a prayer to be united with her again one day soon before her childhood had been completely outgrown.

Billy was the first to wake up; filling every room with his shrills of delight. All through the night, the softly falling snowflakes had blanketed the land and as far as the eye could see it had transformed the world into a bed of glistening whiteness. Billy had never before viewed such a vast expanse of snow; the previous winter he had played with the children out in the street when it had snowed, but in the crowded, dirty streets of the East End it took little time before the snow lost its purity, becoming contaminated with the grime and horse droppings which lay beneath it. The drastic change of weather, however, put an end to the planned working day, at Harberton Mead, but was the perfect opportunity for everyone to let down their hair and spend the day sledging, snowballing and building a huge snowman. Faye watched from the window as she nursed Bobby; pleased that the snow had fallen when it did, giving everyone the chance to have some fun and see another side to Harry Fairbanks. For the first time since the night of the fire, Billy had, at last, become a playful young four year old again and stopped his fretting.

It took another ten days before the temperatures lifted and the thaw set in; ten days where work had temporarily been forgotten. The arrangements inside the house had now been completed with everyone pleased with their rooms, although there was a list of furniture requirements which needed to be purchased and Granny Isabel and Faye had compiled a long list of groceries on a larger scale than they would normally have purchased when living in Wentworth Street. Granny Isabel felt as though she was now living in the middle of nowhere. There wasn't a nearby corner shop or a handy costermongers wheeling his barrow along the road here in Oxford and even though Faye constantly tried to assure her that they were just a ten-minute ride to the city and there were a couple of grocery shops in the nearby villages of Marston and Headington, both within easy walking distance when the weather became more clement, Granny wasn't yet convinced.

It took a couple of difficult months before Ed and Rob had managed to buy and refurbish enough furniture to make any clear profits and only just enough to allow the newly founded company to stay above water. It caused a nervous atmosphere within Harberton Mead with everyone living in fear that the business would collapse before it had even had the chance to get off the ground. Granny Isabel was the only optimist amongst them, she had already decided that if furniture and fine arts failed, she and Faye could bake enough pies to start their own East End pie shop in the heart of Oxfordshire. Faye, however, didn't share her optimism.

Through their travels around Oxford, Ed had met a retired cabinet maker; John Wick had regrettably sold his business in Bicester a few years ago in order to spend his twilight years on an extended holiday in the Scottish Highlands, but without any warning, his wife, who he'd considered to be a picture of health, suddenly collapsed and died a week before their planned departure. John Wick was delighted when Ed had suggested that he could join them at Harberton Mead; after living alone since becoming a widower, companionship and feeling useful again were more appealing than any money he could earn. Harry was in favour of the idea too, and John Wick soon became an important member of the team and a real favourite with Granny Isabel.

CHAPTER THIRTY-SIX

By the summer of 1864, the newly founded company had become an eminent household name for folk wishing to purchase good quality second-hand furniture at reasonable prices. Collectors of fine art and antiques were also frequent callers to the converted stables adjacent to Harberton Mead house. The path ahead was taking on a rosy glow and with the added glorious summer weather; everyone at Harberton Mead was in high spirits. The house had now been fully furnished, most of which were items refurbished by Ed, Rob and the extremely gifted John Wick. While Faye and Granny took care of most of the cooking and the running of the house, it was only Ed and Rob who paid a weekly minimal sum from their earnings to Harry for their rooms. The house ran like clockwork and although the underlying personal problems had not yet been tackled, they had not been forgotten, especially by Harry. It was a balmy August morning when Faye decided she'd take the cart into Oxford's market and purchase half a dozen hens and a rooster; she couldn't understand why Harry had never kept his own brood of chickens before, there was certainly enough space. Rob and John Wick had already constructed a strong fox proof coop at the rear of the house with Billy's expert help; he was as excited as Granny about the arrival of the newcomers and it had become a new breakfast ritual for Billy and Granny to debate over names for the hens with the list growing daily. Granny stayed at home, complaining of how sitting under the scorching sun all morning would bring on one of her headaches, but Billy, behaving like the perfect little gentleman, accompanied his ma and sat proudly, up high, on the horse cart, quite pleased that Granny was going to take care of his sissy brother for the morning. Now a chubby nine-month-old, Bobby was generally a happy baby providing he had a full belly, he was of a larger build than Billy, which Faye put down to the healthy country air. Like Billy, he adored his Granny Isabel and only had to make the tiniest of voices to bring her running to his side.

"Look Ma, there's that old man again!" exclaimed Billy as he pointed to the, now familiar, heavily built man who quite often stood leaning against the dry stone wall, glaring up at the house.

"Shush, Billy, he'll hear you and stop pointing too, that's very rude you know!"

"Pappa said we're not allowed to disturb him, he said that he's troubled…what does that mean, Ma? Is he a *baddie* man?"

"Maybe he has had a sad life and wants to be left alone, Billy, now tell me, what are your favourite names which you and Granny have chosen for our hens," urged Faye, wanting to distract Billy as they passed by the stranger. The odd man had first shown up in June. He could quite often be seen standing in what appeared to be his favourite spot, looking up towards Harberton Mead, but whenever Harry, Ed or Rob attempted to approach him, with the sole purpose of introducing themselves and to enquire after his welfare; he hastily rushed off in the opposite direction. Ed had asked around locally, discovering that the stranger had recently moved into a cottage at the top of Headington Hill, but kept himself to himself. He was regarded as a recluse who was, apparently, not short of money. Twice a day, at lunchtime and again in the evening a hansom cab would collect him and bring him back to his home again a couple of hours later; an inquisitive neighbour had quizzed the cab driver as to where his mysterious journeys took him every day and was informed that he went to dine in the Clarendon Hotel, explaining why he was such a generously proportioned man.

Gently encouraging the horse to break into a trot, the stranger didn't attempt to hurry away as he normally did, but oddly enough, he bowed his head slightly in polite acknowledgement of Faye. For a split second, she was tempted to stop and speak to him, but the sudden remembrance of the evil Reverend Glover reminded her of how devious and untrustworthy men could be, sending an instant rush of goosebumps across her skin.

With the fine summer weather, the Oxford market was bustling with costermongers and farmers. The air was aromatic with the copious mouthwatering varieties of provisions which were for sale; the cries of the costermongers as they shouted their prices, all competing against one another was deafening. Wooden pens, holding sheep, goats, cows and pigs, prompted Billy to squeal with joy, he'd never seen so many animals together in one small space before and wanted to touch every single one of them. Faye, however, was in a hurry to return; should Harry decide to go out, then Granny Isabel and Bobby would be alone in the house. The mere thought caused Faye to become anxious whilst the stranger was lurking around near Harberton Mead.

"Come along, Billy, let's choose some lovely hens to take home and I want you to pick out the most handsome cockerel. Then, we will buy some butter, cheese and eggs, a bag of sweets for my favourite boy, and hurry home to Granny and Bobby."

"Can we buy them some sweets too, mamma?"

"We will buy dear Granny Isabel some of her favourite Queen cakes and a quarter a pound of her favourite Damson drops, and you, my precious can have some marshmallows!"

Billy's eyes lit up, "Can you buy me a sausage too; I'm a *little* bit hungry," he timidly pleaded.

"*Goodness me*, Billy Lopez, you only finished your breakfast two hours ago! "

"Granny says that I'm a growing boy!"

"Hmmm, does she?" laughed Faye.

After a minor dispute, with Billy failing to understand why they couldn't purchase six of the brightly coloured cockerels, rather than the dull, brown hens, Faye convinced him that the beautiful cockerels were far too noisy in the mornings and after he'd heard how much '*cocka-doodle-doo-ing*' one colourful chicken would make, he'd be happy with the peaceful brown hens. It was only the bribe of a sausage which convinced him to agree with his ma. As soon as the cart was loaded up with the livestock and supplies, they made their journey back to Harberton Mead.

Relieved to find that the stranger was no longer hanging around, Faye had a fleeting image of him sat inside the hotel dining room, consuming plate loads of victuals; he was certainly built like a house.

The scorching midday sun was becoming unbearable; Faye panicked as she remembered the farmer's stern instructions that the chickens needed plenty of water, especially in the current heat.

"Hello," she called out as she arrived at the back of the house, near the stables. Ed came out immediately looking as hot and as flustered as Faye felt.

"Faye!" he exclaimed, always pleased to see her, "did yer 'ave a successful morning at the market, then?"

"Yes, but these poor birds, are in desperate need of water before they perish!

Billy climbed down from the cart and ran in through the back door, reappearing seconds later, struggling to carry the full jug of water in his small hands as it spilt over his legs and feet. He sensed his mother smiling proudly at his quick action.

"Well done Billy, good boy! Now, let's get these poor creatures out of their cramped pens so they can quench their thirst!"

Billy furtively took a gulp of water from the metal jug, as Ed and Faye released the squawking birds, which didn't appear as thirsty as Faye had feared; they immediately began scratching and pecking at the dry ground, amusing Billy as he sat down to study the latest arrivals to Harberton Mead.

"That man was down by the wall again this morning, did *you* see him, Ed?"

Ed shook his head, slowly; Faye couldn't help but notice the look of worry on his face.

"Who is that bleedin' cove, an' what the hell does he want with us?"

"Do you think that he might be one of Harry's old enemies?"

"That's what I thought, but 'Arry said that 'e don't recognize 'im,"

"I was going to speak to him, but I lost my nerve."

"I wish e' would give one of us the chance ter speak...'e always does a runner whenever me, Rob or 'Arry try approaching 'im."

"Where is Rob, by the way?"

"Gone down ter Cowley Road ter pick up some bits an' bobs that an old lady is getting rid ov...belonged to 'er late 'usband who passed on over fifteen years ago, apparently, but she's only just got 'round ter parting wiv 'em."

"Ah, that's very sad...*Oh my goodness*, I must go and check on little Bobby; I hope he's been a good boy for poor Granny!"

" You go on in Faye, an' I'll unload this lot, I wouldn't worry 'bout Granny, she's never 'appier than when she's wiv those fine boys ov yours!"

The following week, the news that a large estate near, Chipping Norton was being closed down with much of its contents to be auctioned, reached the attention of Harry; it was the perfect opportunity that they'd been waiting for and would make a huge difference to their business if they could purchase a large bulk of the items. The family who'd lived there for more than five generations had finally given in to the struggle of maintaining the grand Estate and with there not being a successor in the family to inherit, the now elderly couple had taken the decision to dramatically downsize. Harry, Ed and Rob were euphoric, it was just what they needed to lift the business even more, but it all rested on whether or not Harry could convince the bank to lend him the funds needed for such a large purchase. Since his financial ruin six years ago, Harry had had little to do with the bank and although he was now bringing in money on a regular basis, he banked it all at home in his newly acquired safe and had closed his bank account. The likelihood of the bank lending him any funds wasn't looking good, but ever the optimist he was determined to give it his best shot.

Later that day, Harry's forlorn face told everybody the disappointing news as he returned from Oxford. After all the excitement and anticipation, they were back to square one. Sensing his sombre mood, Billy snuggled up next to him on the couch as ways were discussed as to how they could raise some quick funds, "Why is your face cross, Uncle Harry? I've still got one marshmallow left if you want it." Billy pulled out the paper bag from his pocket; the sweet had melted and was stuck to the bag. Harry smiled, as he tousled Billy's hair; he adored this cute lad as though he was his own. "You are a very kind boy, Billy, but I think you should have that one, as it's your last and since they are your favourite and I'm not cross Billy, only annoyed with the *stuffy old bank manager* who won't let me borrow some money."

Turning Harry's words over in his head, Billy decided that his ma's suggestion to feed the chickens sounded like the perfect escape from the grownup's glum chatter.

"Uncle Harry, I have to go and feed our chickens now," he announced, skipping towards the door.

Outside, Billy discovered that John Wick was already feeding the chickens with the crusts of his sandwich. He ran up to him, hoping that he'd share some bread with him.

"Why don't you eat the crusts, Mr Wick, Granny says that they make your hair curly!"

John Wick chuckled, "Look at my head, young Billy, you can count my strands of hair on your fingers...think I'd look a tad silly if they were curly, don't you?"

"Is *that* why you don't eat them?"

"That's one reason, young Billy, but these noisy girls have been shouting at me all morning for a few crumbs of Granny Isabel's tasty bread!"

"Uncle Harry is very sad and a bit cross too," Billy blurted out, as he joined John Wick in feeding the hens.

"Is he indeed? Is that why nobody has left the house to come and do some work?"

"I think so...Uncle Harry said that the man in the bank was *stuffy*...is that a bad word, Mr Wick?" Billy never failed to entertainment John Wick with his boyish innocence.

"Here, I've got a pocket full of breadcrumbs that

you can feed to those greedy hens."

"I'm not sure which one is, Queenie and which one is Dorcus, but that one with the biggest crown on her head is definitely Rosie. What d'you think I should call the others and the cockerel, Mr Wick?"

"How about you give that cockerel, a good strong name like Arthur or Henry?"

Billy looked serious as he considered John Wicks' suggestion, "I'd best ask Granny first, else she might be cross with me. Thank you, Mr Wick."

Throwing the handful of breadcrumbs in the direction of the hens, Billy ran off towards the house already calling out to Granny Isabel in his enthusiasm.

CHAPTER THIRTY-SEVEN

"Can I have a world in private Harry?" requested John Wick, as the men eventually emerged from the house; Ed and Rob were ready to get back to the workshop and Harry had been dragged out by Billy, who insisted on taking him to see the chickens.

 "Of course you can, my good man, just give me a minute while I become more acquainted with our new feathered members of the family!" John Wick couldn't hold his excitement a second longer and he didn't mind Billy's young ears hearing what he was about to propose to Harry, "I hope you won't think that I've been sticking my nose in on matters which are none of my concern, Mr Fairbanks, but I couldn't help but overhear how the bank manager refused your loan request, earlier today. I'd like to help. I have eighty pounds sitting in the bank, doing very little and I'd be honoured if you'd accept a loan from me. You can repay me whenever you are able to. I know it will make a great difference to the business if you can purchase some of those grand items over at the sale in Chipping Norton".

Harry was taken by complete shock; he eyed Billy, knowing full well that the young rascal had been talking to John Wick and telling him about his trip to the bank; he'd have to be careful of what he disclosed in front of the boy in the future. But, in view of the outcome of his careless chatter, Harry could feel nothing but delight and showed even more enthusiasm when Billy chatted away about each individual hen.

"My dear fellow, you have brought a great deal of goodness to our young and growing business and I can't thank you enough for all of your expertise, but this most generous offer is truly appreciated more than you can imagine. Are you quite sure that you're ready to risk investing your life's savings into the business, John?"

Up until the day when Ed had asked him if he would like to take on some work at Harberton Mead, John Wick hadn't seen a day's happiness since his wife had passed away, he could never have anticipated that he'd do another day's work after selling his own business. He simply presumed that he'd while away his days in loneliness waiting for the inevitable to take place. Working at Harberton Mead had given his life a whole new meaning, he felt useful once again and embraced the company of his new fellow-workmen; he enjoyed his chats with Granny Isabel, Faye and especially young Billy, who never failed to put a smile upon his face with his amusing antics and funny conversations; he was beginning to feel like part of this unconventional family.

"I'm more than *quite sure*, Mr Fairbanks..."

"Oh please, call me Harry, John...you are a fully-fledged member of our business now and I'm not just saying that because you have made such a generous offer. Your workmanship is sublime and quite honestly, it's mostly down to your finishing touches that we've sold so many items of furniture."

"Thank you, Harry, but you have in return given me a new life...I can't thank you enough and it's an honour and the greatest of pleasures to work here. I will go immediately to the bank and make the necessary arrangements." John felt as though he'd grown two feet taller all of a sudden as he listened to Harry's compliments; he felt youthful again, as though he'd been given a new lease of life and he had the oddest of feelings that his new adventure at Harberton Mead was only just beginning.

"Splendid, come to my study as soon as you return, I will draw up a repayment plan, with interest of course; these matters of finance must be attended to properly."

Harry peered down at young Billy, giving him one of his stern looks, "Now young man; you and I need to have a little chat about *not* listening in on the adult's conversations!"

"Don't be too harsh on the lad, Mr Fairba...Harry; he does wonders at lifting everyone's spirits with his comical antics!" pleaded John Wick.

Harry ruffled Billy's hair, as he viewed his

worried look, "Come on Billy, let's talk *chickens!*"

Thankfully when the day of the sale at Chipping Norton arrived, two days later, the recent soaring temperature had taken a plunge, making everyday life at Harberton Mead more bearable and everyone less snappy. With constant nagging, Billy had persuaded Rob to allow him to go along on the journey, much to the relief of Faye, who'd been feeling under the weather for a couple of days. It was still early days, but she was keeping her suspicions, that she was with child again, strictly to herself for the time being, but her morning dash to the bathroom was as good a confirmation as any.

They set off in the wagon immediately after breakfast for the twenty-mile journey. Granny Isabel and Faye had prepared a huge hamper of food and drinks, with Granny's main concern being that little Billy might become extra hungry on such a long journey.

With most of the morning chores completed and Bobby taking his morning nap, Granny's sharp eyes had detected how weary and pale, Faye was looking and she insisted that she should join Bobby for a nap, while she busied herself in her search through every cupboard and drawer for jars which could be used for the pickling and preserving of the fruits from the forthcoming harvest. Not wanting to lay in bed, Faye took to the rocking chair on the veranda, relishing in the

cooler breeze which wafted up the hill, gently
blowing her fair ringlets which had escaped
from her bun. It took little time before she
noticed the familiar sight of the stranger; as
usual, he was leaning against the dry stone wall,
looking up towards the house. A strong feeling
of panic immediately took away Faye's
weariness; all the men had gone out for the day
and she wondered if he'd watched them leave.
Only last week, Rob had spoken to Constable
Morris about the man, but he'd merely told him
that there was no law against leaning on a wall.
She had to keep vigilant and watch his every
move in case he decided to approach the house;
Granny Isabel would be as useful as little Bobby
if brute force was needed, mused Faye as she sat
up straight, her eyes fixed firmly ahead of her. A
new wave of nausea washed over her. Her
hands were sweating and all she could think of
was The Reverend Glover...what if it was *him*, it
had been over five years since she'd last seen
him and as far as she could remember, this
stranger was probably about the same height.
She wished now that she'd kept in touch with
Mrs Glover, the occasional correspondence
would have kept her informed as to The
Reverend's whereabouts and his state of mind if
nothing else, but after leaving Woodstock, she
wanted to put that dismal episode of her life
completely out of her mind; as much as she felt
sorry for Mavis Glover, writing to her would

only bring back all of those nightmarish recollections.

Five, ten and twenty minutes passed by and he hadn't moved an inch; standing like a stone statue, motionless, Faye wondered if he even blinked an eye. There was no denying it, Faye was scared; especially as she'd now convinced herself that he *was* Barnaby Glover, maybe still intent on making her his bride. She shivered, her hands were clammy. More than anything, she wished that one of the men had stayed behind. With the passing of another five minutes, Faye's fear turned to anger; this man was ruining her day and one way or another, she had to get to the bottom of the matter; after all, she tried to reassure herself, he might just be an old man who held some kind of precious memories of Harberton Mead in his heart, perhaps he'd worked at the house years ago, met his first love here even. *'Now, be brave and look brave,'* she told herself as she left her seat and began to casually stroll down the field, *'you've dealt with far more intimidating situations and people than this in the past; married life has turned you into a pathetic wilting flower, and that just won't do.'* As she neared the stranger, he made no attempt to leave. Faye stared hard at his face; his bone structure was hidden beneath a covering of fat, three large rolls rested upon his expensive silk cravat, the tangle of broken purple and red blood vessels beneath his skin had turned his flabby cheeks into a shade of puce. He was built like a haystack, but thankfully, he was not Barnaby Glover. He doffed his black bowler as she neared him, revealing a crown of sparse and frizzy grey hair. He smiled; his teeth were perfectly aligned and only slightly stained for a man who had obviously past the half-century mark. Her lack of saliva seemed to have paralysed her tongue; she couldn't decide what tone of voice she should adapt for the stranger.

"Good morning, Mrs Lopez!" he declared confidently, well-spoken and with a broad smile. Thrown by his first words, Faye could only continue to stare, searching hard into his face but already positive that she had no idea who this man was.

"Good morning," she finally said in a small voice.

His smile remained, "I watched your handsome young lad leave with his father earlier; a fine boy indeed."

So he had been watching, thought Faye already feeling the beads of sweat pushing to the surface of her skin.

"I presume that his young brother is resting up at the house." This man was far *too* familiar and well-informed with her affairs, considered Faye.

"*Who are you?*" insisted Faye, crossly, "and what do you want with *my family*?"

He ignored her question, "You have three beautiful children, Faye Lopez."

He had intended to shock her by his statement and he'd certainly succeeded.

She paused, warily before answering, "You are mistaken, Sir, I only have two sons."

"And one *exceptionally* beautiful daughter," he replied, calmly.

"I'll ask you again; *who are you?*"

"It is of no consequence, who I am, but know that I mean you no harm; only good and that it will be in your best interest to trust me."

Faye felt the yellowing grass beneath her feet spinning, she knew she was about to swoon and sat down, breathing deeply in a bid to suppress passing out completely in front of this mysterious man. He stepped briskly to her side, "Here, drink some of this, please; it is the finest brandy," he held out his hip flask but no matter what he'd just said, Faye didn't trust him; it could be laced with laudanum or worse still.

"No thank you, I'll be fine in a minute or two." She noticed an underlying smirk on his face and sensed he could read her thoughts. He was a clever man that was certain.

"Very well, but you should remain sitting for a little longer."

"What do you know of my daughter?" continued Faye.

"*My dear Mrs Lopez*, it would be far easier if you were to ask me what I don't know about your daughter. In truth, I know everything."

"You speak in riddles, Sir and if I were to speak

the truth, then I *do not* trust you."

"Then answer me this, do you wish to see your daughter?"

Feeling every muscle in her body becoming tense, Faye wanted to shout at this hideous looking man; he seemed intent on upsetting her and she couldn't for the life of her understand why. Did he really know what he claimed to, she questioned herself, or was he merely calling her bluff?

"Of course I want to see my daughter, that's a ridiculous question!"

"Then meet me at the foot of Headington Hill, tomorrow morning, early, around dawn, at five o'clock. Come alone and don't mention a word about anything to a living soul."

"That's quite out of the question, I have two sons and a husband, not to mention my daily chores...I can't just up and leave at the break of dawn and besides, as I've already said, *I don't trust you.*"

The stranger's expression suddenly changed; a stern and more serious face stared directly at Faye.

"She has your eyes, and your hair, you know? You will find a way, Mrs Lopez; you are an affectionate mother and no mother in her right mind would ignore such a golden opportunity as I am offering you. Should you decide not to turn up, I will not bother you again and you will be left with the guilt of missing the chance to spend a little time with your delightful six-year-old daughter."

The second he'd finished his sentence, he turned his back on Faye and sauntered away. She remained sitting on the grass, confused and deeply troubled but at the same time, she had a strong feeling that when dawn arrived the following morning, she *would* be waiting at the foot of Headington Hill.

"Well I must declare that I ain't the only person who's got a passion fer pickling an' the likes!" announced Granny Isabel, as Faye returned to the kitchen. "I managed ter finally get that little cupboard in the pantry open, while you were napping and uncovered enough bloomin' jars ter serve the whole of Oxf'rd. *Just look at 'em all!*"

The entire kitchen table was covered with an assortment of gleaming washed jars. Faye tried to look as excited as she knew Granny was expecting her to be, but the recent events were deeply troubling her and she was a terrible actress.

"*Oh good Lord*! Me darlin' girl! What in the world 'as 'appened? Yer look awful! Are yer sickening fer something? Too much sun on yer head...That's it, no more chores fer you terday, yer needs plenty of Rosie Lee and rest. Thank God the men are out fer the day!"

Granny Isabel rested her palm on Faye's brow, a look of concern upon her kind, wrinkled face.

CHAPTER THIRTY-EIGHT

Later that day, when the men returned from Chipping Norton, their jubilant smiles and loud excited chatter was immediate proof of the successful day they'd had. They unloaded the wagon of its precariously piled high, finely crafted furniture, once again, amazed at the sheer amount they'd purchased; it was more than they could have wished for and was guaranteed to bring them an excellent return. Faye felt more like an outsider as she observed their euphoria. Deeply troubled by the meeting she'd had with the stranger, that morning, she was in a quandary as to what she should do and if she should confide in anyone. Her instincts told her that to disclose her secret to anyone, would be as good as ditching the chance of ever seeing her long lost daughter, but inside she was scared and still unsure as to whether she could trust a man who'd been behaving so oddly over the past months. The alternative, however, would leave her unsettled and questioning her actions; possibly for the rest of her life. Sometimes risks had to be taken, she tried to convince herself. If she told anyone, she knew that they would either prevent her from leaving or do something to jeopardize the stranger ever returning, but sneaking out secretly would be an act of selfishness and if the stranger turned out to be some kind of monster, what then? Her thumping head had become a tangled mess from thinking about every possible scenario. The daunting possibility, that he was an acquaintance of Barnaby Glover had also occurred to her. Perhaps, simply using her daughter as bait to lure her away from Harberton Mead and back into his evil possession.

"Are yer feeling unwell, me sweet darlin'? Yer've not eaten a thing on yer plate," enquired Rob, worriedly, as they were all seated around the table.

"Reckon she's been out in the sun fer too long!" voiced Granny Isabel, "it was a right scorcher the day she went in ter Oxf'rd."

Both Ed and Harry were in agreement that Faye had been doing far too much and needed to take it easy for a few days. John Wick nodded in agreement; he didn't feel it appropriate to make such personal remarks about a young woman he'd not known that long and it wasn't often that he joined them all at the dinner table. Today however was a day to celebrate. The future of the business was looking extremely promising. In his usual style, Billy was entertaining everyone around the table with his constant chatter and comical remarks. With the fine spread which Granny and Faye had prepared, he was in his element and finding it difficult to keep his polite manners under control, aware of his ma's watchful eye looking down on him. He had felt like a proper man today, going out on a business trip with the men and now, all he really wished for, was a pair of long trousers, just like his Pa's. He would ask his ma, later when she had a wider smile upon her face.

It had been a long and exhausting day and with the men eagerly awaiting the arrival of the morning when they could re-assess their purchases and sieve through the ornaments, cameos and miniature oil paintings with a fine-tooth comb, an early night was favoured by all. Bobby was fast asleep in his cot as Faye slid into bed, relieved to be in the quiet darkness, where she could reflect on her day and put together a plan for the following day, without any interruptions. Knowing that Rob would soon be joining her she closed her eyes, pretending that she was already asleep and prayed that Bobby would sleep a few more hours before hunger woke him. Although convinced that there would be no sleep for her on this night, when Bobby did finally begin to holler loudly, Faye struggled to wake from her deep slumber. As quick as she could, before Bobby managed to disturb Billy and Rob, Faye put the red-faced hungry infant to her breast. The morning light slowly began to creep into the bedroom, reminding Faye that if she was going to trust the stranger, she'd have to hurry before it was too late and the chance might be lost forever. She had to go and no matter how many reasons she came up with, against going, in her heart she already knew that they were pointless. Bobby soon fell back to sleep, Faye kissed his soft cheeks, "I love you so much my darling," she whispered into his tiny ear. Like two peas in a pod, Rob and Billy were both sleeping in exactly the same position; Faye smiled to herself, she hoped she was doing the right thing, but it was too late for second thoughts now. Quietly and quickly, she dressed; a sensible navy blue day dress and a straw bonnet. She scribbled down a few words on paper, just to let Rob know that she would be out for the day on a matter of urgency and for him not to worry. It was a silly thing to say, she thought later as she crept out of the house, the moment Rob read her note she knew that everyone at Harberton Mead would be out of their minds with worry. Once again the feeling of nausea had swept over her and as nervous as she felt, she knew that it was the growing baby inside her that was the cause. Taking one last glance back at the sleeping house before it disappeared from her sight, Faye said a prayer as she hurried along the dry track, 'Oh Dear God, please keep me safe and deliver me safely back to my family again and forgive my sins. Amen.'

There was no sign of the stranger, but as the foot of Headington Hill came into view, she saw an ominous luxury black coach with its two black beasts standing motionless. The knot in her stomach tightened. She felt hungry all of a sudden, starving even, but knew that her constricted throat wouldn't allow a single morsel to pass it. An austere driver sat up high, his head looking straight ahead of him. As she reached to within a few steps of the coach, the door suddenly flew open and just as Faye had expected, the stranger stuck his head out; a broad smile of victory seeming to shine from his face.

"*Good morning Mrs Lopez*," he declared, rather too triumphantly for Faye's liking.

"Morning," she replied, glumly, feeling like a foolish rabbit about to enter the poacher's trap.

"I'm *so* delighted that you've made the right decision. You won't be disappointed, that, I can assure you."

The stranger pushed down the folding steps with the toe of his highly polished boot, he held out his gloved hand to assist Faye who quickly boarded, wanting to move quickly just in case Rob had already woken and was trailing behind her. Everything about the stranger was immaculate, his attire was of the highest quality, his speech was eloquent and his manners faultless. Faye sat nervously in the softly padded coach; if she wasn't feeling so nervous and nauseous she might have appreciated the sheer luxury which surrounded her. She leant back against the cushioned interior, her eyes gazing downwards to avoid direct eye contact with the stranger. The small voice inside of her head, nagged her continuously, *'are you completely mad, Faye Lopez? Do you realise that you've just walked out on your family and everyone in the entire world who cares for you, to risk your life with a total stranger, who you know nothing about?'*

"Please don't be nervous, Mrs Lopez, all will be well; trust me." It was as though he could read her thoughts. He hit his silver-handled cane against the roof of the coach, *"Drive on!"* He bellowed and Faye knew that now she'd just have to trust that her strong instincts to embark on this journey were not about to fail her. After a few minutes into the journey, the stranger drew the curtains on each side of the carriage. The bright sunshine still allowed enough light to penetrate through them and into the carriage, but it was now apparent that he didn't want to disclose their destination.

"It's better if you don't know where we are heading to," he said calmly.

"We'll my instincts tell me that we are travelling in the direction of Wheatley village." It was a stupid statement thought Faye, the second she'd opened her mouth, but her nerves were getting the better of her.

"Do you know, The Reverend Barnaby Glover, by any chance?" She had to know if he was somehow involved in any way in this charade. Faye observed the stranger's facial expression, feeling immediate discomfort by their closeness. He looked especially flushed today and his copious layers of clothing were excessive for a warm summer's morning and not helped by the stuffiness inside the coach. He ran his chubby fingers around his tight collar, which was clad with layers of silk cravat before hastily dabbing the dripping sweat from his brow with a crisply, starched handkerchief. He cleared his throat, *"The Reverend Glover?* I have heard of him, but am not acquainted with him. I do know, however, that he proved to be unworthy of his title and caused you a great injustice in the past."

"What exactly *do you know, Sir?"*

"My dear, Mrs Lopez, during the past few years, I have made it my business to know everything, especially where you are concerned. I will, however, end this entire cloak and dagger mystery very soon and inform you of exactly who I am and why I have made it my paramount business to do what I have done. I have little time left in this world, and I intend to seek my own justice before I depart."

His words gave Faye the impression that he was an honest man and meant her no harm; his eyes had displayed a sadness when he'd spoken, slightly off guard, leaving Faye feeling more intrigued with him, rather than fearful of him. Every now and again he would take a sip from his hip flask, but never once offered Faye any, as he'd done on the previous morning when she'd nearly passed out. Faye noticed how his hands shook a little, she wondered if it was nerves or some ailment which was causing it, concluding it to be the latter.

"So what else do you know about me...and why can't you at least tell me your name, I can hardly call you *Mr Nemo*, now can I, I might get into trouble by *Mr Charles Dickens*?"

It was the first time that the stranger looked relaxed; he threw his head back against the padded coach interior and laughed loudly until he began to splutter and choke.

"Ah, Mrs Lopez, it has been many, many months since I have laughed from my heart, you are indeed like an expensive tonic. No, we certainly can't risk upsetting the talented Mr Dickens. I presume that you've read *Bleak House* then? An excellent piece of literary genius, I must add."

"I couldn't agree more...are you feeling quite well? You do look rather flushed. Maybe you should remove your jacket; it has become quite warm in here."

He listened and took heed of Faye's advice.

"How long will it take to reach our destination, Sir?"

"About two hours, but we will take a short rest halfway."

Faye was astonished, she'd not anticipated travelling so far from home, she felt a rush of butterflies fluttering through her stomach and her thoughts went immediately to her young boys. She already missed them and longed to hold little Bobby in her arms.

CHAPTER THIRTY-NINE

"I just don't understand...where could she 'ave gone to...she must 'ave left long before six, yer know. I thought she'd gone ter the privy when little Bobby woke me with 'is screaming...but she's nowhere in the 'ouse." In a dishevelled state, Rob marched up and down the drawing-room. Between them, Billy and Bobby had managed to wake everyone under Harberton Mead's roof and all sleep and sense of peace had now vanished. Everyone was worried sick about Faye. "It's just not like 'er ter go anywhere wiv out telling me before'and!" Rob raged.

"Have you checked in all the obvious places in case she left you a letter, informing of where she was going?" asked Harry, worriedly.

"I want my mamma...I want Mamma!" sobbed Billy, as the tears streamed down his red face.

"*Billy!* Stop being a sissy, will yer!"

"Oh, Roberto, 'ave a heart, for *God's sake*, the poor little lad wants 'is ma...it's only natural," warned Granny Isabel, as she hugged the crying boy.

"I can't fer the life of me think of where she might 'ave got to, but she was acting a bit odd yesterday," confessed Granny Isabel, "I just put it down to 'er being out in that scorching sun fer too long, it had made the poor lass quite nauseous too."

"Roberto!" joined in Ed, still half asleep, "Did yer actually bother ter check if she left yer a message?"

Rob shook his head, "The little uns were making too much ov a bleedin' racket, an' as I said, I thought Faye was somewhere in the 'ouse!"

"Yer daft bleedin' bugger...go an' bloody well look then!"

Five minutes later, Rob re-appeared clutching the note; everyone's eyes were upon him.

"It don't say much, just that she's had ter go out urgently, we're not ter worry an' she'll explain when she gets 'ome! Why didn't she wake me up an' tell me?"

"Because, old chap, she obviously knew that you would stop her from leaving!" stated Harry.

Ed had been quietly amusing Bobby, but a thought had suddenly sprung to his mind, "Per'aps she went ter Wheatley village, ter visit someone, maybe 'er business was ter do wiv 'er past, an' fer obvious reasons, thought she'd go by 'erself."

"She still could 'ave told me," insisted Rob.

"I say that we all 'ave some breakfast an' carry on as normal, Faye's a sensible lass an' she knows 'ow ter look after herself. If we sit 'round fretting all day, it will only make the babies more worried 'bout their ma an' it won't make 'er come 'ome none the faster!"

"I quite agree, Granny Isabel," stated Harry.

"I'm not a baby..." protested Billy, "I went out

with the men, so I ain't a baby...Bobby is the baby!"

"Calm yourself, young man, nobody said that you were a baby, in fact, I was going to give you a choice of either helping me with the accounts up in my study or helping your pa and Uncle Ed in the workshop."

Billy wiped his wet face with the back of his podgy hand, as he concentrated on Harry's words.

"What does accounts mean?"

"Ooh, numbers, sums and money, my dear little fellow!"

Like a real gentleman, Billy assured Harry that once he'd begun school next year, he'd be able to help with the accounts, but for the time being, he thought he'd be far more useful in the workshop.

Rob, couldn't manage any breakfast; his mind was totally disturbed; he knew it was going to be the longest day where his mind would be miles away.

"Let's go an' check out yesterday's *fine booty*," suggested Ed, eagerly. "That'll take yer mind off yer worries, Rob."

"I'm going to join you; I don't feel that the exquisite furniture was given my full undivided attention yesterday. Think we'll forgo sums for today, what d'you say young Billy?"

With all the men out of the house and Bobby sat in his high chair, happily licking the porridge from his fingers; in a trance-like state, Granny

Isabel began to clear away the breakfast dishes. She had a bad feeling in her gut and sensed that Faye was in some kind of trouble. She would have confided in her if there was any truth in what Ed had suggested, but wherever she'd gone, Granny knew that she'd been sworn to secrecy by someone.

"Oh Bobby, me little darlin', 'Ow are we ever going ter get through this day?"

Bobby merely chuckled; he was plastered up to his elbows in porridge, with another helping covering his face and enjoying every minute of breakfast.

After half an hour's rest at the coach house, Faye and the stranger were now on the final leg of the long journey, the temperature was steadily rising and with the flawless bright blue sky, it looked to be another fine summer's day. Faye had eaten a modest meal and gulped down two glasses of water in the inn and her nausea had thankfully subsided. The stranger, however, appeared overtired and was finding it difficult to keep his eyes open. He'd looked so much fresher a couple of hours ago, thought Faye, and had gone downhill very quickly.

"Don't feel that you are obliged to remain awake on my account, Sir. Feel free to take forty winks."

He gazed at her, with a half-smile, "I know that love is said to conquer all, Mrs Lopez, and I hope you won't find my words too impertinent, but in my opinion, you could have done so much better than that rough speaking Spaniard who you married."

Faye was instantly shocked, she'd not expected this well-mannered man to make such a dreadfully, rude comment.

"Well actually, I find your insults to be *extremely rude*. Do you take some kind of unhealthy pleasure in interfering in other folk's lives? *That rough speaking Spaniard* has a heart of pure gold and he is who he is, with no pretentious airs and graces. I have loved him since the very moment we met and I really *do* feel great sorrow for anyone who lives without experiencing such a love in their life."

He was silent for a while, knowing he'd upset his companion.

"Did I mention that your daughter goes by the name of Faye Fairbanks," he eventually divulged, "It would be better if you didn't disclose the fact that you are also called Faye...maybe keep to Mrs Lopez."

The swarm of butterflies returned to Faye's stomach; she knew that they must be very near to their destination by now and couldn't quite believe that she would soon see her daughter. Her hands were sweating and the feeling of light-headedness had returned.

"*And what shall I call you?* What will *they* call you, in fact?"

"They will all call me by my name, which I will tell you now, as I think we are now too near your daughter for you to do anything silly."

"I'm not in the habit of doing anything silly, apart from putting my trust in a complete stranger!"

"Well, I might not be quite that stranger to you when I tell you that I am, *Mr Lyle Dagworth*."

He watched as Faye took a sharp intake of breath, "You are a liar; Mr Dagworth died. My Rob and Mr Ed Hall stumbled upon his house auction when we were still living in London!"

"Yes, I sold everything but that is in no way proof of my death, Mrs Lopez. It seems to me that your husband and his friend were foolhardy and made their own wrong presumptions. After the terrible fate of my beloved Marjorie, my life became pointless; I have no living relatives and more than enough money to see me comfortably through another lifetime. I never imagined that I would pine for Marjorie the way I did; my life and my world were empty. I found myself sinking into a dismal black hole; food became my only comfort, as you can probably see, but it also became my enemy by having detrimental effects on my heart. Then one day I decided that if I was going to leave this world, there was some unfinished business which needed my attention first. Do you know that Harry Fairbanks was willing to sell your daughter to my wife and I, for a staggering six hundred guineas? He still owes me *one hundred* guineas, you know, but that is of no importance anymore."

"It was Harry Fairbanks, who rescued her; he believed me to be dead, as did the undertaker and possibly a hurried doctor," interrupted, Faye in Harry's defence. "If it hadn't had been for Harry Fairbanks' insistence that I was covered with a blanket, I might not even be sitting here with you now. He saved my life, *Mr Dagworth*, and also saved my husband and son from burning to death in a house fire, last year."

"Your hero is my enemy, I'm afraid. He was the cause of my wife's desperate suicide; she had set her heart on becoming a mother to your daughter, Mrs Lopez and never recovered from the huge disappointment. I know for certain that if Harry Fairbanks hadn't shown up in my life with his money making scheme, my Marjorie would still be alive today and I would be a happy man."

"I had set my heart on being a mother to my daughter! And in all fairness, Mr Dagworth, that's not true. I know that it's easy to paint a rosy picture of what might have been, but I heard that your wife was already in a fragile state of mind, before Mr Fairbanks even mentioned a word about my daughter to you. It wouldn't have been fair on my daughter too, with all respect, *Mr Dagworth*; could you imagine what it would be like to have a six-year-

old daughter at your age?"

Lyle Dagworth took no offence from Faye's words, he laughed in admiration of her honesty. "Well, my dear Mrs Lopez, thankfully, she is still in my life. I befriended the family a couple of years ago, my carriage conveniently, needed a new wheel a few yards away from Mickleham Farm..."

"Careful Mr Dagworth," interrupted Faye, "you've just given away the secret location!"

"You are indeed a sharp-witted woman, Mrs Lopez; I can see that your daughter has inherited many of your characteristics!" laughed Lyle. "Anyway, let me continue before we find ourselves upon the doorstep. Whilst my carriage wheel was being repaired, during my conversation with Jasper Heath, he's the head of the household, by the way, it came to light, that he'd recently suffered a bad harvest and was in desperate need for a new plough and a strong Shire horse. He also wanted to build an extension on to his farmhouse, for his ever-growing family; two of his sons were due to marry and bring their brides to the farm."

"So you gave or loaned Jasper Heath enough, or probably more money than he needed and became like one of the family!" declared Faye, in a cynical tone.

"That young girl grew in my belly, I gave birth to her in such hardship on the roadside...and she has been used like some kind of lucky chip in a game of roulette! Has anyone ever considered *my* feelings or the fact that she should be with her real mother! Mr Dagworth, you consider yourself to be doing me such a good turn by bringing me here today...You believe your sins to be forgiven by this favour, but you could so easily have united me with my daughter years ago and caused everyone concerned a lot less heartbreak! Now it is *too* late! "

"No, no, that's not true at all, you don't understand. It's complicated. Very complicated; everyone living at Mickleham Farm is either living a lie or living with a lie!"

"I don't understand, Mr Dagworth, you're talking in riddles once again, please explain." The beads of sweat were now pouring from Lyle's forehead and his face had become a brighter shade of crimson. He suddenly picked up his cane and struck the silver handle against the roof of the carriage. As the driver immediately pulled hard on the reins and called out to the cantering horses Lyle simultaneously drew back the tiny curtains inside the carriage. Green farmland surrounded them on both sides.

"Let's continue this conversation outside of this stifling carriage, hopefully, there will be a slight breeze."

Outside they sat down upon the grass, stretching out their numb legs as they appreciated the fresh air. Lyle took regular sips from his hip flask which in turn caused Faye to lick her dry lips.

"*Driver!* Do you have any water with you, my

good man, my companion is parched!"

The driver dutifully climbed down from his lofty driving seat and produced a tin cup full of tepid water.

"Now, Mrs Lopez, let me continue with my explanation. Delia Fairbanks is Jasper Heath's housekeeper; he is a widower and has been led to believe that she too is a widow and that Faye is her daughter. Mrs White, who used to be the cook at Harberton Mead, which you are probably already aware of, now poses as Delia Fairbanks' widowed mother and consequently, grandmother to your daughter. They have been living this deceit for six years now and after all this time, nobody would ever deduce them be anything other than devoted grandmother, mother, and daughter. You will see for yourself in due course. Jasper Heath confided in me of the feelings he harbours for Delia; he loves her, much to his surprise, as he never in his wildest dreams thought he'd ever love again since the departing if his wife, eight years ago."

"And does she feel the same for him?"

"That, my dear Mrs Lopez is a tricky question. She claims that her only purpose in life is to devote herself entirely to raising young Faye, but I have seen that wistful look in her eyes, I have witnessed the way she admires Jasper's every action. She is a prison to her feelings Mrs Lopez; should she confess she would have to disclose everything to Jasper...would he still feel the same about a woman who has deceived him for so long and made a mockery of him. He can't possibly marry her too since she is already tied to the *honourable, Harry Fairbanks!*"

"There's no need to take such a tone of voice when you mention Mr Fairbanks, you know, after all, she was the one who walked out on him. He was devastated and left a broken man and it didn't help when you paid him a visit and pounced upon him like a wild animal!"

Lyle let out a slight laugh, "I should have finished him off then and there; would have solved many problems."

"Harry Fairbanks is a *good* and *decent* man with a heart of gold; his only shortcomings are that he was weak when it came to gambling, but he has well and truly learnt from his mistakes. He makes a lot of people very happy you know and even though he won't admit it anymore, I'm convinced that he is still madly in love with Delia and regrets ever treating her in the way he did."

Lyle listened intently, suddenly realising that there were even more than two sides to every story.

"Do you know, Mrs Lopez, you have just opened my eyes to the fact that I have been viewing the entire situation from one angle. They have no idea at all of my involvement with Harry Fairbanks; to them, I am merely a wealthy London businessman who has taken an interest in their lives. Maybe *there is* a chance of me doing some good before I meet my Maker."

"I wonder if Delia does still love Harry?" said Faye in a small, wistful voice.

"Let us continue on our way, time is catching up with us. There is much to think about. Now, if you are in agreement, I will say that you are the daughter of a neighbour who wished to accompany me today. I will refer to you as Mrs Lopez at all times."

"More lies, *Mr Dagworth* ...watch out that you don't become tangled up in them!" declared Faye, tutting and shaking her head.

"Please Mrs Lopez, try to remember that the purpose of this journey is for you to see your daughter, but there is much to be done and I'm now feeling quite optimistic that together you and I might act as a catalyst in the lives of our friends and family."

"Hmm, well, there's one thing you should know about me, Mr Dagworth and that is, that I detest liars and after today, I refuse to lie for you."

CHAPTER FORTY

"*Ahh*, blast this damn plane!" bellowed Rob, as a jagged shard of wood pierced his hand, causing his blood to flow copiously. He hurled the heavy metal planes across the workroom, accompanying his angry action with a few choice words.

"Yer mind ain't focussed on the job terday, is it, Rob?" stated Ed.

"Maybe he should take the rest of the day off, he's got a lot on his mind today," added John Wick. Ed let out a deep groan.

"Don't reckon we've gotta lot ov choice anymore ...just look at the state ov 'is 'and. Get yerself inter Granny, she'll know what ter do wiv that injury!" ordered Ed, unsympathetically.

Although they were all trying to carry on as normal, everyone at Harberton Mead had only one worry on their minds and that was the whereabouts and the safety of Faye. Rob made his way towards the kitchen, with his hand wrapped in the handkerchief which John had promptly handed him, he felt light-headed, it was the sight of blood; he was bleeding heavily and by the time he reached Granny Isabel there wasn't a white spot left on the handkerchief.

"*Goodness gracious, what in God's Blessed name has happened?*" she cried out in distress. Billy who was sitting at the kitchen table burst into tears before quickly jumping down from the chair and scurrying out of the kitchen screaming loudly, *"Uncle Harry, Uncle Harry*...My pa has cut his hand off!"

Harry had been sat on the veranda, unable to concentrate on anything at his desk; he'd been quietly contemplating the past years, trying to come up with any clue as to where Faye might have gone. He had a disturbing feeling about this day and knew he'd not be able to relax until Faye had returned safely to Harberton Mead. His reverie was suddenly broken as he heard Billy's screams; he was soon on the veranda with a look of sheer terror in his innocent young face and tears pouring from his soulful dark eyes.

"Uncle Harry," he sobbed, "I want my mamma, please go in the wagon and find her. Pa is bleeding...*lots!*"

With decades of life experience to rely on, by the time Harry had calmed Billy down and arrived in the kitchen, Granny Isabel had already packed the gaping wound with flour and tightly bandaged Rob's hand. Still appearing a little washed out, but glad that he could no longer see any blood, Rob gestured Billy to cuddle up to him.

"I want mamma to come home," he said quietly, his head buried into Rob's chest.

"Me too, son, me too."

Granny Isabel handed him a pink lollipop and a bag of stale bread,

"Reckon those chickens need feeding, young Billy...and we still need ter come up with a name for hen number six, so think on while yer outside."

The sweet lollipop was more than enough to put a temporary smile upon Billy's tear-stained face. He kissed his pa's cheek and ran out of the kitchen.

"What a day! What a bloomin' day!" declared Granny Isabel, shaking her head in disbelief.

It was approaching midday when the carriage came to a halt outside Mickleham Farm; the journey had taken longer than expected, with the long discussion between Faye and Lyle taking up almost an hour.

"Don't be nervous, now; try to enjoy this long-awaited moment, and treasure it, my dear girl," encouraged Lyle Dagworth.

The farmhouse had an attractive frontage; on the far side of the building, lilac wisteria hung gracefully from the roof to the lower windows. There were numerous clay pots of various sizes positioned everywhere, all bursting with colour. The sound of chirping birds seemed to greet them as they stepped down from the carriage and not a minute had passed before the voice of a young girl could be heard,

"Uncle Lyle, Uncle Lyle!" A petite six-year-old came skipping out from the open door towards them, her long, fair plaits bounced up and down.

She was beautiful, thought Faye, as she froze, barely unable to catch her breath. She wanted to reach out and pull the child into her embrace, but she knew she was nothing more than a stranger to her young and cheerful daughter.

"My dear, sweet Faye, look how you've grown since I last saw you and I swear that you become prettier with every visit!"

Young Faye's cheeks blushed; she looked up at Faye, "Is this your lady friend, Uncle Lyle?"

Lyle chuckled, "This, my adorable, little Faye is Mrs Lopez, the daughter of a very dear neighbour of mine."

"Hello, Mrs Lopez, it's very nice to meet you," she affirmed, politely.

"It's lovely to meet you too," uttered Faye, her voice cracking with emotion. "Uncle Lyle has told me so much about you."

A plump, grey-haired woman came out to join them, her smile was warm and friendly; Faye immediately knew that she was Mrs White and felt as though she already knew her from the stories which Harry had recalled.

"I do believe that your psychic powers told you I was baking your favourite scones today Mr Dagworth!"

"Ah, Mrs White, you are indeed a miracle worker, I was only dreaming about those golden mouth-watering scones of yours last night...can you believe it. Allow me to introduce my neighbour, Mrs Lopez."

"Any friend of our dear Mr Dagworth is always welcome, Mrs Lopez." For a brief second Faye was worried that Mrs White had spotted a similarity between her and young Faye. Her stare was prolonged.

"Have I met you before, Mrs Lopez, only your face looks very familiar and I used to live in Oxford too, you know."

"Well, perhaps we did meet, maybe at the market or simply in passing."

"What about your parents, perhaps I know them...Do you resemble your mother? I never forget a face you know."

"Come now, Mrs White, poor Mrs Lopez is tired after our long journey and she certainly didn't expect to be met by *Sherlock Holmes*!"

"Oh you are a comedian Mr Dagworth," chuckled Mrs White, "I do beg your pardon, Mrs Lopez, please take no notice of my weakness to pry," she said jovially.

Delia Fairbanks was inside, relaxing and completely unaware of the visitors; Jasper Heath and his three sons were busy, working out in the fields and Noah and William's wives had gone into Dorking for the day to be fitted with new dresses for the forthcoming harvest celebrations. *"We have visitors, Delia!"* announced Ruth White, as she ushered them into the large, inviting kitchen. Delia jumped up, quickly patting down the flyaway strands of hair and smoothing out her dress. She was a fine-looking woman, thought Faye, as they were introduced. Smooth flawless skin, pretty fair hair and softly spoken; Delia had a warm and welcoming smile which immediately made Faye feel at ease. Young Faye was skipping excitedly and asking Delia if she should run out to the fields and announce that Uncle Lyle and his friend had arrived. Faye clandestinely watched as Delia issued the excitable girl with a kind but warning look, telling her to behave like a polite young lady in front of the guests. Faye felt immediately dismayed when she heard her daughter calling Delia Fairbanks, *'mamma'*. If only they knew, she mused, sadly.

They sat at the large table which took centre place in the roomy kitchen, Mrs White prepared the tea and placed a tower of warm scones, butter and jam in front of them, while Delia and Lyle chatted about the bountiful harvest that was anticipated and the glorious weather that they'd been blessed with of late. Faye sat quietly, praying that Delia or Mrs White wouldn't suddenly ask her any awkward questions; she already felt like a complete fraud. But she relished in watching her beloved daughter, having to pinch herself to make sure this day was really true and not merely just another dream. Billy and Bobby looked completely different from her, they had definitely inherited all of their father's dark Spanish looks, but Faye could still remember her own reflection when

she was a child and her daughter reminded her
so much of herself at a young age. It was clearly
obvious that Delia adored her '*daughter*'. Little
Faye sat close to Delia at the table; every so often
she'd look up at her and smile lovingly to her or
stroke her face with her petite hand.

"Uncle Dagworth! Mamma and Grandma are
going to take me to the Dorking fair, it's in two
weeks...would you like to come too? Your pretty
neighbour can also come, if it's convenient, of
course." She directed her wide smile at Faye,
who had to blink rapidly in order to stem her
tears from falling. "Oh, Mrs Lopez, do you have
dust in your eyes?" she asked, as she hurriedly
left Delia's side to offer Faye her help, "Uncle
Jasper told me what to do, cos he always gets
dust in his eyes, out on the fields; you have to
pinch your eyelid and pull it out a little and
move your eye; *all at the same time!* Here, I'll help
you if you like!"

Young Faye's small fingers were already gently
touching Faye's eyelids.

"*Faye, leave Mrs Lopez, alone for goodness sake,
before you cause her some harm!*" scolded Delia.
Finding the scene amusing, Lyle sat laughing
out loud. Faye gently took hold of her daughter's
hands in hers and for a few beautiful seconds,
time stood still as she relished in the close bond.
She wanted to hug her and cover her sweet,
pretty face with kisses, but she could only look
deep into her eyes and thank her for being so

caring.

Lyle Dagworth had now ceased his laughing and viewed the close interaction, nervously before quickly intervening, "I nearly forgot, my dear little princess, I purchased a bag of sweets for you in Oxford." He handed Faye the bag from his pocket and received an immediate hug from the child. "Thank you Uncle. Can I go out to play Mamma?"

With Delia's permission, Faye skipped out through the open back door as Mrs White called out, warning her not to disturb her Uncles who were all busy.

"I won't Grandma," she replied, over her shoulder.

"They'll all be in for lunch soon," stated Delia. "You *will* join us, won't you Mr Dagworth and Mrs Lopez; Jasper will be so happy to see you."

"We have a long journey back to Oxford and Mrs Lopez has two handsome young sons waiting for her, so I'm afraid we'll have to decline your generous offer on this occasion, my dear Mrs Fairbanks, but I *will* take a stroll outside and pass a short time of the day with my dear friend before we leave. Would you care to join me, Mrs Lopez?"

With the insistence of Delia and Ruth, Faye was persuaded to remain with the women and partake of another cup of tea.

"I won't be long; Mrs Lopez, then we will embark on our journey back to Oxford,"

declared Lyle as he stepped out of the back door.
"How old are your sons, Mrs Lopez?" enquired
Delia.

"Billy is nearly five, and Bobby is just nine
months old."

"Oh, what a handful!" declared Ruth White, her
ample cheeks wobbling as she spoke.

"Have you known, dear Mr Dagworth long?"
Faye was beginning to feel nervous, knowing
that these two women were intent on unveiling
as much of her business as possible in the short
time before Lyle Dagworth returned.

"Oh, I have known him for a good many years.
Your daughter is a credit to you, Mrs Fairbanks,"
stated Faye, hoping to turn the focus of
conversation around. "You have a *lovely farm*,
such a beautiful home for a child to grow up in."
It was quite obvious how Delia delighted in
talking about Faye, her smile widened and there
was a distinct sparkle in her eyes. "Faye is our
life, and makes every day worth living, she is
like a warm ray of sunshine, isn't she, mother?"
Mrs White was quick to agree, "Oh yes, since my
poor Delia lost her husband and prior to that her
dear father, God rest his soul, it has been little
Faye that has inspired us to look positive; we
really landed on our feet when we came to work
here at Mickleham Farm."

Putting on an expression of shock, Faye
exclaimed, "You only work here...goodness, I
thought you were the farmer's wife!"

"Well, no, Mrs Lopez, you are mistaken," replied Delia in a sad tone.

"One day, she just might be; who knows? God works in mysterious ways, as we've learnt from experience!" declared Ruth White, elatedly.

"*Mother*, please; Mrs Lopez will think of us as fortune hunters."

"Oh Delia, don't be so silly, Mrs Lopez is a woman of the world and a mother too...I'm sure she understands."

Delia's furtive warning glare to Ruth White didn't go unnoticed by Faye.

"Pardon me if I'm speaking out of turn, but are you in love with the farmer by any chance?" Faye was unable to resist the question.

"They *do* love each other and that's a fact!" announced Ruth, abruptly.

"Then, I can't see a problem...why don't you marry? "

"Let's just say, it's complicated, and leave it like that." It was clear that too much had been said and Delia wanted to change the subject, quickly. Lyle Dagworth's impeccable timing shifted the tense atmosphere as he stepped over the threshold, hand in hand with young Faye.

After an awkward goodbye, Faye and Lyle were soon sat back in the carriage. Faye choked back her tears; it had been an emotional couple of hours, leaving her feeling raw and broken-hearted. Lyle sat solemnly, his head bowed as he fiddled nervously with his fingers and thumbs. "Aren't you going to close the curtains, Mr Dagworth," Faye asked, cynically.

"I do apologise, Mrs Lopez, that *was* rather silly of me, I'm sure you know where we are, anyhow."

"Somewhere near *Dorking*, Mr Dagworth!"

"Forgive me; I thought that taking you to visit your daughter would be a move in the right direction. I only wished to bring a little justice to the world before I depart."

Ten minutes elapsed before Faye found herself able to answer Mr Dagworth, she was in an emotional state and knew in her heart that she would never take Delia's place in young Faye's life. She was a happy little girl and she absolutely adored Delia. They cherished each other and Faye had no right to steal away her happiness. Delia was her mother in every possible way apart from the fact that she'd not given birth to her.

"I *am* glad that I've met her at long last, Mr Dagworth and thrilled to see what a beautiful, happy and fortunate child she is. Delia Fairbanks has certainly given her more love than many natural mothers would have done. They are a happy little family and I wouldn't dream of doing anything foolish to jeopardize that. She will remain forever where she had been since her birth...tucked securely away in the deepest part of my heart."

Lyle Dagworth reached out and took her hand, "You are a brave, courageous and selfless human, my dear Faye Lopez. I admire you, greatly."

"There is one task which I'd like to do though; I'd like to tell Harry of Delia's whereabouts and explain the situation to him. I'm sure he would welcome a divorce after all these years and maybe he too can start a new life, everyone deserves some love in their life, don't you agree, Mr Dagworth?"

A sinister smirk covered Lyle's face, "If my plan succeeds, Delia Fairbanks might find herself to be a free woman sooner than she could have imagined."

In her tired and overwrought state, it took a few minutes for Lyle's words to register; she felt her blood run cold.

"*Mr Dagworth!* What on earth are you suggesting? You can't possibly be intending to do what I think you are...*surely not...you mustn't, you simply mustn't*. You're a sick man and by your own account, close to the grave. How could you possibly rest in peace with blood on your hands?" Overwhelmed by Lyle's intentions, Faye could barely contain herself, she felt the bile rise to the back of her throat; she felt faint and had an urgent thirst all of a sudden. "I beg of you, *Mr Dagworth, don't be so foolish*. Mr Fairbanks is a *good* and *decent* man."

"**No, no**, he *murdered* my wife, my darling

Marjorie. She would be sat at my side now if it wasn't for bloody Fairbanks."

"That's not true, Mr Dagworth and if you are totally honest and pause for a while to reflect, you'll recall that your wife was a sick and desperate woman; in all fairness, do you think that being handed a newborn baby when she was suffering from such melancholy would have been the cure to her state of mind. Would it really have been fair on Faye too?"

Lyle Dagworth sat sulking until they arrived at the coach house, where it was a relief for Faye to refresh herself and part company with Lyle for half an hour. She prayed that her words would make Lyle change his mind about his intentions and knew that she'd have a heavy responsibility once she arrived home. She longed to hold her sons in her arms and kiss them both...It had been a gruelling day, which still wasn't quite over and she'd yet to face the reaction of everyone at Harberton Mead.

CHAPTER FORTY-ONE

The glowing summer sun had just set as Lyle
Dagworth said goodbye to Faye. She'd alighted
from the carriage in the same place as she'd
boarded it that morning, which now seemed
more like a month of Sundays ago. It was a
pleasant, balmy evening and the moment that
Harberton Mead came into sight there was a
sudden surge of activity as everyone who was
seated on the veranda stood up and began to
wave and cheer. There was nothing anyone
could do to prevent Billy from running as fast as
his short legs would allow, down the field.
Tripping up a couple of times, nothing would
deter him and he simply jumped back up,
determined to be the first to reach his beloved
ma. Faye's heart swelled with love for him as she
took in his serious, handsome face, full of
concentration and his father's dark hair cut in
exactly the same style too.
"Mamma, Mamma!" he yelled out, his feet now
barely touching the ground. "Where have you
been? Pappa had a *really bad* accident; there was
a *huge* puddle of blood, but he's all better now,
Granny fixed it for him!"
Faye kissed and hugged him, with tears
streaming down her face.
"My darling Billy, my little man, Mamma has
missed you *so, so* much!"

Rob was quickly by her side, the strained face he'd been wearing all day now relaxed.

"Your poor hand!" exclaimed Faye, sympathetically as she held the bandaged limb. "Nothing ter worry yer sweet little head about, all is right in the world now that yer back 'ome, but where did yer go...we've all bin worried out ov our heads 'bout yer!"

Engulfing her in his embrace, with Billy hugging her legs, they froze beneath the inky sun-streaked sky, locked in their love.

That evening after a late supper and after Billy had finally fallen asleep; Faye sat with everyone in the drawing-room and told them everything about her day, not omitting any details. It was a heartbreaking story, which didn't leave a single dry eye in the room. Sympathy was abounding for Faye, who, after all the years of patiently waiting and yearning to be united with her daughter, had shown such strength by keeping her identity a secret. Everyone was shocked by the news that Lyle Dagworth was not only still alive but practically living on their doorstep. It was unbelievable how much he'd changed in appearance and that nobody, especially Harry had recognised him. It left Harry in a sombre mood; he'd never imagined that Lyle Dagworth held him responsible for the ruin of his life *and* his wife's death. Hearing that, even though, the man was so sick, with little time left in this world but was intent on ending Harry's life, left a bitter taste in his mouth. He felt uneasy and knew that he'd be living on his nerves for the foreseeable future, while Dagworth remained his neighbour. The knowledge that Delia loved another and that yet again it was his fault that she was denied happiness struck another painful arrow into his already broken heart. It had pained him so much as he'd listened to Faye's breaking voice when she'd spoken of her beautiful daughter; that too was all his fault; if he'd not been so caught up in his gambling debt, and given Delia more of his attention, she would never have left him in the first place and now she had obviously wiped his memory from her heart and mind and was in love with another. Harry suddenly felt as though he had more enemies than friends and had left a trail of destruction behind him as he'd gone through life. How many people cursed him and wished him dead, he pondered.

The following day, Harry decided that no work would be done and that they should all enjoy a huge picnic out on the land and enjoy a day of leisure. Persuading Rob in allowing him to bring his favourite hen along, nobody was able to stop laughing as they viewed the hilarious sight of Billy leading his favourite hen, Rosie along by a length of string tied loosely around her neck. "I'm going to buy young Billy a dog or a goat perhaps," declared Harry, feeling sorry that his only pets were a flock of hens.

"*Not a bloomin' goat!*" exclaimed Granny Isabel, "they eat everything in sight, including the washing when it's hung out ter dry!"

"Very well, I'll bear that in mind. Would you like your Uncle Harry to buy you a puppy, young chap?"

Billy's face lit up with joy, "Yes please, Uncle Harry!"

"Reckon yer best start thinking of names then, cos yer still ain't given that last poor hen a name yet!" stated Granny.

"I *have* thought of a name, I just forgot to tell you...but I know Uncle Ed will like it."

"Oh, no Billy lad, yer can't call an 'en, **Ed**, that ain't a gal's name, yer know!" proclaimed Ed.

"I know, Uncle Ed, I'm going to name her *'Daft Bugger'!*"

Once again Billy had everyone in stitches, even Bobby joined in, without understanding the joke, but his chuckling proved to be contagious.

Sandwiches, pies and cakes were eaten in abundance and Granny's delicious lemonade was greatly appreciated in the ascending temperatures. Games were played, jokes and amusing stories told but not a word relating to the previous day was mentioned, even though it was still on the forefront of everyone's mind. Faye found a quiet moment and tenderly whispered in Rob's ear that she was growing their third child in her belly. He was delighted and would have announced the good news immediately if Faye hadn't begged him to keep it their special secret for a little longer. Several times during the day, Faye and the others noticed how Harry kept drifting off in his private thoughts; she felt so sorry for him and hoped that she might be able to work some magic along with her powers of persuasion to bring about a peaceful solution to the dire situation. Harry was like her older, protective brother; she owed him so much and hated to see him so disturbed and forlorn.

A few days elapsed before Faye was feeling energized enough to think about a plan. Meanwhile, in his modest cottage in Headington, Lyle Dagworth was making his own plans and now feeling as though he was living on borrowed time. He would soon be joining his darling Marjorie, the strains and pressures of his lonely existence would, at last, come to an end and this world would be gone forever from him. As he sat in the tiny back garden, enjoying the warmth of his final summer, he reminisced about the men and women who'd been part of his life. His mother; she was the most perfect woman he'd ever known; she had guided him through his early years, making a fine job of it. His father, however, had always been like a weak shadow in the distance and had passed away during Lyle's early adolescence. He couldn't remember ever crying or feeling sad over the loss of him, only relieved that he was left with his mother entirely to himself. It was later when he was in his twenties when he'd suddenly realised how he needed the manly strength and guidance of his father. It was then that he'd actually mourned his death and shortly after that his dear mother, still in her prime, died after a brief illness.

The huge void in his life was soon filled by the shy and beautiful Marjorie; she had instantly captured his heart and six months after their first meeting, they became husband and wife. Every day was like a honeymoon until Marjorie's string of miscarriages began. As she became weaker in mind and body, becoming a mother was her one and only priority in life and for a few happy months, it looked as though the dark days had finally come to an end. Marjorie was carrying their child and the doctor had assured them that everything was looking satisfactory and they would soon be holding the child they'd dreamt and prayed for. But like everything in their life, it ended in tragedy, with the sudden death of their precious daughter.

Lyle wiped away his tears and blew his nose, before dozing off. His brief and fretful nap turned into a nightmare; every single face from his life was as large as life and shouting furiously at him. He watched helplessly as Marjorie fell from the bedroom window, she called out to him for help, but Harry was unable to reach her. Harry Fairbanks was larger than life and was holding *his* baby Phyllis in his arms. Lyle opened his eyes; his weak heart pounding and sweat dripping from his body. Thankful to find he was surrounded by the blossoming summer flowers in his garden Lyle suddenly realised that he now had little time left in which to put his affairs in to order.

His reverie was suddenly broken by the distant hammering upon his front door. He dragged his body from the low garden chair and expecting to be met by his physician, was thrown into a state of nerves at the sight of Harry Fairbanks. The two men stood motionless, locked in a stare. A wave of jealousy swept through Lyle, Harry Fairbanks was looking healthy and young; in fact, he looked in better shape now than he'd done six years ago when their paths had first crossed.

"I thought it was about time we had a heart to heart, Mr Dagworth."

Lyle had been expecting Harry to show up, but not this soon and certainly not unaccompanied.

"You'd better come in Mr Fairbanks."

Harry entered the cottage, warily; his eyes clandestinely searching just in case there were any harmful weapons in sight.

"Can I offer you some refreshment, Mr Fairbanks?"

"Please, *Mr Dagworth*, could we simply revert to addressing each other less formally?"

"Hmm, I suppose it will do no harm, Harry."

"Now, I'm afraid that I no longer employ a butler, but I can pour you a fine Scottish whiskey, Harry and if I recall it *is* one of your weaknesses!"

"That's most generous, *L.D.* thank you. I was very sorry to hear about your wife, L.D. Please accept my belated but sincere condolences; she was a fine lady."

Lyle made no comment as he opened the sideboard door, taking out two glasses and a crystal decanter of whiskey.

"How are Mrs Lopez and her family?" he enquired.

"They are all *very* well, L.D."

"Is she aware of your whereabouts today Harry?"

"I told *no one* L.D. Why should I have? I'm merely paying an overdue visit to an old and dear friend. You should have informed me that you were living so close by, L.D. especially in view of your ill health. I hope you'll allow all of us at Harberton Mead to assist where we can and you *must* join us for dinner at your convenience; sample some of Granny Isabel's scrumptious culinary delights!"

"Oh yes, the *old woman* from Wentworth Street!"

Lyle made a disapproving grunting sound, "Did Mrs Lopez inform you about my intention to kill you, Harry?"

Harry released a tensed laugh, "I'm sure you didn't mean it; merely words said in the heat of the moment, we've *all* done it, *L.D.*"

"No, my dear fellow, they were *definitely not* words in the heat of the moment, I *do* intend to end your life and I am going to tell you exactly why!"

"*My dear fellow*, during our last meeting, you managed to detain me in my sick bed for a week with the beating you inflicted upon me, isn't that enough to call it quits between us!"

They sat on opposite sides of the circular mahogany table in preparation for serious talks. Harry noticed how Lyle's hand shook slightly as he poured out two glasses of whiskey. As Lyle took a large swig of his drink, Harry's fears that the whiskey might be poisoned were laid to rest; he took a gulp from his glass.

"Harry, old chap, for all the hardships you've caused me over the years, you should be glad that you are still breathing God's fine air."

"*My dear fellow*, why do you insist on putting the blame upon my shoulders for all of your misfortunes and tragedies? My one and only mistake in life was having a weakness for gambling and being unlucky at the gaming tables, hardly worthy of a death sentence, I should think."

"What about the murder of my dear Marjorie? I was preparing to buy your wonderful home and live in harmony with her, but *you* even managed to ruin that for me. You caused the only woman I have ever loved, apart from my dear mother, of course, to throw herself from a height to her untimely death!"

"*My dear L.D*, I was at home nursing the wounds inflicted by you! I was nowhere near your wife. I *can* understand that perhaps you might be harbouring a feeling of guilt and it's an easy option to pass the blame onto me. Believe me, Lyle; I was absolutely devastated when I heard about the tragedy."

Lyle refilled the half-empty glasses; his face was puce and strained with grief. Harry picked up his glass; the small room was stuffy and Harry was feeling too overdressed and uncomfortable. He gulped down the whiskey, coughing as it caught in his throat.

"Lyle, I have a proposition to put to you. How about we bury the past and start afresh. I would be delighted if you'd move in with us all at Harberton Mead. We are a mixture of all sorts, from every walk of life and from the very young to the very old. I'm sure you'll be happy there and you will be well cared for and I could do with another business head on our team. By the way, I have already set the ball in motion regarding Delia and she will soon be free to marry the farmer. I do still love her, but know in my heart that there could never be a future for us; her heart belongs to another lucky man now."

The sincerity of Harry Fairbanks was blatantly obvious to Lyle and it struck him all of a sudden that he'd misjudged this man: Faye Lopez was quite correct in her analysis of him and he was left feeling ashamed and foolish.

"*Oh Dear God!*" he suddenly cried out. "*My dear Mr Fairbanks...can you ever forgive me...what have I done?* Your offer is most generous and one which I would gladly accept under different circumstances...but I fear it is too late..."

"Come now my dear fellow, there is nothing but a misunderstanding between us which can now be buried...we shall *forgive* each other."

Harry was becoming very worried about the sudden change in Lyle; he appeared over-anxious and misty-eyed, he was sweating profusely and his flabby face looked as though it would soon burst. All of a sudden he lunged forward and for a split second Harry thought he was about to strike him, causing him to spontaneously jerk backwards into his chair. Lyle violently swiped the half-full glass of whiskey across the room; it smashed noisily against the wall, as Lyle buried his head into his hands, sobbing loudly like a small child.

"*Quickly, Fairbanks!*" he cried out " go and find a doctor...*I poisoned the whiskey*. I'm so sorry...I'm so sorry..."

Harry remained seated, totally shocked by Lyle's revelation, he felt fine and wondered if this was some kind of sick joke.

"But *you've* been drinking from the same decanter Lyle..."

"Oh, my dear chap, what do I have to live for...I'm a dying man..."

"So you thought you'd take me along with you?"

"I had nothing to live for until you made me such a generous offer...Once again, I have made a huge mistake...The story of my life I suppose."

CHAPTER FORTY-TWO

Completely dumbfounded, Harry sat staring at Lyle, unable to gather any rational thoughts; he swallowed hard, wondering if his death would be a vile and long drawn out one. He felt fine so far. Lyle suddenly broke from his sobbing; lifting his head up, a brilliant thought had dawned on him. He squinted at the minuscule carriage clock which monotonously ticked away time upon the mantlepiece and then pulled out his golden *Hunter* pocket watch.

"What time is it, old chap?"

Comparing his own pocket watch with the mantlepiece clock, Harry quietly stated that it was eleven forty. A glimmer of hope seemed to light up Lyle's face.

"What time should we expect to depart this world?" asked Harry sarcastically. "Tell me, L.D, exactly *what* and *how much* poison did you lace that whiskey with?"

"That is of no consequence to you Fairbanks, unless you are an apothecary, but my point is, that Doctor Temple always calls in on me, without fail, *before* midday. He will be sure to know of an antidote."

"Was it cyanide? Because I doubt there would be little hope for us... "

"*No, no, it was arsenic!*"

"If you weren't a sick man, I would pound you to

a pulp, Dagworth, while I still have the strength, but now I shall leave you to your doctor and take my leave. I'd prefer to die amongst those who love and care for me.

"Please don't leave me, Harry, I beg of you. Would you deny a dying man his last wish?"

Harry began laughing and continued uncontrollably until tears ran down his face, feeling as though he was on the verge of hysteria. "Have you forgotten, LD, that thanks to you, I am also a dying man, and *my* last wish is to leave your company."

Lyle laughed at his foolishness, "*You* have a chance...but, as for me, well I already have a weak heart...I will not survive this that's for certain."

Doctor Temple appeared at the window, his knocking upon the front door had gone unheard and being concerned about his patient he'd walked around to the back of the house.

Within seconds he was being informed of what had happened, finding it difficult to comprehend why these two men appeared to be in such high spirits, though.

"In my thirty years as a doctor, I've yet to witness two men laughing themselves to death!" He picked up the decanter; it was nearly empty making his initial prognosis was that these men were both drunk.

"How much arsenic did you add to the whiskey, Mr Dagworth?"

"Not quite the entire bag full, just under four ounces I'd estimate!"

"*Impossible!*" he declared. "Believe me, you would not be sat here conversing with me if you'd consumed such a huge portion.

"Do you still have the remainder of the bag, Mr Dagworth? I'd like to see it!"

Doctor Temple followed Lyle into the kitchen, where Lyle removed the bag from behind the sink. There was a small amount of the deadly rat poison still remaining. The doctor rubbed it between his finger and thumb.

"Give me the smallest pan you have, Mr Dagworth, and light an oil lantern please, make sure to leave off its chimney." Lyle followed the instructions and watched with intrigue as the Doctor mixed the arsenic with a little water and proceeded to heat up the mixture. It soon became like a lump of thick dough upon the spoon. Doctor Temple sniffed the compound and smiled to himself.

Harry, who had now joined them in the kitchen, immediately noticed the tension ease from Doctor Temple's face.

"Take a sniff of this Mr...I do apologise, we have yet to be formally introduced..."

"Harry Fairbanks from Harberton Mead house," announced Harry.

"I have heard a great deal about you Mr Fairbanks, but what are you doing socialising with an old dog like L.D. who endeavoured to end your life. This is a very serious business. I hope you realise, Mr Dagworth and one which I will have to report!"

While Lyle stood puffing out of breath Harry took a wary sniff of the *'Poison'*. He was quite surprised by its rather pleasant aroma.

" *Astonishing!* It has a distinct odour of biscuits to it....*how bizarre!*"

"Mr Fairbanks, you'll be quite relieved to know that if it *had* been arsenic powder, the kitchen would now be filled with the most unpleasant stench of garlic. *Mr Dagworth*, you were thankfully sold flour and *not* arsenic!"

As the euphoria immediately set in, Lyle and Harry gripped each other in a strong embrace, both so delighted to be alive and with the knowledge that they were not about to die. Doctor Temple immediately ordered his patient to be seated, noticing how flushed and out of breath Lyle appeared.

"I will have to get to the bottom of this, Mr Dagworth. Where did you purchase this so-called *arsenic* from?"

"Green's, the ironmongers, in St Clements."

"Doctor Temple, I beg of you to keep this unfortunate incident to yourself; it was nothing more than a huge misunderstanding between us and Mr Dagworth has agreed to accept my offer to move into Harberton Mead house where he will be taken great care of and be under the watchful eye of our very own Granny Isabel!"

The Doctor rubbed his chin as he stared down at the sorry sight of poor Mr Dagworth."

"Do you mean to tell me that even after Mr Dagworth was willing to end your life, you would trust him under your roof!" asked the astounded Doctor.

"Mr Dagworth and I have had our share of ups and downs in the past, but as the saying goes, 'April showers often bring May flowers' and I feel that our friendship is about to flourish and we'll always have this little incident, that I must insist we keep secret, LD, to joke about. I trust my dear old friend *even more* after today!"

Unable to stem his flowing tears, Lyle felt utterly ashamed of himself; he wished he'd taken more notice of the sound advice from Faye Lopez, but he was arrogant, foolish and hungry for revenge. Harry Fairbanks was, by far the better gentleman than he was.

"Harry, my dear fellow, I would completely understand if you wished to withdraw your generous invitation, after today's events."

"Nonsense, old chap, you will move into Harberton Mead and that's final. You will fit in like a vital cog in a clock."

In all of his practising years in medicine, Doctor Temple had never experienced such a peculiar and unbelievable day. He left Lyle's cottage assuring the two men that he'd not breathe a word of what had taken place but was intent on a speedy trip to Green's ironmongers, praying

that arsenic powder was not being sold as flour,
the consequences of which didn't bear thinking
about.

Harry made the return walk to Harberton Mead,
with a multitude of thoughts spinning around in
his head. It had certainly been a strange
morning, one which he'd never forget, for the
rest of his days; it could have turned out so
different, he mused, as he appreciated every
sight and sound on his journey. It was indeed a
sheer joy to be alive and he confided in himself
that he'd never complain about anything in his
life again. It had suddenly occurred to him,
whilst under the impression that he'd never see
his dear new family and Harberton Mead again,
that he'd not yet updated his last will and
testament; it would now be his top priority.
As he turned into the driveway he was met by
Faye and Billy, they were busy picking the first
of the sun-ripened blackberries. The familiar
sound of young Billy's continuous chatter put a
huge smile on Harry's face.
"I hope those are going in one of Granny Isabel's
pies!"
Faye jumped, startled by Harry's sudden
appearance, expecting him to arrive home from
wherever he'd been in a carriage or on
horseback.
"I picked *the biggest* one, Uncle Harry!"
announced Billy, excitedly.

"Did you have a successful morning Harry?" enquired Faye. "You *do* look as though you have, if not a little flushed. *Have you been drinking, Mr Fairbanks?"*

Harry burst out laughing, "My dear Faye, it is always, *Mr Fairbanks* when you are scolding me; you are such a treasure, dear girl. Actually, I've just come from Lyle Dagworth's cottage."

Faye gasped, *"What were you thinking*, Mr Fairbanks, you know how he is so determined on revenge...you should have at least taken one of us with you! You didn't even tell anyone where you were going...Thank God you're home safe and sound!"

If only you knew, Faye Lopez, mused Harry as he waited eagerly to disclose his news.

"And how *is* Mr Dagworth today?"

"He is a sick man, Faye, and that is one of the reasons why I've insisted that he comes to live with us...we can't possibly allow him to live out his final months all by himself; he is a very lonely man and you never know, the change and having company around him might actually be beneficial to his health."

"Can I go and feed my chickens some blackberries, Mamma?" interrupted Billy.

"Of course you can, darling, there are certainly plenty on the bushes, but only give them two each, otherwise we'll have Granny telling us off!"

"That's better," Faye sighed, "now I don't have to be so careful of my wording. You do realise, that he might have simply agreed to live here so that he can carry out his devious plan with ease. How will you ever manage to sleep under the same roof with someone who wishes you nothing but harm, wishes you dead in fact and has not been at all secretive of his intentions."

"Calm yourself, my dear Faye, L.D and I have reached a new understanding, we are now like brothers and the past is the past and will remain there where it rightfully belongs. He will not harm me; that I can guarantee you."

Faye stared curiously at him, "What exactly did happen this morning, Mr Fairbanks...you do appear incredibly relaxed and there is a hint of a twinkle in your eye if I'm not mistaken!"

"My dear Faye, you are indeed a true romantic female!" laughed Harry. "Now I will inform the others at supper, but in the meantime, I think an afternoon nap might be favourable. By the way, I hope young Rob is not using his injured hand today, it needs to be kept quite immobile you know otherwise it could start bleeding again *and* he must be sure to keep it clean, we don't want any nasty infections; take good care of your husband Faye, he is one of the kindest men that I've ever had the pleasure to know!"

"Don't worry, Harry, he's strictly on gentle, left-handed polishing until he's fully recovered."

"Jolly good, make sure he keeps it that way...oh I forgot to mention that I'm going to fetch young Billy his puppy tomorrow, I bumped into an acquaintance who's eager to find homes for his nine puppies!"

"*Harry Fairbanks*, you do have a heart of pure gold, but make sure you only bring one puppy home with you; don't allow their sad eyes to persuade you otherwise."

"Come now, Mrs Lopez, what do you take me for?"

"I take you for the kind and generous man that you are, Mr Fairbanks and my future plan is to go in search of a suitable match for you, it's the least I can do!"

"Now that does sound promising, but right now I can't afford to even think of such possibilities...and I do quite enjoy being a single man! Why don't you and Billy accompany me tomorrow, then the dear lad can choose his very own puppy!"

When supper had been consumed and everyone was full from Granny's mouth-watering blackberry pie and creamy custard, Harry announced the news of the impending arrival of Lyle Dagworth, once again shocking everyone; just like Faye, they couldn't understand why Harry would want to invite this man to live at Harberton Mead. But they all trusted his judgement and after all, it was Harry's house, and he was free to invite whoever he wished to live there. Billy had his own special announcement, and couldn't contain his excitement that he was soon going to have his very own puppy.

"Please let me tell 'em our news, Faye, it seems like the right moment some 'ow," whispered Rob.

"Oh, Rob, I swear you're worse than our Billy at keeping secrets. Go on then, you win and I'm only being so soft on you because of your poor hand, I hope you realise!"

Rob and Faye's news was a delight to everyone, although Billy was more excited at the prospect of a puppy rather than another baby brother or sister.

When everyone had retired to the drawing-room to relax, Faye and Rob insisted that Granny Isabel should also relax after her busy afternoon of cooking, leaving them to clean away the aftermath of supper. They rested for a while in the fading light, enjoying a rare private moment together.

"Oh Rob, I'm so happy, everything seems to be going so well in our lives, and I know I should be grateful for all of our blessings..."

"I sense a but..." interrupted Rob as he took hold of Faye's hand, "I know 'ow yer heart breaks fer little Faye, but yer must remember that she's, alive, healthy and wiv folk who adore her; just remember those black days when yer thought she'd not survived. We never know what the future might bring Faye...just look back on all the ups an' downs that we've bin through since our first meeting on the corner of Angel Street, where I met me very own special angel! Who would 'ave ever imagined us ter be living in such a grand 'ouse, 'ere in Oxf'rd?"

Faye let out a slow sigh as she looked into Rob's cloudy eyes,

"I love you, so much, *Roberto Lopez*."

"I love yer too, *Mrs Lopez*, more than you could ever know! Now, how 'bout we get this mess cleaned up an' join our lovely friends in the drawing-room; sounds as though our Billy is being *'the entertainer'* as usual!"

"Just think, Rob, this time next year, Bobby will be following in Billy's footsteps and we'll have our *third* baby...I'm going to pray for a girl, a beautiful little sister for our boys!"

Rob cupped Faye's face in his left hand; he was the luckiest man in the world and his heart ached with love for his beautiful wife. He planted a gentle kiss upon her lips,

"An' I'm gonna pray that you an' our newest arrival will both be as fit as fiddles!"

EPILOGUE

During the following ten years, there was a great deal of change at Harberton Mead; weddings, births and sadly funerals, but the most significant change came about because of the devastating fire in 1870 when the fine-looking house was completely burnt to the ground. Nobody knew how the fire had started but thankfully everyone escaped unharmed. With so many expanding families now sharing the dwelling, it made far more sense to build individual houses. The land was plentiful and the furniture and antique business was now thriving and continued to be a popular and notorious name throughout Oxfordshire and its surrounding counties. Billy, who was growing into a strapping young man began working alongside his pa at the age of thirteen, a year after he'd finished his schooling. Harry had insisted that all of the children from Harberton Mead should learn a trade which would be a benefit to them and to the business.

Before his death, Lyle Dagworth had enjoyed a peaceful eighteen months at Harberton Mead; he was adored by everyone, especially Billy who would spend much of his time chatting to his heart's content with his Uncle Lyle; he would sneak cakes and slices of pie out from under

Granny Isabel's nose as a special gift for him and in return, Lyle had purchased a huge supply of Billy's favourite sweets which he treated him to, daily. Lyle had helped Billy in the training of his adorable black and white puppy which was named Wilfred and during his time at Harberton Mead the three of them became inseparable. It was a sad day when Lyle was discovered lifeless in his bed one morning, but Doctor Temple, who had continued to call on him once a week since he'd moved to Harberton Mead, was quite convinced that he'd not have lived this long if he'd remained alone in his cottage. Harry and Doctor Temple would often have a secretive laugh about what had happened in the past but he'd requested that Harry kept it a secret, even though Lyle had passed away, just in case it caused any damage to his good reputation as a doctor. During Doctor Temple's investigations, it had come to light that the ironmonger's twelve-year-old son had forgotten to fill in the order form correctly and to avoid a confrontation and a harsh punishment from his father he'd temporarily filled the arsenic container with flour until the following week's delivery arrived. A most fortunate week it turned out for Harry and Lyle and for the multiplying rodents of Oxford, Doctor Temple had joked.

Lyle Dagworth bequeathed the largest share of his estate to young Faye Fairbanks; he believed it was what his darling Marjorie would have wanted and it would mean that her future life was financially secure. He left a substantial and equal amount to both Rob and Faye and to Harry Fairbanks. A healthy share was left to Ed, who had become a close friend of Lyle's in his final months, and equal amounts to Billy, Bobby and Elsie Lopez to be put into a trust until they reached the age of twenty-one. His generosity had made a huge difference in many people's lives; he was indeed a man of much wealth who chose to live out his final years modestly and with those whom he loved and who he felt most comfortable with. There was a small clause in Lyle's will which was intended for Harry; from the hundreds which he'd inherited, Harry was to donate a hundred guineas which he still owed to a local workhouse. He also wrote an enigmatic message reminding Harry to always take extra care when purchasing flour. Harry was left watery-eyed from laughter and sadness.

It was four months after the passing away of Lyle Dagworth, in the summer of 1866 that Harry Fairbanks remarried; he was forty-four years old and still possessed the young and handsome physique of a man in his thirties. Marie Trent had made an instant impression upon Harry during her elder brother's house clearance. Edward Trent was settling down in Africa with his family after leaving his regimental post. He was in urgent financial need to enable him to purchase vital farming land and was hence selling his entire house contents and property. Before his departure, Lyle had constantly nagged his dear friend Harry to marry Marie, declaring how she was the perfect match for him; Harry's one regret was that he'd not brought the wedding forward so that Lyle could attend. Marie was a spinster in her mid-thirties and until recently she'd been the companion to a distant cousin. She was an extremely amiable woman in both appearance and nature and soon became like an older sister to Faye. A year after their quiet wedding, Marie gave birth to the first of their three sons.

With Harberton Mead becoming more like a nursery, what used to be Lyle's room was turned into just that.

Faye had at last born her long-awaited for daughter who she named Elsie, she was dark-haired with olive-toned skin, a complete contrast from her first daughter. It seemed like all of her children were to take after Rob in their appearance. It was just eighteen months after the birth of Elsie that Faye gave birth to twin girls. Anne and Jean were identical and exceptionally beautiful with heads of dark curly hair and the deepest chestnut eyes.

Granny Isabel had never been so happy as when Harberton Mead was filled with young children she would insist that the Good Lord had rewarded her for being so patient throughout her entire life when she'd never once objected to the fact that she wasn't blessed with children of her own.

Ed Hall also married; he and Miss Sharp got off to a wobbly beginning when they had argued about the price of the weekly grocery bill.

Every week, Ed would take the wagon into Oxford and collect the grocery supplies for the ever growing population of Harberton Mead house, it was always Miss Sharp's father who dealt with the larger accounts and although Ed had often greeted Miss Sharp as she tidied the shop and stocked the shelves, it wasn't until she'd temporarily taken over the shop when her father was ill that Ed had actually held a proper conversation with her.

In his usual rough manner, Ed had complained, crossly and after already experiencing a difficult day, Miss Sharp crumbled into tears; it was then that she poured her heart out to Ed.

"I'm so sorry Mr Hall, but I can't be expected to do everything...Pa sees me as a man, half the time, he thinks I'm as strong as an ox and that my skin is as thick as the hide of an elephant. You should see how he treats my four sisters...them with their pretty dresses and dainty hats; they're full of airs and graces and they're not even allowed to pick up a bag of sugar in case it strains their delicate bodies...I've just been left behind to fill my dear ma's shoes and be a blooming dog's body because according to every member of my family *I'm* not the marrying sort..I'm plain and hefty and no man would ever wish *me* to be his wife...I was put on this earth just to serve my pa and the customers of Oxford and be told that I'm stupid too, just because my sums aren't always up to scratch!"

"Hey, *hold on a minute Miss Sharp*, I never said you was stupid...I just know that me bill is usually 'alf the price!"

"Yes, Mr Hall you are most likely correct, it's just been a *wretched* week and I've had more than enough of everyone's criticism."

"Why don't yer let me take yer out fer lunch terday, Miss Sharp?"

"Oh, I couldn't possibly...there's stock taking to be done and the floor to sweep and the accounts to verify...I barely have time to eat a morsel in my lunch break..."

"Course yer could, I'll 'elp yer in the shop, then you'll be on top ov things; just show me what yer want doing."

"Well, I don't know how father would feel about that, he doesn't take kindly to outsiders behind his counter."

"I've got an idea...I'll take me goods back ter Harberton Mead an' then return...give yer time ter think about me suggestion, an' if yer still ain't too keen on the idea, then I'll just 'ave ter treat meself to a fancy lunch an' wish that yer was by me side!"

It was the start of blossoming romance and by the time the first snowdrops were pushing up through the bleak ground, the following spring, Heather Sharp and Ed Hall were walking down the aisle. They were never blessed with any children of their own, but their cottage door was always open to Faye and Rob's brood and Harry and Marie's three boys, although Harry was rather concerned of the possibility that his sons might pick up Ed's East End accent. Faye put his mind to rest telling him that he was worrying needlessly. None of *her* children had picked up Rob's rough accent over the years and he was their father, she had stated.

Soon after Harry and Delia's divorce was finalised, Delia finally agreed to marry Jasper Heath; he had asked her countless times over the years and although he was quite sure that Delia loved him, he couldn't understand why she continued to refuse his offer of marriage. She would insist that it was her pure devotion to her daughter that stood in the way, but even with Jasper's sincere declaration that he loved little Faye as though she was one of his own, which he felt *was* the absolute truth; Delia continued to turn him down. He'd watched Faye grow up since she was a baby, she was a huge part of his life and meant the world to him and he was more than willing to take on the role of a real father to her.

On that surprising day when Delia and Jasper had been on a trip into Dorking while Faye was at school, it was in the tea room where Jasper decided to propose once again. Delia had poured the tea; it was still quite early in the afternoon and there was only an elderly couple in the tea room with them. Jasper reached across the table and touched Delia's arm; their eyes met, which never failed to excite Delia; she yearned to be in his arms and feel his kiss upon her lips but she knew that by telling him the truth she risked losing everything, not just for her but for her darling Faye and dear Ruth White who she owed so much to.

"Just look at us, anyone in the world would look at us and assume that we are husband and wife! Why won't you marry me Delia? My darling, Delia, what is holding you back? Don't you trust me?"

Delia felt a rush of goosebumps across her skin. She glanced at Jasper's rugged face, well worn and leathery from enduring every kind of weather out on the land; he wasn't the well-groomed, immaculately dressed man that Harry Fairbanks had been, he was much older too, but he was genuine and sincere and she knew that he loved her with all his heart and soul. His heart was in the right place and he didn't have a malicious bone in his body. But, would he still harbour the same feelings for her after she'd told him the truth about herself and after he'd realised how she'd deceived him for so many years?

"There is nothing I'd delight in more than becoming your wife Jasper, but there is an *awful lot* that you don't know about me..."

"I don't care about what I don't know about you my beloved, we have the rest of our lives to discover each other! Oh, Delia, you can't imagine how happy you've made me...I've waited a long time for you to say yes..."

"Please Jasper; you must listen to me and to what I have to tell you…"

Jasper detected the seriousness in Delia's firm voice and the stern look upon her face. He hadn't thought that anything could ruin this moment but was suddenly overcome with a strange and ominous feeling.

"Very well, my darling, go ahead and tell me what exactly it is that I don't know about you...my ears are waiting."

Delia took a deep breath and a sip of tea; her hands were unsteady all of a sudden and Jasper became quite worried by her uncharacteristic nervousness; he'd never before witnessed her like this.

"Dear Jasper, I want you to know that I have loved you for many years now; the pain it has caused me on every occasion when I've had to decline your marriage proposals has been crippling to me and I have ached to say yes to you. I also want you to know that if, after you've heard my story, you wish me to leave Mickleham Farm; I will understand completely and will leave immediately."

"*God, Delia*, what in heaven's name are you going to tell me; I'm feeling as nervous as you look and I don't like it!"

"On that day, when you offered me and Ruth White a job at Mickleham Farm..."

"*Your mother*...why *Ruth White*, all of sudden?"

"Jasper please don't interrupt, I don't want to lose my nerve! Now, as I was saying...yes that day...It was the day on which I walked out on my husband. Ruth White was my former cook and my baby was an orphan girl rescued from the roadside where she'd been born; her poor unfortunate mother had not survived. My husband is a compulsive gambler and after an empty marriage of six years, the one shining light in my life was *little Faye*. I loved her from the moment I began caring for her and couldn't bear the thought that she was to be sent to and raised in the workhouse. So the day after the bailiffs arrived at my home and took nearly every item of furniture and items of any value and when the local constable was scheduled to take baby Faye from me, I decided to leave. It was also when I discovered that my husband had stolen my only possessions which were rightfully mine; my collection of gold jewellery!"

Delia quickly stole a glance at Jasper's face and as she'd predicted he was wearing a look of total shock. She took another sip of her tea before continuing. Jasper didn't even attempt to put in a word.

"*Jasper*, when we set out, it wasn't our intention to trick and lie to anyone and in fact, we were making our way to London; we weren't even waiting to be hired when you showed up in Dorking...you simply presumed, because we were standing close by to that group of poor folk hoping to be hired. It was actually all Ruth's plan, which she devised *after* you'd offered us work...in fact...*I* was *totally* against her silly plans but at the time, I was so terrified of having Faye taken away from me, that I saw it as the only safe way of guaranteeing she'd remain mine."

"What about this Harry Fairbanks....your *husband*... did he not seek to locate you?"

"He may have done, I can't be sure of what he's been doing with his life since I left...probably gambled himself into debtor's prison...but he must have discovered, quite recently, where I live and I presume that *he* wishes to re-marry since I was contacted by a solicitor stating how a divorce was about to be set in motion and of course I had no objections to that, in fact, it was the best news I could have received."

Jasper was stunned, and speechless. The tea room had become full without them noticing.

"Should we leave here, Jasper, we could take a stroll if you like or we could go back to Mickleham Farm and I will pack up my belongings."

With scarcely a word spoken between them, Jasper paid the bill and Delia followed him out to the busy Dorking High Street. He rested his arms against the black metal railings and looked down onto the passing carriages and riders as they passed along. His eyes were glistening with unshed tears.

"That's a lot to take in over a pot of tea, Delia," he uttered, in a shaky voice. "I have so many questions but at the same time, I'm not sure that I want to know the answers. I wish that Ruth *was* your real mother and that Faye *was* your real daughter."

"Faye *is* my daughter...in every way, apart from the fact that she didn't come from my body. I'm completely devoted to her, Jasper; you of all people should know that!"

"I do...but it's illegal, Delia!"

"Oh, who is to ever find out? And what of it, I've given that child love and care and a good life, so far; a thousand times better than what she would have received from being raised in the workhouse!"

"What about Ruth White? Has she illegally adopted you as her daughter and you, her, as your mother, when she was once your employee?"

"Ruth White was employed by my husband...She has always been far more to me than the mere cook; I never knew my mother, but Ruth makes a fine and caring one. We are simply three females who all love and need each other and have taken the roles which we all yearned for but never had....and a mere divorce from my scoundrel of a husband doesn't change that, it simply makes me a free woman."

"You're quite right, Delia, I don't think it will change anything and it hasn't changed the way I feel about you either. I love you Delia, with all of my heart and I'd be nothing more than a fool to let you disappear from my life. Let's get married, the sooner the better! *Everything* will turn out fine in the end, my darling Delia."

Printed in Poland
by Amazon Fulfillment
Poland Sp. z o.o., Wrocław